Whisper
My Name

Also by Jane Eagland

WILDTHORN

MACMILLAN CHILDREN'S BOOKS

First published 2010 by Macmillan Children's Books
a division of Macmillan Publishers Limited
20 New Wharf Road, London N1 9RR
Basingstoke and Oxford
Associated companies throughout the world
www.panmacmillan.com

ISBN 978-0-330-51139-1

1 3 5 7 9 8 6 4 2

A CIP catalogue record for this book is available from
the British Library.

Typeset by Nigel Hazle
Printed and bound in the UK by CPI Mackays, Chatham ME5 8TD

For Sheila

ONE

1881

Meriel decided to place her deckchair as far as she could from Mrs Fitzgerald's, but still within earshot. She wanted everyone to know that it wasn't *her* choice to be with that lady. Ignoring the little children playing deck games and the clusters of adults sitting or strolling about, she chose a spot at the very edge of the awning. It was as close to the ship's rail as she could get, though there wasn't much chance of a breeze. She settled down, making sure her carpet bag was by her side.

From this position, if she looked up, she would see the smudge that was India thinning on the horizon. But she would not look up. Instead she kept her eyes on her book, her beloved battered copy of Shakespeare's plays, holding it like a shield to stop anyone coming to speak to her. She was only pretending to read. Really she was trying to hear what they were saying, Mrs Fitzgerald and the other ladies.

'Burra memsahibs' Mamma would have called them, laughing with Papa, meaning that they thought themselves superior to everyone else.

Meriel's chin trembled, despite herself. She clenched her jaw and listened hard.

'What a pity about her hair.'

Were they talking about *her*? The back of her neck prickled where her hair had been cut short.

'I always think red such an unfortunate colour.'

They *were* talking about her.

'How old?' enquired one of the ladies.

'Twelve.'

'I thought she looked old to be going Home.'

'Going Home'. That was what everyone called it, even when they'd hardly spent any time in England.

A languid voice said, 'No wonder she's so pale. Stayed out too long.'

The other ladies clucked in agreement.

'What was her mother thinking of?'

'Back-of-the-veranda schooling, I suppose.'

'And that dress . . .' The speaker tutted.

Meriel gripped her book, murder in her heart. She was admittedly far too hot in her dress. Hastily cut down from an old mourning gown of Mamma's, it made Meriel's skin itch and was too short in the sleeves. Her mother, who had loved beautiful fabrics and was always eager to hear news of the latest fashions from England, would never have let her wear such an ill-designed, ugly thing. But it had been Mamma's once, and Meriel stroked it protectively as she listened.

Although Mrs Fitzgerald had dropped her voice, Meriel still heard snatches of what she was saying. 'Artist . . . portraits . . .' She was obviously talking about Papa, and now she was saying something about Indians, Meriel couldn't hear what, but the ladies were making little sounds of disapproval and out of the corner of her eye she could see them fluttering their hands and leaning forward, greedy to hear more.

She knew that look – she'd seen it on the faces of the ladies at the Club, where everyone went to hear the latest news and pass the time in pleasant conversation. But it wasn't pleasant to be stared at, to see people whispering behind their hands as they had started to do some time ago when she and Mamma went in. She'd asked Mamma about it, and Mamma had said, 'Take no notice; it's just some silly people with silly ideas in their heads,' but Meriel was glad when, after braving it a few times, they gave up going to the Club.

Now, straining her ears, she heard '. . . lost her mother . . . rabies.' At that there was a satisfyingly sharp intake of breath from all the listeners.

Sensing that they were looking at her with renewed interest, she sat up straighter.

Though she was as miserable as it was possible to be, in some ways it was gratifying to be the focus of attention, to be connected with such a drama.

She hated Mrs Fitzgerald. She'd made out that she was doing Papa a great favour by agreeing to look after Meriel on the voyage and see that she was safely delivered to her destination. Really, from the moment they came on board, she couldn't wait to pump her charge, asking nosy questions about Mamma and Papa. Of course Meriel wouldn't tell her anything, so now, she guessed, Mrs Fitzgerald must be passing on gossip she'd picked up at the Club.

She pricked up her ears again when she heard Mrs Fitzgerald say, 'Sir Osbert Swann'. The other ladies made impressed noises, but to Meriel's frustration no one said anything useful and soon they moved on to other topics.

Meriel was desperate to find out more about Sir Osbert, who was Mamma's papa and hence her grandfather. All she knew was that he was an important scientist, famous for research into areas that had scarcely been investigated before. He lived in London, alone since her grandmother died, which happened shortly before she, Meriel, was born.

Now that she thought about it, it was strange that her parents never talked about him, at least not in her presence. Not even when every year, on her birthday, he sent a letter asking all sorts of questions about her. She could tell her parents thought the questions were odd, but they said it was good of him to take an interest in her. And he'd made it clear he was hoping to see her one day. Mamma would write a reply and afterwards she always seemed sad for a while. But nothing more was said about him until the terrible day Papa had announced that Meriel was going to live with her grandfather.

'Why do I have to leave? Why can't I stay here with you?' Over and over again she had asked her father the same questions, hoping to wear him down.

And over and over again Papa had explained patiently that she couldn't stay in India without Mamma to look after her.

'Anila will take care of me.'

It seemed that suddenly she was too old for an ayah – a nursemaid – and besides, he said, Anila wouldn't be able to teach her as Mamma had done.

'I could go to one of the hill schools. And come back in the holidays.'

Papa shook his head and said it wouldn't do. She should be glad she was going to have an English education.

Meriel tried everything she could think of – shouting and stamping her feet, sobbing and pleading with him – but it was no use.

In the end she turned on him and said, 'Mamma would never have sent me away. You want to get rid of me, don't you?'

Papa's face crumpled then. Clasping her to his chest, he said, 'Oh, my Meriel. I don't want you to go.'

'Then don't make me.'

'I must. It's for your sake, my darling. I don't want to lose you too.' His voice cracked, and she knew he was thinking of Mamma.

She nearly weakened then, but over his arm she caught sight of her bags packed and waiting to go. She would never forgive him. And she would not cry.

Nor did she. Not when they boarded the ship in Bombay, and Papa, in tears himself, said goodbye in the neat white cabin. Not when, still hoping that he might change his mind, she hurried to the side of the boat and watched him walk away from her, down the gangplank. Despite the huge number of people on the quayside, she could see him distinctly. He never stopped waving as the ship drew away and the strip of water between them widened, until finally she couldn't see him any more. Even then she didn't cry.

Thinking of this now, Meriel clutched at her locket, twisting it on its chain, and slumped down in her chair.

The horrible tight feeling in her chest shifted a little, but she refused to give in to tears. Blinking fiercely, she turned to the back of her book and found the picture of Ellen Terry Mamma had cut out of a magazine. Dressed as Portia in *The Merchant of Venice,* the actress seemed to look at her with a clear, kindly gaze, rather like Mamma's own. To think that before she came to live in India, Mamma had actually seen Miss Terry, who she said was the best actress in the world, perform on the stage in a London theatre.

Meriel smoothed the picture with her fingers. Then she turned the pages and read:

> Viola: *What country, friends, is this?*
> Captain: *This is Illyria, lady.*
> Viola: *And what should I do in Illyria?*

With a sigh, Meriel turned her head and stared out at the ocean. There might be dolphins or flying fish, people said. But just now all that lay in front of her was a great expanse of water heaving up and down, empty as far as the eye could see.

What should I do in England? she thought.

Mamma had gone and she would never see her again,

never again feel the soft touch of her hand, or hear her voice, or talk with her about Ellen Terry or anything else. Meriel's father didn't want her and now she was on her way to a strange country, to live with a stranger, an old man she didn't know.

Everyone else might be going Home, but she no longer had a home to go to.

TWO

When Meriel first caught sight of England she couldn't understand why everyone else on the ship seemed so excited.

Grey. As they approached the quay at Southampton that was all she could see through the veils of cold rain: grey docks, grey buildings, under a grey sky. Even the people waiting on the dockside in their drab clothes had grey, drawn faces.

Her new cloak that had seemed so warm in India suddenly felt too thin. She shivered, overcome by homesickness for the light, the warmth, the bright colours of India under a vivid blue sky. She didn't want to get off the ship. Wildly she thought of hiding somewhere on board; if she did that, eventually the ship would take her back. But Mrs Fitzgerald led the way down the gangplank and she had to follow.

It was strange in the train – the carriage was full but there was a deathly hush. People sat stiffly, staring straight ahead of them as if they were pretending they were alone.

Once they'd left the town behind and there was nothing to see but dull, rain-sodden countryside Meriel closed her eyes, pretending that she was travelling back to Calcutta, pretending that none of this was actually happening, and she managed to keep it up until someone tapped her on the knee. She opened her eyes and Mrs Fitzgerald pointed out of the window. 'London.'

No one else was showing the slightest interest, but Meriel sat up straight in anticipation and craned her head to look.

'You'll love London,' Papa had said. 'It's a splendid city. There are so many things to see, so many exciting things to do.'

But as she stared through the soot-streaked glass at the rows and rows of grim little houses squeezed together, the cramped backyards where grey rags of washing flapped forlornly in the drizzle, she felt betrayed all over again.

When they arrived at the terminus and walked out into the street the din nearly took her breath away, and there was an unpleasant, pungent smell in the air: London smelled like . . . like a stable. Everywhere she looked there were horses, pulling carts and wagons and carriages – and, horrified, she saw that the road was a river of manure. A scrawny boy dressed in ragged clothes was trying to sweep a path through it for people crossing to the other side, and Meriel felt sorry for him.

They took a carriage – a 'cab' Mrs Fitzgerald called it – to Kensington where Meriel's grandfather lived. Mrs Fitzgerald chattered on in a toadying way, saying things like, 'Oh, your grandfather is such an *eminent* man.' She remarked that Sir Osbert was very rich and said that Meriel was a lucky little girl to be going to live with him. Meriel didn't feel lucky. At the thought that very soon she would be meeting her grandfather, her mouth went dry and she gripped the handle of her bag more tightly.

'Here we are,' Mrs Fitzgerald announced.

Meriel saw a very tall narrow house, in a row of other tall narrow houses, all looking the same in the drizzle: dark and forbidding. She followed Mrs Fitzgerald up a flight of steps to the dark green front door where the lady boldly rapped the brass knocker.

The door was opened by a girl not much older than Meriel. She had a pleasant face and she too wore a black dress, buttoned very tightly, only hers had a stiff white collar. She wore a white apron and a white cap under which her hair was smoothed close to her head.

Meriel felt a little comforted. Perhaps this girl would be her friend.

As she entered the house she smiled at the girl, who was holding the door open, and said, 'Thank you.'

The girl made a slight bob in return.

'Come along, dear,' said Mrs Fitzgerald sharply.

Meriel trailed after her along a dim hallway, noticing chilly-looking white statues, dull prints on the walls, a pair of antlers sprouting overhead . . .

The girl showed them into a room.

'Give the maid your cloak and bag,' instructed Mrs Fitzgerald.

Meriel smiled at the girl again as she handed over her cloak, but she refused to give up her bag. She wasn't letting her most precious possessions out of her sight.

Once the maid had left Meriel stared about her. It was

a grand room, but with a cold kind of grandeur that made her shiver. Compared to the bright whitewashed rooms of their bungalow it was gloomy and oppressive – the tall windows with their thick blinds and dark crimson velvet curtains let in very little light. Suspended from the ceiling, which was decorated with plaster fruit and flowers, was an elaborate chandelier. It hung over a long table swathed in a crimson cloth. Against one panelled wall there was a sideboard covered end to end with silver objects – serving dishes, cruets, sauceboats and other items she didn't know the names of. Ranged against the other walls were at least a dozen very uncomfortable-looking chairs with carved wooden backs.

Meriel wrinkled up her nose at the faint smell of fish that hung in the air. If one day she had a lot of money, she decided, she would make a prettier, more cheerful dining room than this. She noticed that among the solemn portraits in ornate gilt frames that hung on the walls, one haughty gentleman was staring at her reprovingly, as if to say, 'What are *you* doing here?'

She told herself not to be silly. It was more likely that he was frowning at Mrs Fitzgerald, who was gazing wide-eyed at the display of silver, probably taking mental notes for her next gossiping session.

The door opened. Meriel swallowed. Her heartbeat quickened as she faced the newcomer.

'Ah!' he exclaimed, striding swiftly across the carpet. 'At last.' Ignoring Mrs Fitzgerald, he fixed a monocle in his eye and gazed down at Meriel.

He was much taller than she'd expected, and lean, and he held himself very upright. He had a full head of thick white hair and a trim beard to match. His expression was not exactly welcoming. Under bushy white eyebrows his keen eyes examined her almost greedily. She had seen an eagle once, kept by a maharaja for hunting, which had looked at her in just the same way.

She shifted uneasily, but just then Mrs Fitzgerald coughed, breaking the silence. Her grandfather looked startled, as if he'd forgotten that the lady was still there. 'Ah, yes, Mrs um . . . Thank you for taking care of my granddaughter.'

'Not at all. I—'

His interruption was polite but firm. 'I expect you'll be wanting to be on your way.' And he gave a sharp tug on a brass handle sticking out of the wall.

'Oh.' Mrs Fitzgerald was clearly crestfallen. 'Yes, of course.' She smiled at Meriel. 'Goodbye, my dear. Be a good girl and make your grandfather proud of you.'

Meriel scowled.

'Goodbye, Sir Osbert. So delighted to make your acquaintance.'

But he had already turned away and was scrutinizing Meriel again.

The maid arrived to show Mrs Fitzgerald out. As the door closed behind them Meriel was surprised at how dismayed she suddenly felt. Mrs Fitzgerald was annoying, but she was the only link Meriel had with the life she'd left behind. Now, abandoned in this grand unfriendly house, facing a fearsome old man she didn't know, she felt a long, long way from home.

Suddenly he barked, 'What have you done to your hair?'

Caught off guard, Meriel stammered, 'It-it was cut off, for the hot weather – we didn't go to the hills this summer . . .' She trailed off. Didn't he know she and Mamma hadn't moved to Darjeeling as usual because Mamma had been too ill? An image filled her mind, Mamma as she was very near the end, her face whiter than her pillow, her eyes staring wildly. Meriel had clung to her cold hand and cried her name, but Mamma hadn't known her.

Meriel was horrified to find her eyes filling with tears. Furious with herself, she blinked them away.

Her grandfather emitted a displeased 'Humph'. Then, 'Too pale,' he muttered almost to himself, and added, 'but at least she speaks quite well. No chi-chi accent, thank goodness.'

Meriel bristled immediately. Chi-chi accent? At home snobbish English people used that expression to show their disapproval of the way Eurasians, people of mixed race, spoke. But it didn't matter how people sounded as long as you could tell what they were saying. That's what Mamma and Papa had always told her.

'What are your undergarments made of?' Her grandfather's second question made her stomach contract.

'Cotton,' she whispered. Why did he want to know?

Her grandfather's brows drew together in a frown. 'Wool,' he said firmly. 'That's the thing – natural undyed sanitary wool, summer and winter. I'll get Mrs Grimston to sort it out for you.'

Meriel breathed again. But she was dreading further questions. She was cold and tired and she would have given anything to get away from his cold, assessing eyes. The ordeal was not over yet, however. Fixing her with a hard stare through his monocle, he beckoned.

'Come.'

THREE

Still clutching her bag, Meriel reluctantly followed her grandfather back along the hall into his library, which was lined with dark wooden panelling and contained more books than she'd ever seen in one place. An imposing desk stood in front of the window. The room smelled of cigars and was decorated in the same dark, heavy style as the dining room; even the fire glowing in the hearth failed to make it cheerful.

'Sit down.'

Meriel made a move towards a leather button-backed armchair near the fire.

'Not there. Here.' He indicated an upright chair.

Gingerly she sat down, wondering what was coming next. As her grandfather opened a drawer in his desk and took out some paper she watched him covertly, looking in vain for any resemblance to Mamma. Her hand strayed towards her locket.

He came and stood in front of her, too close. Then to her amazement he whipped something from his pocket and wrapped it round her head, pulling it tight.

She sprang up. 'What are you doing?' Heart thudding in her chest, she stared at him wide-eyed.

'I'm measuring your head,' he said, as if it were obvious.

'What! Why?'

Without answering, he pressed down on her shoulder until she subsided onto the chair again.

Unwillingly she submitted to being measured, her mind still racing. He was obviously mad. Why hadn't Papa warned her? How could he have sent her to live with this hideous old man? But then she remembered it would have been a very long time ago when Papa last saw his father-in-law. Perhaps he'd changed over the years.

Without asking if she minded, he proceeded to measure her arms from shoulder to elbow, from elbow to fingertips; he measured her ears, her nose, the distance between her eyes and then made her stand up so he could measure her height and the breadth of her shoulders. He recorded all the figures on a piece of paper with a silver pencil.

Whatever the reason for this bizarre behaviour, Meriel didn't like it. His clothes smelt of tobacco and mothballs and she didn't like being breathed on, being handled by him. She wanted to tell him to stop, but she didn't dare.

At last he seemed to have finished. Pulling up a chair to a small table, he sat down, gesturing at her to do the same. Then he put a fresh piece of paper, a pen and an ink-bottle in front of her. 'Write!' he commanded.

Meriel looked at him, nonplussed.

'Did you not hear me?'

'But what would you like me to write?'

'Anything.'

After a moment's thought Meriel picked up the pen, dipped it in the ink and wrote, 'My name is Meriel. I am twelve years old.' She looked up at her grandfather, wondering if that was enough.

Retrieving the paper from her, he scrutinized it, frowning. 'Hmm. Not very neat.' He darted a glance at her through his monocle. 'Your mother had beautiful handwriting.'

Her heart leapt. It was the first time since she'd arrived that Mamma had been mentioned. But to her disappointment his lips tightened and he put the paper to one side without further comment.

Pulling his watch from his waistcoat pocket, he said, 'Now, I'm going to say a word and I want you to say the first word that comes into your head. I'm timing you to see how fast you are.'

That didn't seem so daunting. She'd always liked playing word games with Mamma and Papa. She waited, ready to jump in.

'Umbrella.'

'Monsoon.'

'Cow.'

'Krishna.'

She'd been as quick as lightning, but her grandfather frowned as if he didn't much like her answers.

He gave her the next word. 'Loyalty.'

'Anila.' It was true. Her ayah would have done anything for her, would have put herself in danger before she'd let any harm come to her beloved 'Meriel-baba'.

Her grandfather tapped the table sharply. Had she missed a word? 'I-I . . . beg your pardon?' she stuttered.

'Truth.'

Her head was beginning to ache. It had been a very long day and she didn't want to play this silly game any more. She pressed her lips together and stared mutinously at her grandfather.

Putting down his pen, he gave her a cool appraising glance.

Meriel squirmed, but she said stoutly, 'I'm tired. I want a wash and a rest.'

Her grandfather raised his eyebrows. 'Do you now?' He leaned towards her across the table and Meriel shrank back. 'Listen to me very carefully. Now that you're here, you can forget those impertinent ways. You've spent too many years with Indian servants. As I expected, you're spoilt.'

'I'm not.'

The eyebrows knitted together. 'And in this country children know their place. Seen and not heard, that's the way. You'll do well to remember it.'

Meriel swallowed. He had spoken quietly, but with a tone that chilled her to the marrow.

At long last he lowered his gaze. Opening one of the files from the pile by his elbow, he took out a document and passed it across to her.

'Read this to me.'

How ill-mannered he is, thought Meriel. Doesn't he know about saying please? Still, she bent to the task eagerly. She was a good reader, Papa and Mamma were always saying so, and however unpleasant he was being she wanted to show him what she could do.

But she was dismayed to see that the passage before her was hand-written.

'In this study I have . . .' She faltered, squinting at the minute, spiky writing. And he'd complained about hers!

'Endeavoured,' her grandfather interposed.

'. . . endeavoured to prove that genius is he-hered—'

'Hereditary.'

She didn't understand why he was giving her such a sarcastic look. She battled on. '. . . by showing how frequently . . .'

'*Distinguished.* You're mangling my words. "How frequently distinguished men have remarkable relatives".' Taking the papers from her, he shook his head. 'Hopeless.'

'That's not fair!' she said, tears pricking her eyes. 'I can read very hard words when they're printed. Listen!'

She fumbled in her bag for her Shakespeare, and flicking rapidly to the page she wanted she stood up and declaimed:

The quality of mercy is not strain'd,
It droppeth as the gentle rain from heaven
Upon the place beneath: it is twice blest;
It blesseth him that gives and him that takes:
'Tis mightiest in the mightiest—

'That's enough,' snapped her grandfather, leaping to his

feet like a folding ruler springing open. 'Give me that book.'

Reluctantly she passed it to him. As she did so, her precious magazine cutting drifted out and landed on the carpet.

'What's this?' he asked, bending to pick it up.

Meriel swallowed. 'That's Ellen Terry.'

Her grandfather looked at her as if she'd offered him a maggot. Speaking with slow deliberation he said, 'I know perfectly well who it is, thank you. I can't believe you have been allowed to keep a picture of that immoral woman.' And with a swift flick of his wrist he tossed the picture onto the fire.

'Don't!' cried Meriel, but it was too late. Her beloved idol was already curling and turning to white ash. The look she gave her grandfather was intended to strike him dead, but he didn't see it. He was leafing through the Shakespeare.

'Hm,' he said, 'most unsuitable. This is the full version, unexpurgated.'

Meriel didn't know what 'unexpurgated' meant, but as her grandfather moved in the direction of the fireplace again she panicked.

'No!' she shouted, springing up. Snatching the book away from him, she clutched it to her chest. 'You can't burn this!' she cried. 'It was Mamma's, don't you see? Mamma's!'

Her grandfather's eyebrows rose. 'Eleanor's?' he said, in a different tone of voice.

'Yes. It was a present from Papa when they married.'

'Ah, of course. I might have guessed.' Her grandfather shook his head. 'It's not a suitable book for a little girl. Why don't we put it here on the shelf, until you're older.' His whole manner seemed to have changed this time at the mention of Mamma.

'No,' said Meriel, glaring at him and hugging the book as if her life depended on it. 'Mamma gave it to me. It's *mine*. You're not having it.'

After studying her for a moment he shuffled the papers together. 'We'll leave it for now. I'll do some more tests tomorrow.'

Tests? Meriel didn't like the sound of that. 'Papa said I was going to have an English education. Am I not going to school?'

Her grandfather seemed to have lost interest in her now. After a few seconds he looked up from the papers. 'School?' he said, sounding surprised. 'No. You've a governess – Miss . . . What's-her-name. You'll find her in the schoolroom, I expect.' He waved his arm vaguely towards the door, dismissing her.

'Sorry – I don't know where that is.'

With an impatient sigh her grandfather pulled the bell by the fireplace. Then sitting down at his desk, he took no more notice of her until the maid appeared when, without looking up, he said, 'Take Miss Meriel to the schoolroom.'

*

Outside in the hallway, Meriel caught the maid by the sleeve. Startled, the girl stopped in her tracks.

'Please,' said Meriel, 'what's the governess like?'

The maid looked taken aback. Before she could say anything a loud nasal voice brayed, 'Parks, what are you doing loitering here?'

Both girls turned. To Meriel, the tall figure bearing down on them was nearly as alarming as her grandfather. The man's nose quivered disdainfully as he regarded her with a cold dead-eyed look.

The maid bobbed her head. 'I'm just showing Miss Meriel to the schoolroom, Mr Ponsonby.' She sounded scared.

'Well, hurry up about it.'

The two girls scampered up the stairs. When they reached the first landing and Meriel judged they were out of earshot she said, 'Who was *that*?'

'Mr Ponsonby. He's the butler, but he also acts as Sir Osbert's valet.'

'Oh. I thought he was someone important.'

'He likes to think he is.' The girl's hand flew to her mouth and her eyes rounded with fear. 'Sorry, miss, that just slipped out.'

'His eyes are just like a cod's,' Meriel observed. '*Parks, what are you doing?*' It was a perfect imitation of the butler's clipped nasal voice.

The girl looked shocked and then she spluttered into giggles.

As they continued up the stairs Meriel found out that

the maid's name was Sally. Sally revealed that there were five other servants in the house apart from herself, Mr Ponsonby and the governess: a housekeeper, a cook, a footman, another housemaid and a kitchen-maid, plus a coachman and groom in the mews at the back.

By now they had climbed so many stairs Meriel's legs were starting to ache. After the bruising encounter with her grandfather she felt wary of the governess and too tired now to cope with someone else who might be challenging.

She had never had a governess before. Mamma had taught her, although lessons, taking place whenever possible in the garden in the shade of the neem trees, were never demanding. And if something better presented itself, like a picnic or a chance to ride elephants, as when Papa was commissioned to paint a nawab's portrait, then lessons were abandoned.

Thinking of this now, Meriel felt her lip begin to tremble. She clenched her jaw and was glad when they finally reached the schoolroom at the top of the house. Sparsely furnished, with an odd assortment of furniture including a blackboard and a globe standing on a faded threadbare carpet, it was much less grand than the rooms downstairs. A feeble fire, much smaller than the one in her grandfather's library, sputtered in the hearth.

The governess, who turned out to be called Miss Allen, was young, but not nearly as beautiful as Mamma – quite plain, in fact. Her dress was plain too, and severe-looking, but she didn't seem quite sure of herself. Actually she seemed nervous. Good, thought Meriel. Miss Allen wouldn't be able to make her do anything she didn't want to.

'Sir Osbert keeps very regular hours,' said Miss Allen, once the introductions had been made. 'He rises early and walks in the park before breakfast. He expects you to be at your piano practice by half past six.'

'Piano practice!' Meriel said. 'But I don't play the piano.'

The governess looked taken aback. 'You don't? That's unusual for someone your age. However, your music lessons are on Wednesday afternoons; your grandfather has arranged for a piano teacher, a Miss Catchpole, to come to the house. And you'll go to a drawing class for three hours every Friday.'

Meriel was astounded. She didn't need drawing lessons. Papa had shown her everything she needed to know and then let her please herself about what she drew and painted. But before she could say anything, Miss Allen continued, 'Lessons start at half past seven in the morning. Lunch is at half past twelve. After lunch you will rest and then we will walk in the park.'

'Doesn't my grandfather have a garden?' asked Meriel, thinking wistfully of the bungalow compound with its purple bougainvillea and scarlet hibiscus.

'Oh no,' said Miss Allen. 'Gardens are not common in this part of London. But the park is pleasant, as you'll find. After tea you will have lessons for two more hours.'

Meriel didn't like the sound of this regime at all. How could there be so much to learn?

Miss Allen added, 'And of course there will be occasions when your grandfather wants to see you.'

Yes, thought Meriel bitterly, when he wants to measure me and do his strange tests.

Miss Allen handed Meriel a piece of paper. 'Sir Osbert thinks you might need some guidance about what is expected of you, so he's drawn up some helpful rules.'

Glancing at the paper, Meriel read:

Do not talk to the servants.
When walking, take short steps.
Swing only one arm at a time.
Do not eat too fast.
Do not talk while eating.

There was more, a lot more, but Meriel stopped reading. She was about to say what she thought of Grandfather's rules when Sally reappeared with a bowl of bread and milk. Meriel ate this dull supper at the round schoolroom table, under Miss Allen's watchful eye. She felt too exhausted to say much, but she resolved that next time she ate she would make a point of talking continuously, even with her mouth full.

When the governess suggested that after all her travelling she might like to go to bed early Meriel readily agreed. She couldn't wait to be alone. It would be strange without someone to help her, but she was determined to manage. 'I'll see myself to bed,' she said firmly.

Miss Allen hesitated, but Meriel scowled and the governess gave in. Showing Meriel how to turn down the gas, she left her. Hah! thought Meriel, she's easy to manage.

Her new bedroom, just off the schoolroom, was even smaller than her bedroom at home. When she opened the wardrobe there were her clothes neatly folded inside. Her trunk must have come from the station and someone, Sally perhaps, had unpacked it and left a jug of hot water on the washstand.

She undressed, put on her nightgown and washed, noticing after she'd rinsed her face and hands that the water in the basin was now black. Then, despite the cold, she didn't get into bed straight away but opened her bag.

One by one, she took out the things inside it.

First the photograph of Mamma. She was sitting on the veranda, her face partly shaded, but her smile was clearly visible. Meriel placed the photograph on a low chest of drawers together with Mamma's silver-backed brush. She traced the pattern in the silver, remembering how she'd been allowed to watch while Mamma got ready for parties. She would help Mamma choose which necklace to wear, and when Mamma had kissed her goodnight she would breathe in her perfume, a lovely smell that stayed with her even after Mamma had left the room.

Sighing, she turned back to her bag and took out the wooden tiger Anila had given her as a parting gift. She smiled. She knew why her ayah had chosen this.

One day they had been talking about reincarnation and Meriel had startled Anila by saying immediately, 'I would like to come back as a tiger.' When Anila asked why, Meriel said it was obvious. Tigers were beautiful and fierce and wild.

The photograph of Papa she put in the wardrobe without even glancing at it.

Opening her inlaid box, which released a faint smell of sandalwood, she ran her fingers through the few rupees, making sure that her mohur was still there. She remembered the moment when the Prince of Nayagarh had bestowed the gold coin on her, praising her for behaving so beautifully while he was having his portrait painted by Papa.

She let her fingers rest a moment on Mamma's red leather-covered notebook. Papa didn't know she had that. She'd taken it from his drawer because it comforted her to know she could see Mamma's handwriting whenever she wanted to.

Shivering now, she kissed Mamma goodnight, not once but twice, then she made herself turn off the gaslight and climb into bed. The homesickness that had been lurking ever since she left Bombay hit her like a wave. Even though she was much too old for *Nini, baba, nini* – Sleep, baby, sleep – she wished she was lying under her mosquito net with Anila sitting beside her singing to her as she used to when Meriel was little.

But Anila was far away in India.

She clutched her locket, which had been Mamma's.

Mamma had told her that it was Papa's first gift to her, before they were married. He'd chosen this one, he'd said when he presented it to her, because the entwined phoenixes were like them, and that whatever happened, their love would live forever.

Did love live on after someone died? Meriel wondered. How could it when the person wasn't there to be hugged and kissed any more? She sighed and shifted on the lumpy mattress.

Her thoughts turned to the next day and the tests her grandfather had mentioned. Horrible old man with his tape measure and watch. That stuff he had written about genius being hereditary and illustrious men – what did it all mean? He hadn't said anything about Mamma apart from that one mention of her name. He hadn't even said that he was sorry. Perhaps he didn't care. Perhaps that was why Mamma and Papa never talked about him. But if that was the case, why had Papa made her come here?

She didn't know who to hate most, Papa or her grandfather. *He* obviously wasn't interested in her, at least not in what she thought or felt. 'Seen and not heard'. Hah! She was shaken by a sudden surge of fierceness.

She only had herself to rely on. Very well. She would be like the tiger, solitary and fierce.

FOUR

1885

It was dark when I woke on the morning of my sixteenth birthday, and cold – dawn was more than an hour away.

As I often did at this time, I thought of home. Some memories were as vivid as if I'd left only yesterday. If I were there now I would open my eyes to sunlight, crows cawing outside the window and from further away the early-morning sounds of the bazaar, the muezzin calling from the mosque. I would be listening out for Anila's soft footfall, the jingling of her bracelets as she brought my banana, a daily pre-breakfast treat.

Stomach rumbling, I lay listening to the hushed house, a silence not just the result of the early hour but imposed by Grandfather: everyone trained to move quietly in the passages and on the stairs and to speak in muted voices. The housemaids even had to clean out the ashes with sticks rather than pokers because they made less noise. So I wouldn't hear Sally bringing my hot water until she tapped on the door, the first event in the day's routine that had been mapped out for me, the monotonous rigid routine that imprisoned me like a fist squeezing me tight.

But not for much longer, I told myself. A year more of this and then I'd be free of it, free to dress as I wished, to go to interesting places and do interesting things, to go to the theatre! And I'd be able to meet interesting people.

People I could talk to about the things that mattered most to me.

Because I was tired of being a tiger, of pretending that my own company was enough, that I didn't need anyone.

Just one more year to get through, but meanwhile I could prepare for it. I had decided that from today things were going to change.

But the changes didn't happen straight away.

I pulled a face when I saw my breakfast – it was the same as always.

Miss Tippins, sitting on the other side of the schoolroom table, said, 'What's the matter, Meriel?' Her mouse nose twitched and her eyes grew larger behind her spectacles.

'I'm tired of rumble-tumble. I'd give anything for a nice spicy dhal and rice.'

'Scrambled eggs, dear. Remember you must use English words.'

I stretched my eyes in mock exasperation. Silly old Tippy. 'Rumble-tumble' *was* English, but it was the word we'd used at home and I knew my grandfather had told her to discourage me from talking about India. He'd told all the governesses that, as if he thought that if I didn't talk about it, I'd forget it.

Of course that made me even more determined to remember.

'Happy birthday, Meriel.' Rather shyly my governess

pushed a small tissue-wrapped package across the table.

It was a bookmark worked in cross stitch. The stitches were rather wobbly and uneven, which wasn't surprising given her poor eyesight.

I feigned a smile. 'Ta! I mean, thank you.'

Tippy was always telling me off for using slang I'd picked up from Sally, but apart from that she wasn't a bad old stick. When I was tired of previous governesses I'd behaved dreadfully to make them leave, but Tippy had lasted for over a year. Grandfather probably thought it was because she was older and more experienced, and so had more control over me. Well, little did he know . . .

After breakfast I presented myself in the library. In the normal course of events summons from Grandfather were unpredictable – that's partly what made me dread them, because I couldn't prepare myself for them, but today I didn't need to be told. It was the ceremony of the annual measuring.

As I'd got older I hated it even more – being prodded and pushed around by Grandfather's liver-spotted hands, their blue veins standing out like knotted cords, and smelling his breath so close to my face. This morning, I could tell, he'd had kippers for breakfast. But no matter how hideous it was, I always did what he wanted. I'd learned early on that the more I protested, the more frighteningly remote he became. And I couldn't have explained why, but I'd never got over the feeling that he might be capable of doing anything to get his own way.

While he busied himself with his tape measure I looked to see if there was anything resembling a present on the table, but there were only the usual neatly arranged books and papers.

'Five foot five,' announced Grandfather. 'Taller than your mother.'

He rarely mentioned Mamma so I waited, hoping he'd say more. But as usual he said nothing further on the subject. For the millionth time I thought how strange it was that he wouldn't talk about Mamma, and that she hadn't talked about him. I wondered if they'd quarrelled about something.

Grandfather went across to his desk and from a drawer took out a polished wooden box. I brightened up.

For my last three birthdays my presents from Grandfather had been a geometry set, a magnifying glass and last year he had given me a scale ruler which neither Tippy nor I knew how to use. This year's was a special birthday though. And the box looked promising.

But when he opened it instead of the bracelet nestling on velvet I was hoping for, I saw a dirty-looking roller, a tube of something and some blotting paper.

Here we go again, I sighed inwardly.

Over the years, as well as routinely testing me on my schoolwork, he'd carried out many other bizarre tests on me. He'd investigated my hearing with a special whistle he'd invented; he'd made me sniff rose oil to see how sensitive my sense of smell was. Often he made me do horrible things, like tasting salt solutions of different strengths. That one had made me feel sick.

He would ask peculiar questions like, 'If I say the number nine, what do you see?' and 'What colour is the letter D?' and no matter what I said, he recorded it all carefully with his silver pencil.

When I'd first arrived and didn't know any better it had made me feel special to be helping with what I assumed was important scientific research, and I thought if I pleased him he might want to spend time with me, talk to me, take me to interesting places. I thought he might come to like me.

But it didn't happen. I realized that to him I wasn't a granddaughter, but a subject to be investigated. He never asked my permission; he just told me what to do as if I had no more feeling than an automaton. He never praised me or looked pleased at anything I did.

The worst thing about it was that I never understood what the tests were for, because he never explained. They didn't make any sense to me and it made me feel like one of Monsieur Pasteur's laboratory rabbits. I sometimes wondered, with a shiver, what would happen to me if the day came when Grandfather had no further use for me.

Now I watched as he squeezed black stuff from the tube on to the roller and coated a glass slide with it. Then he said, 'Give me your hand.'

Reluctantly I held it out.

He grasped my index finger and pushed it onto the slide, rolling it from side to side.

I wanted to pull my finger away, but he held it firmly and pressed it down on a piece of paper. When he let go I was surprised to see an intricate pattern left behind.

He did the same to all my other fingers and both thumbs, then put some turpentine on a rag. 'There, clean your hands with that.'

I didn't mind the smell of turpentine – it reminded me of helping Papa when he was painting – but I didn't want it on my hands. Wrinkling up my nose, I said, 'Pooh! It stinks.'

He gave me a sardonic glance.

I rubbed at the ink stains until I'd managed to get most of them off and I was hoping this was it for the day, but then Grandfather produced another box and disconcerted me by saying, 'Happy birthday, Meriel.'

It was a shallow oblong box, just the sort that could contain a necklace or a bracelet. I couldn't help grinning at him as I took it, and he responded with a rare wintry smile. But when I opened it it took all my acting skills not to reveal my true feelings. The box was full of pen nibs.

'Thank you,' I said dutifully. What a fool I'd been to expect anything nice.

'And *this* has come from your father.' He passed over a long packet.

I was tempted to say I didn't want it, that I was surprised he'd even remembered my birthday, but my curiosity was too great. I tore it open and a letter fell out, which I slipped into my pocket without a glance. It would only say the usual things, how much he loved me and was missing me.

There was also a piece of cardboard folded in half. Inside was a peacock feather, its iridescent green and blue brilliant in the dull light of the library. My heart twisted. At once I was back in the palace gardens of the Raja of Bamra; I could see the peacocks strutting past the lotus pools, feel the cool air from the fountains on my face . . .

A cough from Grandfather brought me back to reality. He was pretending indifference but I could see him eyeing the feather with a look of fastidious disdain. 'Off to your lessons now, young lady,' he said abruptly, and he went over to his desk.

I was expecting this. As far as Grandfather was concerned, the fact that it was my birthday made no difference to the routine of the day. But I had a surprise for him.

Touching my locket for luck, I rose. 'May I speak with you?'

He turned with a pained look. 'Well?'

I took a deep breath, my insides feeling a little shivery. Gripping the table to steady myself, I said, 'You know I am sixteen today, Grandfather.'

He raised his eyebrows in a query.

'Please may I move into Mamma's bedroom, the one she had when she was my age. And – I'd really, really like to have the use of the morning room.'

I'd had my eye on this small room for some time. With its light blue wallpaper and white woodwork, it was the prettiest room in the house. My grandmother would have overseen household affairs and written letters there; as far as I knew, it hadn't been used since her death.

Grandfather was frowning, but as he often did this when he was thinking it wasn't necessarily a bad sign. After a long pause he said, 'I can't see the harm in your having your mother's bedroom –'

I was amazed that it had been so easy, but then he sometimes did that – time after time he'd be strict and horrid and then every now and then, for no reason that I could see, he'd be unexpectedly agreeable.

'– but as to the morning room . . . no.'

'But no one uses it. It's such a waste.' The words burst out of me before I could stop them.

Grandfather's cold eye surveyed me through his monocle. 'I won't have that room disturbed, do you hear me?'

I flinched. Careful, I told myself. Another second and he'll change his mind about the bedroom.

I nodded and his shoulders relaxed. His eyes strayed towards his papers, so hastily I said, 'There's something else. You are very generous in the matter of clothes and other things –'

This was stretching it. The truth was every time I needed anything I had to ask the governess, who had to ask Grandfather and sometimes he'd agree, but more often he wouldn't.

'– and I'm very grateful, but I was wondering whether it wouldn't be a better idea for me to have an allowance now.'

Waving his hand as if to shoo away an irritating fly, he sat down at his desk.

'A small allowance,' I added quickly. 'Because when I am married and have a house of my own I will have to manage the housekeeping money, and I was thinking it would be difficult if I hadn't had any experience.'

He looked at me then, a long level look. I held my breath as he started tapping the desktop. I had worked out my approach very carefully. An appeal to practicality sometimes succeeded with him. Also I knew, because he'd told me often enough, that his ambition for me was to be the wife of an intelligent and successful man and produce a brood of intelligent and successful children, preferably sons.

As it happened I had other plans, but for now I was keeping them to myself.

The tapping ceased. I waited on tenterhooks for his pronouncement.

'That's not a bad idea. Yes, we'll do that. Starting today, as it's your birthday.' He gave me another ghost of a smile. Taking a key from his pocket and unlocking a drawer, he drew out a tin cash box. He counted out some money, wrote something in a notebook and locked the box away.

'Spend it sensibly, mind, for there won't be any more until next quarter. Get the governess to check what you're buying.'

I forced myself to keep smiling at him as he dropped the coins into my palm. 'Thank you, Grandfather.'

Two guineas. Not as much as I'd hoped for, but better than nothing. I quickly pushed the coins into my pocket in case he changed his mind.

Now for my final request.

I said, 'There's just one more thing.' I crossed my fingers behind my back, praying that this wasn't a step too far. 'I think I'm old enough now to go about without a chaperone, don't you?'

Grandfather's head reared up, his monocle glinting dangerously. 'Nonsense. Of course you're not.'

'But I've seen other girls of my age and younger walking out alone.'

He gave me a hard stare. 'It's of no interest to me what other parents allow. I will not have it tittle-tattled that Sir Osbert Swann's granddaughter goes about unchaperoned.'

So it wasn't my safety he was concerned about, but his reputation. Anger began to smoulder in the pit of my stomach, but I did my best to keep my voice cool and unwavering. 'I will write to Papa. I'm sure *he'll* give me permission.'

'No doubt he will.' His tone was icy. 'Your father's sense of propriety leaves much to be desired. But that is by the way. As long as you are under my roof—'

'Papa is still my legal guardian, wherever I live.' Defiant, I stared him in the eye, suddenly exhilarated by my own recklessness.

There was a long silence. I was determined not to be the first to look away, even though inwardly I was trembling. I couldn't tell – I could never tell – what was going through his mind. That was what was most frightening about him.

In the end he said quietly, 'Very well. Write to your papa and we will see what he has to say.'

I should have been jubilant. But there was something about his expression when he mentioned writing to Papa that unnerved me.

'In the meantime, your governess will continue to accompany you on your walk. Now –' he looked pointedly at the clock – 'the morning is passing, and you have schoolwork to do. Your progress to date is far from satisfactory. Given that you will have children one day, what kind of example would a mother set who thinks that "*la journeé*" means journey and "*travailler*" is to travel?'

He'd been inspecting my schoolbooks again. They were nothing to be proud of, but what did it matter? 'I should think it was more important for a mother to love her children than worry about her French.'

A muscle in his cheek twitched but he went on as if I hadn't spoken. 'And your performance on the last set of tests was shameful.'

This was true too, but was the point of swotting up a lot of stuff that I'd forget immediately the test was over?

'In fact, you know what your trouble is, young lady?'

No doubt he was going to tell me.

'You don't apply yourself. If you did, you'd have no trouble remembering. But in any case, all this is beside the point. I have work to do and so do you. Off you go, my girl.'

Uttering a dark curse under my breath I flounced towards the door, but there I stopped, my hand on the knob. He *wasn't* going to have the last word. I launched my parting shot. 'Do you know something? I'm glad I only have to put up with all this for another year.'

'What did you say?' His voice was like steel.

My heart began to race. 'That I'll only be here for another year. When I'm seventeen I'll go back to India.'

'Has your father said so?'

'No, but . . . that's what all the girls do.' The look on his face was beginning to scare me. He seemed almost to be gloating.

'I'm afraid, my dear, you are sadly mistaken. Other girls might go back to India, but you are not other girls, you are my granddaughter, and you will be staying here with me.'

'But Papa –'

He shook his head. 'Even if your papa wanted you back, I'm afraid that because of his extravagant, disreputable way of life, he cannot afford to pay your fare. The only way you will get back to India is if I pay for you to go. And that I'm not going to do.'

I stared at him open-mouthed.

My grandfather bared his teeth in a wolfish smile. 'Now I think you'll find Miss What's-her-name is waiting.'

FIVE

I managed to drag myself out of the library, but I took only a few steps before collapsing onto the chair that stood beside the hall table.

I felt as if the breath had been knocked out of my body. All I could do was sit doubled over, fighting for air. There was a fierce pain in my chest, but I clenched my jaw and squeezed my eyes tight shut so no tears would escape. I didn't want Grandfather to hear me sobbing.

Inside my head one thought kept beating, like a terrible drum: *You're not going back to India. You're not going back to India.*

When the pain subsided a little I forced myself to stand up and go upstairs. But instead of going into the schoolroom, where I knew Tippy would be waiting with a pile of deadly dull books in front of her, I went into my bedroom, closing the door behind me quietly.

Phoebe the housemaid had already been and gone – my basin had been emptied of soapy water, my nightgown, which I'd left on the floor, had been neatly folded and the bed had been made. Dumping my birthday presents on the chest of drawers, I crawled onto my bed like a wounded animal and reached out blindly for my pillow. I buried my face in it, and the pain in my chest rose up into my throat and dissolved in tears. I sobbed and sobbed till my pillowcase was soaked.

My life, my wretched life in this house, had to go on. Pointless piano practice; tedious lessons; those stupid tests; dull, dull afternoon walks in the park; hours and hours alone or with only Tippy for company . . . the days stretched ahead of me, on and on without end. Why did Grandfather want to keep me here? Trapping me like a – like a fly in a web. Yes – the servants and I were all flies and Grandfather was the black spider at the heart of house, controlling us all.

I sat up and blew my nose. The idea of Grandfather as a spider – a strange, mad kind of spider who spent his days counting, measuring, calculating – cheered me just a little, but oh, how my heart ached for India. The only reason I'd been able to survive all this time without losing my sanity was that I'd believed my sentence would end next year and that I'd be going back.

There was a tap at the door. 'Come in,' I called.

Sally appeared. 'She's wondering where you are.'

'Miss Tippins?'

'Yes. I guessed you'd be in here.' She came closer and, seeing my tear-stained face, said sympathetically, 'Has he been peppery again?'

'Much worse than that.' I hugged my knees. 'Oh, Sally, he won't let me go back to India.' As I said it another sob shook me.

She tried to look sorry. 'That's a shame, miss. But to tell you the truth, I've never understood why you've harped on about that dirty place. It's much too hot for the likes of us and full of snakes and wild animals.'

I stared at her. How could I convey to her what India was like, what it meant to me? How, above all, I wanted to go back to the place where I'd been happy, where I'd been at the centre of my world, surrounded by people who admired me and praised me and loved me? I said simply, 'It's my home.'

And this time she nodded. She *did* understand that. I could see it in her eyes. She knew what it felt like to have to leave your home, your family, and go into a cold, alien world where you weren't allowed to do what you wanted but other people told you what to do all the time.

'And there's something else . . .'

'Miss?'

'Well, I have this dream . . .' I stopped. I'd never told anyone before. But she was nodding encouragingly so I took heart. 'I . . . I want to be an actress.'

Sally clapped her hands together. 'Cor, miss! That'd be splendid.'

'Wouldn't it! And one day I intend to have my own company and tour round India.'

Sally's eyes widened. 'Do they have theatres there?'

'Course they do. Once or twice Mamma and Papa took me to the Corinthian Theatre in Calcutta. I've never forgotten the last play I saw there. It was called *The Lady of Lyons*. Have you seen it?'

Sally shook her head.

'It's spiffing. Pauline, the main character, is tricked into marrying a gardener's son, but in the end she falls in love with him.' I struck a dramatic attitude.

Tell him ev'n now that I would rather share
his lowliest lot, walk by his side, an outcast,
work for him, beg with him, live upon the light
of one kind smile from him, than wear a crown!

Sally looked slightly bemused, but as she always did she applauded enthusiastically. 'But, miss – if you want to be an actress, there's loads of theatres here in London.'

'Yes, but can you see Grandfather letting me join one? He won't even let me see a play.' I sighed. 'He won't let me do *anything.* I asked if I could go out without a chaperone. You can guess what he said.'

Sally clucked sympathetically.

'At least he's stumped up some money, but I can't spend it without Tippy twittering at me. I've told you what it's like going shopping with her.' Flinging myself off the bed, I seized my nightgown and wrapping it across my chest I took a few mincing steps as if showing off a new dress. *'Oh, Meriel, do you think that's suitable? What will Sir Osbert say?'*

Sally laughed. I looked out of the window – the sky was blue, the sun was shining – and thought wistfully of the afternoon I might have had. Why did I have to do lessons on such a lovely day? Why should Grandfather spoil everything?

'Sally, you know that shop you're always telling me about, the one you said had tip-top window displays? Not too far away?'

'Whiteley's?' Her eyes gleamed. Going to look in its

windows was her favourite occupation on her afternoon off.

'Yes, that's the one. How do I get there?'

Entering the schoolroom a few minutes later I put on my brightest smile. 'Oh, Miss Tippins, Grandfather says that as it's my birthday I'm excused lessons this morning.'

'Really?' I caught the look of relief that flashed across her face.

'Yes, and he says that I can move into my mother's bedroom, so I'll do that now. You're free to do as you please.'

Her eyes gleamed. 'Oh! In that case I can finish the sketch I started on Sunday.'

Poor old Tippy. When she accompanied me to Miss Cutting's for my art lesson she listened to every instruction with rapt attention. But her efforts were terrible – not being able to see properly, she had no notion of perspective, and everything was rubbed out and redrawn till the paper was grey.

She was rummaging through her portfolio before I'd even left the room.

In my bedroom I paused a moment. What did I need? My brush, some hairpins, my best dress . . . I gathered up as much as I could carry and hurried downstairs to the floor below.

Once or twice before, I'd sneaked a look in there. Now, having dropped my things on the bed, I flung my arms out and twirled round, revelling in the fact that I had every right to be there.

Mamma's was much larger than my old bedroom, and brighter, being at the front of the house. I'd be able to look down on the street and see who was passing. It had pretty rose-sprigged wallpaper, a big brass bedstead with a lace bedspread and thick rugs on the floor. No more mornings standing shivering on the cold oilcloth. There was a low couch and a proper dressing table, with, joy of joys, a toilet mirror! At last I'd be able to look at myself properly instead of trying to see my reflection in some window.

On the dressing table, laid out as if waiting for me, was a matching set of china: tray, ring-stand, trinket box and a hair-receiver. I could save all the strands from my brush and make myself a bracelet. Best of all, in the corner there was a full-length looking glass. I could practise being different characters and rehearse scenes from plays.

Sitting at the dressing table, I wondered why Mamma had left all these dainty things behind. Undoing the silver top of a jar which still had a little cream in it, I sniffed and caught the faintest trace of scent. My throat tightened at the smell, familiar even after all this time.

I looked in the drawers, hoping Mamma might have left something else, but they were empty apart from some yellowing newspaper liners.

I pulled myself up short. I was wasting precious time.

I put on my dress. Thank goodness it was fairly new and quite a decent colour – dark green. And despite

Tippy's feeble protests, I'd persuaded the dressmaker to make it longer than usual so it was nearly full length. I surveyed myself in the mirror, turning round to see what it looked like from the back. Hopelessly flat, when I wanted to look like a fashionable lady.

I paused, searching for inspiration. Perhaps a petticoat? Then I remembered the newspaper in the drawers. Crumpling the pages up together, I contrived a kind of pad, one end of which I managed to tuck into the waist of my petticoat at the back. This time the mirror showed me a much more satisfactory view – though the padding didn't exactly form a shelf as it was supposed to, no one would guess I wasn't wearing a proper bustle. Just so long as it didn't slip out!

Now for my hair. I sat down at the dressing table. I had no idea how to put it up in the elaborate style I wanted. The best I could do was pin up my plait.

I was sticking hairpins in at random, hoping it wouldn't look too bad, when I suddenly caught sight of my face. I stopped, arms raised, and stared at my reflection.

After all this time, it was strange to see myself, no longer a child; to think, this is what a stranger would see.

Wide mouth. A bit too wide? Long, straight nose. A bit too long? Would they see the tiny scar on the bridge of my nose, where as a toddler I'd tripped on the veranda steps?

My eyes. What would they say about them? Papa said they were an unusual colour – amber, he had called it. Teasingly he used to declare I had dangerous eyes. I tried narrowing them and then widening them – but I couldn't see it. How could eyes be dangerous?

The only thing I was sure about was my hair. I didn't care what people said about red hair, I liked it and it was thick and long now, and a glorious glossy red, like Ophelia's in Millais's painting, one of my favourites. But as to everything else . . .

I addressed the room behind my reflection. Am I pretty, Mamma? Of course the room stayed silent.

But then it happened. That old sensation – of someone standing close behind me, caressing my head. I stared into the mirror as if I could will myself to see whoever it was. But there was no one there.

It wasn't the first time I'd felt it. It had happened before – at home in India, especially when I was looking in a mirror. I'd never told anyone about it. They might think I was mad or possessed. And anyway, I didn't feel frightened. Someone was with me – that's what it felt like – and it was comforting. I felt safe, peaceful, as if all my rage and longing were soothed away . . .

It made me think of the story one of my governesses had told me about humans originally having four arms and legs and two faces. But the gods thought men were becoming too proud, and as a punishment they were cut in half and ever afterwards each half felt incomplete and looked for its other half.

The story intrigued me, but it made me thoughtful as well, because even though I didn't believe it, it made sense of a feeling I'd had sometimes. I'd tried talking to Sally about it, asking her if she ever felt that part of herself was missing. 'As if somewhere in the world there's someone who's like you and if you met them you'd feel whole, like they're the other half of your soul or something.'

She rubbed her nose as she always did when something puzzled her. 'Do you mean like a sweetheart, miss?'

'I don't know. Maybe.'

Sally obviously didn't have the first idea what I was talking about, but then I wasn't sure I did either.

Now I pulled a face at my reflection. It was time to seize the day, as Tippy would say.

Giving my hair a final pat, I rubbed my cheeks and bit my lips to make them redder, snatched up my gloves and I was ready. I didn't have a decent hat; I'd have to go without.

Touching my locket once, for luck, I opened the door and listened. No sound from above, where Tippy would be bent over her drawing, rubber in hand. No sound from several floors below where, in his study, Grandfather would be writing his latest paper to present to his fellow scientists at the Royal Society.

The house was hushed and still, just as Grandfather liked it.

But where were all the servants? Fingers crossed that I wouldn't meet any of them, I quietly hurried past the empty guestroom, down the first flight of stairs, past Grandfather's bedroom and his bathroom where he had a cold shower every morning, down the second flight and past the drawing room. Now came the difficult part.

I opened the door to the servants' staircase and listened. Two floors below I could hear a faint clatter from the kitchen, but there was no sound of footsteps on the stone stairs. Holding my breath, I went down them as quietly as I could, my heart beating fast at the daring of what I was about to do.

I reached the ground floor, paused a moment – all was quiet – and then started my final descent. Ahead lay various dangers – Mrs Jubb, who according to Sally was more like a dragon than a cook, the housekeeper Mrs Grimston, who had a very tart tongue . . . and, worst of all, Ponsonby, the butler. He'd have no qualms about sending me back upstairs *and* reporting me to Grandfather.

I was nearly halfway down when I heard footsteps hurrying up towards me. For a moment I froze, then started to retreat, but it was too late. Someone came round the corner and ran into me, with a squeak.

It was Sally. Thank goodness.

'Lor, miss! You gave me such a fright!'

I put my finger to my lips. 'Shh, Sally, not so loud.'

She took in what I was wearing, and my hair, and her eyes went round. 'You're going out now?'

'Yes, please don't tell on me, Sally.'

'Course not. But you be careful, miss. Don't get lost.'

'I won't.'

'And mind you don't bring a follower home!' She winked.

'What, a beau?' I struck a lovelorn attitude. '*Oh, Miss Garland, what a crusher you are!*'

Sally giggled. 'Got to go – your grandfather rang. Watch out for Ponsonby. He was in a fearful wax this morning.' And she clattered past me and on up the stairs.

I carried on down. Good old Sally – she was a real pal. I half wished she was coming with me.

I made it to the back door unchallenged and ran up the area steps. I whisked past the mews, where Grandfather kept his carriage and horses, slowed to a more respectable pace as I passed the mews of neighbouring houses, nodding at a groom as if it was perfectly normal for a young lady to be walking through the yard, and once I had reached the street at the end and rounded the corner I was able to breathe again.

For the first time in my life I was out in London alone.

SIX

It couldn't be simpler – Sally had told me to go straight through Kensington Gardens and keep going when I reached the other side. There were few people about, but those I passed didn't look at all shocked at seeing a girl out on her own; in fact, they took no notice of me. I told myself sternly that my fear someone might recognize me and insist on taking me back to Grandfather's was irrational. No one would know who I was.

It was a beautiful day with a crisp chill in the air that was bracing. Somewhere someone was burning weeds, the blue smoke drifting in the air; not far off a barrel organ was playing; a fat tabby cat was sunning itself on a step. My spirits rose.

It was fun to rush along the Broad Walk for the sheer pleasure of being out and about or to dawdle watching the children kicking up crisp leaves. Much more fun than walking sedately with Tippy, having a stilted conversation in French.

It didn't take me long to reach Westbourne Grove, where the footpaths were already thronged with shoppers.

One of the few pleasures of shopping trips with Tippy, even to the dull shops we visited, was the opportunity it gave me to watch fashionable ladies in the street and observe how they wore their clothes and carried themselves.

My governess was continually chiding me for staring and for delaying us.

Today I could indulge myself in peace, noticing for example how two ladies alighting from a carriage made an elegant descent to the pavement. But as I looked at the wonderful outfits parading past, I suddenly felt self-conscious; my best dress, I realized, was hopelessly, shapelessly unfashionable, my hair ridiculous.

But there was nothing for it. Squaring my shoulders, I stuck my nose in the air and strode on purposefully like the smart ladies around me.

Whiteley's was even better than I'd imagined from Sally's description: huge windows one after the other all down the street, each one filled with marvels. I lingered longest at the windows where the latest fashions were displayed. Wistfully I gazed at the low-cut evening gowns in lustrous satin. What wouldn't I give to wear something like that? But they must be very expensive. My two guineas shrank to nothing, but I comforted myself with the thought that there must be something to buy in a shop that promised to provide everything.

Once inside the wide doors, my eyes were dazzled by the shininess of everything – the mirrored surfaces, the crystal chandeliers. Even the shop assistants, smartly dressed and wearing eager-to-please expressions, looked shiny. And the air was full of a heady mixture of scents from all the perfumes, creams, lotions and soaps on display.

In a daze I drifted from one polished counter to the next, where the goods were displayed like so much treasure: gloves, bags, necklaces, bracelets, brooches . . .

It was almost too much.

And here, where I least expected it, the familiar longing came over me – not just for a companion, someone like Sally who liked a bit of fun – but for someone to share the experience with, who would understand and feel it in the way I did.

But there wasn't anyone like that.

I made myself focus on the counters again. The prices were clearly marked and I could afford to buy *something*. But what should it be? I needed everything – new boots, pretty underwear instead of the ghastly woollen monstrosities Grandfather insisted on, a proper corset so I would be the right shape and dresses, of course . . . but they were too expensive. Something smaller then, but what?

Wandering further into the shop I found myself at a booth covered with posters and advertisements. All at once a familiar name leaped out – Ellen Terry, appearing in *Faust* at the Lyceum. Ellen Terry – Mamma's favourite actress. It must be a theatre-ticket booking agency! For ten shillings I could watch this wonderful woman performing on the stage. I would be able to see for myself exactly what Mamma meant.

I was so tempted. Of all the things I'd seen so far today, this was what I wanted most. But Grandfather would never allow me to go, especially if 'that immoral woman' was appearing. I stood there imagining all the things I might say to try to persuade him, but I knew it was hopeless.

Heartsick, I turned away and nearly fell over a board displaying pictures of ladies' heads. It was, I realized, the hairdressing department and all at once I knew what I wanted to do with my money.

Before I could change my mind I marched in. An elegant young woman sitting at a table looked me up and down and said, 'May I help you, miss?' Her face was perfectly polite, but there was something sneering in her tone.

I bridled. 'I'd like a frizzled fringe and my hair putting up.' Sally had told me a frizzled fringe was the most fashionable way to wear your hair at the moment and I'd seen lots of them today. But struck by a sudden thought I added, 'Can you tell me how much that would cost?'

Consulting a tariff, she smiled unpleasantly. 'That will be three shillings and sixpence.'

Three shillings and sixpence! A big chunk of my two guineas! I swallowed. But my heart was set on this. 'Right. That's what I'd like.'

'You don't have an appointment?' The young woman sighed and then looked down a list. 'Monsieur Alphonse may be able to fit you in, if you're prepared to wait.'

As I took a seat it briefly crossed my mind that Grandfather might not be too pleased about my hair. That's if the old coot noticed. But there was going to be a fearful row about my coming out anyway; this would hardly make it worse.

I watched the hairdressers at work, noting carefully

what they did so I could get Sally to do it for me. One thing was certain – I was never going back to a childish plait again.

An hour later I emerged feeling as pleased as punch.

True, I'd had to put up with the impertinence of 'Monsieur Alphonse', an affected young man with well-oiled hair. He recoiled from my plait as if it were a rat. But who was he to give himself such airs? My French might not be up to much, but I could recognize a genuine French accent when I heard one. Once or twice when he forgot himself he sounded just like Hannah, our kitchen-maid. Whatever his name, I was fairly sure Monsieur Alphonse came from the East End of London.

A delicious smell made my mouth water and I suddenly realized how hungry I was. I found the provision department and watched while a lady in an extraordinary hat – it appeared to have a whole dead pigeon on it – made her selection from rows of expensive chocolates.

And here was a counter displaying cakes – pink iced confections, little pastries with toasted almond toppings, meringues oozing cream . . . My mouth watered. At Grandfather's, cake was always 'wholesome'; in other words plain and boring: seed cake, pound cake. This was a real treat, but which should it be?

I chose an almond pastry and a bag of gingerbread jumbles and waited impatiently while the wooden canister containing my money went humming along the overhead wires to the distant cashier and returned with a loud ping.

I knew of course, having had it drilled into me, that a lady was never seen eating in public. Hah! Having received my change, I wandered on, munching on my purchases, until, turning a corner, I stopped transfixed. I hadn't seen bananas since I'd left India and here they were, piled high.

And what was this? Okra, root ginger and green chilli peppers and spices – cardamom, cumin, turmeric. It was just like the bazaar. Shutting my eyes, I breathed in deeply, as if somehow I could absorb the smell into my very being. As I did so homesickness overwhelmed me, a feeling so sharp it took my breath away, and all the bitter disappointment of the morning came flooding back.

'Miss? Miss? Please, excuse me.'

I opened my eyes. And stared. There before me, like a vision, stood an Indian gentleman of princely bearing in a dazzling white kurta fastened with jewelled buttons. What on earth was he doing in a department store in London?

He bowed his turbaned head graciously and I realized I was blocking his way.

In the face of his courtly splendour I suddenly felt silly again. What must he be seeing? Not the elegant young lady I so wanted to be, but a tearful child in a stupid, ugly dress with a newspaper bustle, gingerbread crumbs round her mouth and sticky gloves. I'd eaten too many jumbles too quickly and I felt slightly sick.

Blushing, I muttered, 'Sorry, sorry,' and fled from the food hall.

As I rounded the corner I ran smack bang into something very solid. There was a surprised 'Oh!' followed by the horrible sound of something smashing on a hard floor. When I dared to look I saw a middle-aged lady dressed in a loosely gathered salmon-coloured gown, with a kind of pie-frill round her neck, staring down at what looked like at least a hundred fragments of porcelain scattered around our feet.

I looked from her shocked red face to the shocked pale face of the shop assistant; then my eyes slid to the display of Japanese vases. I swallowed as I read the price on the ticket.

The next moment a frock-coated gentleman with a distinct air of authority had swept over. 'Madam, have no fear. I saw what happened and it certainly wasn't your fault.'

He turned to me. 'You silly child! Whatever were you doing running about like that? You knocked the vase right out of this lady's hands.'

'Oh, I'm sorry, I'm so sorry,' I babbled, looking round at them all.

The gentleman's expression remained frosty. 'You'll pay for this, of course.'

'Yes, of course. That is . . .' I could feel my face reddening. Stomach churning, I fumbled for my purse, even though I knew I didn't have enough money.

'Come along. We haven't got all day.'

At this point the middle-aged lady came to life. Casting a shrewd glance in my direction, she said to the gentleman, 'Thank you, but I can deal with this. I'm sure you have other pressing matters to attend to.' Her firm tone permitted no further discussion.

'Oh, right. If you insist, madam,' he said, clearly disgruntled. 'Simpkins!' He addressed the poor assistant sharply. 'Don't just stand there gawking. When you have attended to this lady, sweep this mess up.'

'Yes, Mr Oliver.' She bobbed at his departing back and I turned to face the lady.

To my amazement she was proffering a note to the assistant.

I rushed forward, crunching porcelain fragments under my feet, and held out a handful of coins. 'Please, take these. I'm afraid it's not enough, but if you let me have your address, I'll send you the rest, I promise.'

The lady smiled. 'That's very sweet of you, but it was an accident after all. And I'm afraid it was partly my fault.' She pointed at a sign by the display that read: Please do not touch. 'See? I shouldn't even have been holding the vase.'

I couldn't believe how forbearing she was being. 'No, it was my fault, truly, and I want to pay for it.'

'Very well, if it makes you feel better. But I won't take your pocket money – you might need it. Why don't you get your people to send me a cheque?'

A horrible feeling swept over me as I envisaged having to explain to Grandfather what had happened, but I managed to say, 'Right, yes, I will.'

With another quick glance at me she took out her pocketbook. As she was writing she said, 'What's your name, dear?'

'Meriel . . . Meriel Garland.'

She looked up with the oddest expression on her face and then stared hard at me. 'Good heavens! How extraordinary.'

SEVEN

Puzzled, I waited for the lady to say more.

Breaking into a smile, she said, 'Meriel, my dear child. As soon as I saw that hair I should have recognized you.' And to my utter amazement she pulled me to her in a warm embrace. It was like being hugged by an eiderdown especially as she obviously wasn't wearing any stays, but mercifully she let go of me before I was smothered.

I stared at her, taking in her broad brow, soft cheeks, kindly brown eyes. Who on earth was she?

She stood regarding me fondly for a minute or two and then she chuckled. 'You don't know who I am, do you?'

Dumbly I shook my head.

'Forgive me, my dear. Whatever will you think of me? I'm Mrs Jolly, Everina Jolly.'

Seeing the name meant nothing to me either, she added, 'I'm a friend of your father.'

'Oh.' That was the last thing I expected to hear. How did she know Papa?

Her face wreathed in smiles, Mrs Jolly was rattling on about the coincidence of running into me – 'How fortunate!' – and how she liked Whiteleys – 'More convenient than trekking up to Oxford Street, don't you think?' – and only drew breath after saying, 'Have you had lunch, dear?'

'Yes,' I said, still uncomfortably full of jumble.

'Did you try their curry? Don't, it's disgusting – no idea how to do it properly.'

So she must know Papa from India. I almost told her how much I missed curry, proper ones like Azad used to make, but, still not sure of her, I held back. Instead I remarked, 'I was surprised to see an Indian gentleman here, earlier.'

Mrs Jolly waved a hand airily. 'Oh, you'll run into lots of them round here. Didn't you know, this part of London is known as "Asia Minor". Stuffed full of Anglo-Indians too. That's why I like it – wouldn't board anywhere else. I feel at home here.'

I felt drawn to her. And even more so when she said, 'Now, my dear, you mustn't think of paying for that vase. I insist.' But when I'd thanked her and she said, 'Are you in a rush? Or have you got time for a chat?' I hesitated.

If she was so attached to India, perhaps she'd understand my feelings about it, and it was a temptation to pour out my resentment against Grandfather for not letting me go back, to share the unfairness of it all. But I was embarrassed enough already about the vase – I didn't want to make a fool of myself again. And nice as she seemed to be, there was something about her that reminded me of Mrs Fitzgerald, that awful woman who'd brought me to England. I feared Mrs Jolly too was the kind of person who might try to take you over. And indeed the next minute, without waiting for an answer, she said, 'Come on then, my dear,' and seizing my hand, she sailed off, dragging me along in her wake, like a passenger boat towing a dinghy.

She pushed open a door marked 'Ladies' Retiring Room' and drew me in. Ladies were sitting about in armchairs, some reading magazines, some chatting to their neighbours.

'Now, let's sit down, shall we? We have so much to talk about.'

'You said "board here"?' It seemed safer to get her talking about herself.

'Yes. Quite nice rooms – I rent them from a widow – husband was in the Indian Civil Service. I won't be going home till after Christmas. My girls – I have three of the minxes, all younger than you – are at school here. I came over with Minty to settle her in and to see how the other two are faring.' She leaned towards me and said, 'It's very hard, you know, being torn between husband and children, but then of course you'll know all about that, won't you? You must miss your dear papa dreadfully.'

'Mmm,' I said non-committally. And then to divert her, 'Where is home for you?'

'Why, Calcutta, of course.'

'Oh!' My heart jumped. 'That's how you know Papa?'

'Yes. Gussie – that's my husband, Augustus, Mr Jolly – he's the principal of the School of Art, where your papa works. You didn't know?'

Embarrassed I stuttered, 'I'm afraid – I don't think Papa has mentioned—'

'Of course not. Why would he? Far better things to talk about,' she said heartily. 'Now let me see . . .' She paused to think. 'We lived in Calcutta at first, then we had a spell in Bombay. We went there in seventy-seven, so you would have been, what . . . ?'

'Eight.'

'That's it then.' She waved her hand triumphantly at me. 'The last time I saw you, you were eight. It was such a lovely day – we had tea in the garden. I remember it well, because, you see, I'd come to say goodbye.'

She must have known Mamma!

I tried to remember. Papa and Mamma had so many friends, but now I thought about it, I had a dim recollection of someone who might have been Mrs Jolly coming to the house with two small girls.

'Were you and Mamma close?'

'I thought so. I certainly counted her among my dearest friends.' Shaking her head, she sighed. 'Poor Eleanor. A dreadful business.' She gave me a searching look. 'It must have been very hard for you.'

In the face of her kindly sympathy, my resistance melted. It had been so long since I'd had anyone to open my heart to. Out it all poured – how at first I hadn't understood the situation, thinking that a dog bite wasn't that serious . . . 'And Mamma was all right at first, you know, perfectly herself . . .' How she then became ill, not very ill, just a headache and feeling tired and not wanting to eat . . . 'So you know, I still didn't realize, I thought she was going to get better. I didn't know she was dying . . .'

I took the handkerchief Mrs Jolly passed me and wiped my eyes. Then I told Mrs Jolly how they had tried to keep me from Mamma at the end, but I'd escaped from Anila and run in and seen her, delirious, terrified, thrashing about . . . 'And do you know the worst thing? Her jaw was paralysed. She was dying of thirst, but she couldn't drink and – she couldn't speak to me, not one word.'

I looked up to find that Mrs Jolly too was dabbing her eyes. There was a hush in our immediate vicinity, and even though the ladies nearby started talking almost at once, I was sure they'd heard me and my face went hot.

Mrs Jolly blew her nose loudly and gave me a watery smile. 'Tell me, my poor child, how is it at your grandfather's?'

Papa must have told her what he'd arranged for me. I'd already said too much, given too much away. I looked round the room and caught sight of a clock. 'Goodness, is that the time? I'm sorry, I must be getting back.' Mrs Jolly caught my hand as I stood up.

'My dear, do you have to go? I could pop a note in the post to your grandfather and you could come back and have tea with us. And afterwards I have a few friends coming over. You'll enjoy it. I'll say we'll have you back for ten and then no one will worry.'

I hesitated, wondering if I dared. I didn't think Grandfather would be too pleased but then I was already going to be in trouble so what difference could it make?

'Good, that's settled then,' said Mrs Jolly, as if I'd agreed, and she started gathering up her bags.

EIGHT

As we entered Mrs Jolly's living room, three girls, all dressed alike in embroidered smocks of brown holland, sprang up and greeted us excitedly, all talking at once.

'Mamma! Perfect timing. The water's nearly boiled.'

'Hello, would you care for a muffin?'

'Do you like mongooses? I do. Mine killed a snake.' This last from the smallest, who I guessed must be Minty.

After introducing me to the girls, Mrs Jolly turned to an Indian woman who had risen quietly from a seat by the fire. 'My treasure, Varali.'

Her bangles softly clashing, Varali greeted me with a salaam. She gave me a shy smile when I responded in the same way. In her orange sari, with her gleaming dark hair, she reminded me so much of Anila. And as I looked round the crowded room I saw several familiar things: an Indian brass-topped folding table, a carved screen, a string of wooden elephants parading along the mantelpiece . . . A lump came into my throat, but luckily at that moment Amy announced, 'Tea's ready!'

Grandfather would have been appalled. There was a whole loaf on the table, the jam pot had a sticky spoon, the milk jug was chipped . . . But for the first time in four years I felt at home and soon joined in the merry chatter.

'Do you know my grandfather has actually done experiments to find out how to make the perfect cup of tea?'

'No! Really?' said Mrs Jolly.

'Yes, and he gives the housemaids what for if they don't do it right. "*I've told you before – the perfect cup of tea needs water of two hundred and twelve degrees and takes exactly eight minutes to brew.*" '

The girls giggled at my imitation.

'And he's always harping on about genius being hereditary – I'm sure he regards himself as a genius – but then he complains about my poor schoolwork. So it doesn't look as if the theory has worked in my case!'

The girls started talking about their day at school and I told them some tales about the tricks I'd played on my governesses, like the time I'd slipped a spider into Miss Jeek's porridge. I acted out her shocked reaction – a loud scream followed by, '*I can't bear it! Take it away, Meriel! Eugh! I'm going to be sick!*' and they shrieked with laughter. Having such an appreciative audience gave me a warm glow.

Mrs Jolly laughed too. 'Careful, Meriel. Don't go giving them ideas. They're as mischievous as monkeys as it is.'

Eventually she announced the girls' bedtime. They protested, and it was only when I promised to come again that they allowed themselves to be shooed out by Varali.

Mrs Jolly started reminiscing about India then, nothing too personal or painful, and I was drawn into conversation, comparing memories of different places. While we talked, Varali served a supper of spicy Indian dishes. It was the most scrumptious meal I'd eaten in a long time. Either Mrs Jolly didn't know or she didn't care about the rule of not talking while eating. She chattered on, referring frequently to Mamma and Papa. She and her husband must have spent more time with them than I'd realized and I gathered she still saw Papa quite often.

This made me feel uncomfortable – she knew more about Papa than I did, but she seemed to assume I knew these things too. The truth was I had only the vaguest idea of how he spent his time. I never read his letters properly – I skimmed through them looking for the magic words *Come home.*

I didn't feel like telling Mrs Jolly about this morning's great disappointment now. I'd bared my soul enough for one day. Besides, Varali had come to clear away the dishes and I began to wonder what lay ahead.

'Are there many people coming tonight?'

'Just half a dozen – a friendly bunch, though whether they are the sort your grandfather would approve of, I have my doubts. Lavinia Lashbrook, for example – have you heard of her?'

I shook my head.

'She writes novels – rather amusing in their way. Sensational, you know. She likes to shock, but she's a good soul at heart. But I'm afraid I don't know very many lords and ladies.'

'How do you know Grandfather is such a toady?'

Mrs Jolly laughed. 'I gathered it from something your mother once said. I expect your grandfather would think my cousin Hugh Neville acceptable – he works at the Natural History Museum – but I'm afraid he and his wife are off to the opera tonight.'

'The opera!'

Perhaps I sounded envious because Mrs Jolly asked, 'Do you like opera, Meriel?'

'I don't know – I've never been.' On impulse I added, 'What I'd really love is to go to the theatre. I've not been since I came to England. Mamma and Papa used to take me when the travelling companies came to Calcutta, but—'

There was a ring at the doorbell.

'That'll be Cecil.' Mrs Jolly smiled indulgently. 'He always comes early for fear of being late.'

A young man in a huge floppy bow tie shot into the room as if propelled, but seeing me he came to an abrupt halt and his mouth dropped open.

'Mr Utterby, let me introduce my friend, Miss Garland.'

'Ah! *Les pwemières fleurs qu'elles sont parfumées!*' And giggling nervously, he gave my hand a limp, damp shake.

'I'm sorry?'

'Verlaine. Do you . . . Do you like poetwy, Miss Garland?' He spoke in a curious way, hesitant at first and then rushing on in a burst, revealing prominent teeth.

'Er, yes.'

'I . . . I adore the Fwench poets, don't you? To capture moments of extweme sensation . . . I . . . I am a poet myself.'

'Oh.' I really didn't know what to say to him, and the way he was looking at me was embarrassing. But at that moment several people arrived and Mrs Jolly beckoned me over. I was glad to escape Mr Utterby's attentions.

I guessed at once who one of the newcomers was even before she announced herself.

'Miss Lashbrook, but do call me Lavinia. I can't abide silly convention.' Pressing my hand warmly, she glided off.

She was certainly a striking sight. With quantities of dark hair piled high on her head, she was sporting an outfit to rival Mrs Jolly's in its oddness – a red silk robe with a high neck and long loose sleeves, worn over a flowing yellow dress. She looked like some high-born lady in a Renaissance painting. She wasn't young. In fact, none of these people were anywhere near my age. But it didn't matter – this was much better than an evening by myself or with Tippy.

Mrs Jolly introduced me to her nieces. Miss Russell, a rather serious young woman, said hello, then went to talk to a shabbily dressed elderly man. Not very friendly, I thought.

Her sister Daisy was prettier. I noticed with a stab of envy that she had dimples when she smiled. She asked me how I knew Mrs Jolly, and while we were talking I became aware of a pair of dark sardonic eyes surveying me from across the room.

'Who's that?' I asked Daisy in an undertone.

'That's Mr Foyd. Be careful. He is sure to want to paint you.' She giggled.

Was she serious? I'd like to have my portrait painted, but perhaps not by Mr Foyd, with his sticking-up hair and his fierce black eyebrows.

'And who's that with your sister?'

'Oh, that's Herr Blumstein, dear old thing. He lodges upstairs.'

Mrs Jolly raised her voice. 'Now then, everyone, let's get started. We need to clear a space.'

I watched bemused as the chairs and occasional tables were pushed back. What was going on?

'And now we need to divide into two parties.'

There was a sudden movement in our direction as Mr Utterby rushed across the room, followed at a more leisurely pace by Mr Foyd. The next second Miss Lashbrook appeared at my side.

'Ah,' said Mrs Jolly. 'It would be better if we were evenly divided. Daisy dear, would you mind being in our group?' And as Daisy moved she went on, 'I thought we'd do scenes from Shakespeare tonight.'

I nearly clapped. What fun!

This was obviously something they'd done before as, without further explanation, Mrs Jolly led her group out on to the landing. As the door was shutting I heard Miss

Russell say, 'I will do whatever you say, but I won't play a man's part.'

What a ninny! I'd act anything if someone asked me. I looked at my companions expectantly.

'What shall it be then, Arthur?' Miss Lashbrook smiled coquettishly at the artist. Oho, I thought. She likes him.

But he was staring at me and I felt myself blushing. Why? He was old, at least thirty, and he had splashes of paint on his trousers.

He murmured, '*Crimson and Gold*, that's what I'll call it.'

Miss Lashbrook oozed closer to him. 'Are you planning your next painting, Arthur?'

'Mmm.'

'How would you like me to wear my hair?'

'What?' He started. 'Not you, Lavinia.' He looked at me. 'That hair, those eyes, yes – *Crimson and Gold*, perfect.'

I blushed again. But his admiration gave me a little thrill. Then I noticed the look on Miss Lashbrook's face and I gave her a sheepish smile.

Rather brusquely she said, 'We must get on. Which play?'

'*Wo– Womeo and Juliet*?' suggested Mr Utterby with a sideways glance at me.

Mr Foyd made a rude noise. 'Not that,' he drawled. 'Too much love and death. What about a comedy?'

'How about *Twelfth Night*?' I suggested. Mr Utterby

with his receding chin and lank hair, was perfect for timid Sir Andrew Aguecheek.

'A wemarkable idea!' Mr Utterby flashed his teeth at me. 'But which scene?'

'Are we to act a whole scene?' I was surprised. There was no sign of a book anywhere.

'No, no. We choose a scene and mime it.' Miss Lashbrook made an expansive gesture. 'The others have to guess which it is.'

After some discussion we settled on the scene where Olivia declares her love for Viola, mistaking her for a young man, followed by Sir Toby Belch's attempt to get Viola and Sir Andrew to fight.

I don't think Mr Utterby liked being cast in the role of Sir Andrew, but Miss Lashbrook bullied him into it, declaring that she would play Olivia, Mr Foyd should play Sir Toby and that I should be Viola.

Privately I thought this was the best part. There was the serious bit where I had to remind Olivia I was there to present my master Orsino's love, and then the comedy of pretending to be a bold young man while being terrified of being killed.

As we rehearsed, my main difficulty was not laughing at Mr Utterby, who during the fight scene would keep looking at me like an adoring puppy rather than a frightened knight.

At last the others returned. They went first and it was obviously meant to be a serious scene, but I had to work hard to stop myself laughing.

After some embracing, Daisy's sister died first, not a very convincing death as, stiff as a poker, she sank gradually to the floor. The illusion was further spoiled by her continuing to fidget with her skirts as if she was afraid of exposing too much ankle. Daisy, trying not to giggle, mimed talking to something in her hand and then, laying her hand on her breast, she died very prettily. Herr Blumstein marched in with a solemn face, whereupon Mrs Jolly laid *her* hand on her breast and died dramatically by throwing herself backwards, but cunningly she managed to land on a convenient sofa.

We clapped enthusiastically.

'So many deaths one might think it was *Hamlet*, but for all the kissing,' drawled Mr Foyd. 'Do you know what it was, Miss Garland?'

'Cleopatra's death from *Antony and Cleopatra*?'

Everyone congratulated me and then we performed our scene. I might not be very good at French, but this was something I *could* do and it went well, I thought, though it took a while for the others to guess which play it was taken from.

Afterwards there was a lull in which Miss Lashbrook spoke out. 'You seem to have a natural talent for this, Miss Garland. Have you acted before?'

'Oh yes. At home in India we often had evenings of amateur theatricals, and I learned Shakespeare by heart with my mother.' My voice trembled and I was aware of Mrs Jolly's eye upon me, but it was Mr Utterby who spoke.

'Oh, would you care to tweat us to a speech from your wepertoire, Miss Garland?'

'Would you like me to?' I looked round. Everyone was nodding encouragingly so I ran rapidly through the possibilities and chose the speech where Juliet is looking forward to her wedding night with Romeo. I loved it – it was so passionate: 'Come, night; come, Romeo; come, thou day in night . . .'

I gave it my best, aware from the hushed stillness that I had their full attention.

There was a beat of silence when I finished. Then everyone clapped and Mr Foyd even called, 'Bravo!' It felt wonderful.

As general conversation broke out Mrs Jolly came over and said, 'Sorry, Meriel, but it's ten o'clock. I've sent Varali for a cab.' Already? I couldn't believe the time had flown so fast.

After I'd taken leave of everyone, Mrs Jolly accompanied me downstairs. She gave me a warm hug. 'I'm so glad we met. You must tell your papa, next time you write. He'll be pleased, I know.' Releasing me, but retaining hold of my hand, she gave me a tender look. 'Poor dear Eleanor, she would be so proud of you.'

I smiled at her, moved by her words.

'It's been so lovely to have you. You'll come again?'

I didn't hesitate. 'Yes, please!'

NINE

6 Queen's Gate Walk
Kensington
22nd October 1885

Dear Papa,
Thank you for your letter & the peacock feather – & thank you very much for the postal order. I didn't find it until after I'd been shopping but next time I hope I can buy myself something very nice.

For once I had some fun yesterday. I met your friend Mrs Jolly in Whiteleys & she took me back to her house & I had a fine time. We mimed scenes from Shakespeare & I acted and everyone said I was very good.

BUT because I went out without asking permission, on my own, and missed my music lesson, there has been a frightful row. Grandfather behaved like the Spanish Inquisition. Truly, Papa, I was frightened. He kept asking, 'Who else did you meet?' as if I'd made a secret assignation. He's said I must never again go out without the governess (who will only let me buy boring things like hat elastic & flannelette nightgowns) & if I do, the first thing he will do is stop my allowance (which he has only just started giving me)! He didn't say what else he would do, but he implied I wouldn't like it.

I have to do extra lessons today & I've been made to put my hair back into a plait, after I'd had it put up in a very elegant style by the hairdresser.

Papa, can you not see how badly I am treated? I hate it here. But Grandfather says I won't be able to come home next year. It isn't true, is it? If I thought it was, my heart would break. Please tell me it isn't so. But in the meantime will you write to Grandfather & tell him that I have your permission to put my hair up, wear long dresses, go out on my own & generally be treated like a young lady. I am sixteen now, after all.

The only thing that saved me from being banned from Mrs Jolly's is that Grandfather knows her cousin who is something important in the Natural History Museum. So I can look forward to some more nice times at least until Mrs Jolly returns to India. But what will I do then?

Please, please, Papa, let me come home with Mrs Jolly.

Please, Papa.

Your ever-loving daughter,

Meriel

TEN

Once I had recovered from my encounter with Grandfather my high spirits returned. This time Papa would respond to my appeal, for sure, and meanwhile I had Mrs Jolly's to look forward to. Every day I expected a note from her and I thought I'd go mad if it didn't come soon.

Poor old Tippy – she was at her wits' end.

Normally we had a settled routine. After some persuasion on my part, we'd reached a compromise. I'd do the minimum of schoolwork necessary to satisfy Grandfather, then I'd practise acting or read the scandal sheets Sally passed on to me while Tippy sucked peppermints and read romances from the public library – the kind Grandfather thought led to 'softening of the brain'. She sometimes lent them to me, and they weren't bad, though I preferred sensation novels, which Tippy kindly borrowed for me on her ticket. This comfortable arrangement suited us both, but Grandfather would have been merciless if he'd caught us so we had to be on our guard for his visits to the schoolroom.

Every now and again, more frequently recently, he'd descend on us without warning. Keeping his eye on us, I suppose. It made me shiver the way he'd stand there watching us, me in particular, without saying a word. But so far he hadn't caught us out. A squeaky board on the landing warned us if anyone was coming, and we had time to snatch up the schoolbooks and look as if we were doing what we were supposed to be.

However, since the evening at Mrs Jolly's, I couldn't concentrate at all. I kept imitating the people I'd met at her house and repeating the things they'd said. I talked so much and laughed so much that finally and astonishingly Tippy actually shouted, though it came out as more of a squeak, 'Miss Meriel, will you *please* stop playing the giddy goat!'

It was funny, like seeing a mouse lose its temper. But when she said, 'What if Sir Osbert hears you?' it pulled me up short.

The last thing I wanted was to provoke Grandfather. I certainly didn't want him to change his mind about letting me go to Mrs Jolly's, but nor did I want another confrontation like the one after my birthday escapade. I hadn't exaggerated to Papa – I *had* been frightened, not so much by what Grandfather said, though that was bad enough, but by his unspoken menace, the ferocious intensity of his eyes when he said I was never to go out alone again.

So I tried to calm down, and in the meantime I was practising Ophelia's mad scene, getting Sally to stand in for the other characters whenever she could, though this wasn't very successful because she couldn't help giggling and that set me off too.

And then one morning she appeared with an envelope. I leaped up so fast I knocked over the inkstand.

Tippy let out a volley of squeaks, but ignoring her and the stream of ink spreading over the table, I tore open the envelope.

Mrs Everina Jolly would consider it an honour if Miss Meriel Garland would accompany her to the Lyceum Theatre on the evening of December 21st to see 'Faust' . . .

'Yes! Yes! YES!' I shrieked.

Sally and Tippy, who were mopping up the mess, looked up, startled. Seizing a bemused Sally round the waist, I danced round the room, singing, 'I'm going to the theatre! I'm going to the theatre!'

Hot and out of breath, I relinquished Sally at last, and flinging myself into a chair I read the letter again.

'Meriel . . .' Tippy began.

'Just a minute, there's more.'

Mrs Jolly was also inviting me to her house for the evening in two days' time.

I stood up to follow Sally out of the door.

'Where are you going?'

'I must show this to Grandfather.'

Tippy shook her head. 'Do you think that's a good idea?' And she looked at the schoolroom clock.

She was right. Half past ten in the morning was just about the worst time to interrupt Grandfather. I would have to wait. But how on earth could I go back to the river systems of Europe when every part of me was fizzing with excitement?

There was only one thing I might be able to think about.

'Miss Tippins, I'd like to learn about Faust. Can we do that? Now?'

I wasn't surprised at the look on her face. It was the first time I'd ever shown an interest in learning anything.

'Of course, Meriel. Of course we can.'

Two days later on the dot of eight o'clock I alighted from Grandfather's carriage and rang Mrs Jolly's bell. Annoyingly Grandfather had insisted that Tippy come with me. But nothing was going to stop me enjoying myself tonight.

Mrs Jolly greeted me with her warm smile. 'Hello, my dear! And I see you have a companion.' I introduced the governess and straight away Mrs Jolly started telling her how impressed they'd all been by my acting. Tippy gave me an anxious, reproachful look. Abruptly I excused myself and went to greet Herr Blumstein.

While we were talking I surveyed the room out of the corner of my eye. Miss Lashbrook and Mr Utterby were chatting by the mantelpiece. The latter, seeing me, broke into a toothy grin, which I ignored. No sign of Mr Foyd. No Daisy Russell or her sister either, but a girl I didn't know sitting by herself on the sofa.

She was about my age, but very plainly dressed in a boring grey gown and she seemed withdrawn and self-contained. In fact, with her dark hair, pale oval face and serious expression, she looked like a nun.

Mrs Jolly came up and taking me by the arm said,

'Excuse me, Herr Blumstein. May I borrow this young lady?'

Steering me over to the sofa, she said, 'Miss Casson, may I introduce Miss Garland. I knew her when she was a little girl in India, but she's been in London a while now so I'm sure you two will have much to talk about.' And she sailed off.

I couldn't help feeling irritated. Mrs Jolly meant well, but why did adults assume young people would like each other just because they were of a similar age? And this girl didn't exactly look like one for larks, as Sally called them. But it was stupid to sit there looking at one another and not saying anything.

'Have you known Mrs Jolly long?' I asked.

'I don't know her at all.'

That was all she was going to say?

'So why are you here?' It wasn't polite, I knew that, but I was determined to make her speak.

'I'm here with my guardian, Mrs Quinn. She knows Miss Lashbrook.' She nodded towards the window and turning I saw someone I hadn't spotted before, a mound of a woman dressed in rusty black, spilling out of a small armchair. She had a face like a bulldog's, eyebrows that looked painted on and I think she was wearing a wig.

For a moment I almost felt sorry for the girl. Even Grandfather might be better than that funny old bird.

'And do you like amateur theatricals?'

'No! I'd hate to have everyone looking at me.'

Good. She wouldn't be a rival then.

'What *do* you like?'

She looked sideways and for a moment I thought she wasn't going to answer. But eventually she said, 'I'm fond of music.' She spoke in a cool way, as if to say, 'Don't ask any more, for I shan't tell *you*.'

Luckily Mrs Jolly rescued us from this tedious conversation, by addressing the company. 'Now that we're all here, we can make a start. Lavinia thought it would be . . . interesting, to say the least, to do something different tonight.'

'Indeed,' burst in Miss Lashbrook with enthusiasm. 'We should mark the day.'

What did she mean?

'But,' Mrs Jolly went on, quelling Miss Lashbrook with a look, 'before we do, has anyone prepared something to entertain us?'

'I have.' I leaped up.

'Twemendous,' cried Mr Utterby.

I'd planned for this carefully. I'd collected some twigs from the Gardens, to represent Ophelia's flowers. I'd also tied my hair back loosely. I patted my locket for luck, and then, as I faced my audience, I gave my ribbon a tug so my hair fell down and spread over my shoulders. Tippy gasped, but I ignored her and launched into Ophelia's song.

I knew singing wasn't my strong point, but it didn't matter if I sang out of tune – it was quite a good way of suggesting Ophelia's madness. Even so, I skipped quickly through the snatch of song and started on the speech, handing out twigs as I spoke. Miss Casson shrank back when I offered her the pretend pansies so I laid them in her lap. When I finished there was a loud burst of applause and I swept a deep bow, loving every minute of it. Noticing Miss Casson gazing at me, I made a cheeky little bow to her and she immediately looked away.

'Thank you, my dear,' said Mrs Jolly. 'That was splendid. Anyone else?' She looked round but as no one made a move, she went on, 'In that case, I'd like to welcome our two special visitors, Mrs Quinn and Miss Casson. We are in your hands, Mrs Quinn.'

That lady now hauled herself out of her armchair with some difficulty. Supporting herself on a cane she said in a husky voice, 'Thank you for inviting us on this night when the veil between the living and those who have passed is as insubstantial as air – an auspicious time for spirit communication.'

Of course. It was October the thirty-first. All Hallows Eve. Despite myself a shiver ran down my back.

I told myself not to be silly. I'd read about this spirit nonsense in the newspapers Sally passed on to me. It was all the rage – people flocking to see famous mediums who could do all sorts of things including, apparently, floating out of windows. Utter rot. And it didn't look as if we were going to do any more acting.

I scowled at the visitor. Why did she have to come and spoil things?

Judging from the murmur of anticipation that greeted Mrs Quinn's words, no one else was objecting. When she beckoned us to gather round the table, which had been cleared of its clutter, everyone else took their place eagerly. Only Tippy and I were left standing. She was looking worried. With a glance at Mrs Quinn, she stared pointedly at me, trying to signal with her eyebrows. Any minute, if she got up her courage, she would say we should leave.

I wasn't going to be treated like a child. Turning my back on Tippy, I marched up to the table and sat down with the others. Tippy hesitated and then came and joined the circle, looking round anxiously.

Mrs Quinn asked Herr Blumstein to turn down the gas. At once the room became a shadowy cavern, only the fire glowing, like a red eye. I heard a nervous giggle that sounded like Mr Utterby. Despite myself, I was half intrigued. Would anything happen?

Someone struck a match and lit the candle that had been placed in the centre of the table. At once everyone's faces appeared, illuminated but made unfamiliar by the flame.

'We will start with a hymn,' Mrs Quinn wheezed. '*How strange it is on the further shore . . .*' In a hoarse rumble she began to sing and everyone else joined in, a ragged chorus.

I didn't sing because I didn't know the words. I noticed Miss Casson's voice soaring above the rest, a high, pure sound.

'And now a reading from the first letter to the Corinthians, chapter thirteen, verse twelve.'

I hadn't noticed that Mrs Quinn had produced a Bible. In the darkness I smiled to myself, thinking how

Grandfather, a declared atheist, would disapprove of what was happening now.

In her husky voice Mrs Quinn read, 'For now we see through a glass, darkly; but then face to face: now I know in part; but then shall I know even as also I am known.'

At this there was an appreciative murmur round the table. But the reference to seeing through a glass had reminded me of that strange sensation I sometimes had when I looked in the mirror. Surely it couldn't be a spirit, a ghost visiting me? A shudder ran through me at the thought.

I told myself not to be stupid. That experience was reassuring, and besides, I'd felt it long before Mamma died. It couldn't be a spirit.

'Let us all hold hands,' instructed Mrs Quinn.

I was glad I was sitting between Mrs Jolly and Herr Blumstein. I didn't mind holding hands with either of them. Mr Utterby would have been a different matter.

'Now what happens?' Miss Lashbrook's loud question made me jump.

'We wait,' Mrs Quinn said quietly. 'We try not to disturb Sophie's concentration.'

Sophie? That must be Miss Casson. I looked at her with renewed interest; she had her eyes closed, I noticed.

A restive silence fell. Someone coughed, and Mr Utterby giggled again. Only Mrs Quinn and her ward were still.

Bored now, I studied the rings glinting in the candlelight. Mrs Jolly wore just one, a plain gold band. Mrs

Quinn wore the most, heavy jet rings on nearly every finger. I'd have liked Miss Lashbrook's snake ring for myself. I swallowed a yawn and wished I'd let Tippy take me home.

Miss Casson seemed to be in some sort of trance now. Her face, shining out of the darkness, was a smooth, translucent mask and she was swaying slightly, backwards and forwards.

And then she spoke. 'Someone is here.'

A shiver ran through me.

Miss Casson tilted her head as if she was listening. 'Does the name Florence mean anything?'

'Cwumpets!' exclaimed Mr Utterby, who was sitting next to Miss Casson. 'It's Gwandmamma!'

A ripple ran round the circle.

'She says . . .' Miss Casson broke off, screwing up her eyes as if she was concentrating. 'She says, "The drawer – look in the drawer again."'

'My pen!' said Mr Utterby. 'Gwandmamma gave it to me, and I've been looking for it evewywhere.'

Someone gasped. Across the circle Tippy's little mouse-face was looking apprehensive.

'Without it, I can't wite.' Mr Utterby was explaining. He leaned towards Miss Casson. 'Will you ask her – if I find it, will my muse weturn?'

'She hears you,' said Miss Casson. 'She says, "Yes."'

There was a communal sigh as if everyone had been holding their breath till now.

Did this girl really have the power to talk to the spirits

of the dead? While the circle broke into a quiet murmur I watched her closely. She had resumed her swaying, but suddenly she stopped and seemed to go rigid.

Mrs Quinn hushed us.

'There is someone else here.' Miss Casson spoke so quietly we all leaned towards her. 'A little girl. She has fair curls.'

Miss Casson's eyes shot open and she stared blankly ahead. And then from her mouth came an extraordinary sound – a little girl's voice crying, 'Papa!'

'*Mein Gott*,' breathed Herr Blumstein. '*Lieselotte! Meine kleine Lotti*.' His grip on my hand tightened.

I swallowed. This was madness. But indisputably, out of Miss Casson's mouth, the child spoke again. '*Ich liebe dich, Papa*.'

'*Ich liebe dich auch, liebling*.' Tears were running down Herr Blumstein's whiskery face and a lump rose in my throat.

'*Gute nacht, Papa*.' The little voice was fainter now.

'Lotti!' he cried, his voice breaking.

'Be comforted.' Miss Casson spoke in her own voice now. 'Your little girl comes every night to say goodnight to you. She says she is with you *für immer und ewig* – forever and always.'

'*Für immer und ewig*,' repeated Herr Blumstein. He let out a great sigh. Then he released my hand and rummaged in his pocket. Pulling out a vast spotted handkerchief, he wiped his face.

'Extwawdenwy,' Mr Utterby murmured.

I'd had enough of this. It was too strange and upsetting. But then Miss Lashbrook said, 'Can Miss Casson try some automatic writing?' She sounded eager, as if this was just a game to her.

'Certainly,' rasped Mrs Quinn. 'But nothing is guaranteed, you understand.' Rummaging in a capacious bag she brought out some sheets of paper and a pencil and placed them in front of her ward.

Miss Casson hadn't moved since her last utterance, but sat there still, rigid and staring.

'You may release your hands,' said Mrs Quinn softly, and we did so. I thought Mr Utterby looked rather regretful to be letting go of Miss Casson's slim white hand.

Once more we waited. And then, as if in a dream, Miss Casson picked up the pencil and her hand started moving across the paper. We all craned forward to see. At first the pencil made big loops, followed by some scribbles.

'Does it say anything?' asked Miss Lashbrook.

'Hush.' Mrs Quinn raised a finger. 'Help her by concentrating.'

Without looking down, Miss Casson took another sheet of paper. Her face, chalk-white now, was drawn, and her hand visibly trembled with the effort as she pressed hard on the paper.

As I watched the large letters form, my mouth went dry and the hair rose on the back of my neck. For even though they were upside down, I could make them out.

M E R I

For a moment time seemed to stop. I sat paralysed, feeling nothing but a kind of sick horror.

With a sharp 'snap', the pencil lead broke.

Letting go of it, Miss Casson slumped forward, to a general exclamation, followed by an outburst of voices. Above the hubbub, Mrs Jolly spoke in a clear, calm voice.

'Herr Blumstein, would you be so kind as to turn up the lights?'

I blinked as the hissing yellow gaslight returned, but still I felt incapable of movement.

I was only dimly aware of Mr Utterby fussing over Miss Casson, of Mrs Quinn calling for a glass of water, of Miss Lashbrook looking at the piece of paper and saying, 'But what does it mean?'

I *was* aware of Mrs Jolly's warm hand on my arm. Of Tippy's frightened eyes staring at me across the table.

They alone knew my first name. But no one here could know that only two people in the world called me 'Meri'.

Papa . . . and Mamma.

ELEVEN

Giving my arm another pat, Mrs Jolly started to bustle about, clearing the table, summoning refreshments. Tippy leaped up to help her. But I stayed where I was, staring at Miss Casson. She had revived enough to sip some water, but her face had a faint green tinge.

Mr Utterby was still fluttering over her and Herr Blumstein was hovering with a look of fatherly solicitude, but she was ignoring them both. Eyes cast down, she seemed focused on her glass of water.

Though the paper had been tidied away, in my mind I saw the letters as clearly as if they were still in front of me. Had they formed my name by chance? Or was it some kind of trick?

At that moment Miss Casson glanced up and caught me staring. I couldn't interpret the look in her dark eyes – it was enigmatic. But I thought, She knows something.

And I felt as if someone had lightly run a finger down my spine.

Miss Lashbrook was pressing Mrs Quinn to take tea or coffee. But she wheezed, 'Thank you, but we must get home. Sophie is tired now.'

Mr Utterby was dispatched to summon a cab; there was a flurry of retrieving Mrs Quinn's fur cape and finding her stick.

While everyone's attention was diverted I seized my chance. Slipping round the table, I whispered to Miss Casson, 'If I wanted to see you again, how . . . ? I mean, could I? Where would I find you?'

But at that moment Mrs Quinn put her gloved hand on the girl's shoulder.

'Come, Sophie, the cab is here.'

Too late. Without another word she rose and allowed Mr Utterby to wrap her in a cape. But as she followed Mrs Quinn towards the door she looked back at me and with a slight nod of her head gestured towards the table. Then she was gone.

I looked at the table. A small pile of visiting cards lay there. Checking to see that Tippy wasn't looking, I slipped one in my pocket.

'Tea, Meriel?' Mrs Jolly called across the room.

'Meriel!' Miss Lashbrook pounced. 'Is that your name? The message – it must have been meant for you! Don't you think so?'

Everyone was looking at me and I could feel my colour rising. 'I . . . I don't know.'

'How exciting. We must have another seance, Everina.'

'Perhaps,' said Mrs Jolly non-committally. But she wasn't looking at Miss Lashbrook – she was looking at me.

At that moment Varali came in to announce that our carriage had come.

Downstairs, I was about to follow Miss Tippins out

when Mrs Jolly put her hand on my arm. 'Are you all right?'

I nodded. I wasn't, but I was afraid that if I tried to speak I would break down in tears.

'What happened earlier – it's probably of no significance. You won't take any notice of it, will you?'

'No,' I managed to say.

'Goodnight then.' She engulfed me in one of her hugs, and it was so comforting I hugged her back.

On the way home I knew Tippy wanted to speak – she kept darting glances at me – but I refused to meet her eye. Eventually, plucking up her courage she leaned forward and said, 'Meriel, dear, do you not think—'

'I'm tired. I don't feel like talking.'

She subsided with a little quiver.

It was mean of me, but I did feel worn out – too drained to think, too drained to feel.

I turned my head and looked out of the window at the sky above the chimney pots. It was a still, clear night. If there were any spirits abroad, there was no sign of them in the starry heavens.

Once in bed, I examined the card I had picked up.

MRS MYRTLE QUINN
CELEBRATED MEDIUM

11 PEMBROKE TERRACE,
EARL'S COURT

'LIFE IS ETERNAL'

So Mrs Quinn was a medium too. Why hadn't she performed tonight, if she was so celebrated? None of it made any sense to me. Perhaps if I saw Miss Casson again, I could ask her . . . what? What was happening when she wrote the letters?

But I could hardly say to Tippy, 'Let's not go to Kensington Gardens today, let's go and see a medium instead.' And even if I could get there, I wasn't sure I wanted to hear what Miss Casson might say.

I heard the clock strike eleven then twelve before I fell into a restless sleep. All night, it seemed, unfamiliar disembodied faces kept coming at me and voices hissed and whispered words I kept straining to catch but couldn't hear. I was in the grip of a terrible fear – there was something I had to do at once and if I didn't do it something dreadful would happen. But I didn't know what the thing was. That was the worst of it, the not knowing . . .

The next morning, bleary-eyed and listless, I dutifully set about my piano practice. I kept expecting Tippy to appear and when Sally brought the breakfast tray to the schoolroom I asked her if the governess was ill.

She shook her head. 'Sir Osbert sent for her.'

I froze in the act of pouring milk into my cup. 'Do you know why?'

She shrugged. 'You look like you need cheering up. Well, listen – you know that earl who was trying to divorce his wife and put her in a madhouse? He's not been allowed.'

'Oh.' Usually I relished hearing all the latest scandal, but today I was only half listening. My mind was on Grandfather and Tippy.

Sally tried again. 'Didn't you enjoy yourself last night?'

'It was all right.'

Seeing I wasn't in the mood for talking, she took herself off.

I picked at my breakfast. If Grandfather was asking about my studies, that wasn't a problem. But what if he was trying to find out what happened at Mrs Jolly's?

When Tippy came in she looked unusually flushed. Abruptly she announced, 'Your grandfather wants to see you.'

'What have you said?'

She wouldn't meet my eye.

'Listen, if you've said anything about last night, I'm going to tell him.'

'Tell him what?' she quavered.

'Everything. About your not making me work . . . and reading novels . . . and being such a duffer at maths.'

'Oh, Meriel dear –' She put a trembling hand on my arm. 'Please don't. If I lose my place here, I may not find another one.'

I relented immediately and felt ashamed of speaking as I had. It wasn't her fault if she hadn't managed to hold out against Grandfather's interrogation. I found it hard enough myself.

'I was only joking. I'm sorry for scaring you.' I left the room rapidly before she became mushy with gratitude.

I paused at the library door before knocking. How much did he know?

Unusually, Grandfather was not at his desk immersed in papers but was looking out of the window. He turned as I entered, his brows corrugated in a frown.

I swallowed and my heart began to beat faster.

For a long moment he studied me. In the silence I could hear the loud tick of the clock on the mantelpiece.

Finally he spoke. 'I have made allowances for you, Meriel, on more than one occasion. After all, you cannot be held responsible for the deficiencies of your upbringing – I speak, of course, of your father and his patent inadequacies. But this time you have gone too far.'

I clenched my hands, my fingernails cutting into my damp palms.

'I understood that Mrs Jolly's associates were suitable companions for you. But now I find that, for example, the Nevilles were not present last night, but instead you were in the company of some . . . *people* –' he almost spat the word out – 'of a most insalubrious type, and what is more, you were engaged in dubious activities.'

'Grandfather, I couldn't have known who was going to be there or that they were going to hold a seance.' I hated my pleading tone, but I was desperate to mollify him.

'Granted. But the minute you realized what was afoot you should have had a cab called and come home.

Instead, I understand from Miss Tippins that you participated, leaving her no option but to join in.'

'But it would have been impolite not to take part.'

I might have been a fly trying to stop a juggernaut for all the notice he took of me.

'This *spiritualism* is nothing but trickery and imposture, executed by vulgar charlatans to gull the credulous and superstitious. I am surprised, Meriel, that a granddaughter of mine should be persuaded to take part in such feeble-minded nonsense.'

I went to speak, but he held to his course. 'As if this wasn't bad enough, I gather that you showed off in front of these people in a most shameless way and that on your previous visit you also engaged in some sort of performance?'

'We acted scenes from Shakespeare,' I said quietly.

'Did persons of the male sex take part in these scenes with you?' He contrived to make 'persons of the male sex' sound like a loathsome disease.

'Yes.' There was no point in denying what he already knew.

'Tchah!' Striding to the door, he said, 'Come.'

Oh Lord, what was he up to now? I stood rooted to the spot, my heart thudding, but then I heard him unlocking the dining-room door.

Reluctantly I followed him and stood on the threshold looking in.

'Here,' he ordered, for all the world as if I were a dog.

When I slunk nearer he gripped my shoulder so tightly it hurt.

'Look,' he said, gesturing at the portraits. 'What do you see?'

A lot of boring old fatheads, I thought. But of course I didn't dare say it.

'These illustrious gentlemen are your ancestors. Their genius has been passed down from generation to generation. While I am as yet in doubt as to whether it has passed to you . . .'

I wanted to seize his monocle and twist the cord tight around his neck.

'. . . nevertheless you come from a long line of Swanns, every one of whom has been regarded with the utmost respect and esteem by his peers. I wish you would remember that and not bring dishonour on your family.'

'I'm a Garland, not a Swann.'

'That is evident. I'm afraid you have the taint of your Irish father in your blood.'

I flared up at once. I couldn't help it. 'I'm sick of you being nasty about Papa. I'd rather live with him than you any day. If I'm such a trouble to you, why don't you send me back to India?'

He smiled, exasperatingly unruffled. 'Oh no, missy. That I won't do.'

'Why not? You obviously don't like me so why do I have to stay here?'

His jaw tightened and for a second his eyes held an expression I couldn't fathom, but then his usual coldness returned. 'I've wasted enough of my time this morning. Go back to the schoolroom and think about what I've said.' He made for the door, then stopped.

'You will of course have no further communication with Mrs Jolly nor with any of the persons you encountered at her house.'

I felt as if a horse had kicked me in the chest. I opened my mouth, but no sound came out.

'And this subject will not be mentioned between us again.'

TWELVE

I went straight to my bedroom. Phoebe was in there picking up clothes I'd scattered about. She looked scared when she saw my face.

'Leave that for now,' I said.

'But when should I do it, miss? Mrs Grimston—'

'Bother Mrs Grimston!' I snapped. 'Come back later.'

'Yes, miss.' She dropped the petticoat she was holding and scurried out.

I snatched up a pillow and beat it wildly on the unmade bed, thump, thump, thump, cursing Grandfather, Tippy, everyone and everything. A white storm of feathers whirled round me, but I didn't care. I carried on until my arms were tired, then flung myself onto the bed and wept angry, anguished tears.

No more amusing evenings, no more acting to an appreciative audience . . .

Then – a fresh wave of pain – my theatre trip, my one chance to see Ellen Terry . . . gone.

When my tears were exhausted I carried on lying there, a damp, miserable heap.

After a while I was roused by the sound of a timid knock at my door. 'Meriel?'

Tippy. 'Go away. Traitor.'

The door opened. 'Meriel dear –'

With a snarl I sat up and flung a pillow at the

worried face peering round the door. It retreated hastily.

Swinging my legs round, I sat on the edge of the bed. My head ached from crying and my eyes felt swollen. I dragged myself over to the dressing table. What a sight – my face all blotchy, my hair a tangled mess.

I stared at my reflection. What are you going to do now? My reddened eyes looked back at me, blank and hopeless.

And then it happened. That sensation again. As if someone was standing behind me, so close I could feel their warmth. And that light, tentative caress . . .

I whirled round.

There was no one there. Of course not. How could there be?

My eye fell on Mamma's photograph. I picked it up. Her clear eyes looked out at me from her lovely, unchanging face.

A vision of Miss Casson, her staring eyes and the letters forming under her hand, appeared in my mind.

'Was that you, Mamma, at the seance? Were you trying to reach me?'

Mamma smiled up at me.

Perhaps there could be no harm in speaking to Miss Casson and finding out what she had to say. If there was nothing in it, as I suspected, it would set my mind at rest.

I had no idea how I was going to manage it, but just the thought of taking action lifted my spirits a little. After splashing some water on my face and tidying my hair, I wrote a note to Mrs Jolly explaining what Grandfather had decreed and rang the bell for Sally.

As soon as she appeared I said, 'Sally, you're the only person in this house I can trust. I can trust you, can't I?'

'Yes, miss, of course.' She came closer, eager to hear what I had to say.

'My grandfather has forbidden me to see Mrs Jolly.'

'Oh no, miss.'

'Yes, I'm really mad about it. So will you post this letter for me . . . secretly?'

'Of course.' She slipped the note into the pocket of her apron.

'And will you look out for any letters that come for me? I know – you could hide them in my copy of Shakespeare. I'll leave it on top of the chest of drawers.'

'Right you are, miss.' She grinned, obviously enjoying being a part of this conspiracy.

'One more thing. Do you know where Pembroke Terrace in Earl's Court is?'

'No, but I could find out for you.'

'Please do, but you'll be discreet, won't you?'

'Trust me.' With a knowing wink, she left me.

That was all I could do for now. I sighed. Nothing for it now but Tippy and a tedious lesson about Charles the First. Execution wasn't such a bad idea . . .

The very next day at bedtime I found a letter from Mrs Jolly hidden inside the Shakespeare. She was sorry about what had happened and she said she'd put her mind to thinking of a solution. She was sure there would be one.

I wasn't as optimistic. Still, it was nice of her to write so quickly and it made me feel slightly better to know we could keep in touch.

Several days passed, and no solution to escaping from the house came to me. I thought I would go out of my mind with boredom. Everything got on my nerves: Tippy prattling on in her efforts to jolly me out of what she called 'an attack of the dismals'; the rain drumming ceaselessly on the window. Even Sally's quips and gossip failed to cheer me up. And I was too depressed to practise acting. What was the point now?

Only one thing, a very odd occurrence, broke the monotony.

One afternoon, as dusk was falling, I went to my room to fetch a clean handkerchief. The door was unlocked, which was strange as I was sure I'd locked it, and when I opened it I had a horrible fright. Someone was in there, a dark figure in the gloom, standing by the dressing table.

'Grandfather?'

He started, as if he'd been miles away. When he turned I was astonished. Perhaps it was just the effect of the shadows, but he looked . . . sad.

He stared at me as if he didn't know who I was, and then his face cleared. 'Ah, Meriel.' He put down one of Mamma's china trinkets and glancing round the room said, 'You like it in here? Everything to your satisfaction?'

In a state of wonder I answered automatically, 'Yes, Grandfather. Thank you.'

'Good, very good.' And without another word he drifted out of the room.

If Sally had seen him, she'd have tapped her head and said, 'Cracked.'

I didn't know what to make of it, but I soon forgot all about it because the next afternoon when Tippy and I returned from our walk and Sally was helping me off with my wet coat she slipped me a piece of paper. She did it neatly, but with such suppressed excitement I was sure Tippy would notice. Luckily the governess was busy taking off her galoshes and fussing about the drips we were making in the hall.

Examining the note later in my bedroom I found that it had pencilled directions to Pembroke Terrace scrawled on it. The street wasn't far away – I could walk there – but I was still faced with the problem of leaving the house undetected.

I was struggling in vain to come up with a plan when I had a stroke of luck.

The next day at lunch Tippy put down her knife and fork and said, 'Meriel dear, I'm afraid I feel rather unwell. I suspect I've caught a chill.'

She did look pale.

'I'm sorry, but we will have to forgo our walk this afternoon. I think I'd better lie down.' I tried to look suitably disappointed. And then she said, 'What distresses me most is that I may not be able to take you to the lecture this evening. And I know how much you enjoy them.'

Dear deluded Tippy, please don't recover in time for the boring old lecture.

'So how will you pass the afternoon, Meriel?'

'Oh, I shall study, Miss Tippins.'

Of course I did nothing of the kind. I stared out at the rain. This was my chance to go to Pembroke Road, but since my birthday, on Grandfather's instructions, the back door was kept locked. The only other way out was through the front door, but Grandfather would hear it and he'd only have to look out of the library window to see me . . .

And then I had a brilliant idea. If Tippy was too ill to take me to the lecture, perhaps Sally could take me instead.

I couldn't believe how easy it was. Grandfather was pleased at this evidence of my interest. Sally was less delighted, especially as it was still raining when we left the house.

'It would be your grandfather's evening at his club,' she grumbled as we splashed along the wet footpath. 'I was looking forward to a ride in the carriage. We'll get soaked waiting for the omnibus.'

We'd turned the corner by now. 'Listen, Sally, we're not catching the omnibus because we're not going to the lecture.'

'What?'

'Yes. You see, Mrs Jolly isn't the only person Grandfather has forbidden me to see.'

'Really?' From the excitement in her voice I knew my plan had worked. She thought I had what she would call a 'sweetheart'.

'So we're going to Pembroke Terrace.'

Her face lit up. 'Are we? Blimey, miss, that's a clever dodge.'

'You won't tell on me, will you?' I was taking an enormous risk, I knew. The thought of Grandfather finding out made my blood run cold, but I was determined to discover what Miss Casson might have to tell me.

Sally's widened. 'Heart alive! Course not, miss.'

Pembroke Terrace was a dimly lit street of small houses, one or two with signs saying 'Apartments' in the fanlight above the door.

'Are you sure this is the place, miss?' asked Sally, eyeing the peeling stucco of number eleven, the rubbish littering the small front garden.

'Oh yes,' I said brightly. Inside I didn't feel nearly as brave. This was a mad idea. But having come so far, I had to go through with it. 'Will you come back for me at seven o'clock?'

She nodded stoutly. 'I'll wait over there, miss.' She pointed across the road to where light and raucous sounds were spilling from a public house.

I fumbled in my pocket and found a florin. 'Here,' I said awkwardly.

Sally grinned. 'Thanks, miss.' And with a cheery wave she left me.

Before I could change my mind I strode up the path and knocked. I was shaking out my umbrella when the door was opened by a skinny girl in a mob cap so big it fell over one eye.

'You're just in time,' she trilled. 'They're starting in a minute.'

Before I could ask what she meant, she'd seized my umbrella, whipped off my coat and pushed me through a door.

I found myself in a small, stuffy room crowded with people, mostly middle-aged or elderly women, who all turned to look at me. I wanted to flee, but I made myself bow graciously to them. One or two inclined their heads in return, then, to my relief, they resumed their conversations.

A hoarse voice said, 'Ah, Mrs Jolly's young friend, isn't it? Miss . . .'

'Garland,' I said to Mrs Quinn, who had appeared at my side. Who were all these people? What was going on?

'Your governess is not with you tonight?' Mrs Quinn's little eyes, almost hidden in rolls of fat, regarded me brightly.

'Miss Tippins? Oh no. I came with my maid.'

'Your maid?' Mrs Quinn glanced over my shoulder.

'She's taken this opportunity to visit a friend,' I improvised hastily. I was looking round the low-ceilinged room, which was crammed with chairs and ugly ornaments. There was no sign of Miss Casson.

Disappointed, I said to Mrs Quinn, 'Is your ward not here?'

'She will come down very soon. She rests in the afternoon. Her gift, as you know, is great and such a gift takes its toll on a delicate constitution. Especially one that, alas, has had to bear so much.'

I raised an enquiring eyebrow, but it was unnecessary – Mrs Quinn was only too eager to tell me more.

'Sophie's father, Count Casso, died when she was very small and her mother, my great friend Isabel – we were at school together, you know – brought her little Sophia back to England. She could no longer remain in Italy, where she had been so happy.' Mrs Quinn shook her head, causing her bulldog jowls to tremble.

'What happened to Miss Casson's mother?'

'It was a great tragedy. On a night of thick fog, she was run down by a cab.'

'Oh no. How horrible.' Tears welled up in my eyes.

'Indeed. Poor little Sophie, to lose both her parents. What could I do, but take her in?' Mrs Quinn sighed. 'It was my idea to change her name because, you know, there is so much wicked prejudice against foreigners.' She laid a plump hand on my arm. 'I know Sophie's secret is safe with you. I can always tell when someone is to be trusted.'

I was flattered. At last here was someone who treated me like an adult. And my interest in Miss Casson, Sophie, was piqued. We had more in common than I'd thought.

At that moment I noticed her slipping in through a

folding door that stretched across one side of the room. Had she seen me? I wasn't sure.

I excused myself to Mrs Quinn and started fighting my way between the chairs towards Miss Casson. Perhaps we could go somewhere to speak in private.

But just then Mrs Quinn said, 'Come, friends, let us gather round.'

Not another seance.

'Come, Miss Garland,' said Mrs Quinn.

I hesitated. But then I wondered when I would get another chance to come here. Perhaps this wouldn't take long and I could speak with Miss Casson afterwards.

Reluctantly I took my seat beside a gaunt-faced elderly gentleman. I hoped nothing disturbing would happen this time . . .

THIRTEEN

Mrs Quinn turned down the gas, but this time she didn't light a candle. I wished she would. It was unsettling being among strangers in the dark. After the singing of a hymn I didn't know, Mrs Quinn threw her arms wide and wheezed, 'Friends, take comfort. Know we need not fear our passing for there, at the gateway to the other side, our loved ones gather to welcome us home.'

A collective sigh followed her words. I didn't want to be drawn into this, I really didn't, but I couldn't help wondering, Was Mamma waiting for me? Would I one day feel her arms around me again?

'Join hands,' rasped Mrs Quinn quietly. In the darkness my hands were taken; I could feel Mrs Quinn's little finger linking with mine and on the other side the dry touch of the elderly gentleman's skin.

Mrs Quinn continued. 'Listen to the silence and you will hear them, the dead who wait for us to attend to them. Listen and hear them speak . . .'

In the silence I strained my ears. Was that a rustling voice I could hear, like a breath stirring dead leaves? My pulse quickened.

There was a faint tinkling sound behind me as if someone had rung a bell in the corner of the room. I craned round in that direction, but I couldn't see anything.

The next moment I jumped. Something had brushed my face, as if a cobweb had touched me. I sensed a movement in front of me and a damp, earthy scent filled the room.

'The spirits have sent us a gift,' said Mrs Quinn. 'That is a propitious sign.'

I tried to see what was on the table. It looked like . . . chrysanthemums? How had they got there?

'We will attempt a manifestation,' said Mrs Quinn. 'Sophie, my dear, are you willing to try?'

A ripple of excitement ran around the circle and there was a sudden flare of a match as Miss Casson lit an oil lamp. She pulled ajar the middle two panels of the folding door and, going into the room beyond, she sat down on a chair placed some way back from the partition.

'Colonel Avery, will you do the honours?' asked Mrs Quinn.

'Certainly, madam.' The elderly gentleman next to me stood up. To my astonishment, she passed him some cords.

He went through the folding doors and bent over Miss Casson.

'Miss Garland, as a newcomer to our gathering, would you like to check that Sophie is fastened securely?' Mrs Quinn nodded at me encouragingly.

Everyone was looking at me expectantly. Embarrassed, I stood up and went beyond the folding door, where I found myself in a dining room with a small fire burning in the hearth.

Miss Casson looked at me gravely, giving no sign that she knew me. I saw that the colonel had bound each of her wrists to an arm of the chair. Feeling self-conscious, I checked the fastenings.

'No way she can escape, eh?' said the colonel.

'No, sir.' I couldn't help feeling sorry for Miss Casson. The cords were so tight they must be cutting into her delicate wrists.

The colonel took the lamp and I followed him back into the other room, where people had rearranged their chairs to face the partition. Mrs Quinn quenched the light and once more we were plunged into darkness. When my eyes adjusted I could just about see where Miss Casson was – her white collar and cuffs and the lower part of her face were faintly visible in the firelight.

'Now we must help Sophie,' said Mrs Quinn. 'This is hard for her, even dangerous. Pray, if you are so disposed. But otherwise please sit quietly and help her by concentrating – focus all your energies on summoning the spirit.'

The colonel shut his eyes at once. I couldn't see what the others were doing, but a stillness fell on the gathering. I certainly wasn't going to pray or even shut my eyes. I was desperately curious to see what would happen.

'Ah . . . look . . .' said Mrs Quinn very softly.

At first I could only make out the dark shape of Miss Casson in the chair. But then something began to move, about where her shoulder would be. Something thin and white started to extend from her body.

It was an arm!

I could see the pale gleam of Miss Casson's cuff where her hand remained fastened to the chair.

An icicle slid down my back.

On Miss Casson's other shoulder another arm began to appear, shining in the darkness.

And then I held my breath as a white figure rose up from Miss Casson's body and drifted away from her. It didn't have a distinct form, rather it was a kind of luminous mist. As it floated closer to the partition, the others let out a muted gasp. The figure had a head, but where its face should have been there was nothing, only a dark empty space.

I shivered. Was it really a spirit?

The shape hovered before us, then withdrew. It floated back towards Miss Casson and gradually diminished as if it had been absorbed by her body.

As the last speck of whiteness disappeared, Miss Casson jerked convulsively.

My heart jumped and I heard several shocked exclamations. Now that the apparition had gone, the darkness seemed blacker than before. I imagined ghostly fingers creeping towards me and I had to bite my lip to stop myself crying out. It seemed an age before Mrs Quinn managed to find the matches and relight the lamp.

The circle of faces sprang into view. I realized I was clutching the colonel's hand and I murmured an apology as I loosened my grip.

'Well,' said Mrs Quinn, 'we have been blessed indeed

tonight. Perhaps it is the presence of our visitor that has encouraged our spirit friends to come.'

She smiled a ghastly bulldog smile and everyone looked at me, nodding and beaming.

'Miss Garland, please will you release Sophie?'

I swallowed. The last thing I wanted to do was go in that room, but everyone was waiting.

When I stood up my legs felt shaky. Taking the key and the lamp I went through the doors. Sophie was sitting just as we'd left her, but her eyes were shut and she barely seemed to be breathing.

'Miss Casson?'

She didn't respond at first, then her eyelids flickered open. Her dark eyes were turned in my direction, but rather than seeing me she seemed to be gazing past me, towards the corner. I couldn't help glancing in that direction, but there was nothing stirring in the shadows.

I set the lamp down and in trying to unfasten the cords my fingers brushed against Miss Casson's skin. It was cold and clammy. My hands were trembling so much I had trouble untying the knots, but eventually I managed to release her. As she stood up she lurched and I put my hand out to steady her. Catching my eye, she seemed to know who I was and raised her eyebrows. I wondered if she was trying to communicate something. If only we could just speak to each other. But with a last glance at me, she returned to the gathering in the next room.

Reluctantly I took the lamp back and sat down again at the table. The circle of hands was re-established.

'As circumstances seem auspicious, I will see if I can make a link,' rasped Mrs Quinn, extinguishing the light again. 'It may be that some of your dear ones are waiting to communicate with you.'

I immediately wanted to leave, but the pressure not to break the silence was too great. Mrs Quinn had already shut her eyes and people leaned in closer, concentrating.

Beneath my palms the table began to vibrate.

What was happening now?

'Have we a spirit in our midst?' intoned Mrs Quinn.

Three sharp raps made me jump. Something had knocked on the table.

'Yes!' exclaimed Mrs Quinn. 'Do you wish to speak to someone?'

Three more raps.

'Dolly, is it you?' asked the colonel.

Two raps sounded out. I felt the colonel's hand quiver then lie still. Two raps must mean 'no'. But what or who was making the sound?

'Does someone else want to try?'

A pause, and then a breathless voice from somewhere to my right said, 'Is that you, Arthur?'

Three raps again. A yes!

'Speak, Mrs Nisbet,' said Mrs Quinn. 'What is it you wish to ask?'

'The money, Arthur – is it truly all gone?'

A pause, then three slow, rather muffled raps.

The woman uttered a sound like a half-choked sob. Then she seemed to rally. 'I forgive you, Arthur dear.'

Another collective sigh rippled round the circle. I didn't join in. I couldn't believe this woman's husband was really communicating with her. But if he'd lost all their money, she was a fool to forgive him.

'I love you, Arthur. Do you still love me?'

Three distinct raps.

I could hear sniffing, as if someone was weeping. Then silence.

'He has gone,' announced Mrs Quinn. 'I will try again.'

I began to feel desperate. I couldn't get at my watch, but it must be nearly time to meet Sally. I'd have to leave even if I hadn't spoken to Miss Casson.

I felt Mrs Quinn's hand go rigid. 'My guide is here,' she said in a tight voice. 'Cha-O-Ha, do you wish to speak?'

A pause, and then from her mouth a deep male voice said, 'Peace to all. I come with message. Someone here wish to make connection.'

A stir in the circle.

'This person ask for Ma– Muriel?'

I went cold.

'Do you mean Meriel?' asked Mrs Quinn in her own voice.

A pause.

'Meriel,' said the man's voice.

A cry stuck in my throat.

'He say, do not be sad. He happy. They both happy.'

'Who? Who is it?' I cried.

Another pause. I thought my heart would explode, it was thudding so furiously.

'He say . . . Papa.'

'No!' I wailed, leaping up. 'No, it can't be.' In a paroxysm of terror, I stumbled out of the room, banging myself on the chairs that were in my way.

'Miss Garland.'

I whirled round. It was Miss Casson, who had come up silently behind me in the hall.

'My papa's not dead. He's not!'

She put her hand on my arm, but I shook it off. 'Don't touch me! I don't know who you are or what you're doing, but it's wicked.' I burst into tears.

She whispered something, but I was sobbing too much to hear her. Glancing behind her, she said a little louder, 'Don't be upset. Come back tomorrow night. I'll be alone.'

'Tomorrow night?' I spoke in my normal voice and she shushed me. I hissed, 'If you think I'm coming back here again, you must be mad.'

I looked around for the coats. They were piled up on a table and I threw one after the other on to the floor until I found mine. Fumbling at the knob, I opened the front door and ran down the steps. As I started across the road, I heard Miss Casson call out, 'Tomorrow night! I'll be here.'

I burst into the crowded public house. A man whistled and another said, 'Lost your way, darling? Want me to show you where to go?' Several others laughed uproariously. Steeling myself, I pushed through the throng, ignoring the winks and comments. Where was Sally? Surely she hadn't left without me?

Then I spotted her at a table talking to another young woman . . .

'Sally.'

Startled, she broke off her conversation. 'Oh, it's you, miss. This is my friend—'

'Sorry. We've got to go.'

'But I haven't finished my beer yet.'

'There isn't time. Come *on*, Sally.'

Without waiting to see whether she would follow, I plunged back through the crowd. Outside I drew breath, glad of the fresh air after that horrible stuffy room. Sally appeared and I set off at such a pace she had to run to catch up with me.

'You all right, miss?' She peered at me anxiously.

I realized I was shivering. 'Yes, I'm fine.'

She flicked another look in my direction, but she didn't say any more. I was too shocked to speak, too shocked to think, really. I walked along in a daze, relying on Sally to find the way.

Just as we approached Queen's Gate Walk she said, 'That lecture – what was it supposed to be about?'

I stopped. 'Lecture?' For a moment I couldn't think what she was talking about. Then I remembered. 'Oh.'

'Cos someone might ask.'

'I haven't the faintest idea.'

FOURTEEN

I went straight to my room when we got back. I sat in the armchair staring ahead of me, seeing nothing. I couldn't hold off the thoughts any longer. What if Papa *had* died? It was possible. Even now the dreadful news might be on its way. If only I could contact Papa quickly. But he wouldn't yet have received the letter I'd sent two weeks ago.

There was a knock on the door and Sally appeared with my supper tray. 'Do you want this in the schoolroom, miss, or in here?'

'I don't want anything, thanks,' I said, an idea occurring to me. 'Sally, do you know how to send a telegram?'

'I've done it before, miss.' She looked at me curiously.

I wanted to tell her what had happened, but it was too risky. She might let it out without meaning to and there would be awkward questions to answer.

'If I write something, could you send it?'

'The post office will be shut now, miss. I'll try and slip out tomorrow.'

It was the briefest message that I scribbled on a page of my pocketbook. 'Are you well? Meriel.'

I tore out the leaf and gave it to her.

'What address is it for, miss?'

I clapped my hand to my head. Fool! I took back the paper and added Papa's name and address. Then I counted out three sovereigns. 'I don't know if this is enough . . .'

'I'll come back if it isn't.'

I gave her a grateful look. What a good creature she was. 'Has anyone asked about the lecture?'

She grinned. 'Not downstairs, miss. They're all busy gossiping about that member of parliament's wife that's been found guilty of adultery.'

I smiled half-heartedly. I wasn't in the mood for scandal tonight. 'I have rather a headache, Sally. I think I'll go to bed soon, but I'll see to myself.'

'Goodnight then, miss.'

'Goodnight.'

It was true about the headache. But despite everything that had happened, I fell into a deep, dreamless sleep. When I woke the next morning, for a second I felt rested and calm. And then I remembered.

When she brought the breakfast Sally said, 'Are you feeling well, miss? You look a bit under the weather.'

'I'm all right, thank you.'

'Miss Tippins is still poorly, bless her. She says you're to carry on as usual.'

It was a strange day. The fog didn't help. Thick and yellow as pea soup, it lingered all day, filling the schoolroom with an eerie light and making me feel shut in. And it was funny without Tippy. I didn't see anyone apart from Sally when she brought my meals. I was relieved when she told me the telegram had gone off all right and there was even some change. But all day a sense of dread lay like a heavy stone behind my ribcage, squeezing my breath. I hated Papa for abandoning me, but I didn't wish him dead . . . no, not that.

I felt too restless to settle to anything. In the end desperation drove me to do something about the hotchpotch in my wardrobe and drawers.

The mechanical nature of the task – separating collars and handkerchiefs, pairing up stockings – calmed me, but it left my mind free. I didn't know what to think. Last night I had been certain I didn't want to see Miss Casson again. Today? I wasn't so sure. She was the only person who might help me make sense of these weird happenings.

Noticing that my locket was twisted on its chain, I straightened it and then folded my hand protectively around it. I stood for a moment, caught in indecision, and then I made up my mind. Tonight I would go to see Miss Casson, but if she wasn't alone I would leave immediately. I would not attend another seance.

I went over to the window and saw that the fog was still thick. Good – that would conceal me, if anyone should look out. There was only one way to do this. The back door was locked and the front door was too risky – it was one of the evenings Grandfather entertained his friends. Even though most of the visitors were boring old men, scientists and academics, I sometimes sat on the stairs listening to the sounds of voices and the clinking of glasses and wished I could join them. Tonight though, I would be glad that Grandfather was too deep in cigars and conversation to give me a thought.

Though I was on edge, I tried to appear my usual self when Sally came into the schoolroom to collect my supper tray.

As she was leaving I asked, 'How is Miss Tippins?' I'd heard the servants going in and out of the governess's room and whispering on the landing.

Sally pulled a face. 'Not well, miss. Not well at all.'

I was surprised. I thought Tippy just had a cold. Though I was happy not to have lessons, I was missing the old stick and her funny ways.

Sally added, 'Mrs Grimston says, if she's no better tomorrow, the doctor had better be called. I'm going to sit with her now.' She went out.

Already the doorbell had rung several times. I didn't dare fetch my coat from downstairs so I put on my shabby old cloak that I'd laid aside ready, then, tiptoeing to the window, I raised the blind.

I'd often complained as I shivered my way through lessons, but now I blessed Tippy's passion for fresh air. The sash window slid up easily without a noise, letting in a swirling billow of fog. Now for the hard part.

I swung my legs over the sill. The fire escape ran down beside the window and I could reach it with one hand and foot. But I had to swing my body across the gap. Seconds ticked by as I froze on the windowsill, imagining my hands slipping, the sickening plunge, my body smashed and broken on the stone flags five storeys below . . . Don't be silly, I told myself. You won't fall.

I clutched the cold metal and pushed myself out into space.

I made contact and clung to the fire escape for a second, catching my breath. Then, fog choking my throat, I began to climb down. The narrow ladder seemed frighteningly flimsy. With every step I expected it to come away and fling me backwards. The descent seemed interminable and I was longing for it to be over, but I didn't dare go fast in case I missed my footing.

At last I reached the bottom and could breathe again. My legs were trembling and I'd never been more glad to feel solid ground beneath my feet. But I had to hurry – at any moment someone might come out of the back door. With nightfall, the fog had turned a murky brown and I felt, rather than saw, my way up the steps. Setting my sights on the haze of light at the end of the mews where the street lamp was, I cautiously made my way towards it.

After that I aimed for the next street lamp, and then the next, my eyes and throat stinging from the acrid smog. It was eerily quiet. At the corner a dark shape loomed at me and my heart leaped into my mouth.

It was a policeman – in fact, two policemen. They looked at me searchingly.

'Goodnight, constables,' I said brightly, trying to sound as if it were perfectly natural for me to be out alone at this hour.

'Goodnight, miss.'

I went on, expecting every moment to hear a shout after me, but none came.

So far, although it was hard to see where I was going, I'd been confident of my route, but at the end of the next street I paused. Which way? Right or left?

A figure suddenly sprang from the fog. I jumped back with a cry. Confronting me, palm held out, was a boy dressed in rags, with a bruised face and filthy, matted hair. Grunting, he peered at me, gesturing with his hand. Heart racing, I fumbled in my pocket and gave him three pennies, but he shook his head, making horrible growling noises. In desperation I flung another couple of pennies at him, then took to my heels and ran.

I stopped a few minutes later when the great bulk of a building emerged from the gloom, its facade blank apart from a forbiddingly dark doorway. Had we come this way last time? As I was hesitating, I heard the sound of muffled hoofs. Thinking of Miss Casson's mother, I pressed myself against the rough wall. A cab passed, its wheels inches away, and stopped just ahead of me under a street lamp. A man leaped down and I shrank back into the shadows, watching. Ringing the doorbell, he turned to the driver.

'Give us a hand here.' Together they dragged something from the cab and hauled it to the door.

As they passed under the lamp I put my hand to my mouth.

It wasn't a sack of coal or potatoes as I'd supposed, but a human being. Glimpsing her skull-like face, I thought she was an old woman, but then I saw the fair hair straggling loose over her shoulders – she was young.

I stood rooted to the spot. Why was she in such a state?

The door opened and another man, tall and broad, looked out. 'What's to do?' he asked.

'Four weeks rent she owes me,' said the first man, shaking the woman roughly. 'And I'll have to fumigate the room before I can let it again.'

'We're full, mate.'

'What am I supposed to do with her then?'

The big man shrugged. 'You can try again tomorrow.' And he went back in and shut the door.

The first man cursed. Then he nodded at the cab driver. 'We'll leave her here.' And they propped her up against the wall, got into cab and rattled away.

Sick with horror I approached the young woman, who lay there with her eyes closed looking like a bundle of rags. She needed help. If this was a hospital, surely they'd take her in.

I rang the bell. At the sight of me, the porter frowned. 'Yes, what do you want?'

I gestured at the woman. 'They've left her.'

'So?'

'Aren't you going to let her in?'

He looked at me as if I was an imbecile and then he spat, the gobbet of phlegm landing an inch from my foot.

'You're not leaving her there? It's cruel.'

Alarmingly he stepped forward, raising his arm. 'Piss off, you baggage, unless you want to feel the back of my hand.'

I turned and ran.

I only stopped when I ran out of breath. Clutching the stitch in my side, I listened out for footsteps, but all I could hear was the sound of my own panting. I looked at the rusty railings of the house nearest to me and my heart dropped. I didn't recognize this muddy little street at all.

Sheer panic took hold of me. Papa was dead and I was lost . . . I'd never find my way back . . . I'd end up like that poor woman . . .

I forced myself to take a deep breath.

I could knock at this house and ask for directions. But the front garden was full of nettles and littered with broken bricks, bones and scraps of rag. Perhaps it wasn't a good idea. The best thing to do was go forward and hope I'd soon come to a main road. There might be a policeman there who could tell me the way back to Grandfather's. I'd had enough of the fog and the darkness and being frightened. All I wanted to do now was to retreat to the safety of my room.

I followed the railings, turned the corner and at last saw a street lamp up ahead. When I reached it I looked about and my eye caught a plaque on the wall: Cornwall Gardens. Thank heavens! I knew where I was.

But as I faced towards Queen's Gate Walk, and Grandfather's, something made me pause. I knew the right way to go now. And I might not get another chance . . .

I hesitated. What should I do?

'Meri'. Mamma's voice.

Was I imagining it?

I dithered for three more seconds. Then I made up my mind.

FIFTEEN

When the skinny maid ushered me towards the same room as before I hung back.

But I gave myself a shake. I couldn't give up now. Bracing myself, I went in. All the lamps were lit and the folding doors were pushed back, disclosing the empty dining room. No dark corners for spirits to lurk in . . . And Miss Casson was alone.

As she rose from her seat something flickered across her face. Was it dismay? But then her features assumed their grave, mask-like expression. Perhaps she was regretting her impulsive invitation. But I was here now.

Glancing at the filthy hem of my dress, she drew me to a chair by the fire. 'I didn't expect you to come on such a night. Surely you haven't walked?'

'Why, yes,' I said, trying to sound nonchalant.

She offered me tea and I accepted, glad of something hot after the chill of the fog. While we waited for it, an awkward silence fell. I noticed she was wearing the same dress as before – perhaps her wardrobe was even more limited than mine.

To break the silence, I blurted the first thing that came into my head. 'On the way here I passed a large building, some sort of institution. What is it?'

For a second the mask cracked, and I was sure a look of fear crossed her face, but she recovered herself rapidly.

'I expect you mean the workhouse.'

'Oh yes, of course.' Sally had told me about the workhouse – how it was dreaded by poor people, who would do anything rather than end up there. My mention of it certainly seemed to perturb Miss Casson. I didn't feel easy enough with her to tell her what I'd seen, nor to confess how frightened I'd been.

A pause, during which I looked at the carpet. What should I say? 'Did my dead mother speak to you?' It sounded daft. But the tea arrived, the maid departed and Miss Casson looked at me enquiringly.

There was no alternative but to plunge in. 'I . . . what happened here –' I gestured at the room – 'and at Mrs Jolly's – well, I don't understand it.'

She put down her cup. 'Many people find their first contact with the spirit world unsettling –'

I pulled a face. What an understatement!

But she went on smoothly, 'After a while they take comfort in knowing that their loved ones are happy and at peace.'

'I didn't feel very comforted last night!'

She lowered her eyes. 'No.' She was silent a moment and then she said, 'Sometimes the messages are confusing. It's . . . it's not always easy to understand their meaning.'

'But the message was quite clear! That Papa was happy. Or that's what Cha-whatever-his-name-was said. But I didn't even know my father was dead. If he is.' My voice broke.

She looked up then. For a long moment she regarded me. Finally, glancing at the door, she said, in a lowered voice, 'Sometimes . . . mistakes are made.' Even though her face gave little away, she seemed to be trying to convey more than her words suggested.

'Mistakes?'

She gave a small shrug.

'You mean Papa isn't dead at all?'

She winced, then murmured so quietly I could hardly hear her, 'Perhaps not.'

I wanted to shake her. Couldn't she see how upset I was?

'So how can you tell it isn't *all* a mistake?'

She fixed her dark gaze on me. 'When you have the gift . . . you *know*.'

Why did she keep talking in riddles? I was desperate to discover whether what had happened held any significance for me, but I was afraid she'd just give me enigmatic answers. Taking a deep breath, I tried again. 'The other night at Mrs Jolly's – you were in a trance?'

Sophie inclined her head slightly.

My curiosity got the better of me. 'What does that feel like?'

She looked thoughtful and then she said, 'Have you ever fainted? It's a bit like that at first. You go cold and you feel – how shall I put it? You feel *pale*, if you know what I mean.'

I nodded. Once I'd been playing in the garden at home and disturbed a cobra. It hadn't bitten me, but the fright caused me to faint and I'd never forgotten the feeling.

'Everything around you shrinks away; it's like being surrounded by a thick, cold mist.'

I knew exactly what that felt like.

'As to what happens next, well, it depends. Sometimes I see things.'

'Things?'

A floorboard creaked, making me jump. I looked round, half expecting a ghostly spirit to be hovering in the doorway, but there was nothing there. Then it occurred to me that the maid might be listening at the door.

Perhaps Miss Casson had the same thought. At any rate, waving her hand, she said, 'It's hard to describe.' She'd retreated behind her mask.

'Do you see people?'

She frowned.

'Please. I'd really like to know.'

Our eyes met. I don't know if what she saw in mine reassured her, but after glancing at the door again she said in an undertone, 'Yes. Sometimes I see them, and sometimes . . . I *sense* that they're there – behind me.'

A shiver ran down my spine. That sounded just like my experience when I was looking in the mirror. Maybe someone *was* trying to communicate with me. Someone dead . . .

Miss Casson was looking at me, her head on one side. 'Are you all right?'

'Yes, of course.' But my mouth felt very dry. I took a

sip of lukewarm tea, the cup shaking in my hand. 'When you do that – what's it called? Automatic writing? What – I mean, how does it feel? When it's happening – the writing – do you hear a voice, someone spelling out the letters for you? Or is something guiding your hand?'

'Sometimes I write without knowing I'm writing, and sometimes I sense someone else's hands on mine, guiding the pencil.'

This was it. I had to ask.

'You remember at Mrs Jolly's? When you wrote those letters – M. E. R. I?'

She nodded.

'I wondered – I mean – my name is Meriel.'

She looked at me gravely. 'It's an unusual name.'

'Yes. I was named after my Irish grandmother. It means "sea-bright".' Nerves were making me prattle on.

She was nodding as if something made sense to her.

'What is it? Why are you nodding?'

She gave a slight start as if she'd given away more than she meant to. 'Oh, it's nothing.'

'Do tell me . . . please.'

Finally she said, 'Well, Miss Garland—'

'Meriel, please.' I was tired of all this formality.

She inclined her head. 'Thank you. If you will call me Sophie.'

'Yes!' I spoke impatiently. 'Do go on.'

'When I look at people, I mean ordinarily, not when I'm in a trance, I sometimes see things.'

'What sort of things?'

'Well, when I look at you I see a tawny-coloured gemstone, and now you've explained about your name I think it's amber, which is often found on the seashore, I believe.'

A hand squeezed my heart. She couldn't know what Papa said about my eyes.

She was still studying me. 'And I see – it's not very clear – but something, a proud, fierce creature . . . a hawk perhaps . . .'

'Or a tiger?' Immediately I wished I hadn't said it. It was my secret.

'Yes, that might be it, but it's hard to see – it keeps itself hidden.'

I shifted uneasily under her scrutiny, wanting to get back to the writing. 'So . . . those letters . . . Meri . . . That's what my parents used to call me.' I swallowed.

'Did you sense that it might be a message for you?'

'I don't know – but when you were writing them . . . did you see anyone?'

There was a pause and she stared into the fire, wrinkling her smooth brow as if she was trying hard to remember. In the silence the crackle of the flames sounded very loud.

Finally she looked up and said, 'I'm sorry, no, I didn't.'

My heart dropped.

Until that moment I hadn't realized how much hope I was pinning on this, how much I wanted it to be true – that in some way Mamma was still 'here', perhaps could even tell me about Papa. But after all it seemed what had happened was merely a coincidence of random letters.

That was that then. I might have saved myself all the effort of getting here. I was about to take my leave when she said, 'Would you like to try again?'

My hand jerked, rattling the cup against the saucer. 'What do you mean?'

'We could see if anyone comes through for you.'

'Now?'

Her mouth curled slightly in a smile that vanished immediately.

Was she laughing at me? Nettled, I said, 'All right, let's try.' Although I wasn't at all sure that I wanted to.

She took my cup from me.

'Aren't you going to turn down the gas?'

'No, there's no need.'

'Oh?' I was surprised.

As if she guessed my thought, she explained, 'It's part of what people expect.'

'You mean, like a performance?'

'In a way.' She added quickly, 'Though I'm not acting, of course.'

Her words seemed to hang in the air. I wondered if she was telling the truth. Perhaps she was more of an actress than I was.

'May I take your hands?'

I held them out. Hers were cool and smooth, her nails, I noticed, perfect ovals.

She shut her eyes and I wondered if I should do the same. But I wanted to keep watching. If anything happened, I wanted to see it.

But, though we sat there for what seemed a long time, the only sound came from the coal settling in the grate.

Eventually Sophie opened her eyes. 'I'm sorry. I'm not managing to make a link tonight.'

I withdrew my hands from hers. 'Oh, well.' I tried to sound as if it didn't matter.

But she was looking at me speculatively. 'Do you have anything with you that might make it easier – something your mother gave you, perhaps?'

How did she know that it was Mamma I was hoping to . . . what? Hear from? See? Oh, if only . . . I touched my locket. 'This was hers.'

'May I?' She held out her hand.

I slipped the locket off and passed it to her.

'It's very beautiful. They're phoenixes, aren't they?'

'Yes.' I almost told her all about it being Papa's first gift to Mamma, but I stopped myself. It was private – not for anyone else to know.

And in any case Sophie was concentrating now, her eyes fixed on the locket. After a minute or two she looked at me strangely. 'May I ask what's inside?'

'My hair. When I was born Mamma was very ill. She thought she was going to die and, worried that I would die too, she asked someone to cut off a piece of my hair so Papa would have a keepsake.'

'Do you mind if I see it?'

'Not at all.' But I was puzzled. Why she was curious about my baby hair?

She opened the locket to reveal the curl of soft red hair, bound with a length of embroidery thread. 'How bright it is, and long!'

'Yes. Mamma said she'd never seen such a shock of hair on a newborn. Everyone remarked on it.'

She took the lock in her hand and studied it. There was a long silence. Then she raised her eyes and looked at me with the oddest expression on her face.

'I think this hair has come from two babies.'

SIXTEEN

'Whatever do you mean?'

'I don't think this is just one lock of hair. Some of it is yours, and some of it comes from another baby.'

'What? That's impossible.' I took the lock from her.

'I know it must seem strange, but I am as sure as I can be.'

'But the strands of hair all look exactly the same.'

'The other baby must have had hair just like yours.'

I was so bewildered I nearly laughed. 'Why would Mamma keep another baby's hair? And how could it be like mine?'

Sophie pondered a moment. 'You are an only child?'

I nodded.

'Perhaps your mother had another child before you? A child that died?'

I shook my head. 'No, I was born the year after my parents married.'

'Could a child have been born after you? And died while you were too young to remember?'

I was taken aback. 'I suppose it's possible, but I'd have been told, surely.'

'Perhaps it was too sad for your parents to talk about.'

I stared at her. Was it possible that my parents had shared a secret I was excluded from? That I had had a brother or sister who meant so much to them that they couldn't speak of it? That I wasn't the sole focus of their love?

I felt as if the solid ground had dropped from beneath my feet, leaving the world spinning round me.

'This has been a shock for you.' Sophie was concerned.

'No – that is, I'm just rather surprised, that's all.' I didn't like the way she seemed to know what I was feeling. Especially when *she* gave so little away about herself.

She might be able to tell me more about the lock of hair, but I didn't know what questions to ask. 'Do you think . . .' I began.

The doorbell rang.

Sophie glanced at the clock. 'That will be Mrs Quinn.'

Dismayed, I jumped up. I'd intended to leave before Mrs Quinn returned. I didn't want her to know my business.

Again Sophie seemed to read my mind. She swiftly returned the hair to the locket, snapped it shut and passed it to me. Then she whispered urgently, 'If you can bring me something else, something of your mother's, I might be able to discover more.'

It was tempting, but the thought of sneaking out again at night almost made me despair. 'Can we meet somewhere else?' I asked. 'In the daytime?'

'It's possible. When and where?'

I couldn't think. But then I heard Mrs Quinn's voice

just outside the door and I blurted the first place that came into my head. 'Kensington Gardens? By the memorial. Thursday afternoon at . . . at two o'clock?'

'Saturday,' Sophie said quickly as the door opened.

'Miss Garland.' Mrs Quinn didn't look surprised to see me. In fact she seemed pleased.

'Miss Garland is just leaving,' said Sophie firmly. Her mask of calmness was back on; we might have spent the evening discussing the weather. 'I'll ask Betty to call a cab, shall I?'

I was torn. A cab was expensive, but the thought of walking back through the fog was too hideous to bear. 'Thank you, that's very kind.'

While we waited, I was uncomfortably aware of Mrs Quinn's bright eyes quizzing us, but Sophie adroitly asked her guardian about *her* evening and I managed to escape without giving anything away.

I was so preoccupied by what had happened I almost forgot to ask the driver to stop the cab at the end of the mews. Before I negotiated the hazards of the fire escape again I told myself to concentrate and I managed to climb up and get back into the schoolroom unscathed. After all the shocks I'd experienced, it was a relief to be back in familiar surroundings.

Going straight to my room, I began to get ready for bed, questions spinning in my brain.

Could it be true that there was hair in my locket from a baby brother or sister who was now dead? For a brief wild moment I considered asking Sophie to try to contact the spirit world to see if a message would come through for me from this mystery baby. But would it be able to communicate?

I almost laughed at the ridiculousness of what I was thinking. I didn't really believe this stuff, did I? How could Sophie know for sure about the hair?

It boiled down to whether I trusted her or not. And I didn't know.

The next morning when Sally brought my breakfast she told me Grandfather wanted to speak to me as soon as I'd eaten it. She looked as if she hadn't slept, and I asked her how Tippy was.

She shook her head. 'The doctor's been sent for.'

'Can I see her?'

'Better not. She's really too poorly to see anyone.'

For the first time it occurred to me that my governess might be gravely ill and I felt annoyed that they hadn't sent for the doctor sooner. I hoped they were looking after her properly. And what was going to happen to me?

I soon found out.

In the library, Grandfather glanced up from a document he was plainly itching to return to. 'I did consider hiring a day governess while Miss Tippins is indisposed. But on reflection I decided not to.'

I knew what that meant – he couldn't be bothered with the fuss of finding someone suitable.

'This is a golden opportunity for you to develop a more mature attitude to your studies. You will therefore continue with your usual programme of learning by yourself.'

I almost clapped my hands.

He glowered at me from under his eyebrows. 'Mind you apply yourself, missy. I shall of course be checking on your progress. Ask one of the servants to bring me your school books every evening, and I shall expect to see you every morning after breakfast, without fail.'

'Yes, Grandfather,' I said meekly. 'Am I to be confined to the house till Miss Tippins is well?'

'What?' Grandfather had risen from his desk and was looking for something in a bureau drawer. Without looking round he said, 'Oh no, of course not. I'll speak to Mrs Grimston. One of the maids will accompany you on your daily walk.'

My heart leaped. Let it be Sally. Oh, please let it be Sally.

As far as Grandfather was concerned our conversation was at an end. But I had another question.

'Grandfather?'

'Well?' He spoke testily, still searching through the files.

'Did Mamma have any other children? Apart from me?'

The effect of my question was remarkable. Grandfather really did start as if someone had shot a bolt of electricity through him. I'd read this in books, but never believed it. Turning, he raked me with his eagle glare. 'What made you ask that?'

My heart beat faster. 'I just wondered, that's all . . .' It sounded feeble so, hastily improvising, I continued, 'I just remembered something I heard when I was small, something the servants were talking about. I thought it meant Mamma had had a baby after me, one that died . . .'

He relaxed visibly. 'You must have misunderstood. There were no other children.'

'Are you sure? Because, after all, she was living in India and you were here.'

Grandfather covered the space between us in a second and towered over me. 'Do you think my daughter would have neglected to tell me something as important as that?' He was scowling ferociously.

I shrank back. 'I'm sorry, I—'

'She chose to have you here, in this house, before she went to India. In fact, you were born in your mother's room, the room you sleep in now. I was the first person to see you. If she had had another child, I would have known, she would have told me. You are her only child, do you hear?' His eyes pierced me with a cold intensity that made me quake.

After a second or two he seemed to recover himself. 'I've got a lot to do this morning, Meriel, and so have you, so run along.'

Unnervingly, instead of turning back to his desk, he watched me walk to the door. He was still staring after me as I closed it.

I did go to the schoolroom, but of course I didn't open a single book. I tried to sort out my thoughts. If Grandfather was right, then the hair in the locket was a mystery.

If Sophie was right . . . it was an even bigger mystery. Too many ifs . . . and it was all so painful. I wished I'd never set eyes on Mrs Quinn and Sophie Casson. Everything was confused, shifting . . . I couldn't make any sense of it.

Fate seemed to be on my side for once. It was Sally whom Mrs Grimston told to accompany me on my walks – which pleased us both. Sally was glad to get out of the house and even more pleased when I told her that on Saturday she could go off by herself for a couple of hours. 'I have to meet someone.'

'Do you, miss?' She winked. 'Right, mum's the word.'

I'd come round to thinking that Sophie had to be sincere. What reason would she have for lying? So I was all ready to meet her. I'd put Mamma's photograph and the Shakespeare ready in my old carpet bag.

And then something happened that changed everything.

A telegram arrived from India.

SEVENTEEN

Sophie was already at Prince Albert's Memorial – she saw me coming and waved.

She happened to be waiting at the corner I liked best, with the figures that represented Asia. Usually I nodded at the elephant, but not today. I marched straight up to Sophie, whose smile faded as she absorbed the look on my face.

'Read that.' I thrust the piece of buff-coloured paper at her.

She read the scrawled message and handed the paper back with her inscrutable face on. 'I'm pleased for you.'

'Is that all you've got to say? Don't you realize how worried I've been? I thought he was *dead*. You should know what that feels like.'

She flinched, but her lips remained firmly closed.

'It's all your fault, you and Mrs Quinn, with that stupid message that was supposed to be coming from the other side, or whatever you call it. It was nonsense, wasn't it?'

Sophie glanced at some children, who had stopped jumping up and down the steps of the memorial and were regarding us curiously. She put her hand in my arm. 'Shall we go somewhere else?'

I shook her hand off. 'I'm not going anywhere with you. I almost didn't come today, but then I thought you'd just suppose I was ill or something.' I paused to gather my breath. 'I came because I wanted you to know that you'd been found out. You and Mrs Quinn. You're nothing but –' I searched for Grandfather's word – '*charlatans*. That's what you are and that's all I have to say.' I spun on my heel and strode away, glaring at the nurse who'd rushed forward to rescue her charges and was looking at me as if I was a raving lunatic.

I walked on blindly, seething, and it wasn't till I was halfway over the Serpentine bridge and heard someone calling that I realized where I was, and that Sophie had followed me.

'Miss Garland – Meriel, please wait.'

I turned and faced her through the mist that was rising up from the lake and swirling about us.

'I don't know why you're following me. I have nothing to say to you.'

'Please . . .' She was panting. 'I can explain.'

'Explain! You mean, tell me more lies.'

'No,' she said. 'I want to tell you the truth.'

I glared at her. 'You say it's the truth. But why should I believe you?'

'Please hear me out. And then you can decide whether or not to believe me.'

I could have said no. But something about her desperate tone made me curious to see what she had to say. 'Very well. But let's walk. It's too cold to keep still.'

We crossed over the bridge and took a path along the river, in a silence I was determined not to break. But we'd passed the ferry and the boathouse before she began to speak.

'I hope you will receive what I am about to tell you as a confidence.' Her eyes were anxious as she searched my face.

I shrugged. 'How can I promise that when I don't know what you're going to say.'

Her face fell. 'That's fair, I suppose.' She was silent for a while, seemingly engaged in some inner struggle. Then she burst out, 'Oh, I *will* tell you and risk the consequences.'

Naturally this made me even more curious.

'The message that seemed to come from your father was a mistake. Mrs Quinn acted in good faith, but she must have been misinformed.'

I stared at her, uncomprehending.

'You have to understand that my guardian is not unlike many mediums—'

'You mean she's a fraud.'

Sophie blushed. 'No, that is – well – she once had the gift, I'm sure, but now she is older, her powers are waning. That's why when she is an unfamiliar situation, as at Mrs Jolly's, she prefers me to officiate. But in her own home . . . she has some faithful followers who would be disappointed if she did not perform.'

That was the right word for it. 'When you say "perform" you really mean she's acting, faking, don't you?'

Sophie's flush deepened and she looked troubled.

'But how does it work? How does she know what to say?'

Sophie sighed. 'Since Mrs Quinn finds it hard to make a link with the spirit world, she has to rely on . . . shall we say, more human agencies.'

Exasperated, I stopped dead. 'Will you please stop talking in riddles and tell me what you mean.'

Sophie hesitated a moment, then, as if it was being dragged out of her, she said, 'For example, it was Miss Lashbrook who told her that Herr Blumstein had lost his daughter.'

I was stunned, and then angry. 'Miss Lashbrook is in on the trickery too?'

'Oh no,' said Sophie hastily. 'Mrs Quinn has a way of drawing people out – they don't always realize what they are revealing. Miss Lashbrook is innocent, I assure you.'

'But it was *you* who pretended to be Herr Blumstein's little girl.'

Sophie looked even more miserable. 'I don't like doing it – in fact, I hate it – but I'm afraid I have to.'

How feeble she was. Why didn't she stand up to Mrs Quinn? 'So are you saying Mrs Quinn got the idea from Miss Lashbrook that my father was dead?'

Sophie nodded.

'But why would Miss Lashbrook think that?'

'I imagine she learned something of you from Mrs Jolly and, knowing that you lived with your grandfather, she assumed that both your parents were dead.'

I thought about it. It made sense. And Miss Lashbrook

had probably told Mrs Quinn my first name too. What a hideous old hag the medium was. 'What your guardian does is wicked. How can she live with her conscience? And how can *you* be a party to it?'

Sophie looked even more dejected. She mumbled, 'Mrs Quinn would argue that it's laudable to bring comfort to people who are grieving.'

'So she does it out of the goodness of her heart?'

Sophie blushed again. 'Everyone has to live. And if people are happy to give her . . . *tokens of their appreciation*, shall we say, it would be discourteous to refuse.'

Her words sounded stilted, and I had the feeling that she was just parroting Mrs Quinn.

As we resumed our walk I thought about what had happened at the two seances I'd witnessed. I could see how the so-called messages might all be explained by prior knowledge. But what about the other events? The knocking, the flowers. And that strange and ghostly manifestation.

I asked Sophie and when she said nothing but looked ashamed I knew it was all part of the deception.

'But how? How is it done?'

Sophie sighed. 'The rapping is simple. Mrs Quinn does that – she knocks under the table with her hand.'

'But I was holding her hand all the time. And wasn't the person on her other side doing the same?'

'You were both holding the same hand, leaving the other hand free. It's easy enough to achieve in the dark.'

'And the flowers?'

'Betty is very adept at moving silently.'

'Betty? Oh, you mean the maid.'

Sophie nodded.

'But that . . . being. I saw it with my own eyes!'

'Betty again. Covered in very fine muslin, dipped in a solution of phosphorus and ether.'

'And you – all that convulsing and so on – you were *acting*?'

'Yes,' she said quietly.

'You were very good,' I said bitterly.

We walked on in silence. I was turning it all over in my mind. I'd wanted to believe it so much – that somehow Mamma could still communicate with me . . . It wrung my heart to think it was all trickery.

Suddenly I stopped again and faced Sophie.

'Why have you told me all this?'

She gazed at me, her dark eyes unfathomable. 'Because I think I might be able to help you.'

'Help me? How? And why would you want to help me? We hardly know one another.'

The look she gave me was so penetrating it made uncomfortable. Quietly she said, 'Forgive me for being so personal, but I sense that, in some ways, we are alike.'

What did she mean? *I* wasn't a bit like her.

She put out her hand in a gesture of apology. 'I'm sorry. I've offended you.'

I was even more irritated. How was it she could tell what I was feeling? 'I think you've a cheek saying you could help me. What will you do? If you suppose I'll be taken in again by your tricks, including that nonsense about the locket, you're mistaken.'

She started as if I'd slapped her. 'When I have talked of . . . of stratagems I have been talking of Mrs Quinn –' She broke off, her pale face contorted with anguish. 'Please believe me, Meriel – I hate having a part in it.'

Act or no act, I'd not seen her express so much emotion before.

After a pause she continued, 'I hate it all the more because I *do* have a gift, it seems. I can't explain it, but I . . . know things, without knowing how I know them.'

It sounded like more of the same gibberish to me and I pulled a face.

She turned away, exclaiming, 'Oh, I knew I would not convince you. But it's just – I wanted you to understand the difference between the illusions and the genuine occurrences.'

'Which were . . . ?'

'When I wrote your name, for example. I was as surprised as you were.'

I snorted. 'You don't expect me to believe that! Miss Lashbrook told you my name, didn't she?'

'But not till after she saw the writing. She didn't know it before.'

I stared at her, trying to recall the sequence of events that evening. And now I came to think of it, it was *after* Sophie had written the letters that Miss Lashbrook heard Mrs Jolly calling me Meriel.

But it was impossible, ridiculous to attach any importance to it. 'That could have just been accidental, a coincidence.'

'I don't think so. Although I didn't see anything, I felt a presence. And there is the lock of hair too.'

'*That*,' I spat contemptuously. 'You don't expect me to believe that jiggery-pokery. Anyway, I asked my grandfather and he said that I was my mother's only child. He was quite clear about it.'

She stared at a solitary moorhen bobbing along near the edge of the lake.

'I could try again if you like.'

'*What?*'

'I could see if I can sense any more. Do you have anything else of your mother's with you?'

'No.' After the telegram, of course I hadn't brought the Shakespeare and Mamma's photograph.

Sophie went across to a bench and sat down. Holding out her hands, she said, 'If you give me your locket, I will try again with that.'

She really was extraordinary. So calm and assured.

I slipped the locket over my head. This was absurd, irrational, yet there was a part of me that wanted to see if anything would happen.

I expected Sophie to open the locket to take out the hair again, but instead she held it in her hand and closed her eyes.

The minutes ticked by. Sitting beside her on the damp bench I felt self-conscious especially when a gentleman passing by threw us a quizzical glance. Across the water I could see a stream of shadowy shapes, riders taking their afternoon exercise on Rotten Row, the sound of their hoof-beats muffled. Along the lakeside a moorhen suddenly uttered a high *kikikik* of alarm and then fell silent.

Where we were, a stillness had descended. After a while I started shivering as the cold mist began to penetrate my bones. I was about to suggest we give up and leave when she suddenly made a sound, an audible sigh. She said, 'I can smell perfume.'

I breathed in, but could detect nothing but the dank smell of the lake and rotting vegetation.

'I can see a beautiful orange flower.' Sophie smiled dreamily. 'I don't know its name.'

An image came into my mind – orange flowers floating in a brass bowl. I was straining to remember the name when Sophie said it for me. 'Champak.'

I looked at her in amazement. Champak, of course. The November chill of the park faded and I was back in the shuttered interior of our bungalow, the creaking fan barely stirring the hot air despite the punkah-wallah's efforts, the sweet perfume of the flowers filling the room . . .

'She says they are her favourite flower.'

She? The hairs rose on the back of my neck.

'She says much has become clear in spirit.' Sophie spoke slowly, leaving a brief pause between each word. She tilted her head as if listening to someone just behind her. But there was no one there – only the soot-streaked leaves of a straggly rhododendron.

'Someone is close to you, very close, but as yet unknown,' she said in the same slow way.

'Who, Sophie? Who is saying these things?'

She opened her eyes and looked at me directly. 'I believe it is your mamma.'

'*Mamma?* She's actually talking to you now?' I couldn't believe it.

'Just a minute.' Sophie appeared to listen again. 'She says, "Don't be sad. Think of Pickles."'

'Pickles?' I went cold all over. It *was* Mamma. For how could Sophie possibly know about Pickles? It was years since I'd thought of him myself.

Pickles was a puppy we had for just a few weeks when I was about five. He ate some rat poison, and I was inconsolable until Mamma comforted me by describing his happy afterlife. Was mentioning Pickles her way of telling me that *she* was happy now?

'She wants you to know something important. She says . . .' Sophie's brow furrowed as if she was having trouble understanding what she was hearing. 'She says, remember the children of – I can't get the name – Sida? Sita?' She turned to me. 'Does this mean anything to you?'

I tried to recall the name. 'I don't think so – unless, wait, yes, Anila used to tell me stories about the goddess Sita. Is that what she means?'

Sophie was nodding. 'Sita, yes.' She paused. 'She says she has to leave us now.'

'No!' My cry was involuntary. I waited, tears running down my face, longing for more, but Sophie was silent, tactfully looking away from me towards the lake.

I took in a few deep lungfuls of misty air. I felt overwhelmed, bereft.

Eventually Sophie turned to me. 'Your mamma wanted you to know that you're not alone. And at least you've got something to go on now – the message about the children of Sita.'

I wiped my face with my hand. 'But I've no idea what it means. I can't remember anything about Sita's children.'

'You can find out.' Sophie's tone was encouraging, but then her expression changed and she looked at me very seriously as she handed back the locket. 'But, Meriel, spirit messages are not always reliable, you know. Even if you do discover something about the children of Sita, it might not make any sense.'

I didn't reply. Nothing was making much sense at the moment.

Sophie stood up. 'I'm sorry, I can't stay any longer.'

I remembered what she'd said about 'tokens of appreciation'. Fumbling in my pocket, I held out a handful of coins. Awkwardly I said, 'I don't know how much—'

Sophie looked shocked. 'I don't want any money! But listen, if you find anything out and need more help, I'll be happy to do what I can. You know where to find me.' She shook my hand and walked swiftly away, leaving me staring after her.

EIGHTEEN

I walked slowly back to the gate where I'd arranged to meet Sally. Luckily her mind was too full of the new fur coats she'd seen in Barker's window – 'Astrakhan, I think it was called, with a hat to match, and a whole real fox with its tail in its mouth!' – to notice I was subdued. Or perhaps she thought the meeting had not gone well and was too tactful to pry. In any case, she kept up a stream of chatter that allowed me to carry on thinking, and by the time we reached the house I had an idea.

6 Queen's Gate Walk
Kensington
14th November 1885

Dear Mrs Jolly,
I do hope you are keeping well. We are all in good health here except for my governess, Miss Tippins, who has a bad case of pleurisy. She is keeping to her bed and so I am studying by myself. As I am sure you can imagine, that is very dull at times. To amuse myself, I have decided to write down the stories my ayah, Anila, used to tell me so I don't forget them. But my memory is dreadful. I am working on the Ramayana at the moment and I can't remember who kidnapped the goddess Sita. Also, was there a story about her children? If so, I seem to

have forgotten it. I wonder if you could help me, or perhaps Varali will know? I would be so grateful.

Yours very truly,
Meriel

Two evenings later an envelope appeared between the pages of the Shakespeare. I tore it open and skimmed through Mrs Jolly's greetings and more details about Sita's life than I wanted. Varali, for she was the source of the information, had obviously responded with enthusiasm. But at last I came to the part of the story I was interested in. '. . . exiled and alone in the jungle, Sita was given refuge by a hermit. There she gave birth to her twin sons, Lava and Kusha . . .'

My heart skipped a beat. I couldn't believe it and had to read it again. But even in Mrs Jolly's flamboyant scrawl the word was quite clear: *twin* sons.

I felt light-headed and, my legs turning to water, I sat down heavily on the bed, still clutching the letter.

What had Sophie said? Another baby with hair just like mine?

Was it possible? That I'd once had a twin brother or sister?

My twin. How strange it sounded. Strange and thrilling. But if it were true, why had nobody told me?

A hot and bitter taste filled my throat and, unable to sit still, I got up and paced about. The burning sense that some injustice had been done to me was tangled with an overwhelming feeling of longing. I had to know the truth. But how could I find out?

Grandfather must know. If I'd had a twin we – how strange that 'we' was! – we would have been born here together. But he'd been quite clear about it. 'You are her only child.' Why would he lie to me?

I could ask Papa, but if he'd kept it from me all this time, why would he tell me now?

My pacing had brought me to the dressing table. I gazed at my reflection. Was this why I so often felt someone touching me, someone close? Why I felt so empty, so incomplete?

'Mamma,' I cried to the deserted room, 'is this what you're trying to tell me? That I once had a brother or sister? Please, speak to me.'

Silence.

A horrible lonely silence.

I could feel tears rising again in my throat and, as if to escape them, I ran to the window and pushed back the curtain. The street was empty, not a single person or vehicle to be seen, but the sky was full of bright stars, and over the rooftops opposite the moon shone silver. I hadn't seen such a sky since the night I'd been to Mrs Jolly's.

I clutched my locket. *Mrs Jolly*. Of course!

'A twin?' Mrs Jolly paused in the act of sipping her tea, surprise written all over her face. 'Whatever made you suppose that?'

'Oh, you know, I've been thinking about my life in India. It was something I overheard the servants say.' It was the same lie I'd told Grandfather, but I felt less comfortable lying to Mrs Jolly and could feel my face going red.

Luckily she didn't seem to notice. 'No, my dear, I'm sure your mother would have told me. In fact, I seem to remember our once having a conversation about twins. One of the servants had had them, I think – perhaps that's what you heard them talking about – and your mother and I agreed that it must be difficult to look after two babies at once. She didn't seem distressed by talking about it. That would suggest she hadn't any experience of it herself, wouldn't it?'

'I suppose so.' I felt deflated. I'd convinced myself Mrs Jolly would have the answer.

'I believe your mother envied my having two children – Minty wasn't born then, of course. She wished she'd been able to have more herself. She was afraid you'd be lonely and wanted a brother or sister for you. Is that why you're asking?' She gave me a searching look.

'Oh no,' I said quickly. 'I liked being the only one, you see, because I didn't have to share. I had Mamma and Papa's full attention.'

'And now?'

'I'm sorry?'

'Do you like being the only one now?'

'Oh yes.' Too proud to admit the truth, I added, 'I'm not a bit lonely.'

Mrs Jolly's glance was shrewd, but all she said was,

'More tea?' Pouring it, she went on, 'I do wonder if it isn't dull for you sometimes at your Grandfather's.'

Usually, yes, it was hideously dull, but not at the moment. What would she say if I told her about Sophie and the locket? 'I do miss India.' I wanted to steer her on to safer ground.

'I can understand that, my dear. I'm looking forward to the time when the girls can join us over there.'

Lucky girls, I thought enviously. If only Papa was more like Mrs Jolly.

'Mrs Jolly, do you think my papa is extravagant?'

She laughed. 'On a teacher's salary? Whatever gave you that idea?'

'Oh, nothing,' I muttered, ducking my head.

'That sounds like something Osbert Swann would say.'

I looked up in surprise. How did she know?

Mrs Jolly sighed. 'My dear, I don't want to create ill feeling between you and your grandfather –'

Too late for that, I thought.

'– but it's unfair if he has put wrong ideas into your head about your papa. You are entitled to know the truth. You might not remember, but when he first went out to India, your papa made a name for himself painting portraits of important people.'

'Of course I remember! I went with him sometimes. I was made a fuss of, especially by the Indian princes. Some of the English sahibs weren't so friendly.'

'Exactly! The arrogance of the Heaven-born!'

It was a long time since I'd heard anyone refer to people in the Indian Civil Service by that name. Mamma and Papa used to use it mockingly.

'Your parents were comfortably off then and believed in enjoying themselves, but in a modest way, you understand – hardly extravagant.'

There used to be parties, I remembered now, music and the grown-ups' laughter keeping me awake.

Mrs Jolly leaned forward. 'Do you remember Indians coming to the bungalow? I mean, as friends?'

I nodded.

'That's what caused the trouble.' Her usually affable face darkened to a frown. 'Your father got a reputation as a "Friend of Indians". And as far as many of the sahibs were concerned, that was the end of it. He wasn't "pukka" any more. The portrait commissions dwindled and your poor parents struggled.'

'Is that why Papa started giving drawing lessons again?'

'Yes, but there weren't so many families where he was welcome. When we came back from Bombay we could see how the land lay. That's when Gussie pulled strings to get him the position at the School of Art, and a room there.'

I opened my eyes wide as I realized something. 'Grandfather is very rich. Why didn't he help us?'

Mrs Jolly grimaced. 'I doubt your parents would have told him what was going on. Of course, it's likely that word reached him somehow – London is full of retired

Anglo-Indians – but do you think Sir Osbert Swann, with his ideas about the innate superiority of the English upper classes, would approve of your father's attitude?'

I shook my head.

'No, I don't think so either.' Mrs Jolly leaned forward and gave the fire a violent poke. 'But you know, right from the start, he didn't approve of your father.'

'I've never understood why.'

'Oh, because, of course, he wasn't good enough for Eleanor Swann. Your mamma told me all about it – how your papa had been her drawing tutor and they fell in love. It was wildly romantic. Of course Sir Osbert was furious. His daughter and a penniless nobody – and what was worse, an Irishman! He tried to end the relationship, but your mother threatened to elope.'

'He gave in?' I couldn't believe it.

'He couldn't deny your mother anything, you see.'

'Why not?'

'Because he loved her and couldn't bear to lose her.'

I looked at Mrs Jolly in amazement.

'It's true; he absolutely doted on her. He went to the wedding – he even gave Eleanor away – but he put his foot down about one thing: he wouldn't have your father in the house, not on any count.'

Hot anger flared in my chest. How could Grandfather have been so beastly? How could Mamma have tolerated such behaviour?

'Do you know how I came to be born at Grandfather's? Why was Mamma there without Papa?'

'Your poor grandmamma took ill, and your mamma felt she had to look after her. So your papa went off to India on his own. And then your grandmamma died and I think the shock caused you to arrive sooner than your mamma expected. She was very ill.'

'I know about that.' I thought of the locket with its keepsake hair – the hair that wasn't just mine. 'Do you think Mamma hated Grandfather? Because of his attitude to Papa.'

Mrs Jolly looked thoughtful. 'I don't know. She didn't talk about it. I think she was sad about the rift.'

I remembered Mamma's reaction to the letters Grandfather sent. Mrs Jolly was probably right.

She looked at the clock. 'Well, it's lovely to see you again, my dear, but I don't want you getting into trouble. How long is this walk of yours supposed to be?'

I jumped up. 'Oh golly, I've got to dash. Sally will be waiting for me.'

Back in my room, alone, I had time to reflect. I'd never really thought about Mamma living here in this house, being a girl like me. I couldn't imagine what it must have been like. I tried to picture Grandfather as a doting father. Impossible.

I could imagine the excitement of Papa arriving – the dashing young drawing master. But then what was it like for Mamma to stay here without Papa, looking after Grandmamma, watching her die? I thought of Mamma having meals in the dining room, just her and Grandfather at that long table. In the drawing room, receiving visitors who had come to pay their condolences. Sitting in the morning room, writing black-edged letters.

Is that why Grandfather didn't want the room disturbed? I'd thought it was because of Grandmamma, but perhaps it was because of Mamma. These would be his last memories of her. After that he never saw her again.

I wondered what Grandfather really felt about me. Did he want me because I reminded him of Mamma? Or did he hate me because I reminded him of Papa?

As to what I'd hoped Mrs Jolly could tell me, I'd made no progress. If Mamma had told her all these private things, surely she would have told her if she'd had twins. But she hadn't talked about her feelings for Grandfather. Perhaps there were other secrets she'd kept to herself.

I sighed. So many questions. And I didn't know the answer to any of them. I'd let Sophie know what little I'd found out, but after that, I had no idea.

NINETEEN

11 Pembroke Terrace
Earl's Court
18th November 1885

Dear Meriel,

Twins! That makes perfect sense. I felt that there was a very close connection between the two locks of hair and this would explain it.

And do you not remember the message from your mamma? That someone you don't know yet is close to you. It might indicate that you have a twin who is still alive. Have you thought of that? Someone must know the truth. You were born in your Grandfather's house. Have you asked the servants?

Take heart. We might be able to get to the bottom of this mystery. But be warned – even if you do, you may be disappointed. Remember what I told you about spirit messages. I would not like to see you hurt.

Your friend,
Sophie

The hairs had risen on the back of my neck. It had never occurred to me that if I had a twin, he or she might still be alive.

'*Someone you don't know yet is close to you.*' My heart beat faster, and a trembling excitement seemed to fill my whole body. I made myself sit down on the bed and read the letter through again.

I shook my head at Sophie's warning – she was so cautious and fearful. But her suggestion about the servants was a good one. I should have thought of it myself.

I rang for Sally and when she arrived I asked, 'Do you know if any of the servants have been here a long time – say, since my grandmother died?'

She thought a minute. 'Ponsonby, miss. I believe he's been with your grandfather since before he married.'

'Oh.' I couldn't imagine approaching Ponsonby. Apart from anything else, he was devoted to Grandfather. If there was a secret, he wouldn't reveal it to me. 'No one else?'

'Mrs Jubb, of course. She's always moaning that Mrs Grimston's a skinflint compared to your grandmother.'

Mrs Jubb. My heart skipped a beat.

I could see that Sally was bursting to know what this was all about. She wasn't a tittle-tattle, but once again I couldn't take the risk. 'Thank you, Sally, that's really helpful.'

As soon as the door shut I did a little jig to myself in the mirror. But then I thought of tackling Mrs Jubb and stopped dancing. I hadn't had much to do with her, but according to Sally she was given to 'wicked tantrums'. Would she take kindly to me poking around in the past? More likely she'd send me away with a flea in my ear.

I would have to plan my campaign carefully.

The next afternoon, immediately after our walk, I descended to the basement. Sally had said this was the best time to catch Mrs Jubb alone. Since lunch was long over and she would not yet have started the dinner preparations, she might also be in a slightly better temper.

You expect cooks to be fat, if not jolly. Mrs Jubb was scrawny with twin spots of red in her cheeks and a permanent frown between her sparse eyebrows. When I entered the kitchen she was sitting at the table with a newspaper in front of her and a teapot at her elbow. I couldn't help staring. She'd taken off her cap, and her hair stuck up in tight plaits all over her head. I felt as if I was facing the gorgon Medusa in her den, and the glare she gave me as she growled, 'Yes, Miss Meriel, and what can I do for you?' suggested she'd have liked to turn me to stone.

I swallowed. 'Mrs Jubb, I hope you don't mind, but I wanted to speak with you.'

'Oh yes?' She narrowed her eyes suspiciously. 'Something wrong with your lunch, was there?'

'Not at all,' I said hastily, smiling brightly. 'It was delicious.'

It had been revolting – lukewarm gristle, lumpy mash with black bits in it and hard carrots. Because I'd wanted to avoid offending Mrs Jubb today, I'd choked some of it down.

'The thing is, I'm trying to find out more about my family.'

'Oh yes?' Her thin lips curled; her eyes were like chips of malachite.

I floundered on. 'So . . . I understand you were here when my grandmother was alive?' I thought she wouldn't be able to resist talking about Grandmamma, and then I could lead her round to the subject that really interested me.

Did her hard stare soften for a second or did I imagine it? But she kept silent, forcing me to carry on. 'So I wondered if you could tell me anything about her – you know, what she was like.'

Abruptly she stood up. 'You must ask your grandfather about that. It's not my place to say. Now, if you'll excuse me, miss, I've a dinner to get ready.' She went to the range, picked up an iron pan and clanged it down, a clear signal that as far as she was concerned our conversation was over.

But I wasn't going to be put off so easily. 'Can you just tell me then, were you here when I was born?'

She opened a drawer and clattered the knives about before selecting a villainous-looking one, which she proceeded to clean on the old knife-board. 'No, I wasn't, as it happened. I'd gone to stay with my sister for a holiday, so I missed all the excitement.'

Her sarcasm was unmistakable.

Rather desperately, I flung out, 'Well, who *was* here? Someone must have looked after Mamma.'

She paused, knife in hand, and gave an audible sniff, which made the red tip of her nose quiver. 'There was a person who made it her business to take charge of Miss Eleanor – Mrs Garland as she was by then. Sending back the tray because she said the cloth had a spot on it, claiming that the beef tea was greasy. Pah!' Mrs Jubb bent to her work, the knife blade flashing across the leather surface.

'Who was that?'

'Ada Lightfoot.' She almost spat the name, at the same time making a jabbing motion with the knife.

'Do you know what became of her?'

'Of Ada?' Mrs Jubb looked up bemused. 'I don't know and I don't care. The day she left this house was a red-letter day as far as I was concerned.' She slammed the knife down on the table, making me jump. 'Now, Miss Meriel, Sir Osbert won't be pleased if his dinner's late and I won't accept the blame for it.'

I bet she wouldn't, horrid old hag. It was definitely time to go.

I was on my way to the stairs when the cellar door suddenly opened and Ponsonby emerged carrying two dusty bottles of wine.

'Good afternoon, Ponsonby,' I said, putting on a confident voice and trying to look as if I had every right to be in the basement.

'Good afternoon, Miss Meriel,' he said crisply, giving me his you-shouldn't-be-here look. His eyes flicked past me towards the back door. Perhaps he was wondering whether I'd been trying to escape again. I could tell he was keen to question me, but it seemed he didn't quite dare. He went into his pantry and I fled upstairs.

Later Sally found me slumped on a chair by the window, watching the street, where nothing at all was happening.

'You look glum, miss. Wouldn't Jubb talk to you?'

'No. She said I'd have to ask Grandfather. She did mention someone who was here in those days – Ada Lightfoot. Have you heard of her?'

Sally shook her head. 'No, can't say as I have, miss.'

I suddenly felt sick of my own company. We hadn't had a good gossip for days. 'Are you busy, Sally? Can you stay awhile?'

She pulled a face. 'Sorry, miss. It's Phoebe's night off – I'm needed downstairs.'

When she'd gone I felt more doleful than ever. It all seemed so hopeless.

Before I got into bed I picked up the photograph of Mamma. Silently I asked her, Who is Ada, Mamma? Was she kind to you? Where is she now?

But Mamma's smiling face didn't change. I had no sense of her presence, or anyone else's. No voice whispered my name. I felt completely alone.

I was in a dark house, in a long, twisting passage with doors opening off it. I was searching for someone and I knew that if I didn't find them quickly it would be too late. I kept opening door after door, but each room was empty, just dust floating and settling on the bare floorboards. I grew more and more desperate. At last I went into a room that had a huge cabinet in it. Ornately carved and reaching up to the ceiling, it had hundreds of drawers, rows and rows of them. I opened the nearest one, and pieces of paper spilled out and scattered over the floor. I picked one up. It was covered in writing, but in a strange language I couldn't understand. I looked at another and another, but all were incomprehensible. All the time I knew the answer lay here somewhere, if only I could find it. I opened drawer after drawer, paper flying out and filling the room, words swirling past my eyes, more and more paper, until I knew I was going to suffocate, but I couldn't, mustn't, stop looking . . .

I woke with a jerk, my heart thudding. I fumbled for the matches and lit the candle with trembling fingers.

The flame flickered and grew still. The light fell on the photograph I'd placed by my bed and Mamma's eyes leaped out at me, intent, reassuring. They seemed to say, Don't be afraid, and indeed my breathing slowed, my pulse steadied. And, as I looked into Mamma's eyes, an idea sprang into my head, distinct and compelling.

Putting on my dressing gown and picking up the candlestick, I opened the door and listened. Silence.

Gliding like a ghost, I set off down the stairs. As I came to the landing below I paused and listened again. From Grandfather's room came a low, rumbling snore. Relieved, I carried on, all the way down to the ground floor, where the tall clock ticked in the shadows.

Past the dining room, past the green baize door that led to the basement, and into Grandmamma's morning room. I had never done more than peep in here and it was tempting to have a good look around, but it was too risky. I did pause a second to take in the painting that hung over the mantelpiece. It was of Grandmamma in middle age. She was wearing a flowing blue dress over a crinoline; her pose was rather stiff, with one elbow propped on a broken pillar, but her face was relaxed. She had a look of Mamma, and from her kindly expression I got the feeling that she didn't mind me being in her room one bit.

The hall clock began to chime. Five o'clock. It wouldn't be long before the housemaids stirred. I had to hurry.

Scarcely thinking about why I was doing this, I sat down at the escritoire. It was a beautiful little desk, made from rosewood, and as I let down the top to reveal the leather writing surface and the cunning little pigeon holes and drawers, I felt a stab of resentment at Grandfather for not letting me use it.

Seeing at a glance that the pigeon holes were empty, I opened one of the drawers. I did it tentatively, half expecting pieces of paper to come flowing out as in my dream, but there was nothing in it. I tried the others with the same result. My last hope was the drawer in the centre. I drew it out slowly, willing it not to be empty. But all that was in it was a well-used rubber and a few paperpins. Frustrated, I gave it a shove, but it wouldn't go all the way back – something was sticking. I jiggled it a bit. I was worried about making a noise, but I couldn't leave it like that; it would be obvious someone had been here. I gave it a sharp tug, the drawer flew out of its casing and with it came a grubby, creased piece of paper.

I smoothed it out. It was a letter, written in spidery handwriting. I was moving the candle nearer to the page, head bent over faded ink, trying to make it out, when I froze.

I'd heard the sound of a door shutting below me.

Quick as a mongoose, I pushed the drawer in, closed the flap of the escritoire and darted to the door. Blowing the candle out, I stepped into the passage. I couldn't hear anything now, but that didn't mean I was safe. I ran along the hallway and reached the bottom of the main staircase just as the green baize door opened. Holding my breath, I pressed myself against the wall as light flooded the hall.

Whoever it was seemed to pause a moment, breathing heavily, as if they'd just hurried up the servants' stairs. Then the sound and the light moved away. I risked poking my head over the banister just as the unmistakably tall form passed into the morning room. Ponsonby!

I didn't wait a second longer.

I scrambled up the stairs, one flight, two flights, three, feeling my way in the dark, dreading that any moment a voice would call after me. Rushing into my room, I dropped the candlestick on the dresser, leaped into bed and pulled the covers over my head.

When I got my breath back I pushed the covers aside and listened. After a while I heard a creak from the landing floorboard. It sounded as if Ponsonby was checking the empty guest rooms. Something brushed my door, and then everything went quiet.

I didn't dare to move for what seemed like an age. But eventually, judging that it was safe, I got up and lit the candle. Tense with anticipation, I unfolded the letter I'd been clutching in my fist all this time.

Dear Lydia, I read and my eye skipped to the signature. *Ever affectionately, your cousin Cyril.*

I screwed the letter up and threw it across the room, tears of disappointment pricking my eyes. I'd been so sure it was a letter from Ada Lightfoot. How stupid of me. Believing in a dream . . .

I looked at Mamma's serene face. You probably never were in that room writing letters, were you?

At home in the bungalow, she used to write letters on the veranda. I could see her so clearly, sitting at the table with the blue ink bottle in front of her, thumbing through her red leather notebook . . . Of course! *Her red leather notebook.* I could have hit myself for being so stupid.

That's where she kept addresses. The notebook I'd brought with me from India. I'd forgotten all about it.

Frantically I started searching for it. Sally must have put it somewhere when she moved the rest of my things downstairs. It wasn't in the wardrobe or the chest of drawers. I found it at last in a drawer of the dressing table, under Papa's photograph.

I flicked through the pages till I came to the *L*s. And there it was, in Mamma's dear familiar handwriting: *Ada Lightfoot, 3 Lavender Grove, Battersea, London.*

TWENTY

I felt prickly with excitement at the prospect of meeting Ada Lightfoot. I was sure that at last I was getting close to finding out the truth.

I scrawled a note to Sophie, telling her what I'd discovered and asking her to meet me the next afternoon at the end of Gloucester Road. I was apprehensive about going to Battersea on my own and Sophie's company would be welcome – she understood what this meant to me. I also thought she might be useful – she might *sense* something. But I soon began to regret involving her.

First of all, she was late. It was drizzling, and by the time she arrived my coat was wet through and I was beside myself with impatience. But Sophie wasn't very apologetic, and the reason she gave was feeble – something about having to help Mrs Quinn. And she didn't seem at all excited about finding Ada's address.

'What if she doesn't live here any more? Or she might be dead . . .'

'In that case, you'll be able to talk to her, won't you?'

Her face instantly took on that closed-in expression.

I sighed. 'Look, you said you wanted to help me. Are you coming?'

'Now?'

'Of course now. I'm dying to find out what she has to say. Aren't you?'

'Wouldn't it be better to write first?'

What a wet blanket she was. 'Listen, I'm going. You can do what you like.' I stalked off but had to turn back. 'Which way is the station?'

With a tight little smile she said, 'I'll show you.'

As we went along I stole a sideways look at her. She looked even paler than usual and had dark circles under eyes. I remembered what Mrs Quinn had said about her needing to rest in the afternoons and I felt a bit ashamed of the way I'd spoken to her. At the station I said, 'Look, Sophie, I'm sorry I was sharp. It's just that this matters so much. Are you sure you won't come?'

She hesitated. 'The thing is, I haven't got much time today . . .'

I looked at her pleadingly.

'Oh, all right.'

The railway line ran alongside a long cemetery – rows and rows of grey tombstones and monuments, more than I'd ever seen before in one place, looking abandoned in the rain.

Sophie's eyes met mine across the carriage and I wondered if she was having the same thoughts as me – how lonely it must be to be dead and lying in your grave. I shook myself. Of course she wouldn't think that. For her the dead were sociable spirits with plenty to say to the living.

'Sophie . . .' I stopped. It seemed a bit rude to pry, but

then I thought, Hang it, why not? 'When did you first believe you had, you know, a special gift?'

'I've always known.'

'What, right from when you were small?'

She nodded. 'I could sense people's feelings, but when I said something that revealed this they'd look at me strangely. It dawned on me that other people weren't so . . . aware, and it made me feel different.'

'Did it make you feel important?'

She looked out of the window. We'd crossed the river and were chugging past rows of soot-blackened terraced houses. When she spoke her voice was subdued. 'Not really. It made me feel cut off from other people, isolated. I'd rather have been like everyone else . . .'

'And now?'

She turned her head to look at me questioningly.

'Is that how you feel now, I mean? Isolated?'

'Oh no.' Her quick response reminded me of my own denial when asked the same question by Mrs Jolly. Pehaps, like me, she wasn't telling the truth.

After a slight pause she went on, 'My gift could be useful though. If something was lost, I often knew where it was.' She spoke brightly, as if determined to make light of the subject.

'Golly, that must have made you popular.'

She gave a fleeting little smile but at once became serious again. 'When someone died, I knew they were safe.'

I wondered if she was talking about her parents. I

wanted to ask her about them, but that seemed too intrusive.

'What about you?' Sophie broke into my thoughts.

'Sorry?'

'When did you know you had a gift?'

Was she teasing me? 'What do you mean?'

'Why, acting, of course.'

I blushed. 'You've only seen me perform one speech.'

'Yes, but you were very good.'

Her admiration seemed genuine and I found myself telling her all about my dream to be an actress.

She listened intently and then said, 'You know, you might bring it off.'

'You think so? Can you see into the future as well?'

That little smile again. 'No, but you have the talent and passion and determination . . .'

I liked this image of myself as Sophie saw me. How different from Grandfather's view. 'And you? Do you want to be a famous medium one day?'

'No. *No.*' She looked horrified at the idea. 'I wish I didn't have to do it at all.'

The train was slowing down. We'd reached Clapham Junction.

Outside the station we found ourselves on a main street where carts, drays, dog carts, carriages, cabs and omnibuses were battling each other to make some headway up the hill. I realized I didn't have a clue about where to go.

I confessed this to Sophie and she went to a nearby

cab-stand and spoke to the drivers clustered there. After some banter and laughter, she came back red-faced.

'What did they say?'

'Nothing. Lavender Grove's just up here.' Without another word, she set off.

I hurried after her. She was so strait-laced. A sympathetic listener but you couldn't have a laugh with her, not like with Sally.

'Does a lady called Ada Lightfoot live here?'

The woman who'd opened the door was tiny, bird-like. She even put her head on one side as she said, 'Oh dear, what a shame. I'm afraid Miss Lightfoot recently passed away.'

I looked at her, dismayed. 'When was this?'

'About three weeks ago. The room's still vacant, but I'll be lucky to find another lodger who gives as little trouble.'

I blew out my breath. I'd come too late.

'I'm sorry,' the woman said. 'Are you a relative?'

'No, just . . . a family friend.' There didn't seem to be any more to say. 'I'm sorry to have troubled you.'

When the door was shut I made myself look at Sophie. If I'd been her I probably wouldn't have been able to resist crowing – it *would* have been better to write first – but all she said was, 'What a pity.' She seemed genuinely sorry.

I began, 'I don't suppose you could . . . ?'

'What?'

'You know . . .'

That little smile I was beginning to recognize. 'It's not as easy as that. I mean, Ada would have to want to get in touch with you.'

'I see. That's not very likely, is it?'

'I'm afraid not. Can we go now?' Without waiting for an answer, Sophie set off briskly towards the main road, leaving me to trail behind her. But at the corner I caught up with her.

'I should have talked to that woman,' I said. 'She might just know something.'

The landlady was obviously surprised to see us again, but, wiping her hands on her apron, she invited us in. She took us into a small, musty front parlour, where Sophie and I perched on a shabby horsehair sofa.

I explained that I didn't actually know Miss Lightfoot myself, but that she had known my mother. 'Do you mind telling me what she died of?'

'Well, it was pneumonia in the end, but I'd say the poor old thing was worn out. She was over eighty, you know.'

'Did she ever say anything to you about where she'd worked?'

The landlady thought. 'I can't say as she did. She liked to be private, if you know what I mean, which suited me.' She sighed. 'Poor dear – she took it hard when she needed some attendance towards the end, but really it was no trouble.'

I pulled a face at Sophie. This was getting us nowhere.

'Perhaps her niece could help you.'

'Her niece?' I sat up straighter.

'Yes, Mrs Fillary. I don't know how close they were, but she came to visit the old lady towards the end – she did most of the nursing, if truth be told.'

'Do you know where she lives?'

'I do, as it happens. She left her address, in case any post came for Miss Lightfoot. I'll get it for you.'

She left the room and Sophie and I exchanged glances.

'It's a long shot, but you never know. She might have told her niece something,' I said in a low voice.

'Mmm.' Sophie looked doubtful and I bit back an impatient remark. The landlady returned with the address and we thanked her and took our leave.

Out on the street, I looked at the piece of paper. 'Whitechapel. Where's that?'

'It's in the East End,' said Sophie.

'Oh, that's where Hannah, our kitchen-maid, comes from. Can you get there by train?'

Sophie frowned. 'I'm not sure . . . probably. But you're not thinking of going there? From what people say, it's rather dangerous.'

I snorted. 'Dangerous? Surely they're exaggerating!'

She was looking about, a worried expression on her face. 'Do you know what time it is?'

Reaching inside my coat, I pulled out my watch. 'It's only a quarter past three.'

'Is it? I must get back.'

'What? You mean you're not coming with me?' I couldn't believe it. Just when we were getting somewhere.

She looked discomfited. 'I'm sorry, really I am. I could probably come on another day, if you really want to. Please don't go on your own.'

I hesitated. If Sophie was right about the East End, the idea of going there by myself was daunting, though I'd never admit it. But on the other hand . . .

'I can't wait another day. I'm going today.' And I marched off. She ran after me and soon caught me up, but I wouldn't look at her or speak to her.

At the station she clutched my arm. 'Meriel, listen. I think this is a very bad idea. I really don't think you should go on your own.'

'So come with me.'

A look of anguish crossed her face. 'I can't.'

'Go home then. I'm not stopping you.' I took my place in the queue for the ticket office. I half hoped she wouldn't desert me, but when I looked round a minute later she was nowhere to be seen.

I regretted my impulsiveness when I reached Charing Cross.

As I made my way down the dimly lit stone staircase, spiralling round until I felt dizzy, with every step I felt more anxious. I'd never ridden on a train that travelled underground. How could the driver see his way? I wished I'd waited for Sophie now.

When the train roared out of the darkness and drew up, its brakes squealing, everyone surged forward and I was carried with them, squeezed into a gloomy compartment that was already crowded. An elderly gentleman shifted along to make room for me, and I tried to say thank you, but I choked on the sulphurous fumes filling the air. What with the heat and the smoke from men's pipes, I felt as if I was being asphyxiated.

It was a relief when at last, gasping and gulping the fresh air, I tumbled out on to Whitechapel Road where dusk was already falling.

Having asked directions from a policeman, I pushed my way through the crowds of people who, despite the drizzle, were milling on the footpath and gazing in the windows of the brightly lit shops or pausing by stalls offering an extraordinary variety of things: cabbages, sheet music, trousers, second-hand books, mousetraps . . . Passing a cookshop, I was enveloped by a gust of warmth and mouth-watering smells – onions, fried fish, sausages. The air was filled with excited chatter and laughter, tramcars rattled past ringing their bells, a piano organ ground out 'Home, Sweet Home'. It was as lively and busy as an Indian bazaar, and if I hadn't been so eager to see Mrs Fillary, it would have been fun to linger there.

I'd been mentally checking off the side streets, and before long I came to a narrow opening I thought led to

Lark Street, where Mrs Fillary lived. As I paused on the corner looking for the name, a girl standing there gave me a hard stare. I was startled at her appearance, and couldn't help staring back. She wasn't wearing a coat, but shivered in a low-cut dress of garish yellow and lime-green silk; damp feathers and ribbons drooped from her hat. She had twin spots of rouge on her chalk-white face and her mouth was a bright red gash, but behind this mask she looked exhausted.

'Seen enough, 'ave yer?'

I smiled nervously.

'Listen, this is my patch, so you can piss off.' She stepped towards me threateningly and muttering, 'Sorry,' I fled down the alleyway.

Here there were no cheerful shops or street lamps. The narrow lane, closed in on either side by tall buildings, was a shadow-filled tunnel. A man loitering in an open doorway watched me as I went past, and I could feel his eyes boring into my back as I tried to hurry over the greasy cobbles.

As I turned a corner I nearly cannoned into another man, who stepped in front of me, barring my way.

'What's the hurry, darlin'?' He put his bristly face close to mine, and I could smell alcohol on his breath. 'You're a nice little tart, ain't cha?'

My mouth dried, my insides dropped away.

''Ere,' he said in a thick voice. 'I've got somethin' very nice for yer. You'll like this.' And he started fumbling with the buttons of his trousers.

For a moment I stood paralysed with horror. Then I came to my senses. Giving him a mighty shove that sent him reeling away from me, I ducked under his arm and ran.

I could hear him calling after me, 'Don't be like that, darlin',' but I didn't look back. What a fool I'd been. I should have listened to Sophie.

Panting, I turned another corner and found myself on Lark Street. To my relief, it was deserted apart from a couple of grubby little girls sitting outside the public house on the corner. They looked curiously at me, but I ignored them and hurried along the row of small terraced houses.

Number nine was one of the smarter ones, with neat blinds at the windows and a front door that looked freshly painted. Taking a deep breath, I rang the bell.

The woman who opened the door was like a taper, thin and straight up and down. She had a pale, tired-looking face, her hair was coming loose from its pins and her eyes held a faraway expression, as if she had been thinking about something quite different from the piece of leather she held in her hand. She looked at me vaguely as I hovered uneasily on the step, and then her eyes seemed to come into focus. She took a step back and her mouth fell open.

'Oh my Lord!' she said. 'It's never you, is it?'

TWENTY-ONE

I was taken aback, my prepared speech dying on my lips. I'd never seen this woman before, so who did she think I was?

'Are you Mrs Fillary?'

She didn't answer, but continued to stare at me.

I started to feel uncomfortable. 'Mrs Mabel Fillary?'

The question finally seemed to sink in. 'Oh yes,' she said with a nervous little laugh.

'I believe your aunt, Miss Lightfoot, knew my mother, so—'

Mrs Fillary leaned forward eagerly. 'What's your mother's name, dear?'

'Eleanor Garland.'

She clapped. 'I knew it! Soon as I saw you, I felt it in my bones, you know? Whatever must you think of me, keeping you on the step, and in this bloomin' rain too. Come in, come in.'

Bewildered, I was ushered through the door into a small room lit by a couple of lamps, which gave off a strong whiff of paraffin. But this was almost eclipsed by the smell of leather that hung in the air. It wasn't surprising. Every available surface was covered with the stuff – some in flat cut-out pieces, some sewn together to make what looked like the tops of shoes. There were just two clear spaces in the middle of the piles – two work tables, at one of which a white-faced girl younger than me was sitting at a sewing machine. She'd stopped what she was doing and was staring at me with open curiosity.

Mrs Fillary looked round the room helplessly and waved her arm. 'Do excuse the mess. Oh, this is our Jenny. She's a good little machinist, you know. She can fashion an upper faster than you can say "shoe-leather". I never saw such a girl for—'

'That'll do, Mother.' The girl's cheeks were pink. 'Who's this?'

'Now, Jenny, mind your manners. This is, er . . .'

'Miss Garland. Meriel.'

Mrs Fillary clapped her hands again. 'Meriel! What a pretty name. I never guessed that's what they'd call you.'

More mystified than ever I said, 'I wonder, could I speak to you? Alone?' Out of the corner of my eye I saw Jenny frown.

'Yes, yes, of course, dear. Come through here.' Mrs Fillary led the way into a back room, where she lit a lamp. This seemed to be the family's living room and kitchen combined. It was small and cluttered, but the multicoloured rug in front of the range was bright and everything looked clean.

Mrs Fillary turned as I came forward. 'I'm so pleased to see you're walking so well, dear.'

'I beg your pardon?'

She looked flustered. 'Oh, forgive me, I shouldn't have

mentioned it,' and sweeping some newspapers from a chair, she said, 'Sit down, won't you, please.'

She herself perched on a stool and continued gazing at me, shaking her head as if she couldn't get over the surprise. 'However did you find me?'

'I went to your aunt's lodging and the landlady told me where you lived.'

'Fancy you coming back after all this time . . .'

Coming back? As far as I knew I'd never been here before. I began to wonder if her reason was unhinged.

'It must be . . . what? Arthur's sixteen, so it must be nearly sixteen years since you was here last. Of course you won't remember it. Ahh! What a little dear you was.'

Had I been here as a baby? Or was there another baby who looked just like me? My heart began to beat faster. 'How did you recognize me?'

'I don't know. Your hair, of course, and . . . I don't know. I suppose I always hoped I'd see you again, and what with Aunty talking about you so recently, soon as I saw you there on the step, I just knew.'

This sounded promising. 'I'm sorry to hear about your aunt.' I was trying to work the conversation round to what I wanted to know.

'Oh yes, poor Aunty. It was very sad, but I think she was ready to go. She was worn out and everything had become a struggle, you know?'

'You said she talked about me?' I prompted her.

'Yes, just at the end. Bless her, she felt so guilty about it. Said she couldn't go to her grave without telling someone. I think it eased her soul to confide in me, which I was glad about, but then, you know, I worried about it. I kept thinking I ought to do something, but what could I do?'

Trying not to sound impatient, I asked, 'Mrs Fillary, what did your aunt confide in you?'

'Why – you mean you don't know? They didn't tell you?'

I shook my head in bewilderment.

'Oh.' Mrs Fillary's forehead creased with anxiety. 'I thought that's why you'd come. Now I don't know whether I ought to say anything. Aunty was very clear about it. She said, "Tell no one, Mabel, only Eleanor Garland if she ever comes looking. No one else." '

'My mother's dead.'

'Aw no, is she?' Mrs Fillary clasped and unclasped her hands. 'I'm sorry to hear that. And did you . . .' She looked embarrassed. 'Did you know her?'

'Of course,' I said, more baffled than ever. 'She was my mother.'

She gave another nervous little laugh. 'Forgive me, dear. It must sound strange, but I meant, did you live with her?'

'Yes, of course I did.' Poor woman. She obviously wasn't quite right in the head.

Her face relaxed. 'Oh, I'm so glad. I can stop worrying now.'

She might have 'Doolally tap' as we would have said at home, but she knew Ada Lightfoot's secret and she knew it was something to do with me. I had to find out what it was.

'Mrs Fillary, I know you feel you should keep your aunt's confidence, but since my mother's dead and it concerns me, can't you tell me?'

She clutched her hair with both hands, causing a shower of pins to clatter on to the floor. 'Oh dear me, I don't know.'

Frustration was starting to tighten in my chest. 'Please. I was going to talk to your aunt, but I was too late. Now you're the only person who can tell me what she said. I've a right to know, don't you think?' I gazed at her, willing her to change her mind.

She shifted about on her stool, fidgeting with her hair. Just when I thought I would burst with impatience, she sat up and put her hands in her lap like a child told to be good. 'You're right, dear, and with everyone dead now, I can't see what harm it could do.'

I sat up straighter too, anticipation bubbling up inside me.

'As I said, it was near on sixteen years ago. I hadn't seen Aunty for over a year, not since Mother's funeral, and then one night, it was ever so late cos Robert – that's my husband – had already locked up, there came such a knocking at the door.' Lost in her memories, Mrs Fillary kept her gaze fixed on the range. 'We couldn't think who it could be at that hour. Anyway, I says, "You'd better open it, Robert. Something might be up." So he did and there was Aunty with this little bundle in her arms. That was you, not more than a few hours old.' She turned to me with a fond smile.

'Why did your aunt bring me here?'

'So I could be your wet nurse. I was nursing our Arthur at the time and I had plenty of milk to spare. Bless you, you took to it right away, thank goodness, or otherwise you'd have starved.'

'But why couldn't my mother feed me?'

'That I didn't know till later. Aunty wouldn't tell me nothing – not your name, nor who you was. Ask no questions, Mabel, she said. Just do this for me. You'll be paid handsomely. But I'd have done it for nothing, you know.' Mrs Fillary smiled again. 'You was such a sweet little scrap. We called you Ginger, on account of your hair. I never saw such a mop on a mite before. And my Robert was that taken with you. Soon as he come in from work – he drives the trains, you know – he'd say, "How's that Ginger?" Course he loved Arthur too, goes without saying, but he had a soft spot for you. Heartbroken he was when Aunty came and took you away.'

'When was that?'

'Why, soon as you was weaned. About six months old, you was.'

I leaned forward eagerly. 'Do you know where she took me?'

'No.'

I slumped back in my chair. Of course, that would have been too easy.

Mrs Fillary had that faraway look in her eyes again. 'I

often wondered. I had a foolish fancy I might meet you in the street one day and if I saw a little copper-knob I always had a second look, but it was never you.'

'How could you be sure?'

'Oh, because of . . .' She stopped, flustered. 'Because of your eyes, dear – such an unusual colour!'

I had a feeling that wasn't what she'd been going to say at all.

'And your aunt never told you who I was or where I came from.'

'No, not for all these years. She said, "Don't ask me, Mabel, cos if I tell you it'll be the worse for me and for you too." '

'What did she mean?'

'I never knew till about three weeks ago. She could hardly speak by then, bless her, but she was determined to tell me what had happened. She said your mother, poor lady, was so ill with the having of you she hardly knew nothing about it. And someone, Aunty wouldn't say who, told her to find a wet nurse for you what could be relied on, which of course was me. And this someone told Aunty, made her promise, not to say nothing about it to your mother.'

My stomach tightened. Who was this 'someone'? I was begining to have my suspicions. 'Do you think your aunt kept her promise?'

'I do. And that's why she felt so guilty, see. Poor Aunty . . .' She sighed. 'One thing she did, secret like, was cut off a lock of your hair. "Her dear mother had to have something to remember her by." That's what she said. Did you know about that?'

'Oh yes.' My hand strayed to where my locket hung under my coat.

Mrs Fillary shook her head. 'What she thought, your poor mother, when she recovered – which she did cos of Aunty's nursing, though she wouldn't take no credit for it – as I say, what your poor mother thought, I don't know. Whether they told her you'd died or what, I haven't a clue, cos Aunty didn't know – least that's what she said – but however it was, your mother went off to India without you.'

My heart jolted. But at that moment the door opened. I'd been so engrossed in the story I'd forgotten about Jenny next door. Hovering in the doorway, she said, 'Mother, are you going to be much longer? Else we'll never get our quota done today.' She shot me a disagreeable look.

'Don't fret, ducky, I'll not be long,' said her mother.

Jenny retreated and the sewing machine began to whirr again. 'Don't mind her, Miss Garland,' said Mrs Fillary. 'She's a good girl, but she worries, you know? Got an old head on her shoulders. Now, where was I?'

'You were telling me why your aunt felt so guilty.' I said it automatically, but my mind was full of the last thing she'd said – *your mother went off to India without you.* And if I could, I would have jumped up and danced.

I made myself attend to Mrs Fillary.

'. . . she felt like she'd stolen you from your mother. "It wasn't right, Mabel," she kept saying. "I shouldn't a done it." I told her, "You was only carrying out orders." But you see, for doing it and not saying nothing, she got a nice little pension. Bless her, though – I don't know why she felt bad about it cos she gave most of it to us. "Something for the kiddies," she'd say, cos you know, Miss Garland, I've five of them now and that's a lot of mouths to feed and a lot of feet to find boots for. We couldn't have managed like we have without Aunty's help, but I never knew where the money came from.'

I thought I might know. 'Do you think that's why she kept the secret? She was worried she'd lose her pension?'

'I reckon so. And more bothered about us than herself, you know? But when she knew she was dying she told me your mother's name, "in case she ever comes looking for me" – that's what she said. "You tell her that she had a lovely little girl what was taken from her."' Mrs Fillary sighed. 'Poor Aunty, what a pity she didn't live long enough to see you. And she'd have been so happy to know you was reunited with your mother. I suppose you was taken over to India after you left here?'

'I suppose so,' I said non-committally. I was nearly choking with excitement, but I kept my face neutral.

Mrs Fillary puffed out her cheeks then expelled the air. 'So what was it all about, eh? A mystery, that's what it is. And now we'll never know.' Rising from the stool, she opened the firebox on the range to replenish the coal.

I glanced at the clock on the mantelpiece and jumped up. 'It's been very nice meeting you, Mrs Fillary, and thank you for telling me this story but I'm afraid I have to go now,' I gabbled. It was after five o'clock.

'Aw, d'you have to? Why don't you stay and have some tea with us? Nothing grand like – not what you're used to – but good and wholesome.'

'I'm sorry, I'm expected back.'

'Where do you live now then?'

'In Kensington.'

'You've come a long way. On the train?'

I nodded, moving towards the door, anxious now to leave.

'Can't you just wait till my Robert gets back? He'll be cock-a-hoop to see you. And then Arthur'll walk you back to the station. You didn't ought to go alone.'

It was very tempting. I dreaded facing the streets by myself, but I was already late. 'Thank you, you're very kind, but I really must go.'

On the step Mrs Fillary said, 'You'll come and see us again, won't you?'

'I will,' I said, wondering if I would.

As I turned away she said, 'You're not going down Gaskin Row, are you? If you go the other way and turn left, you'll get back to Whitechapel Road. It'll take a bit longer, but it's safer.'

I thanked her and saying goodbye I hurried down the street. At the corner I stopped and looked back. She was still there, a pale figure in the gloom, waving.

TWENTY-TWO

All the way back in the crowded train my mind was full of what Mrs Fillary had told me.

I believed her – it made sense of everything. And it all pointed to Grandfather. Only he could have authorized Miss Lightfoot to take a baby away; only he could have arranged her pension. She would have known that Mamma had had twins, so presumably the pension was to ensure her silence. But what possible motive could he have for making such an arrangement? It didn't make any sense.

The more I thought about it, the angrier I felt. That he could have done such a thing to his own daughter, the daughter he was supposed to dote on. Poor Mamma! Never knowing that she had two little girls. And my twin sister, nursed by Mrs Fillary and then left behind when Mamma took me to India.

I knew I wasn't the baby called Ginger, I knew I'd gone to India with Mamma, because she'd told me about the journey. She'd said it was the first time she'd ever been so far on a ship, and by herself she might have been frightened, but because she had me to look after she wasn't frightened at all. I could remember her telling me about it as clearly as if it were yesterday. 'You were so good. You slept a lot, and when you were awake I used to stand at the rail holding you and you waved your little fists at the sea and chuckled. I knew then that we'd chosen the right name for you.

'And one night there was a full moon – it was so beautiful I took you up on the deck to see it. You laughed as if all of it – the moon, the stars, the shining path across the sea – had been laid on for your entertainment. And as we watched, a shoal of flying fish leaped from the water, one after the other, like silver arrows. I've never forgotten it.'

Though I couldn't remember it, of course, I felt as if I knew how it had been – the dark water suddenly erupting into flashing silver and Mamma's arms holding me safe . . .

Sitting in the swaying train, I surreptitiously wiped my eyes. And saw, reflected in the carriage window, my double doing the same.

Back at the house the servants were busy preparing dinner. I was able to slip in through the back door, which Sally had left unlocked for me, and reach my bedroom undetected.

I couldn't stop thinking about my sister. I wondered what had happened to her after she was taken from Mrs Fillary's. Where did she go? It might have been miles away from London. It could have been anywhere in the world. Wherever it was – and the question kept beating in my brain – *was she still alive?* Was she even now walking about, talking, laughing?

The thought nearly took my breath away.

I tried to imagine what she looked like. I went over to

the mirror and studied my reflection. I knew she had hair like mine, but would she look just like me?

I wasn't sure I liked the idea of that. It made me feel uneasy.

And would she *be* like me? That would be stranger still.

A sudden longing swept over me. I had to know. I had to know whether she was alive and, if she was, I had to find her.

My twin. My other half.

If I found her, the horrible feeling of loneliness, of being incomplete, would vanish forever.

I stared into the mirror, almost willing her to appear there, but only one reflection, my own, stared back. But then it came . . . the sense of someone just behind me, so close I could feel their warmth, feel them softly touching my head. Tears pricked my eyes, though I didn't know why I was crying, because my heart was filled with gladness.

I hardly noticed Sally bringing in my supper. I responded to her cheery chatter mechanically, mechanically chewed the food without knowing what I was eating. All the time I was thinking about how I could find out more about my sister.

It occurred to me that I could ask Sophie. She'd said she could find lost things – perhaps she could find lost people. But remembering that afternoon, I changed my mind. I couldn't wait until she was free to see me again.

Besides, she wasn't the only person who knew about all this. Of course it was no good asking Grandfather directly. He'd simply deny it. But what if there were some evidence hidden somewhere in the house, some indication of what had happened to my twin?

The next morning I waited till everything was quiet and then crept out of the schoolroom. No one was about on the landing, but there were sounds of coughing coming from Tippy's room. For a moment I was tempted to peep in and say hello, but it didn't seem a good idea to disturb her if she was feeling rotten.

I went down two flights of stairs to Grandfather's bedroom. I'd peeked in there once before, soon after arriving in the house. It looked just the same, spacious but austere. Someone – Phoebe, perhaps – had already made the bed, and there was nothing untidy, nothing out of place. There was nothing personal either – no pictures, or photographs. With its heavy old-fashioned furniture and hushed atmosphere, it was like a museum.

Carefully, worried about making a noise, I pulled out each drawer in the wardrobe, releasing a smell of mothballs. Grandfather's socks, all black, neatly paired; suspenders; thick cream-coloured undergarments – all made from natural undyed sanitary wool, of course . . . I shuddered.

I had a sudden overwhelming urge to throw everything on to the floor, to wreak havoc. Why should Grandfather carry on his orderly life undisturbed when he'd done something so monstrous?

I quickly pushed the drawers shut. There were no secrets here. It was the same in the rest of the wardrobe – white shirts folded on the shelves, stiff collars, a rail of neckties in sombre colours. I looked in the washstand – just the slop pail – and in the small adjoining cupboard, where I found an ancient chamber pot with mosaic-like cracked glaze. I even looked under the bed. Nothing but a few balls of fluff.

With no great expectation, I peered into Grandfather's bathroom. A damp towel on the towel rail and the shower dripping into the claw-footed bathtub. Nowhere to hide anything.

The obvious place to look was the library, but that was much harder to get into since Grandfather spent most of his time there. Tomorrow was Monday though, and every Monday evening without fail he went to his club. Tomorrow I would seize my chance . . .

TWENTY-THREE

I'd never been in the library when Grandfather wasn't there. Entering it without his permission felt like violating a sacred place. I'd taken a candle with me and it cast eerie shadows on the bookcases and left the corners in darkness. For a moment I wondered if I dared do this – what if somehow he could tell I'd been in here?

Banishing my doubts, I set my candle down on the table and went over to the shelves where Grandfather stored his papers, very neatly of course, in beige manila folders. I began taking them out one by one and reading the labels. Luckily Grandfather had written in capitals so it was clear.

I started keenly enough, but I soon lost heart. It was such dry stuff – *An Inquiry Into Pangenesis, Heredity and Intelligence* – hah! – *Anthropometry* . . . I had no idea what half the words meant. And there was so much of it. Besides, what was I expecting to find? A folder labelled *The Stolen Baby*?

Think, Meriel, think.

This wasn't about Grandfather's work – it was personal. If anything was written down, it was more likely to be in a letter or a diary.

I carried the candle over to Grandfather's desk and began to search the drawers. I felt a surge of hope when I came across a packet of letters, but when I looked through them they were all from people congratulating him on his knighthood. Vain old bird. Some old diaries raised my hopes, but they went back only ten years. If he'd kept a diary the year I was born, it wasn't here. And anyway, he only recorded appointments and meetings – there was nothing helpful there.

I shut the drawer with a sigh. I was getting nowhere, and Sally would be on her way upstairs soon to help me get ready for bed. I was about to give up when I had a sudden thought. The tests Grandfather made me do – he wrote all the results down, and who knows what else besides. This was a perfect opportunity to see what he said about me.

I'd seen him put his notes into a folder he kept in his desk. I found it in the bottom drawer, under a large blue notebook, and opened it eagerly. To my disappointment it held only a couple of pieces of paper – figures recording all the measurements he'd taken on my birthday, the results of his most recent investigations, plus the dismal results of last month's tests on my schoolwork – some general knowledge, a fiendish piece of French translation and, worst of all, some horrible arithmetic I couldn't do at all. Grandfather had been particularly vile about that one. He said arithmetic was important for my future role as a wife – I would have to keep control of the household accounts and make the sure the servants didn't cheat me.

Remembering this conversation, I gritted my teeth and closed the folder abruptly. I put it back in the drawer, and was about to replace the blue notebook on top, when a sudden burst of curiosity made me open it.

The pages were divided into columns, the first containing single words or phrases, the second and third, figures, and the last filled with Grandfather's cramped, almost indecipherable, handwriting.

Studying the first column I made out some of the words: *Verbal Reasoning*, *Visual Recall*, *Associative Identification* and then further down more familiar topics: *Spelling*, *Arithmetic* . . . Perhaps this was where he kept a permanent record of my results, transcribed from the pieces of paper I'd just been looking at. But why were there two columns of figures? For the schoolwork, the ones in the second column were mostly higher than those in the third: French: 80%; History: 92%. I pulled a face. Better than my results.

Each column was headed by a strange hieroglyph: λ in the second, μ in the third.

I turned to the first page in case there was an explanation there, but it was the same as all the other pages. It was dated October 1881. I hadn't even arrived here then. This was nothing to do with me.

I was about to close the notebook when I noticed that on that page next to the symbol μ there was a squiggle of writing. I moved the candle closer to see it better, but as I did so, some wax splashed on to the leather top of the desk. Horrified, I dabbed at it, and instantly burned my finger. With a little cry I snatched my finger away and sucked it. What a stupid thing to do! But perhaps I could scrape the wax off when it had hardened, perhaps it wouldn't show . . .

I returned to the notebook, and by screwing up my eyes I managed to decipher the squiggle: NOV. I'd arrived in November. And looking down the first column I could make out: *Height*, *Circumference of Head*, *Length of Arm* . . . These must be the measurements Grandfather had taken the day I arrived!

μ *must* be me. So who was this λ who was a bit of a swot and who'd had measurements taken a month before me? Could it be . . . ?

I looked at the first column of figures. *Height:* 5 foot 1 inch. Just the same as me. *Circumference of head*: 21⅓ inches. My heart beating rapidly, I flicked though the pages: 1882, 1883, 1884 . . . Every year on my birthday Grandfather had taken two sets of measurements. And the figures in the two columns were nearly identical.

I checked the latest entry. October this year, just over a month ago. My column was blank, awaiting transcription of the notes he had taken, but the other column had been filled in.

I sat and stared at those numbers.

My twin. My sister. Alive . . . Could it possibly be true?

The word 'Reading' caught my eye. Struggling with Grandfather's writing, I made out: μ *has more confidence than* λ. *She, however, though shyer, has more natural grace, less consciousness of performing.*

With a shaking hand I touched the page. 'She'. λ *was a girl!*

Here at last was the proof I'd been looking for. It had to be her, didn't it? And if she lived near enough for Grandfather to go and measure her and make her take the same tests as me . . . then I would be able to visit her too.

The thought almost stopped my breath.

I sat there stunned as the minutes ticked by, until eventually I remembered that any time now Sally would be arriving in my bedroom and expecting to find me there.

Reluctantly I shut the notebook and replaced it in the drawer. As I did so, my eye fell on Grandfather's current diary. A sudden inspiration made me check the page for 20th October. Sure enough, in among other jottings, there it was: λ. Grandfather had visited this girl on my birthday.

Trembling with anticipation, I searched ahead in the pages. I found the mysterious symbol again on 2nd December: λ 2.30.

In just over a week's time Grandfather was going to see her again. Here was a chance to find out where this girl lived, yet it was utterly impossible for me to do anything about it. The second of December was a Wednesday and at half past two I would be trapped in my music lesson.

The clock struck nine, jolting me back to the present.

I put Grandfather's diary back, lining it up with the edge of the desk, as he always did. I picked up the candle and then I remembered. The wax! I scraped at the blob and managed to peel off most of it, but a residue could still be faintly seen in the grain of the leather. I moved Grandfather's blotter an inch or two to the right and hoped he wouldn't notice. I took a last swift look round the room to make sure everything was as it should be and caught sight of my schoolbooks on the table. Just in case, I picked one up to take back upstairs with me.

I was shutting the library door as quietly as I could when a cough behind me made me start.

'Miss Meriel?'

My heart was jumping like a frog, but I said coolly, 'Good evening, Ponsonby.'

He held my gaze for a long moment with his hooded eyes before he looked away.

'Is everything all right?' I asked him.

'I heard a noise. I was just checking that all was as it should be.'

'Very good, Ponsonby. Goodnight.'

'Goodnight, miss.'

In a dignified manner I went upstairs, conscious of his eyes following me.

He'd tell Grandfather of course. But I was prepared for that. The more urgent question was how could I find out where Grandfather was going on the second of December?

TWENTY-FOUR

Sleep was impossible. I felt quite overcome – stirred up, yes, but also somehow afraid, as if my world had turned on its head.

This girl who might be my sister – I wondered what her name was. I wondered too whether I should send Papa another telegram, telling him what I'd discovered. But how could I possibly fit the news into a telegram? And besides, there was always the possibility that I was mistaken. I couldn't be sure until I'd set eyes on this girl and seen for myself who she was. But I couldn't think of a single dodge to get me out of my music lesson.

Miss Catchpole would arrive at the house at two o'clock sharp and she would leave at three. Too late. And Grandfather would expect a full report of my progress as passed on by Mrs Grimston.

I tossed and turned and wrestled with the problem until at last I thought of something. Lighting a candle, I got out of bed and wrote a note to Sophie, telling her everything I'd found out so far. Then I wrote:

'I know this is asking a lot, but if you could follow Grandfather and find out where he goes, I would be so grateful. I will repay the cab fare next time I see you. Can we meet next Thursday, 2 o'clock at the memorial?'

I was uneasy about entrusting this task to Sophie. It was a lot to ask. Would she be able to do it? Would I at last know where λ lived?

If only I could do it myself . . .

I wasn't surprised to be summoned to the library the following morning. Just as I expected, Ponsonby hadn't wasted any time.

I kept silent through Grandfather's scathing lecture. He paced about as he spoke of obedience, self-discipline, privacy . . . but eventually he wound to a close and looked at me directly.

'I'm disappointed in you, Meriel. Lately I have been beginning to think that at last you can be trusted to behave properly.'

I was surprised – he sounded genuinely regretful. So I wasn't expecting his next abrupt question: 'Why were you trespassing?'

'I was looking for this.' With a flourish I produced my French workbook from behind my back.

Grandfather frowned.

'I thought I'd probably made some mistakes yesterday and I wanted to see what they were. I know I should have waited for you to return my books this morning, but I was keen to correct them. I wanted to do better in my next tests.' I opened my eyes wide and tried to look as innocent as possible.

Grandfather scrutinized me through his monocle. I gazed back without flinching, and at last he said, 'Well,

I'm glad to see this desire to apply yourself. It's been a long time coming.'

I breathed again. It looked as if my ruse had worked.

'But there were many mistakes in your work yesterday, so you have plenty to occupy yourself with today.'

He passed me my books. I was walking towards the door when a sudden icy question brought me to a halt.

'Have you been in the morning room?'

I rearranged my face, and looked round. 'No, Grandfather.'

He narrowed his eyes, and there was a long moment of silence. At last he waved his hand to dismiss me.

Outside the library I breathed again. That had been a narrow escape. If Ponsonby was trying to get me into trouble he'd been foiled. But from now on I would have to watch my step.

Time dragged horribly through the following week, and by the time Wednesday arrived my nerves were as taut as wires. Sophie had written back to say that she would try to do as I'd asked, but she couldn't promise. Never my favourite moment of the week, today my music lesson was excruciating. The notes seemed to dance before my eyes as I stopped and started and stumbled my way through the first piece.

Miss Catchpole, a fierce elderly woman with a moustache, closed her eyes. 'You are murdering the music, Meriel!' Sweeping my hands from the keys, she told me to start again. 'And concentrate!'

I did try. But all the time, in my mind's eye, I was following Grandfather's carriage through the streets of London, willing there to be a hansom cab close behind, and inside it Sophie, on a mission that I'd have given anything to undertake myself.

How strange to think that somewhere not too far away another girl was about to do the tests on her schoolwork I'd done myself that morning. Oddly, knowing this had made a difference – instead of rushing though the tests, not caring about the outcome and just wanting to get them over as quickly as possible, I'd concentrated and tried to do my best. In a funny kind of way λ had become my rival.

I didn't really understand why. After all, I'd long given up trying to impress Grandfather. How bizarre it all was. If this girl was my twin, then she was his granddaughter too. Was he keeping an eye on her progress, making sure she had a good education as he did for me? If he cared that much, then why was she hidden away?

'F sharps, Meriel,' snapped Miss Catchpole, banging her stick on the floor.

I sighed, and started again.

The next afternoon was cold and grey, with a stiff wind that sent the leaves swirling in eddies. As I waited for Sophie I circled the memorial, taking long strides and hugging myself to try to keep warm.

The minutes ticked by and I grew more and more desperate. At last I rounded the corner and there she was, standing by Asia's elephant looking slightly breathless.

'Sophie! What happened? Did you do it?' I called, rushing up to her.

She nodded and all my anxiety vanished.

'You did? Oh, Sophie, you're a wonder. What happened? Was it difficult? Where did Grandfather go?'

Laughing, she held up her hand. 'Wait. I'll tell you, if you give me a chance.'

We set off down the Broad Walk, where even on this wintry day nurses were pushing perambulators. Small children trussed up in coats and scarves, mittens and hats, were bowling hoops and chasing the pigeons.

Sophie spoke in her usual measured way. 'I made sure I was here by half past one, and I hired a growler and asked the driver to wait at the end of your street.' Sophie's expression, for her, was almost impish. 'I had a good view of your house, but when an elderly man came out and got in a carriage I wasn't sure at first whether it was your grandfather. I thought, what if he's just a visitor?'

'Was he tall, with a shock of white hair and great bushy eyebrows?'

'I was too far away to see his eyebrows, and he had a hat on, but yes, he was very tall, and he was wearing a long black coat. He had a cane and he carried himself like this.' Sophie threw back her shoulders and straightened her back.

'Yes, that's Grandfather. He's always telling me off about my posture.'

'I thought it probably was him, and as his carriage went by I said to my cabman, "Follow that brougham".'

I clapped my hands and laughed. 'How topping! Like a detective policeman in a story.'

Sophie smiled. 'Yes, exactly. The cabman's eyes positively bulged, but he whipped up the horses and we clattered off and soon caught up.'

'Oh, I wish I'd been there. It must have been thrilling.'

'I was terrified he'd notice us. We went through the park, and along Piccadilly—'

'But where did you end up?'

'In Bloomsbury, of all places.'

'Is that so surprising?'

'No, of course not.' Sophie coloured. 'It's just that I know the area quite well.' Her mouth shut tight and her face took on that familiar guarded look.

For a second I wondered what she was keeping to herself, but I was more interested in her story. 'So what happened?'

'Your grandfather's carriage stopped outside a house and he went inside.'

'Did you see anyone?'

'No. I mean, I saw the maid who opened the door, but that's all.'

I kicked a stone lying on the path. Of course, it would have been a coincidence if the girl had been coming out or going into the house just at that very moment, but still . . . 'You managed to get the address?'

Taking out her pocketbook, Sophie showed me the page.

I cheered up at once and clapped her on the shoulder. 'Well done. You're a genius.' Her face went pink.

I carefully copied the address into my own pocketbook: 22 Eldon Square, Bloomsbury. 'What's it like, that part of London?' I was thinking of the stinking gutters and crowded streets of Whitechapel.

'Very grand,' said Sophie. 'A lot of wealthy people live there, and there are some fine squares. Eldon Square is not the most impressive, but it's still a well-to-do area.'

'Oh.' I adjusted the picture in my head.

'You don't sound very pleased.'

'Oh I am.' But I had to admit I felt a little – what? Put out? Of course I didn't want my sister to live in a slum, but it hadn't occurred to me that she might live in a similar place to me – or even better. 'Oh, how much do I owe you, by the way?'

Looking embarrassed Sophie said, 'It all came to one and ninepence, I'm afraid. I came back on the train to save money.'

Wincing inwardly – my stock of money was dwindling fast – I counted out some coins and passed them to her.

'Thank you. So? You'll go there?'

'Yes.' My answer was instant, but as I spoke I felt a twinge of misgiving.

'What is it?' said Sophie, ever quick to sense my feelings.

'Nothing . . . except –' I paused and then went on,

'well, now it's come to it, I feel rather nervous. Isn't that silly?'

'I don't think so. I'd be nervous too.'

On an impulse I seized her hand. 'You will come with me, won't you? You're the only person I can trust.'

She smiled one of her little smiles. 'Yes, of course.'

'Thank you. The sooner the better, I think, don't you? I'm anxious to get it over with. Shall we go now?'

Her face fell. 'I can't.'

I couldn't believe it. Something erupted inside me. 'Why not? You know how important this is, how much it means to me. You said you'd come with me, you said you wanted to help me, but you're always letting me down. You just say these things and—'

'Stop, please.'

The resolute way she spoke was so unexpected I stuttered into silence. She looked me in the eye as calm as anything. 'You asked me to do something for you yesterday and, though it wasn't easy for me, I did it. So how can you say I'm always letting you down?'

Grudgingly I had to admit the justice of what she'd said. 'Well, no, yesterday you didn't, but the day I wanted you to come with me to Whitechapel I ended up having to go all on my own, and today –'

She put out a hand. 'Meriel, you're not being fair.'

'What do you mean?'

'Has it never occurred to you that perhaps you're not the only one who has pressing concerns, who—'

'Are you saying I'm selfish?'

'No, but –' She broke off and looked away across the misty park. Then she turned back to me. 'Look, I understand, I do, probably more than you realize. I understand what an incredible thing this is, what it would mean to find a sister you never knew you had –' She stopped again and I saw, to my surprise, that her lip was trembling. She swallowed, seemed to gather herself. 'And I do want to help you, but I have certain . . . *obligations*. I can't just ignore them, much as I would like to.'

'You mean Mrs Quinn?'

Sophie nodded.

'But she can perform seances herself. She doesn't need you to be there all the time. Why don't you just tell her you have more important things to do?'

'It's not that easy.'

'You haven't the courage to stand up to her, you mean.' Even as I said it, a little voice inside me said, 'Like you stand up to Grandfather, eh?'

A pink flush had appeared on Sophie's pale cheeks. 'You're right. I don't have your courage. I wish I did. But it's not just that. My situation . . .' Her mouth twisted.

'What do you mean? What *is* your situation?'

'I can't explain.'

'You could . . . if you trusted me. You accuse me of ignoring your "concerns", as you call them, but then you won't tell me what they are.'

'I know, I'm sorry. I do trust you, but . . . oh, it's impossible.'

'Why is it so difficult? She's only your guardian. It's not as if she owns you.'

To my horror, her face crumpled and she started to cry.

'Sophie, what is it? I'm sorry, I didn't mean to . . .' I faltered into silence.

She quickly gained control of herself. Waving her hand as if to say, it's over now, she took a breath and said, 'It's not your fault, really. And believe me, I wish I could tell you, but I can't.'

My anger faded away completely as I gazed at her. She looked so pale. So sad.

'As to going to Bloomsbury, I understand why you want to go there immediately – I'd feel the same way – but if you could wait till Monday, I'd be able to come with you then. We can take the underground railway to save money. I really do think –' Sophie looked at me in that grave way of hers – 'it would be better if I came with you.'

'Why?'

'Because you don't know what you're going to find. And . . . it might be a great disappointment.'

I looked at her uncertainly. 'Is this something you can tell? You've seen my future, my destiny?'

Sophie smiled. 'I told you, I don't have that gift. So no, I don't know what your destiny is. I just know that things don't always turn out as we hope. I wouldn't want you to face that on your own.'

I stared at her. She was so thoughtful and I'd been so mean. 'Thank you,' I said gruffly, feeling my colour rising and I went on quickly, 'So we'll go on Monday, shall we? Can you be at the station at half past one?'

Sophie nodded.

'Right. I'll meet you there then.'

I watched her walk away. She was in a hurry, but at the bend in the path she turned and looked back. I gave a kind of half-salute, which she returned before disappearing from view behind the shrubbery.

TWENTY-FIVE

The minutes crawled by as I waited for Monday to come. I didn't know what to do with myself. I couldn't sit still, let alone concentrate, my meals tasted like cardboard and I hardly slept. I was desperate to see λ. But I was scared too, scared that λ might not be my sister at all, but some other girl, nothing to do with me, but some strange whim of Grandfather's. Better to think she wasn't my sister and then I wouldn't be disappointed. But another part of me was scared that she might be my sister after all . . . I felt so disturbed, confused.

I thought a lot about my conversation with Sophie. I came to the conclusion that perhaps she was right – I had been expecting too much of her. But she was so mysterious. Why couldn't she trust me and let me into whatever she was hiding?

Whereas my sister . . . she and I would understand one another perfectly. She was my other half, my secret self, and on Monday I might meet her. My heart dipped with excitement.

But then on Saturday two unexpected things happened.

The first was that at long last Papa replied to my letter.

Calcutta
12th November 1885

My dear Meriel,
I'm sorry you've had to wait so long for this letter. And I'm even sorrier that what I have to say might cause you unhappiness. But, my darling, you will have to be very brave, as I know you can be, and accept that it is absolutely impossible for you to come back to India now or in the foreseeable future. It's hard for me to explain at the moment – I hope that one day when you're older you will understand.

And, my dear, while you are dependent on your grandfather's generosity, it would be wise to fall in with his wishes. I know that some of his ideas must seem irksome and old-fashioned to you, but he is right about some things, and certainly in London it is safer for you to be chaperoned. Try to remember that he means well and has your best interests at heart. If he should decide, for whatever reason, to stop supporting you, then – oh, Meriel – I am afraid to think what might happen.

I was glad to hear you've met up with Everina Jolly and are having fun. Mamma valued her friendship and we used to enjoy the time we spent with her and her husband.

I was puzzled by your telegram, but touched by your concern. Rest assured, I am in perfect health. A little tired, to be sure, but otherwise very well.

I'd better finish now as it's time to go and teach. Please, my darling, be a good girl and try to please your grandfather.

Your ever-loving,
Papa

I put the letter down, feeling . . . what? I didn't know. India and Papa seemed so far away now. What absorbed me at the moment was meeting my twin. Everything else had faded in importance.

Even so, I felt bitter towards Papa. He clearly didn't want me to go home – he didn't want to be bothered with me. And I couldn't see why I had to fall in with Grandfather's wishes. *He means well* . . . Did he? If Grandfather had done what I suspected, then Papa was quite wrong about him.

Sighing, I flipped open a book, but I was still immersed in my train of thought. Of course, if it turned out that λ was my twin, his daughter, I would have to tell Papa. For a few delightful minutes I envisaged Papa having a huge row with Grandfather and insisting that both his daughters should come to live with him in India. But that was a daydream. It quickly faded and was replaced by stark reality. Why would Papa do that? He wouldn't even rescue me.

I sighed again. There was no point in thinking about it now. One step at a time, and Monday was the next step.

But it wasn't.

When I presented myself in the library to hear the results of my tests, Grandfather said, 'Sit down, Meriel.' I went towards the table, but he said, 'No, not there, here.' And he gestured towards the armchair.

I was struck all of a heap, as Sally would say.

Ensconced behind his desk, he regarded me through his monocle, but not with his usual eagle stare. His eyes had a shadowy look about them and his expression was almost . . . *gentle*?

I felt distinctly uneasy. What was going on?

He read out my results, and with each one I grew more surprised and also more pleased. I hadn't done at all badly.

'A distinct improvement, Meriel,' said Grandfather, echoing my thoughts. 'Sadly long overdue, but nevertheless at last you seem to be doing yourself justice and showing signs of that intelligence I would have expected to see in you.'

I grinned. I couldn't help it. Grandfather acknowledging some achievement on my part. It had never happened before. I wondered how λ had performed – had I beaten her this time?

'I feel it is only fair that you should be rewarded in some way.'

I sat up, tingling with anticipation. This was so unlike him. What did he have in mind? Perhaps he was going to increase my allowance. Or perhaps he'd relented and was going to let me go to the theatre after all? Thrilled, I held my breath and paid attention. But he wasn't making any sense.

'. . . going to convalesce with her cousin in Broadstairs.'

'Pardon me, Grandfather, who is?'

'Miss Tippins,' said Grandfather, with a touch of his

usual asperity. 'Given that her health is so broken down, I have decided to dispense with her services. She will not be returning to us after Christmas.'

'Oh.' I was shocked. All along I'd been assuming that Tippy would get better. I was even looking forward to the resumption of our routine – in the mornings, at least. Studying on my own hadn't been as much fun as I'd thought it would be. I was worried for Tippy too – her illness must have affected her severely, if she couldn't return to her duties.

And was I to have a new governess? Is that what Grandfather meant by my reward?

'I have thought long and hard about this, Meriel, and I've come to the conclusion that this is the best thing to do, although . . .' He sighed heavily and turned to look towards the window, apparently lost in thought.

I was on tenterhooks. Eventually, when I couldn't bear it any longer, I said, 'Grandfather?'

He started as if he'd forgotten I was there. What a strange mood he was in! 'Ah, yes, well, at least now you're performing at a level where you won't disgrace yourself, or me.'

I was utterly bemused. 'I beg your pardon, Grandfather?'

'At school, of course. I'm sending you to school.'

'What?' The word exploded from my mouth.

'I thought you'd be pleased. A change of regime, a chance to mingle with other girls of your age . . .'

I swallowed. 'What kind of school?'

'I've been talking to some of the fellows at the club. Marchett's girls are at a Swiss finishing school, Château Bellevue. He thinks pretty highly of it: healthy climate – it's situated in the mountains – good discipline and so forth. And your French will certainly improve.'

I was shocked into silence. A few months ago I'd have probably jumped for joy at the idea of getting away from here, even if it was only to school. But not now. Not when I might be about to find my sister . . .

Choosing my words carefully, I said, 'It's very good of you to suggest this, Grandfather. But, you know, I really don't want to go away.'

His eyebrows lifted in surprise. 'You don't?'

'No, and . . .' I struggled to think of what to say. 'You said yourself that my results have improved. Doesn't that prove that I don't need to go to school?'

'An admirable piece of logic, but it's not merely a question of results, you see. There are other considerations . . .' Once again his gaze drifted towards the window.

I risked prompting him. 'Other considerations?'

There was a pause before he brought his attention back to me. 'Yes, well, for one thing, you're getting rather old for a governess—'

'Actually, Grandfather, I'm not so sure. When Tippy, I mean Miss Tippins, is well enough, I think it would be much better to go on with her. She knows how to get the best out of me.' I injected as much earnest sincerity into my voice as I could.

But though he frowned slightly at the interruption, Grandfather carried on just as if I hadn't spoken. 'A governess is all very well and necessary at a certain stage of life, but these women –' he shook his head – 'they're naturally limited, by virtue of their class. What do they know of society? No, this school is just what you need. It'll give you a final polish, as it were – prepare you for entry into society at the highest level, as befits my granddaughter.'

'But couldn't I go to a school in London? So I don't have to go so far away.'

Leaning his elbows on his desk and resting his chin on his clasped hands, he regarded me gravely. 'Switzerland is, sadly, some distance away, but it's a question of your best interests.' I was taken aback at the kindliness of his tone. 'At a school like this you will mix with a class of society not so easily encountered in England. You will meet the daughters of the European aristocracy. Who knows where it might lead?'

I gazed at him bleakly. His motive was obvious – he was hoping to marry me off to the son of some marquis or whatever they were called. He'd be rid of me, but able to boast to his cronies about his connections. As for me, I'd be stuck abroad and my dream of being an actress would be over. I felt as though all the wadding had been beaten out of me.

For a moment I considered flying into an almighty

tantrum – shouting, kicking, screaming – but I knew there was no point. Whatever I did, he would have his way.

'When am I to go?' The quaver in my voice wasn't put on.

'I'll write to Madame Marmot, the headmistress. I'm hoping you can start in January, though it's part-way through the school year.'

January! Only a few weeks away. It hardly gave me any time at all.

Grandfather shot me a sharp look. 'So aren't you going to thank me? This is why you need this school – I hope they teach you some manners.' The acerbic tone was back.

'Thank you, Grandfather,' I said through gritted teeth.

Without another word, he put the folder containing my results in his drawer, a signal that our interview was over.

Leaving the room, I passed Ponsonby in the hall. He greeted me in his clipped nasal voice and I acknowledged him absent-mindedly as he went in to Grandfather.

I continued up the stairs but at the first landing I stopped, thunderstruck. I looked back at the closed library door.

What if Ponsonby had seen me snooping in the morning room as well as catching me in the library? Perhaps Grandfather had noticed the splash of wax on the desk and realized I suspected him. Sending me to school might be my punishment. On the other hand, he might be getting rid of me to stop me finding my sister! So much for my 'best interests' . . . why, he was a better actor than I was!

In a turmoil of swirling thoughts I carried on up the stairs, meeting Sally on the top landing.

'Sally, did you know I am to be sent away to school?'

'Oh, no, miss.'

'Yes, after Christmas. I'm going to Switzerland!'

'Switzerland? Golly, that's a long way away.' She sounded dismayed, and it comforted me a little to think she might miss me.

'Grandfather says Tippy's too ill to carry on teaching. Is that true?'

'I don't know. She's better than she was. Do you want to see her?'

Tippy was sitting up in chair, swathed in a shawl. I was shocked at the change in her. Her skin looked waxy and behind her spectacles her eyes were bigger than ever. But her shrunken face lit up at the sight of me. 'Meriel,' she exclaimed in a weak voice, 'how nice of you to come to see me.'

At once I felt guilty for not having come before.

'How are you, Miss Tippins?'

'Oh, not so bad now, my dear.' But she broke into a fit of coughing. 'Excuse me,' she wheezed, her eyes watering.

Sally brought a glass of water, and she drank some. As she did so I stole a glance at the room. On the mantelpiece was her sad little collection of ornaments – the shepherdess and her swain and the little girl holding a flower looked as though they wondered what they were doing here.

Tippy returned the glass to Sally with a smile. 'You see how well I've been looked after, Meriel. Everyone has been most kind.'

'But I hear you're leaving us?'

A shadow passed across her face. 'That's right, my dear. I'd hoped to make a full recovery, but this silly old chest of mine won't behave itself. Still, I think I'll be well suited with my cousin.' And she smiled bravely.

Poor Tippy. I didn't believe for a minute that she really wanted this arrangement. 'When are you going?' I asked, thinking I would come and see her again.

'Monday.'

'So soon?'

'The doctor thinks I'm fit enough to travel now. And you're off to school, I understand.'

'Yes,' I growled, 'but I'd much rather stay here and carry on with you.'

She patted my hand. 'That's sweet of you, my dear, but I think you'll enjoy school.' She started coughing again, and Sally gave me a look.

'Well . . . I'd better go and do some work now, Miss Tippins.'

'You'll come and say goodbye, won't you? Before I go.'

'Of course.' I felt truly sorry that I hadn't seen her more often while I could. She wasn't a bad old stick and I was really going to miss her.

Sally came out with me, and when the door was shut I said quietly, 'Listen, Sally, this afternoon I need to go somewhere again. Can we keep to the usual arrangement?' For all the time I'd been talking to Tippy, I'd been thinking.

If Grandfather knew I suspected him, there wasn't a moment to lose. Rather than wait for Monday and Sophie, I would go to Bloomsbury by myself that very afternoon.

TWENTY-SIX

I lurked behind a postbox in Eldon Square, surveying the house from across the street while I worked up the courage to go and ring the bell.

All the way here I'd been trying to think of what to say, how to introduce myself, and I wished now I'd waited so Sophie could have come with me. Eventually I settled on, 'Please may I speak to the young lady of the house.'

But what if λ were one of the servants?

I told myself not to be stupid. Why would a servant be learning French?

Swallowing the pebble of fear lodged in my throat, I marched across the road and rang the bell. After a few moments the door was opened by a maid who didn't look at all surprised to see me. She said, 'Oh, Miss Katharine, have you forgotten your key?' and stood back to let me in.

For a moment I was too astonished to move, but then, gathering my wits, I took several hesitant steps forward and the maid shut the door behind me. I expected her to look at me again and exclaim that she had made a mistake, unleashing who knew what hullabaloo. But she merely went off towards the back of the house, leaving me alone.

I stood frozen to the spot, terrified that any moment a

door would open and I would be discovered. I hadn't the faintest idea what to do.

Unlike Grandfather's chilly entrance hall with its Grecian statuary and boring prints, this one was welcoming, with a colourful rug on the tiles and bright pictures on the walls. But there was nowhere to hide.

And then from somewhere upstairs came the sound of a piano, and a moment later someone started to sing.

I stood transfixed, all the hairs on the back of my neck tingling.

Mamma.

A second later I shook myself. Don't be stupid, Meriel. Of course it isn't Mamma. But the voice, though lighter, did have a similar quality, a haunting loveliness that drew me up the stairs, along a landing, to a door that stood slightly ajar.

I pushed it open a little more so I could see into the room without being seen and stepped closer to the gap.

My heart stilled.

I was looking at myself in that drawing room, playing the piano and singing.

I caught hold of the skin on the back of my hand and pinched it hard. No, this was me, here, standing outside the door.

The girl in there was my identical twin sister.

It was uncanny, as if I was looking at my reflection in a mirror, but a reflection that had a life of its own. She seemed to be alone so I pushed the door further open and took a few steps forward. After a minute or two she happened to turn her head in my direction. She gave a little gasp and the music died away. All the colour drained from her face as she stared at me – stared at me with my own amber eyes.

We couldn't stop looking at one other. It wasn't just my eyes – she had my eyebrows, my nose, my mouth, my chin . . . I felt light-headed, and for an awful moment I wondered whether somehow my face had slipped from me to her. If I looked in the mirror, would I see a stranger? Or worse, a faceless wraith?

Enough, I told myself. Clearing my throat, I managed to say, 'Hello.'

'Hello.' It was a whisper, but I heard it – my own voice answering me.

Still gazing at me in wonder, to my utter amazement she murmured, 'All my life I've dreamed about you, but I never thought you really existed.' Her face changed. 'You are real, aren't you?'

I laughed. 'Yes, I'm real.' I made a move, intending to dispel any doubt in her mind, but then I stopped dead. Because she'd risen from the piano stool and taken a step or two towards me. And she limped. My sister had a limp. In a flash Mrs Fillary's words about my 'walking so well' came back to me.

My reaction must have registered on my face, because my sister blushed, glancing down quickly, but then she raised her eyes and looked at me steadily.

I didn't know what to say. After a moment's

embarrassed silence I went up to her. 'I am real. See?' I held out a hand.

She touched my fingertips and I noticed her hands were just like mine – small and fine-boned. It was the lightest of touches, but I flinched. Perhaps I hadn't quite believed she was real either.

We both smiled. And she had my smile.

'It's so peculiar—'

'Isn't it strange—'

We'd both spoken at once and we laughed. Identical laughs.

I was glad to see she wasn't putting her hair up yet either – it was tied back loosely – but I did notice that her dress, made of a lovely blue silk, was well cut. It was much nicer than any of mine.

Still gazing at my face she said quietly, 'I can hardly believe it, but I think we must be sisters, mustn't we?'

'Yes. I think so.'

'And are you sixteen too?'

'Yes.'

'So we're twins,' she whispered.

It was as if we couldn't tear our eyes from each other. Suddenly, with a sharp intake of breath, I exclaimed, 'You have a scar on the bridge of your nose!'

'So do you!'

'I fell down some steps. I think I was about two,' I said.

'*I* fell down the stairs, probably at about the same age.'

We both clasped our hands to our mouths, our eyes wide. I thought she looked amused . . . and afraid. That was how I felt too. How could the same things have happened to us at the same time? Had we shared other experiences without knowing it?

It really was very, very strange. And I had longed for and imagined this moment, but all my imagining was nothing like the reality. There was nothing for it but to plunge in. 'I'm Meriel.'

'Kitty.'

Kitty. I wondered who'd given her that name. 'The maid thought I was you! She just let me in.' Again we both laughed, but there was an edge of tension, certainly in *my* laugh. We weren't the same – we couldn't be. Even though she existed, I was still me. 'You said you'd dreamed about me. What did you mean?'

'Just that. I've dreamed that there were two of us – doing ordinary things, you know, like talking, or eating a meal, but doing them together, always together . . . And I've often wondered whether somewhere in the world I might have a sister.'

Moved by her words, I told her about the strange sensation I had of someone being close to me, caressing me.

'I've felt that too!' she exclaimed. 'Do you think it's from before we were born? When we were lying so close together?'

'Perhaps.' It was an amazing thought and we gazed at one another for a moment in a rapt silence. I was the first to break it. 'What happened to you? After we were born, I mean.'

'I don't know. Someone must have brought me to England from China—'

'China?'

'Yes, didn't you know?'

I shook my head. It seemed the safest thing to do.

Kitty looked distressed. 'Oh dear. I'm sorry.'

I suddenly sensed that I had to tread carefully, that I needed to find out as much as I could about her before telling my side of the story.

'There's no need to be sorry. But I'd be glad if you tell me what you know.'

'Do you mind if we sit down?' From the look in her eyes I wondered if she was in pain; perhaps her leg was troubling her.

I dropped onto the deep buttoned sofa with a bounce, dislodging a tasselled cushion. It was much more comfortable than any piece of furniture at Grandfather's. I wondered whose house this was. The room, with its honeysuckle chintz, china ornaments and watercolours, was pretty rather than grand, a room you could relax in. But I wasn't relaxed. I kept my eye on the door. What if someone came in and found us? What would I say?

Kitty sat down with obvious relief and folded her hands in her lap. I blurted out, 'What's the matter with your leg?'

She went pink and ducked her head and I was

sorry I'd asked, but then she said quietly, 'I have a club foot.'

She must have seen my puzzlement because she said, 'My left foot was like this when I was born,' and she bent her wrist to show me. 'They tried strapping it up when I was a baby, and I wore a brace for a while – it helped a little, but it will never be completely straight.'

'Does it hurt?'

She nodded. 'Sometimes. Then I can't stand for too long.'

I thought how hideous that must be, not to be able to move about freely, to take big strides when you felt like it, to twirl around or dance. 'Don't you mind awfully? I should.' It was out before I could stop myself.

She coloured up again and twisted her fingers together.

Stupid Meriel. 'You were telling me about China.'

'Oh yes.' She hesitated. 'You know about our parents?'

I shook my head slowly, wondering what on earth she was going to say.

'I can't believe no one's told you. They were missionaries in China and . . .' She paused, shooting me a troubled look. 'I'm sorry, I don't know how to say this.'

'Please, go on.' I was struggling to keep a suitable expression on my face, but my mind was racing. Who'd told her these lies?

'They died from malaria just after we were born.'

'Oh.' I made my voice sombre and looked down so she couldn't tell what I was really feeling.

'Yes, it's terribly sad, isn't it?' She was quiet for a moment, thinking. 'I've often wondered what they were like, of course . . .' She paused, giving me a quizzical look. 'It's odd that we got separated, don't you think? I wonder how it happened.'

'Mmm,' I said, non-committally. 'So when you were brought to England, you came here?'

'Yes, I've been so lucky. Mamma and Papa are so kind.'

I sat bolt upright. 'Mamma and Papa?'

She blushed. 'The Chirks, I mean. I've always called them that. And why not?' Her tone was defensive. 'They are as dear to me as any parents could be.' Her face changed and her hand went to her mouth. 'I hope you don't think I've betrayed the memory of our real parents?'

'No, of course not.' But she had disconcerted me. Of course she didn't know who our real parents were, but even so . . . I felt that Mamma and Papa would have been hurt.

She was looking at me anxiously.

'It's all right, really it is,' I said, trying to sound reassuring.

Her face relaxed.

'So how long have you lived with . . . the Chirks, did you say they're called?'

'All my life, from the time I was six months old.'

I stiffened. It fitted exactly with what Mrs Fillary had said. After leaving her, Kitty must have come straight here. 'And do you have any brothers or sisters? I mean, do the Chirks have any other children?'

'No. There's only me, so I've been spoilt.' She smiled. 'But I've always wanted a sister, and here you are! It's amazing, wonderful.'

I smiled back automatically, but I wasn't sure I shared her feelings. And it hadn't occurred to me that my sister might be content with her life. If I'd thought about it at all, I'd have assumed she felt the same as me – dissatisfied, yearning for something. The truth was I hadn't thought – not beyond the hope of finding her; I hadn't given any consideration to what her life might be like or what would happen next.

'Mamma and Papa will be so pleased to see you, I know. Papa's still at the university, of course, but Mamma's here. Shall we go and surprise her?'

'No!' I sprang up in alarm. I wasn't ready for that. I added hastily, 'Don't you think this will come as quite a shock? Perhaps we shouldn't tell them yet, not before we've thought of what to say.'

She looked as if she didn't agree. 'But—'

'Please, can't this be our secret, just for now?'

She stared at me for a second or two and then her face cleared. 'All right.'

I felt a little thrill. Already we'd formed an alliance.

Kitty said, 'There's so much I want to ask you. I want to know everything. How did you find me? How long is it since you've known about me?'

'I –' I stopped. Everything was happening too fast. I

needed to digest what Kitty had told me and work out exactly what I was going to say. 'It's a long story. I'm sorry, but I don't think we've got time for it now. I'm expected back soon.'

'Oh. Where do you live?'

'Kensington.'

'Really? To think we're both here in London and I didn't know. Have you lived here a long time?' Her eyes searched my face. 'And who do *you* live with?'

I knew I was being unfair, but I couldn't help it. 'I'm sorry . . . I really must be going.'

Her face fell. 'But you haven't told me anything about *you* yet.'

'I know. Next time I will, I promise.' I remembered what the maid had said about her forgetting her key. 'Are you allowed out without a chaperone?' I heard the envious tone in my voice, but I couldn't help it.

'Only to the postbox. And I walk with Papa to the university on fine mornings and come back on my own. It's just round the corner. Why?'

'Oh, I was hoping we could meet somewhere out of the house, where we can talk freely, but I can only get away in the afternoons.'

She was thinking. 'I could meet you one afternoon. Richard could bring me.'

'Is Richard your footman?'

'No – he's a distant relative of Mamma's, the son of her second cousin. He lodges with us.'

From the way she spoke I knew at once that she was

fond of this Richard. Something twisted in my stomach. How many more people were there in her life, people that she loved?

'If you don't tell him why, would he be prepared to bring you to near our meeting place and then leave you to come on alone? And not tell anyone?'

'Why can't I tell him?'

'You can, but not yet. Not till we've worked everything out. Would he do that?'

'I think so.' I could tell from her face that she was baffled by all this secrecy, that she didn't like it. But it was an instinct I felt compelled to follow. Just for now, just until I'd thought everything through.

'Where is a good place for us to meet?'

She thought for a moment. 'How about Regent's Park? The York Gate entrance?'

I would find out where it was. 'We'll meet there. Would Monday suit you? At half past two?'

She nodded.

'Right. And now I must go.' I paused. 'I'd rather no one saw me.'

She glanced at the clock. 'You should be all right. Mamma is writing letters till teatime. If you go down quietly, you can let yourself out.'

'Till Monday then.'

At the door I turned back, suddenly wanting some reassurance that I hadn't imagined it all. But there she was, indisputably, my mirror image. From across the room she smiled at me and I sent her a little tentative smile back.

TWENTY-SEVEN

I managed to leave the house undetected and hurried away in the dusk, scarcely aware of my surroundings my mind was in such a whirl. I kept telling myself, Yes, Meriel, it really did happen. You have just been talking to your sister, your twin sister.

I sat on the train in a daze, reliving snatches of our conversation and wondering why I'd been so reticent, why I hadn't told Kitty anything. I didn't know and I couldn't work it out. I'd imagined I'd be ecstatic, but I wasn't. I was just in a horrible muddle.

I spent the evening turning everything over in my mind. Now it was absolutely clear what Grandfather had done. He'd taken, no, *stolen*, my sister away from Mamma when she was just a few hours old and secretly arranged for her to be brought up in another family. Whether the cock-and-bull story about missionaries in China was his idea or the Chirks's didn't matter; the result was the same. My sister had, unknowingly, been exiled from her true home and lost to us for all these years.

However hard I thought about it, the one thing I couldn't work out was *why* he'd done this. Granted, his behaviour was bizarre at times, and he took his obsessions to extreme lengths, but this? It was unfathomable.

I climbed into bed and blew out the candle, but I was too angry for sleep.

I decided I would go to Grandfather and confront him with what I knew. For once, I held all the power. I pictured the scene: initially he would be shocked, and then, as I gradually revealed my discoveries, he would cower – terrified because he'd been found out – and beg me to remain silent.

I was enjoying this vision when another thought made me take in a sharp breath.

I was assuming Grandfather had done this without telling anyone. Part of my rage was about the way he'd treated Mamma and Papa, especially Mamma. But what if they'd been in on it too? Or – and the thought made my stomach suddenly plunge – what if it had been their idea?

My world tilted. What if I'd been lied to all my life? Because not telling someone something, especially something as important as this, was as good as lying to them.

I felt sick. And then another horror struck me. It could have been me who was taken away. What if it was pure chance that Kitty was taken and I was left? Perhaps my sense that I was unique, special, *loved*, was an illusion.

I stared into the darkness, gripped by a fear that was worse than anything I'd ever known. Everything solid, familiar, real, dissolved, leaving me floating in a boundless void.

By the time I left the house on Monday afternoon I was in such a wretched state I hardly said a word to Sally. On top of everything else, I'd said goodbye to Tippy that morning and that had upset me. I was still in the grip of anxieties about Mamma and Papa and I didn't know whether or not I even wanted to see Kitty again. I was dreading having to tell her what I knew. My only shred of comfort was that I'd decided to keep to the arrangement with Sophie.

I told myself that Sophie could help me to convince Kitty of the truth of my story. But really I wanted Sophie to be there for me – I knew I'd feel steadier and calmer in her presence.

When I met Sophie she gave me a searching look and said, 'Is everything all right?'

'No, it isn't.'

I poured everything out – the news about school, and meeting Kitty. It was a relief to share it with her.

'You didn't tell Kitty anything? About yourself or what you've discovered?'

I looked away. 'I should have at least told her about our parents. I don't know why I didn't.' The more I'd thought about it, the guiltier I'd felt.

Sophie frowned. 'I should think it will be very disturbing for her to learn that her parents didn't die when she was a baby, that she might have had a life with them. Maybe you wanted to protect her from being upset?'

'Maybe.' But I didn't think that was the real reason.

'And of course her father, her real father, is still alive.'

A jolt went through me at her words, and I was quiet for a minute, thinking about what she'd said. For all I was angry with Papa, even hating him at times, he was still *my* father. The idea of sharing him with someone else was disturbing.

'I'll tell Kitty today about our parents,' I said. 'I must. But I don't know what to tell her about how I found her . . . or about Grandfather.' I couldn't tell Sophie what I feared.

'Why not tell her the truth?' Sophie said, as though it was quite simple.

'Because she'll tell the Chirks – I know she will.' I spoke bitterly, remembering Kitty's tone when she'd referred to 'Mamma'. I couldn't imagine her keeping any secrets from them.

'Does that matter?'

'Yes! I've been thinking about it. What if they concocted the plot with Grandfather and I get sent away to school and Kitty carries on having her nice life and that's that!'

Sophie blinked at my vehemence, but before she could say anything I went on: 'Or supposing they're not aware of what he did. They'll be shocked. They might say to Grandfather, "Here, have your granddaughter back," and then we'll both get sent away.'

'Would that be so bad? At least you'd be together.'

'Yes, but . . . Oh, I don't know.' I struck the seat with my hand.

Sophie gave me one of her long, considering looks. Finally she said, 'What is it you really want?'

I thought. Finally I said, speaking slowly as I worked it out, 'I want to say to Grandfather, "Look, I know what you've done, and I want to know why." And I have to know whether he did this on his own. I want to ask him myself, not let the Chirks do it.'

I stared out of the window. I would have to tell Kitty everything, but could I rely on her to keep it a secret? Would she see how important it was to me?

I had no idea. That hope I'd had, that she and I would be twin souls who understood one another perfectly, seemed childish now. She might look just like me, but really I didn't know her at all.

We arrived at the appointed meeting place before Kitty. Although a pale wintry sun was shining, it was very cold. I stamped up and down, as much because I was too agitated to be still as to keep warm, but Sophie waited patiently.

'There she is,' she said at last. 'Oh!' I turned to see what was wrong. Kitty was approaching quite fast, despite her limp, her flame-red hair unmistakable. But she wasn't alone. There was a young man with her.

Kitty saw us and waved, but I didn't wave back and after a second she slowly lowered her arm. She exchanged a few words with her companion and then he set off across the park, taking a path that led away from us.

He must have seen us. I was furious. I'd specifically told her to leave her chaperone somewhere and come on alone.

Kitty approached us looking rather abashed.

My mood was not improved by seeing that as well

as wearing a close-fitting charcoal wool coat, she was carrying an astrakhan purse muff. Thrusting my woollen-gloved hands into the pockets of my childish brown coat, I coldly effected the introductions. 'Miss Casson, my sister Kitty.'

'How do you do, Miss . . . ?' Sophie paused, at a loss as to how to address Kitty.

Kitty said, 'Miss Chirk.'

She *was* adopted then. I hadn't liked to ask. Did it matter? Well, I knew I didn't like it, for some reason, but there wasn't time now to work out why.

Kitty greeted Sophie in a friendly enough manner but turned to me as if to say, Who's this?

'Miss Casson is a friend of mine,' I said stiffly.

There was a pause. Kitty and Sophie were both looking at me, waiting for me to take the lead. 'Shall we walk?' I said curtly, and set off along the path. I had no idea where I was going, but it wasn't the direction the young man had taken.

After a minute or two I realized Kitty was struggling to keep up with me. Sophie, typically thoughtful, was hanging back so I slowed to let them catch up, but I still didn't look at Kitty.

'You're angry with me, aren't you?' said Kitty after we'd walked a few paces in silence.

I rounded on her. 'Are you surprised? I said we must keep this a secret for now, and you agreed. You were supposed to come by yourself.'

Kitty flinched. 'I know, but after you left on Saturday

I was so excited. I was bursting to tell someone. I don't think Mamma or Papa noticed, but as soon as he came home Richard knew something had happened.'

'So that young man was Richard?' I said sourly.

'Yes. He would like to meet you, but we thought it best if you and I spoke first. He's gone to the zoological gardens,' she added.

I didn't care where he'd gone. And as for wanting to meet me . . .

Kitty looked at me earnestly. 'I had to tell him; I couldn't help it. So I thought it wouldn't matter if he saw you. But he's promised he won't say anything. He'll keep his word, I know.' Her confidence in Richard irritated me. I was even more irritated when she added with a flare of spirit, 'Anyway, you brought *your* friend. I beg pardon, Miss Casson, if that sounds rude. I don't mean it to be.'

Sophie looked as if she was about to say something gracious, but I butted in. 'That's different. I wouldn't have found you without Sophie. She's been involved with everything from the start. She has a right to be here.'

I caught on Sophie's face a look of surprised pleasure before she resumed her usual neutral expression and said gravely, 'It's very chilly here. Shall we continue our walk – that is, if that suits you, Miss Chirk?'

As we moved on I wondered if that was a reproach aimed at me because I wasn't walking slowly enough for Kitty.

Feeling very grumpy, I gazed across the lake.

After a few more minutes silence Sophie said, 'The

young man knows about you both now. Would it not be better to move on to more important subjects?'

I scowled. She was right of course.

Shooting Sophie a grateful look, Kitty said, 'So how *did* you find me? You said you'd tell me today.'

'I will tell you,' I said slowly, 'but there's something else you need to know first.'

TWENTY-EIGHT

In the end I just blurted it out.

'You know you told me that our parents were missionaries in China? It's not true. They lived in India – well, our father still lives there, actually. He's an artist, a very good portrait painter, and he teaches at the College of Art in Calcutta, but—'

'Why are you doing this?' A mottled red flush had spread over Kitty's face.

'What do you mean?'

'Making up such a story.'

I stared at her, my mouth agape. Recovering myself, I said, 'But I'm not making it up, Kitty. Truly.'

'I don't believe you. Our parents were missionaries in China.' Tears glistened in her eyes.

I shot a desperate glance at Sophie.

Speaking gently, she said, 'I know this must seem very strange. And if you've been told something, especially by someone you love, and believed it all your life, it's very hard to accept it might not be true.'

'But Mamma and Papa wouldn't lie to me.'

Oh, wouldn't they? I thought.

'They might not have lied. They themselves might have been deceived.' Sophie gave me a meaningful look.

'That's right,' I said. 'It's very likely, actually.'

Kitty looked from one to the other of us in utter bewilderment.

'Listen, Kitty. I know we don't really know each other, but I'm your sister. Why would I tell you something so upsetting, unless it was true?'

'But how do you know our parents lived in India? That our father is an artist?'

I swallowed. She wasn't going to like this. 'Because I lived with them.'

She stared at me, crinkling her forehead, just as I did when I was puzzled.

'I lived with them, in India, you see, until Mamma died.' Something caught in my throat and I swallowed again.

Kitty had gone quite white and I feared she might faint. She seemed paralysed, unable to speak. If someone had just told me what I'd told her, I'd have made a fearful fuss, not able to contain myself, whereas she was as still as stone, seeming to absorb this revelation somewhere deep inside herself.

I was frightened by her silence and looked at Sophie for help.

She put her hand on Kitty's arm. 'Breathe, Miss Chirk.' She produced a small bottle of smelling salts from her bag and waved it under Kitty's nose.

It worked. Kitty gave a little start and seemed to come back to herself. We helped her over to a bench. Somewhere in the distance a lion roared and I wished I was in the zoological gardens, like Richard, rather than here having to cope with Kitty.

Sophie tugged at my coat sleeve and I realized that Kitty was staring at me imploringly.

'I beg your pardon?'

'When did . . . our mother die?'

I could see the effort that 'our' cost her. 'Four years ago.'

'Oh.' She looked down at her boots, one of which, I saw, had a much thicker sole than the other. I looked away feeling as though I'd seen something I shouldn't. How hideous to have to wear such an ugly thing.

Kitty stirred and looked up at me. 'I don't understand. Why didn't I live with you?' she asked in a tremulous voice.

I could imagine how she felt. Hurt and rejected. Well, that's how I would have felt if it had been me. Perhaps I could persuade her that it could just as easily have been me; it wasn't as if I was chosen and she wasn't. Unless – I stiffened – unless it was something to do with her foot. Grandfather was such a snob – perhaps he couldn't accept that a member of his family wasn't perfect.

She was waiting for an answer. I had to tell her. I licked my lips. 'I don't know *why*, but I think I know what happened. Someone comes to see you, doesn't he? An old man with white hair and a beard. And bushy eyebrows. He gets you to do tests and does weird things like measuring you, doesn't he?' I deliberately didn't say the name.

For all I knew, Grandfather might go under an alias when he visited the Chirks.

But Kitty said at once, 'Sir Osbert?' She sounded surprised. 'You know him?'

I nodded. 'I know you're going to find this hard to believe, but that man is our grandfather. Our mother's father.'

She stared at me, 'Our *grandfather*? But . . . how can that be possible?' Her voice was as thin as a reed. 'He's never said so; he's never given any indication that we were related. Papa told me he was a scientist – I assumed he worked with Papa at the university. He's never *said*.' Her eyes narrowed, just like mine when I was suspicious. 'How do you know this?'

'I live with him now, Kitty. I've lived with him since I came to England, since Mamma died.'

Kitty uttered a little gasp, her colour coming and going. I glanced at Sophie, wondering if we'd need the smelling salts again.

'He's never said anything about you,' she said finally.

'He's never told me about *you*.' I smiled ruefully. 'He doesn't know I've found you.'

Kitty looked from me to Sophie and back again, her expression utterly bewildered.

'But why has he kept us apart? Why hasn't he said anything?'

I shrugged. 'I've no idea. But I want to find out, if I can.'

Kitty fell silent, her eyes on a pigeon pecking at the

grass. But I doubted that she actually saw it. She was very pale, and I noticed she was shivering. Sophie must have noticed it too, because she said, 'If you feel able to, I think we should walk on, don't you?'

Kitty rose to her feet obediently, but instead of moving she looked at me and said, 'Do Mamma and Papa know? That he's my grandfather, I mean. Or about you.'

Her tone was plaintive, and I was pretty sure what had been going through her head – the same questions as afflicted me. Who knew about our separation? Who'd been concealing the truth from us?

'I don't know. Come on, Kitty, you're cold. We must move.'

We left the circular walk. As we crossed the lake on a suspension bridge, two swans glided silently towards the shelter of the nearest island. We took a path to the right that climbed an open slope covered with grey, frost-stiffened grass. I worried that Kitty would tire quickly, but she stumped along gamely and I was glad to see some colour returning to her face.

As we walked I told her as simply as I could what I knew or suspected about how she came to be living with the Chirks. I didn't reveal my anxiety about our parents and whether they had anything to do with Grandfather's actions. I don't know why I kept that back – perhaps it was just that I desperately didn't want it to be true. Kitty listened without interrupting, sometimes staring away across the park, sometimes frowning down at the ground.

When I'd finished she didn't say anything for a long

while. I wasn't surprised – it was a lot to take in. Finally she turned to me and said, 'How long have you known about me?'

'A month, that's all.'

'And what made you suspect I even existed?'

'I . . . I was looking in Grandfather's desk and I came across some papers.'

Sophie, walking on the other side of Kitty, shot me a look, part surprised, part reproachful. I could feel myself blushing, and I hoped Kitty would think it was guilt about prying.

It was a spur of the moment decision not to tell her about the hair in the locket and Sophie's part in my discoveries. For one thing, I wasn't at all sure that she would believe me – it sounded so far-fetched.

'Incidentally, Kitty, do you know what these mean? Have you ever seen them before?' Taking out my pocket-book, I pencilled a large λ and μ on a clean page and showed it to her.

She shook her head. 'What are they?'

'I don't know, but I think this one refers to you.' And I told her about Grandfather's notebook.

'We could ask Richard. He might know.'

There was something about her tone that grated on me. What made this young man so special?

'Oh, look, he's there!' Kitty exclaimed, sounding glad. She waved.

Richard, lounging on the rail of the bandstand, raised a hand in greeting.

'You will come and meet him, won't you?'

'I'd rather not.'

'Oh, do,' said Kitty. 'He wants to meet you.'

I glanced at Sophie, who shrugged as if to say she didn't object.

'Very well,' I said grudgingly, 'but, Kitty, just before we do, we need to think about what's going to happen next.' I realized with some consternation that I hadn't given this any thought at all.

She looked at me wide-eyed. 'What do you mean?'

'Well . . . do you want to meet up again?' I supposed that was the next logical thing to do. I wasn't sure that it was what I wanted.

'Oh yes!'

'In that case we need to arrange where and when.'

'Well, you'll come to the house, won't you? And meet Mamma and Papa.'

'*No!*' I threw Sophie an agonized look. This was just what I'd feared. 'Listen, Kitty, you can't tell them. Not yet.'

'Why not?'

'Because . . .' I waved my arms about. 'Something bad might happen,' I ended lamely.

She laughed. 'Of course it won't. Mamma and Papa will be delighted to see you. I know they will.' Her expression became serious and she put her hand on my arm. 'If you're worried about Sir Osbert, you needn't be. Mamma and Papa won't let anything bad happen. And they have a right to know that he's lied to them.'

She'd obviously made up her mind that the Chirks were innocent of any involvement.

'Please, Kitty, don't tell them. Promise me you won't,' I pleaded, but at that moment a cheery voice cried, 'Hull-oh!' and I turned to see the young man, Kitty's friend, striding towards us.

Raising his hat, he said, 'Hope you don't mind my butting in, but I was getting jolly cold up there.'

I scowled. I did mind. Richard's voice was striking – deeper than I would have expected, musical, compelling. He was older than us, but not by much, tall with long dark hair that brushed his coat collar.

He stood there looking from Kitty to me and back again. 'I wouldn't have believed it. *An apple cleft in twain . . .*' His dark blue eyes were alive with amusement and he had a charming crooked smile, but he was too cocky for my liking.

Sophie looked puzzled.

'It's from *Twelfth Night*,' I told her. 'The moment when identical twins are discovered.'

The young man raised his eyebrows. 'You know your Shakespeare, then, Miss . . .'

'Garland,' I said coolly, but I felt discomfited by his gaze – it was so alert and direct. 'And this is my friend Miss Casson.'

'How do you do, Miss Garland, Miss Casson? Richard Darnell.' And he gave a little bow.

He turned to Kitty. 'How are you, Kitten? Not too tired, I hope.' There was genuine concern in his voice.

'No, I'm not. But, oh, Richard, you won't believe what Meriel has told me. I can scarcely believe it myself.'

'Oh? Is it good news or bad?' He glanced in my direction.

I kept my lips firmly pressed together.

'I don't know.' Kitty sounded woebegone and I saw that she did look washed out.

'Why don't we go home now? You can tell me on the way.' He glanced at Sophie and me. 'Are you ladies coming in our direction?'

'No, we're not,' I said abruptly. 'Come on, Sophie, or we'll be late.' I threw a goodbye at the two of them, Kitty and Richard, and stalked off.

Sophie caught up with me. 'I think it's quicker if we go down the Broad Walk.' She indicated the path that the others had taken.

'I don't want to walk with them. We can get out this way, can't we?'

As we hurried along Sophie asked, 'What's the matter? Why are you so angry?'

'Because she's going to blab everything to him. What right does he have to know our business? He's not even a relative.'

She threw me a meaningful look.

'Why are you looking like that? Oh, I see. You're not a relative either. But that's different.'

'Perhaps it isn't, to Kitty. Besides, I expect she needs to talk to someone about it – it's such momentous news.'

'She could talk to *me*.' I glared balefully at a magpie who chattered back at me before flying off.

'Well, perhaps she would have done, if you hadn't rushed off.'

I rolled my eyes at her. She was always so reasonable. 'Anyway, it doesn't really matter about him. I know she's going to tell the Chirks.'

'I think it's very likely. What are you going to do?'

'I don't know. Perhaps I'll just go back and confront Grandfather and have done with it.'

Sophie raised her eyebrows. 'Is that wise? Especially when you don't know what arrangement, if any, he has with the Chirks.'

She was right, of course. I kicked at a stone. 'This was supposed to be so . . . so wonderful and it's not.'

Sophie gave me one of her looks. 'Do you not think you might be expecting too much too quickly?' she said tentatively. 'After all, you and Kitty have only just met.'

I stared at her and then sighed. 'Maybe you're right.'

'Why don't you write her a note?'

'Yes, and I'll tell her if she wants to see me again, she's got to do what I want.'

Sophie smiled. 'Maybe you could word it a little more tactfully?'

Of course, when I calmed down I saw that Sophie was right, as always. I needed Kitty to understand why she must not tell the Chirks. So I wrote her a polite and friendly note suggesting we meet on Thursday afternoon at the same time and place. *I will come alone*, I put, *because we have important things to discuss.* Surely she'd take the hint. I hesitated about how to finish it. I couldn't bring myself to write 'With love'. In the end I settled for *Yours cordially*.

I'd done all I could. If only it wasn't too late.

But in the middle of Wednesday morning Sally appeared with a letter. I didn't recognize the handwriting, the note inside was very brief.

Dear Meriel,
Please come tomorrow afternoon. Mamma and Papa are looking forward to meeting you.
Your affectionate sister,
Kitty

TWENTY-NINE

The maid who opened the door went saucer-eyed at the sight of me, although she must have been warned about my arrival because she immediately said, 'Miss Garland? The family are expecting you. I'll show you up.' All the way up the stairs she kept turning round to look at me.

Although my stomach was churning, I tried to keep my face neutral. I was determined not to give anything away until I knew how much Kitty had told the Chirks. What sort of people were they? How would they react?

These questions had been nagging at me ever since I'd received Kitty's note. I'd been in two minds about coming, but I had to know how things stood. I'd tried to comfort myself with the thought that at least they wanted to meet me first – they hadn't turned up on the doorstep demanding to see Grandfather – but I still felt tense. I wished Sophie was with me.

When I entered the drawing room I saw Kitty first. She was sitting on the sofa wearing another lovely dress, in green silk. From her expression I knew exactly what she was feeling because I'd often felt it myself – guilty about what she'd done, but defiant.

I gave her a hard stare then deliberately looked away. I wanted her to know I was furious with her.

A round bespectacled man bounced at me across the carpet and seized my hands. 'My dear . . .' he began, then broke off in confusion. 'Oh, forgive my familiarity, but when Kitty told us – in short –' he broke off again, apparently overcome with emotion. Pulling out a large white-spotted red handkerchief, he mopped his brow. There was a lot of it to mop as the top of his head was bald.

A small dumpling of a woman rose from the sofa and joined us. 'What my husband means, Miss . . . Garland, isn't it?'

I nodded.

'What my husband means, Miss Garland, is that we were both shocked, utterly shocked, by what Kitty told us. And I hope you don't feel that this is presumptuous of us, but our hearts went out to you, didn't they, Francis?'

'They did, my dear; they did indeed.'

Side by side, they surveyed me with a remarkably similar look of fond concern.

I felt embarrassed. But I noticed that they hadn't done that looking-from-me-to-Kitty-and-back-again business. It was as if they'd already accepted that we were identical twins . . . or maybe it wasn't important. I was glad about that. But – I glanced at Kitty but she wasn't giving anything away – just what exactly had she told them? How much did they know?

Mrs Chirk suddenly started and said, 'Oh dear, we're forgetting our manners. We are the Chirks, of course, and – oh, my dear, may we call you Meriel? Such a pretty name! But do you mind, because we feel, well –' she broke off with an embarrassed laugh – 'you are one of the family, so to speak.'

'I don't mind.' It was partly true. I didn't mind being called by my Christian name: what I wasn't sure about was being 'one of the family'.

I caught Mrs Chirk giving her husband a look of delighted surprise when I spoke. Was she reacting to the fact I sounded just like Kitty? He shook his head at her slightly and said to me, 'Do have a seat, my dear.'

'Oh yes.' Mrs Chirk bustled to plump up a cushion on one of the armchairs for me, and when she was satisfied that I was quite comfortable she sat down beside Kitty on the sofa again.

Mr Chirk didn't sit down but stood in front of the fireplace and surveyed us all. I was expecting him to speak, but it was his wife who said, 'It grieves me to think of it. You poor girls, to grow up apart like that. To be deprived of your childhood together, of the joys that sisters share. We said, didn't we, Francis, that it was such a pity.'

'We did, my dear.' Mr Chirk nodded at his wife.

'And to think how often I have regretted that our Kitty doesn't have a brother or a sister . . .'

'Mamma.' Kitty spoke in a soft voice, putting her hand on Mrs Chirk's arm. In response, Mrs Chirk laid her hand on Kitty's and left it there.

Lucky Kitty, I thought bitterly. I realized then why I'd reacted badly when I'd heard that she was adopted. I was jealous. The Chirks wanted her, that was very clear, whereas neither Papa nor Grandfather wanted me.

'And as for Sir Osbert . . .' Mrs Chirk shook her head. 'We'll never understand why he did it, will we, Francis?'

There was a slight pause and I swivelled my head to look at Mr Chirk. 'No. No, we won't, my dear,' he said hastily, but I wondered why he'd missed his cue. Did he know or guess something that his wife didn't?

But she was continuing as if she hadn't noticed. 'Such a cruel deed to separate you girls! Forgive me, I know I shouldn't speak ill of your guardian before you, Meriel, but that is what I think. Still, I can't condemn him totally because he gave us our Kitty – do you see, Meriel? I'm sorry if that sounds selfish. It *is* selfish, but she's brought us so much joy.' She caressed Kitty's hand and I gritted my teeth. But then she looked across at me with a kind, sad smile.

'Just fancy, in all the time he's visited us, not to tell us, not to betray your existence by a single look or word, Meriel! I can't bear to think of you growing up without the comfort of a mother's love. If only we'd known about you, we would have gladly taken you as well, wouldn't we, Francis?'

While Mr Chirk gave his response pat this time, I glanced at Kitty. Mrs Chirk's remarks were puzzling. And my sister was looking uneasy. Hadn't she told them the whole story?

Suddenly Kitty jumped up and declared, 'Oh, Mamma, Papa, I'm afraid I've not been totally candid with you.'

My stomach lurched. 'Kitty!' I said urgently.

But she took no notice of me. Wringing her hands, she said, 'Please forgive me.'

Mr Chirk went to her at once and gave her a hug. 'My dear girl, what is it?'

Instead of answering, she burst into tears.

Mrs Chirk looked at me. 'Do you know what this is about?'

I shook my head. After all, I didn't know what Kitty had said, and I didn't see why I should help her out.

Finally, speaking through sobs, she managed to say, 'According to Meriel, Sir Osbert is our grandfather.'

Mrs Chirk gasped and Mr Chirk exclaimed, 'What?'

They both turned to me. I had no choice now. 'It's true,' I said.

Mrs Chirk spluttered, 'But I don't understand. How can that be possible? It can't, can it, Francis?'

Instead of answering straight away, her husband took out his handkerchief and mopped his brow again. I had the distinct impression that he seemed uncomfortable and I wondered if he'd known all along. 'I suppose it could be possible, my dear.'

'I don't believe it. Surely he would have told us. Our Kitty, his granddaughter?! Why would he have concealed such a thing?' Mrs Chirk was appealing to me now.

'I don't know why he didn't tell you, but it *is* true.'

'I think, my dear,' said Mr Chirk, speaking carefully, 'that we must try to accept that it is so. Why would Meriel make up something like that?'

Mrs Chirk stared at her husband and the colour drained from her face.

Kitty limped back to the sofa. 'I'm sorry I didn't tell you yesterday, Mamma.'

I was sorry she'd told them today. What was the point of telling the truth? All she'd done was upset the Chirks.

Mrs Chirk uttered a little cry.

'What is it, my love?' said her husband.

'Oh, Francis, does this mean that Kitty doesn't belong to us after all? That if Sir Osbert decides to take her back, we can't do anything about it?'

Kitty cried out, 'No!'

Grandfather couldn't take her back if she was adopted, could he?

We all looked at Mr Chirk.

He took off his spectacles, polished them with his handkerchief and replaced them. 'Oh, my dears,' he said, 'I don't know how to tell you this. I didn't know, I swear I didn't, that Sir Osbert was Kitty's grandfather, but –' He made to take off his spectacles again, but then left them where they were. Taking a deep breath, he said, 'When Sir Osbert first told me about Kitty all those years ago – and forgive me, my love, for keeping it from you – he said he was distantly related to her and therefore took an interest in her welfare. And when he arranged with me that we could have her, we signed an agreement . . .' Here he paused, seemingly unable to carry on.

'An agreement?' echoed his wife faintly.

'I'm afraid so.'

'What does the agreement say, Papa?' Kitty's voice was firm. I had to admit she was braver than I'd thought.

'It says – well, it doesn't matter what it says – what it means is that ultimately any decisions about Kitty are Sir Osbert's, not ours.'

THIRTY

Following Mr Chirk's revelation, Mrs Chirk gave a little moan and her hand flew to her throat. Kitty, white-faced, pressed her lips together and was silent.

'Why didn't you tell me?' Mrs Chirk's brown eyes reproached her husband.

'I'm sorry,' he said. 'I know I shouldn't have kept it from you, but you were so overjoyed to have Kitty. I didn't want a shadow to darken your happiness again.'

I wondered what he was talking about. He was looking anxiously at his wife, but she seemed lost in her own thoughts.

'I see now,' she said slowly. 'I've never understood why you set so much store by Sir Osbert's advice. I thought it was because you respected him. But he was controlling how we brought Kitty up, wasn't he? And he had every right to do so.'

Here she started weeping and I looked away, feeling uncomfortable. These things were private, no business of mine. But she was right about Grandfather. 'Controlling' was exactly the word for him. It made me feel a little better to know that Kitty hadn't escaped his influence altogether.

I glanced across at her. To my surprise, she was sitting bolt upright and looking at me, an intent look that I couldn't interpret.

'Meriel,' she said, 'do you think Sir Osbert does have this right? Do you know whether it was given to him by . . .' she hesitated, 'by Papa?'

'What?'

'No!'

Both the Chirks had exclaimed at once and were now staring at her, Mrs Chirk's expression puzzled, her husband's hurt.

'She doesn't mean you,' I said to Mr Chirk. 'She means our real father.' I sighed. It was impossible to go on pretending. Kitty had seen to that. 'Our real father, who's an artist in India. Who's alive,' I added, probably unnecessarily.

The impact of my words was electrifying. Ellen Terry at her finest could not have had such a dramatic effect on her audience.

'What on earth do you mean?' Mr Chirk sounded breathless.

Into a pin-drop silence I spilled my story, trying to keep it as brief and simple as possible.

When I'd finished there was a short pause and then Mrs Chirk turned to her husband. 'Did you know *this*?' she asked, her voice wafer-thin.

'No, my love, I didn't.'

I believed him. Which confirmed that the Chinese missionary tale was an invention of Grandfather's. Well, well.

Mrs Chirk looked at Kitty. 'Why didn't you tell us?'

'I . . . I didn't want to hurt you. *You* are my parents and always will be.' As she asserted this there was a catch in Kitty's voice.

I couldn't help feeling pleased – it meant Mamma and Papa were *my* parents; I didn't have to share them with her.

Mrs Chirk took her hand and squeezed it. Mr Chirk removed his spectacles and polished them. Replacing them, he said to me, 'Well, my dear, can you answer Kitty's question? Do you know whether your father surrendered his paternal rights to Sir Osbert?'

'I don't. As I said, I don't even know if Papa is aware of Kitty's existence.' Again that spectre rose in my mind, the fear that Mamma and Papa had been involved in this, but I quashed it. There was no point in complicating things.

'And does your grandfather know you've found Kitty?'

'No,' I said. 'Not yet.'

'That man is a monster,' Mrs Chirk declared. 'I'm sorry, but there is no other word for him. When you have it out with him, Francis—'

'No!' I cried. 'You mustn't.' It was turning out just as I had feared.

Mr Chirk was speaking to his wife '. . . not a good idea, my love. Meriel is right. We know that Sir Osbert's behaviour is . . . unusual, shall we say. What is not clear is why he has acted in this extraordinary way. If we reveal that we know he has deceived us, there's no telling what he might do. He might take Kitty away from us—'

'But what if he hasn't the right to do that?' Mrs Chirk was as fierce as a lioness defending her cub.

'His actions so far suggest he'd pay little heed to the rights of the matter. '

I couldn't suppress a murmur of agreement, and Mr Chirk glanced at me with a wry smile.

'So do we do nothing then? Just let it go and hope for the best and worry every day that our darling will be snatched away?' Mrs Chirk was holding Kitty tight as if she feared that at any second Grandfather might appear and whisk her off.

Mr Chirk studied his wife for a moment and then, speaking solemnly, he said, 'Kitty, my dear. I'm going to ask you a question and I want you to think about it very carefully. You don't have to answer straight away – take all the time you need.'

Kitty looked at him, her eyes wide.

'If it were possible, would you like to live with your real father?'

'It isn't possible,' I exclaimed. 'Papa won't have her. He doesn't want me.' As I said it, a sickening thought knocked me all of a heap. If Papa didn't know about Kitty, when he found out he *might* want her to live with him. She was quieter, better behaved, more obedient than me . . . or he might take pity on her because she was lame.

I became aware that the Chirks were looking at me in a kindly way and I blushed.

'It may be that the same applies to Kitty,' said Mr

Chirk gently, 'but just now, what matters is what Kitty wants.'

Gentle he might be, but I felt rebuked, and I slunk back into the cushions. Lucky, lucky Kitty to have people asking her what she wanted.

With a glance at me, Kitty said, 'I can tell you that now.' Her voice was quiet but resolute. 'I want to stay here, with you.'

Her answer wasn't unexpected, but although I was pleased I couldn't help feeling a surge of protectiveness towards Papa. It didn't seem fair to reject him when she didn't know anything about him.

Unsurprisingly, the Chirks looked as though they'd just been given the finest present in the world. Mr Chirk said, 'Well, in that case, my dear, I think our best plan is to write to the girls' father and tell him of all that we have learned. Of course, if he knows nothing of Kitty, it will come as a shock. Whatever the case, we will ask him if there is some way we can make an agreement that will ensure Kitty is ours.'

I couldn't help thinking that if Papa had been part of this arrangement all along, he wasn't likely to agree to this, but I kept silent. It seemed better to wait till they found out the truth from Papa, rather than upsetting them now with my doubts.

'I think that's a capital plan, my love.' Mrs Chirk's face was wreathed in smiles. 'But –' she became a lioness again – 'in the meantime, we'll not let Sir Osbert set foot in this house.'

Hooray, I thought, imagining Grandfather's face when he found the door barred against him.

'No, no, my dear,' her husband said hastily. 'We must carry on just as usual. Sir Osbert must not suspect a thing.'

'Oh,' I said as if I'd just bitten on something sharp.

'What's the matter, Meriel?' asked Mr Chirk.

'I can't carry on as usual. I've got to speak to Grandfather about this soon, before he packs me off to Switzerland, to school.'

The Chirks looked puzzled, and Kitty's eyes widened in alarm.

'I don't understand, Meriel,' said Mr Chirk. 'How will speaking to Sir Osbert prevent you from being sent to school?'

'Because I'll say that unless he lets me do what I want, I'll let everyone know about him stealing Kitty from Mamma.' I spoke defiantly. I could tell they were shocked, but I didn't care.

Mr Chirk pressed his hands together. 'I really don't think that would be wise, Meriel. I can understand your feelings, my dear, but Sir Osbert is a powerful man. I wouldn't like to make an enemy of him. If he feels threatened, there's no knowing what he might do. And I'm not just thinking of Kitty. I wouldn't like anything to happen to you.'

I stared at him. For all my bravado his tone made me shiver – it was alarming to have my own fears about Grandfather confirmed by an adult.

'And anyway –' Mr Chirk glanced in Kitty's direction – 'are you absolutely sure that Sir Osbert's actions were nefarious? Are you sure – and I'm sorry, Kitty, if this distresses you, but the possibility has to be faced – are you sure that he wasn't acting with the full knowledge and permission of your parents?'

I hung my head. 'No,' I mumbled, 'I'm not sure.' Out of the corner of my eye I was aware that Kitty was clutching one of the sofa cushions tightly.

'So you see, I think the best thing would be to wait until we hear from your father. Then we'll know exactly how things stand.'

They were all looking at me, wanting me to give in and agree. Kitty's eyes were wide, imploring. 'Please, Meriel,' she said, 'don't say anything.'

I hesitated.

She hadn't listened to me when I'd asked her to keep our secret. But Mr Chirk was right – Grandfather might go to any lengths to achieve his purpose, whatever it was. I might be putting myself in danger.

'All right,' I said grudgingly. The pink marble clock on the mantelpiece chimed the half-hour. I stood up. 'I have to go now.'

'You can't stay for tea?' Mrs Chirk sounded disappointed.

'No, I'm afraid not.'

'Well, come again, any time. And bring your friend Miss Casson with you. We'd like to meet her, wouldn't we, Francis?'

'Indeed.' Mr Chirk beamed.

I forced myself to say goodbye graciously and left them to play at happy families.

Only when I was safely alone in my bedroom could I allow myself to reflect on the visit. I wondered if Kitty knew how fortunate she was. She had every material comfort – a pleasant home, beautiful clothes – but none of that mattered compared to the most important thing: that the Chirks were good, kind people and they obviously adored her; her happiness mattered more to them than anything.

Whereas I . . .

I'd never felt so alone. The knowledge that no one cared for me as Kitty was cared for cut me too deeply for tears.

THIRTY-ONE

During the next day or two I couldn't make my mind up what to do and each afternoon as we trudged round Kensington Gardens I could tell that Sally was surprised I wasn't going off somewhere on my own. She tried to cheer me up with the latest snippets of gossip – for instance, Mrs Langtry was due to appear in a new play at the Prince's Theatre – but hearing about these things made me feel worse. Soon I would be marooned on a Swiss mountain, cut off from theatres, cut off from everything.

The fact that Christmas was approaching didn't help. This time of year was always difficult. It brought back the rituals Mamma and I used to share – making a gift for Papa like a pen-wipe or a comb bag, hanging paper garlands in the mango tree, and when it grew dark on Christmas Eve lighting the small clay lamps. Then we'd all sit together to tell stories, read to each other and listen to Mamma sing.

This year the memories made my heart ache more than ever. And even though I tried not to think about it, I couldn't help tormenting myself with images of what Christmas at Eldon Square might be like: merry festivities with Kitty at their centre, everyone opening presents, pulling crackers, making music, laughing . . .

It was all very well for the Chirks to talk about me

being 'one of the family', but I wasn't taken in. As long as Kitty was happy, it didn't seem to matter what happened to me.

And now I'd thought of it, I couldn't stop worrying about Papa's reaction, especially if he didn't know he had another daughter. I was sure he'd want to meet her. I could just imagine it – Kitty summoned to India while I was left to stew in Switzerland.

On Sunday afternoon Sally brightened up when we reached the end of our street and, having looked round to make sure we weren't being followed, I said, 'I'll meet you at the usual place. All right?'

I walked down Gloucester Road, but instead of continuing to the station to take a train to Bloomsbury, I turned off into Cornwall Gardens. I'd made up my mind. There was only one person I could trust.

When Betty opened the door she explained that Mrs Quinn was engaged with a sitter and wasn't to be disturbed. The parlour door was shut tight.

'It's Miss Casson I've come to see.'

'Oh.' This appeared to put her in a quandary. 'I'll run up and see if she's available, miss.'

After a few minutes she appeared on the stairs and beckoned to me. 'Will you come up, miss?'

Betty showed me into a low-ceilinged attic room that was distinctly chilly. Wrapped in a shawl and wearing woollen mitts, Sophie rose from her seat, looking surprised. 'Hello, Meriel. I didn't expect you today.'

'I only just decided to come. Is that all right?'

She hesitated and then nodded. She was shivering. No wonder. She was wearing the same thin dress as always. I glanced at the empty grate – it was rusty as if it hadn't seen a fire in a long time. Then I took in the rest of the room – the bare floor, the shabby washstand, the stain on the yellowed whitewash from a leak in the roof – it was like a servant's room. And there was nothing personal in it at all – no knick-knacks on the rickety chest of drawers, no ornaments on the mantelpiece. It was as bare as a nun's cell.

'Is this really your room?'

Sophie nodded, her colour rising as if she'd guessed what I was thinking.

Mystified, I thought of Mrs Quinn's silk gowns, her rings – she wasn't a pauper. Why didn't she let her ward have a better room? But out of consideration for Sophie's feelings I thought I'd better not pursue the subject.

Sophie gestured at the chair she'd been sitting on and, as it was the only one in the room, I took it while she perched on the bed. There was a brief pause and then I burst out, 'Oh, Sophie, everything's beastly!' and I told her what had happened at the Chirks and how I felt about it all.

She listened without interrupting, her face grave as usual.

When I finally trailed to a stop she said, 'So you didn't get a chance to speak to Kitty alone?'

'No, but maybe it was just as well.'

She was silent for a moment and then she said, 'Do you think . . . ?' She broke off.

'What?'

'Well, isn't it natural that Kitty would feel closer to the people she knows?'

'But I'm her sister! She should put me first, shouldn't she?'

Sophie didn't answer. She was tracing the pattern of a rose on the faded coverlet and finally she asked, 'So are you saying you don't want to see her again?'

'I don't *know*.' This came out as a wail.

Rain started pattering on the skylight overhead and we both looked up.

I suddenly said, 'Sophie, I've been thinking. Can you . . . Would you try to get in touch with Mamma? Now, I mean.'

She looked dubious.

'Please. I want to tell her about Kitty.'

There was a pause and then Sophie said gently, 'Don't you think she already knows?'

I stared at her, realizing she probably meant that Mamma knew 'in spirit' as Sophie would say. But in any case, I'd made it up about Kitty. The real reason I wanted Mamma was so I could have the comfort of feeling her close to me, so I could ask her what I should do. I fumbled under my coat and taking off my locket I held it out to Sophie.

She looked at me, her gaze troubled. 'I don't think this is a good idea.'

'Please, Sophie.'

Reluctantly she removed one mitt, clasped the locket and shut her eyes.

There was silence apart from the drumming of the rain and the sound of water running in the gutters.

I waited, willing Mamma to come, wanting her to speak through Sophie, longing for her to say something to make me feel better.

After a while Sophie opened her eyes. 'I'm sorry.'

'What's the matter?'

'I can't – your mamma isn't here today.'

The disappointment was like a sour taste in my mouth. 'You're not trying hard enough.'

Sophie regarded me with her dark eyes. 'Meriel, please don't get cross with me. It's not a matter of how hard I try. Whatever Mrs Quinn pretends, the spirits are not at our beck and call. They come of their own volition. And it may be that your mamma has accomplished her purpose.'

'What do you mean?'

'You have found Kitty.'

I looked at her. 'Are you saying that Mamma won't ever come again?' My voice shook and I could feel my throat thickening.

She put out her hand as if to comfort me, but then drew it back.

'I'm sorry,' she said again.

Resting my head on the wall, I looked up. The clouds were dirty rags pressing on the skylight. I shut my eyes. I had never felt so empty.

'There is something I want to say to you,' Sophie said at last.

I opened my eyes and looked at her.

'Some people become . . . obsessed . . . by the idea of contacting their loved ones in spirit. Whether or not they succeed, it becomes an all-consuming passion. In their thoughts, their feelings, they dwell on death. I have seen it happen all too often. And even when they do succeed, that communion, though it might bring comfort for a short while, is never truly satisfying; it cannot recreate the experience of loving the living person. The voices, the fleeting sense of someone there . . . they are mere echoes, shadows . . .'

In the dim light, her eyes looked enormous.

'Since death is inevitable and will come to us all in the end, it seems to me that it is a mistake to fill our lives with it . . . to forget to live.'

There was a long silence during which I turned her words over in my mind.

'Are you saying I should let Mamma go? Stop searching for her?' My voice wobbled and I could hardly breathe for the sudden pain in my chest.

She nodded.

A minute or two passed while I struggled not to cry. When I gained control of myself I was able to look at her. 'Do you believe in God, Sophie?'

'Yes,' she said simply.

'So you think we'll all be reunited with our loved ones in heaven?'

'Yes. Don't you?'

'I don't know. Papa said Mamma had gone to heaven and we would meet her there one day, but I don't know if he really believed it. I think he was saying it to make me feel better.'

There was a silence and then Sophie said quietly, 'I think you'll see her again. But in the meantime you have your memories to hold on to, to comfort yourself with.'

I stared at her. And then I thought about Mamma, not as I had last seen her – pale, cold, like a waxen image of herself – but warm, alive, full of vitality . . . laughing when we rode in a howdah on the maharaja's elephant . . . lifting up the mosquito net to kiss me goodnight, the smell of rosewater lingering long after she'd left me . . .

Something became clear to me for the first time.

My memories of Mamma were inextricably bound up with India. At some deep but childish level, I'd believed that if I went back Mamma would still be there.

But of course she wouldn't. There was no going back to the time when she was alive. That time had passed.

Perhaps Sophie was right. The only place where I could be sure Mamma still existed was in my memories, and she *was* there, alive, inside me. There was no need to search for her. All I could do was go forward and make the best of the problematic gift she'd given me, the gift of my sister.

Sophie stirred. Silently she rose from the bed. Going to the mantelpiece, she struck a match and lit a candle. The flame glowed, chasing the shadows back into the corners of the room, illuminating her face.

I looked at her and I suddenly thought how wise she was and how lucky I was to know her.

'Sophie.'

'Mmm?'

'I – I just wanted to say how grateful I am . . . you know, for all the help you keep giving me.' I felt myself redden and she ducked her head, embarrassed.

'And –'

She looked up.

'I think you're right. I should try to get to know Kitty better. But, please, will you come with me?'

THIRTY-TWO

When Sophie and I arrived at Eldon Square at the arranged time we could hear Kitty singing as we went up the stairs. On being shown into the drawing room we found her sitting at the piano, but it was Richard who was playing.

I was taken aback. I'd assumed we'd be seeing Kitty on her own.

As soon as we appeared they stopped and rose to greet us, but to be polite I said, 'Do finish the song,' and Sophie said, 'Yes, please do,' with an eagerness that surprised me.

We sat down to listen. I quickly realized with a pang that Kitty was far more accomplished than me. Immediately I chided myself for being envious. On the way over I'd decided to try to be nice and not bring up difficult subjects like Kitty doing the opposite of what I wanted her to.

It was partly Sophie's influence. She'd convinced me that maybe part of the problem was that I'd assumed Kitty would be just like me. If I could accept that she might not be, perhaps I'd come to like her for herself.

I glanced at Sophie. She was listening with rapt attention, a faint flush on her usually pale face. When the song came to an end she clapped enthusiastically until she realized she was the only one applauding. She stopped at once, blushing as scarlet as a hibiscus. After bowing with a flourish, Richard joined her on the sofa.

'Do you like music, Miss Casson?'

'Oh yes, more than anything.'

I was taken aback. I had had no idea Sophie was keen on music.

My attention was diverted by Kitty drawing up a footstool to sit by me. 'I'm so glad you came,' she said in a rush. 'I was afraid you wouldn't be able to forgive me, you know, for telling Mamma and Papa about us.'

I opened my mouth, but I couldn't do it. I couldn't say I had forgiven her. Instead I nodded at the piano. 'That was jolly good.'

'Yes, Richard plays well, doesn't he? He's so talented.'

'I meant you – your singing's tip-top.'

'Thank you.'

Her simple acceptance of my praise, without a display of false modesty, made her go up in my estimation.

Her amber eyes were fastened on mine. 'Do you sing?'

'Me? Oh no – well, I mean, I can, but it's awful.'

She laughed. 'I don't believe you.'

'It's true. Look, does Grandfather like you to sing for him?'

'Yes, he does.' She sounded surprised that I knew that, but I'd guessed he might because she sounded so like Mamma.

'Well, he's only asked me to sing for him once. He sat through it looking like this –' I pulled the sort of face someone might make if they were listening to a cat yowling and Kitty laughed. 'At the end he shook his head and said –' I did a passable imitation of Grandfather – '*Not gifted like your mother, more's the pity.*'

Kitty winced. 'That wasn't very nice of him.'

I glanced across at the sofa where Sophie and Richard were deep in a conversation about music. I wondered how Sophie knew so much about it.

Kitty, serious now, asked tentatively, 'Was . . . our mother gifted?'

'She sang beautifully.' Did I mean to rub in what Kitty had missed? Perhaps a little.

But when she said wistfully, 'I'd like to have heard her,' I felt guilty.

'I expect you take after her,' I said, to make her feel better.

'Do you think so?' She was silent for a moment or two, then she said, 'Papa and Mamma have been very encouraging . . . you know, finding the best teachers and everything.'

'And would you like to sing? Professionally, I mean.'

She didn't answer straight away. She looked at me as if she were weighing me up and then she leaned closer and said in a confiding way, 'I've seen Madame Patti sing at Covent Garden and I would love to be like her.'

I hadn't heard of Madame Patti, but it was clear Kitty

felt about her as I did about Ellen Terry. The difference was, she had seen her idol. Was I surprised? No, I could imagine the Chirks encouraging her to do things she enjoyed.

'But of course it's just a dream.' Kitty leaned back, clasping her hands round her knees.

'Why? You could do it . . . if you really wanted to,' I added. I couldn't help thinking her attitude was rather spineless.

'Oh, I couldn't. I'm not nearly brave enough. And anyway . . .' Shifting on the stool, she glanced down at her foot.

At once I regretted my insensitivity. I didn't know much about opera but I could imagine there wasn't much demand for limping heroines.

Abruptly Kitty said, 'What's it like living with Sir Osbert?'

I noticed she didn't call him Grandfather. I didn't feel like telling her the truth. The last thing I wanted was for her to feel sorry for me. 'It's not bad. I don't care for being subjected to his peculiar tests, but you must know what that's like.'

She wrinkled up her nose. 'Yes. I don't like it either. He's rather frightening, isn't he?'

'Oh, I don't know. He's docile enough if you know how to manage him,' I said airily.

'He gives you a lot of freedom, doesn't he? I'm surprised – I thought he'd be very strict.'

'Mmm.' I shifted uncomfortably. I might not want to

tell Kitty the whole truth, but again I felt uncomfortable lying to her.

'Oh!' she said suddenly. 'I asked Richard about those funny symbols you showed me. He said they were the Greek letters *L* and *M*.'

I frowned. '*M* must be me, but why are you *L* and not *K*?'

'Lydia. It's my middle name.'

'That was Grandmamma's name.'

'Was it? Oh. That probably means Sir Osbert must have named me, doesn't it?' She pulled a face.

Or Mamma, I thought, if she knew about Kitty. But I didn't want to bring that up and upset her. To change the subject I asked her if she had a governess now – she did, but only in the mornings – and we compared notes. Kitty spoke fondly of Scutty, Miss Cutler, who'd been her governess for many years, and laughed with amazement at my antics with Tippy's predecessors.

From there we progressed naturally to other topics: we shared the same favourite colour – blue; we both liked chicken and disliked fish, preferred raspberries to strawberries, loved almond paste and detested junket; we both liked reading, though Kitty hadn't heard of some of my favourite authors; we'd both had measles when we were five, scarlet fever when we were seven. We'd both had a tooth out when we were ten, same tooth but on opposite sides . . . The number of coincidences was remarkable.

At first it was jolly to mention something and both say

'yes' or 'no' at the same time, but I began to feel uneasy. With every similarity I felt as if I was losing my sense of who I was.

'Which board games do you like?' Kitty asked.

'I don't know. I don't play board games.' I could imagine the cosy evenings she passed, playing with the Chirks and Richard.

I glanced across at the sofa again. Whatever he was saying, it was making Sophie laugh.

'So what else do you like to do?'

'I used to paint a lot at home, but I haven't done so much since I came to England.' As soon as the words were out of my mouth I regretted them. Kitty was looking at me curiously. I knew what was coming and it was my own fault.

'What's he like? Our father.'

I couldn't answer straight away. 'Father' meant a hard knot of something in my chest, a knot I didn't want to start untying. I tried to think past it, back to the 'Papa' of my childhood.

'He has curly hair, and . . . nice eyes,' I said lamely.

'What else?'

'He's a good painter. At least, I think so, but so do a lot of other people – or they did.' I told her about the 'pukka sahibs' ostracizing Papa.

Her eyes flashed. 'That's awful,' she said. 'So unjust. But, tell me, what's he *like*?'

I didn't know what to say. 'He laughs a lot, or he used to.'

Kitty reached out and gave my hand a sympathetic squeeze. 'You must miss him awfully.'

'Mmm.' I made a non-committal noise and slipped my hand out of hers.

Richard called across, 'I say, Miss Garland, Miss Casson tells me you're a spiffing actress.'

'Are you?' asked Kitty eagerly.

'No,' I said, shooting Sophie a look. 'Well, that is, I like acting, but I don't know how good I am.' Now who was being falsely modest? But I suddenly felt embarrassed.

Kitty was all agog. 'Can you give us a speech? Go on – you've heard me sing.'

'Oh, do, Miss Garland.'

There was a merry look in Richard's eye and I wondered if he was mocking me. Nettled, I stood up. I'd show him what I could do.

I took up my position on the carpet in front of the sofa and became Queen Margaret, from *Henry VI*, Part Three, where she taunts the Duke of York before she kills him. I gave it my blood-curdling best and then, still in character, I skipped plays to *Richard III* and recited:

I had an Edward, till a Richard killed him;
I had a Harry, till a Richard killed him:
Thou hadst an Edward, till a Richard killed him;
Thou hadst a Richard, till a Richard killed him.

With each 'Richard' I looked at him more threateningly, until I had to stop because I was laughing.

They all clapped enthusiastically and Richard jumped up. 'Well done, Miss Garland. Truly a *tiger's heart wrapped in a woman's hide.*'

I couldn't help it – I blushed with pleasure. And I thought, He must know *Henry VI* as well as I do.

When I took my seat again Richard came across. Kitty moved to the sofa and started talking to Sophie while Richard took her place on the footstool.

Having him so close was disconcerting. He was rather pale today and he had dark circles under his eyes. I wondered if he'd slept badly. He was wearing a bottle-green velvet jacket and magenta tie – lovely colourful clothes that Grandfather would have totally disapproved of.

'Miss Garland—'

'Please, call me Meriel.' I felt ridiculously self-conscious, but it seemed absurd to be so formal when he and Kitty were on such friendly terms.

'Surely.' He smiled charmingly. 'As long as you call me Richard.'

I ducked my head in assent, but I didn't return his smile.

'Have you been interested in the theatre long?'

'Forever.' I told him about reading Shakespeare with Mamma, and he seemed genuinely interested so I told him about how I practised scenes from plays, and which ones were my favourites. The more I talked, the more I forgot that I didn't like him very much and I forgot to be cautious. I even told him about my passion for Ellen Terry.

'That's extraordinary,' he said. 'My hero is Henry Irving, and you must know they frequently appear together.'

'Have you seen him on the stage?'

'Once or twice, but not as often as I'd like. You see, I work in the theatre myself.'

I stared at him. What did he mean by 'working'? He looked back at me, an impish expression on his face, his eyes dancing. Surely he didn't mean . . . 'You're an actor?' I said, incredulous.

He waved his hand in a mocking flourish.

I shot a look at Kitty. Why hadn't she told me? Why had she let me make a fool of myself by performing before him?

Richard's eyes were still on me. 'You know, of the girls in the company at the Dionysus – that's where I am at the moment – very few could deliver that speech as you did.'

I must have blushed bright scarlet, my face went so hot. 'You really think so?'

'I do. Have you thought of the stage as a career?'

I suddenly felt self-conscious again. It was all very well to tell Sally or Sophie about my dream. But Richard was a professional actor. He was still waiting for an answer though, and I suddenly thought, Dash it! Why not?

I looked him in the eye. 'Yes. I was hoping to become an actress and I'd like to tour India.' I couldn't bring myself to tell him of my wish to own a company – it would sound far too presumptuous.

'Why take your talent overseas?' he said. 'There are probably more opportunities here in England.'

'Are there? Is it easy, though, to become a success?'

He smiled and I immediately worried that my question had been childish, my ambition silly. But he answered me seriously. 'Not easy, no – it takes hard work, possibly for years, as well as talent, of course, and even then you need luck on your side. It's a risky profession.'

'But you have chosen it.'

'Never wanted to do anything else. Like you, I was smitten early, I'm afraid.'

At his words I felt a tremor of excitement. Not only was he taking me seriously, but he shared my passion. 'What are you doing at the moment?'

'*Romeo and Juliet*.'

'Oh.' I felt breathless. One of my favourite plays.

'And what part do you play?'

'Guess.' He struck a spoony attitude.

'Not Romeo?!'

'Afraid so.' Self-mocking, he grinned his charming grin.

I was torn between envy and the desire to hear all about it. 'I'd love to see the play.'

'Why don't you? It's popular, but I could get you a ticket.'

I shook my head. 'I won't be allowed. I had a chance to see *Faust* but Grandfather put his foot down.'

'Oh, bad luck. It's going to be ripping from what I've

heard. But knowing Sir Osbert, I can't imagine there's any chance he'll change his mind.'

Of course, he must have met Grandfather. 'He won't,' I said bitterly.

He looked at me thoughtfully for a moment. 'I say, if you're allowed, would you like me to show you round the Dionysus? I could take you backstage.'

'*Oh.*' My breath escaped in a gasp. '*Yes, please!*'

He laughed. Then he called across to others. 'Kitten, I've had a jolly idea. Meriel would like a tour of the theatre. Will you join us? And, Miss Casson, you'd be very welcome too.'

Kitty looked only mildly interested. But Sophie's face lit up at once. 'When?' she asked.

'Let's see. Tomorrow's no good. Shall we say Thursday? Two thirty?'

'Oh.' Sophie looked crestfallen. 'I'd like to come, but I'm not sure if I can.'

It was a shame for Sophie, and for a moment I considered suggesting we postpone our jaunt until another day, but I couldn't bear to wait. I looked beseechingly at Kitty. Smiling, she nodded and I bounced out of my chair. 'Thank you, oh, thank you,' I said to the room at large, and everyone laughed.

'I must go and rest now,' said Richard, rising also. 'Prepare myself for tonight's performance. Kitty, will you explain to Meriel how to get there? I'm whacked.'

Everything felt flat after he'd gone. There was so much I wanted to ask him and now I'd have to wait.

As Kitty was giving me directions, the door opened and I turned eagerly, thinking Richard had come back for something, but it was only Mrs Chirk.

'Hello, my dears.' She bustled over and bent down and kissed me, taking me by surprise. She greeted Sophie warmly.

'Now, have you asked her?' Mrs Chirk demanded of Kitty.

'Not yet. We've been too busy chatting, haven't we?'

I looked from one to the other. Asked me what?

'Oh, Meriel,' Kitty looked at me imploringly, 'do say yes. It will be such fun.'

'Bless you,' said Mrs Chirk. 'How can the poor girl say yes, when you haven't told her what it is yet?'

'I know it's rather soon to be mentioning it, but we'd like you to join us on Christmas Day,' said Kitty. 'We can have our dinner in the afternoon, if that's the only time you can come, and Papa says this year we can have a tree, so if you can come on Christmas Eve as well we can decorate it together. And you can help me wrap up my presents. Do say yes.'

Mrs Chirk nodded throughout the speech, adding when Kitty had finished, 'And, Miss Casson, we would be delighted if you would like to join us too. You'd be most welcome.'

I was glad she'd said that, because I was uncomfortably aware that Sophie might be feeling left out.

Sophie said at once, 'That's very kind, but I shall be dining with my guardian, thank you.'

And then everyone looked at me. I took a breath. 'Thank you for asking me. And I'd love to come. But I can't.'

Protests and exclamations of dismay greeted my words.

'No, really. I'm afraid as it's Christmas, Grandfather will want me to spend the day with him.'

Sophie's head jerked up.

'Oh,' Kitty wailed, sounding like a little girl. 'Can't you say – oh, I don't know – that you've just got to have a walk? Sir Osbert's very keen on exercise, isn't he?'

I shook my head. 'I'm sorry. I couldn't disappoint him.'

'Don't press her, Kitty,' said Mrs Chirk. 'It's not fair. But your dutifulness does you credit, my dear.'

I felt myself blush. To hide it I jumped up, claiming we had to go. Mrs Chirk lavished embraces on us and exhortations to come again as soon as we could. Finally I reminded Kitty that I'd see her on Thursday and we managed to get away.

Outside the temperature had dropped and the sky was leaden. It looked as if we were in for snow. As we walked to the station, hunched against the cold, I thought about the theatre visit. It would be marvellous to have a peek behind the scenes and in the company of such a guide . . . but oh, how I wished I could see the play.

Sophie craned her head to look at me. 'Well?'

I rapidly reviewed the afternoon. 'It was good . . . it

was very good. I was wrong about Richard. He isn't at all as I imagined him – not a bit conceited, even though he's already playing leading roles.'

'And Kitty?'

'What do you mean?'

'Did you enjoy talking to her more today?'

I thought about it. 'Ye-es. I suppose so.' If I admitted I still found things difficult, Sophie was bound to say, 'Give it time.' I wasn't sure time was the answer.

There was a pause. Sophie was looking thoughtful. After a minute or two she said, 'I was surprised at what you said – about your grandfather and Christmas. It didn't seem to fit with the other things you've said about him.'

I felt myself going pink. I thought about trying to talk my way out of it, but I knew I wouldn't convince her. 'I was lying.'

She blinked, but didn't say anything. She seemed to be waiting for me to elaborate.

'In actual fact . . . well, you know Grandfather's an atheist? So it makes sense that he doesn't celebrate Christmas, I mean as a religious festival. But he really despises it. He won't send Christmas cards, even if people send them to him, and he hates what he calls the "epidemic of plum pudding" and the "relentless half-witted insistence on merriment". He's just like Scrooge.'

Sophie was listening attentively and she nodded as if to encourage me to go on.

'So . . . you can imagine what our Christmas Day is

like – just like every other day. Grandfather won't want to see me unless he takes it into his head to summon me for some experiment or other or comes to check on me in the schoolroom.'

Sophie looked slightly bemused. 'But doesn't that make you want . . . ?' She stopped.

'To join in the festive frolics at the Chirks's?'

'Yes.'

I looked away from her. 'I shouldn't think there'll be any trains on Christmas Day, do you? And even if there are, I counted my money this morning. There's just enough left for Thursday, that's all. And I don't get my allowance till January.'

She didn't say a word.

'It's true!' But she was giving me one of her looks and I couldn't keep it up. 'Oh all right, if you must know, the real reason is I can't bear the idea of seeing them all so happy together.'

She still didn't say anything, but making a rueful face she pressed my arm in silent sympathy and it helped a little.

After a pause I said, 'What about you? How did you get on this afternoon?'

'I enjoyed myself. The music was splendid, wasn't it? And they were both very kind to me.'

'You seemed to be getting on very well with Richard,' I teased her.

She went a little pink. I was taken aback – I hadn't really meant anything by my remark.

But all she said was, 'I enjoyed talking to him.'

'How is it you're so knowledgeable about music?'

Her faced closed in the old way. 'I just like it, that's all.' Her mouth set.

I felt hurt. I'd just bared my soul, but Sophie persisted in keeping secrets from me. What *was* it she was hiding?

THIRTY-THREE

I easily found my way to the stage door, thanks to Kitty's directions, but though I was late because of the traffic, she wasn't there and neither was Sophie. As I waited, I kept attracting glances from passers-by. I wondered if they thought I was an actress and I posed accordingly, but I quickly grew bored and poked my head round the door.

Just inside, in a glass box, a red-faced little man sat reading the paper; behind him, a scrawny boy was perched on a stool eating a pie. I tapped on the window and the little man opened it.

'Good afternoon. I'm Miss Garland and I'm here to see Mr Darnell.'

He whistled through his teeth and the boy's eyes bulged. 'Cor, yer the dead spit of Miss Chirk, ain't yer? Bert, run up and tell Mr Darnell the young lady's 'ere.'

Gobbling down the last of his pie, the boy sped off. While I waited, I mused gloomily on the revelation that Kitty was known here. Possibly she could come whenever she liked. She was bound to have seen Richard act.

All the while the little man kept staring at me and I was glad when Richard appeared.

'Hello, Meriel.'

I couldn't help giving him a big smile. Then a thought

occurred to me and I said mischievously, 'How do you know it's me?'

He chuckled. 'Because I left Kitty at home, nursing a toothache.' With a glance at the doorman, he lowered his voice. 'You don't mind not being chaperoned, do you?'

'Not at all.'

But just then we heard the sound of quick footsteps and Sophie appeared at the door, very much out of breath. 'Sorry I'm late,' she panted. 'I hope I haven't kept you waiting.'

We both gave the right polite response, but I felt put out. I still felt a bit bruised about Sophie keeping secrets from me. And I'd liked the idea of having Richard to myself and didn't understand why Sophie was so keen to come.

'We'll start at the top, shall we?' Richard smiled at us. 'Do you want to see the star's dressing room?'

He led the way up a steep flight of stone stairs and along another passage. Lit by a single gas jet turned low, it was gloomy, and I noticed the walls were grimy and scuffed. We stopped outside a door with Richard's name on it. As I went in I touched it and a little thrill went through me. Would my name be here one day?

Sophie, following on behind, saw me do it and gave me a funny little smile. I immediately softened towards her – she was so quick to pick up on my feelings.

I didn't know what I was expecting of a dressing room, but it certainly wasn't this. Scarcely bigger than a cupboard, it was horribly stuffy and there was a distinct smell of drains. Sophie wrinkled up her nose and Richard laughed at the looks on our faces. 'I take it you were imagining something grander.'

'Ellen Terry would have a better dressing room than this, wouldn't she?' I exclaimed, looking at the holes in the linoleum. Then, realizing what I'd said, I put my hand to my mouth. 'I'm sorry, I didn't mean –'

Richard laughed again. 'Don't worry, I'm not offended. I expect Miss Terry might be accommodated more comfortably at the Lyceum, but not necessarily anywhere else. This is the reality in most theatres, even for the biggest stars. And everyone else has to squash in together. Is it making you change your mind?'

'No, not a bit.' I moved across to the rickety table under an ancient mirror, drawn irresistibly to what lay there – brushes, thick pencils, a pot of cold cream, a bottle of spirit gum, a tin of powder and – joy of joys – sticks of greasepaint. I picked one up and sniffed it, closing my eyes as I breathed in the smell. 'Mmm.'

I opened my eyes to find Richard grinning at me. I shot him an impish look. I was tempted to try out some rouge on my cheeks, but I thought I'd better not. What if I couldn't get it off?

I looked in the spotted glass. Richard was close behind me and I thought how well matched we were, my head just reaching to his shoulder . . .

My eyes met Richard's in the mirror and I suddenly felt hot. Could he guess what I was thinking?

'Is this your costume?' Sophie was looking at some clothes draped over a stool.

'Yes.' He held up a tunic of red velvet. Wonderingly, I touched it. How marvellous to dress up, to become someone else . . .

There was a cloak to match, a black-feathered hat and shoes with blue ribbons.

'Can I see you in the hat?' Sophie asked, and Richard obligingly put it on and posed.

Surprised, I glanced at Sophie, who was smiling at Richard. She was different today – more relaxed. I remembered how she'd blushed the other day when I teased her about Richard, and I felt a twinge of something . . . an uneasiness.

Abruptly I said, 'I like the ribbons on your shoes. Very droll.' Richard pulled a face. 'They're pretty hideous, aren't they?' He nodded towards the door. 'Shall we carry on?'

As we went along the corridor and back down the stairs I asked, 'If you want to be an actor, how do you start? How did you?'

He grinned. 'I started as a child actor in pantomime.'

I laughed. 'Pantomime? Where?'

'Here in London. When I was ten I came here from Norwich – that's where my family live – to go to school.'

'Ten? Didn't you mind? Leaving your home.'

He gave me a sudden quick look as if he'd caught the feeling behind my words.

'Yes, at first. But the Chirks were so good to me I soon

stopped feeling homesick. And anyway, there are far more acting opportunities here.'

I hadn't realized he'd been with the Chirks so long. If he was about twenty or twenty-one, as I guessed, Kitty must have been a little girl when she first knew him. No wonder they got on so well.

'Did your parents approve?'

He pulled a face. 'Not at first. My father's a lawyer, and he wanted me to follow him. But my godfather, Hugh Avery – I don't know if you've heard of him – he helped me persuade them. He's quite a well-known actor. He got me the pantomime work and then I gradually moved on to other roles.'

'You didn't go to school?'

He grimaced. 'Oh yes, I still had to do that, but I left as soon as I could – when I was sixteen. Mind you, these days, it's as well to have a good education.'

'Is it?' I said, dismayed. 'I thought it wouldn't matter.'

'Didn't used to, but now there's a lot of competition and the better-educated people are favoured.'

I contemplated this gloomily as we passed the stage doorkeeper's box and descended another flight of steps.

'This is the green room.' Richard opened a door and we peered in. An ill-assorted collection of sofas and ottomans covered in faded chintz stood on a carpet that had seen better days. The walls were pale sea green.

'This is where everyone waits to go onstage?'

Richard nodded.

'Is it always green? And if so, why?' Sophie wanted to know.

He shrugged. 'I've no idea.' He was already moving on, and Sophie followed, but I lingered behind. I imagined sitting here, knowing the auditorium was filling up, feeling the buzz of anticipation before the play began . . .

Along the corridor Sophie was talking animatedly about Handel, and Richard was looking engrossed.

I felt another twinge but this time I recognized it: irritation. But it didn't last long because, as soon as I reached them, Richard broke off the conversation and threw open a door. 'This is the property room. Well, that's the idea, anyway. Actually it's just where they put everything there's no room for anywhere else.'

We squeezed in.

'This is amazing,' I said, looking round at the jumble of things packed into the small space. A throne covered in gilt paper, with a bearskin draped over it, lay on its back on a bedstead. A cauldron supported a writing desk on which sat a toy chariot, a jewelled casket and a box of tennis balls.

'Isn't it?' Richard picked up a cylinder. 'Listen.'

He shook it and there was a sound of rain.

Sophie's face lit up. 'What makes the noise?'

'Dried peas.' Richard shook it near her ear and she giggled. I stared at her amazed. I'd never seen her like this before.

'What's this?' I asked abruptly, pointing to a sheet of iron.

Richard gently vibrated it and it made a quiet grumbling noise.

'Oh,' said Sophie, intrigued. 'It's thunder!'

'Let me have a go!' I rattled the sheet and a great booming sound reverberated round the room, causing the others to put their hands over their ears.

I snatched up a crimson brocade curtain and threw it over my shoulder. Removing my hat, I put a pasteboard crown on my head and seized a lance. 'Ta-daa!'

'Joan of Arc?' Richard hazarded.

'*Once more unto the breach, dear friends*,' I declaimed.

He laughed. 'I think Henry would have been wearing armour.'

Sophie smiled, then wandered off, pausing here and there to look at something.

I sank on to a wooden chest. 'How hard is it to get into a company?' I was in earnest now. 'I mean, if I were to think of trying . . .' I gave Richard a sideways look.

He regarded me thoughtfully. 'You're serious about this, aren't you?'

I nodded.

'You do realize that people will look down on you, that you risk being cut off from respectable Society, with a capital S, that you'll very likely never earn much money, and probably be out of work as often as not?'

'I don't give a fig –' I banged the lance on the floor

and out of the corner of my eye I saw Sophie jump – 'for respectable society.'

Richard grinned. 'Good for you! There *are* compensations . . . the company is like a family. There are fallings out, of course, as in all families, but you'll not find more loyalty or better friendship.'

'I can't wait.' I meant it. Whatever the drawbacks, that was exactly what I wanted. 'So, how do I start?'

'Hmm, good question.' Fingering the tasselled fringe of a cushion, he thought for a moment.

My attention was distracted by Sophie. She had paused by a wooden cradle and was lifting out the doll inside, handling it tenderly as if it were a real baby. She held it to her and rocked it, seeming lost in a little world of her own.

'If I were you,' said Richard, 'I'd try to get into Miss Thorne's School of Acting. Have you heard of it?'

I shook my head.

'It's at the Theatre Royal, Margate, in Kent. We went there once on tour and I met Miss Thorne. She's rather formidable but a good 'un, I'd say. I've heard the pupils get a chance to act with experienced actors, and people like Irving and so on attend the performances to look out for newcomers with talent. Ellen Terry sent her son there.'

'Really?' My heart was doing somersaults in my chest. 'And . . . do you think I've got a chance of getting in?' I searched his face anxiously.

He gave me a little smile. 'I don't see why not.'

I could have hugged him. I broke into a huge grin and waved the lance in the air. 'Huzzah!'

Shaking his head, Richard gently took the lance from my hand, removed the crown from my head and handed me my hat. 'Shall we move on?'

I didn't want to. I could have stayed there all afternoon. I longed to hear every detail about Miss Thorne's school, every detail about Richard's life in the theatre, but he and Sophie had already left the room. With a sigh I pulled off the curtain and joined them outside.

Something touched my leg and I looked down to see a tabby cat rubbing itself against me and nudging me with its head.

'That's Garrick,' said Richard. 'He lives here in the theatre.'

Sophie crouched down. She tickled the cat under his chin and he started purring. 'Why do you have a cat?' she asked.

'Can't you guess?' Richard's eyes danced teasingly.

'Mice?' Sophie's eyes widened

'And worse. Are you afraid?' He ushered us along the corridor.

'I'm not,' I said. 'When I was little, at home in India, I had a pet rat, Mr Whiskers.'

Sophie shuddered and Richard's eyebrows shot up. 'That does surprise me. After Kitty found out about the mice, she was nervous about coming backstage again.'

'We're not completely alike.'

He smiled his crooked smile as we stopped outside another door. 'No, I'm beginning to realize that.'

I was aware of Sophie looking from Richard to me, an odd expression on her face.

'We'll sneak a look at the stage, but we'll have to be quiet,' Richard warned, stopping outside a door. 'They're having a rehearsal. The actor playing Mercutio slipped and put his knee out so the understudy has to go on. They're practising the duel.'

Inside, it took my eyes a minute or two to adjust to the darkness. As we stood there I breathed in the atmosphere – smells of canvas, glue and gas. Richard pointed, and Sophie and I looked up. High above our heads in the shadowy space I could see the silhouettes of ladders, narrow platforms, dangling ropes. Richard said in an undertone, his breath tickling my ear, 'The flies.' I nodded, although I had no idea what he meant.

We were in a narrow space at the back of the stage that ran from one side to the other. Long rolls of canvas were piled on one side and India-rubber hosepipes snaked along the floor, which was littered with tiny fibres. Richard beckoned to us. Sophie moved to him obediently and I followed, being careful where I trod and trying not to sneeze as we disturbed the dust. There was a backcloth to one side of us, and beyond it I could hear the clash of metal on metal, grunts and exclamations and at one point laughter, followed by a voice giving instructions. It was, I realized with some astonishment, a woman's voice.

Richard was waiting for us at the other side. 'The wings,' he whispered. The space was cluttered with buckets of water, rolled up blankets and lots of other things. I spotted a spade, a crow bar and several lanterns.

'Hang on.' Richard spoke in an undertone, gesturing at me to stay where I was. Taking Sophie's arm he steered her around the various obstacles. I couldn't see properly because of the shadows, but it seemed to me that she was gazing up at him in admiration. I thought, *Ha! I like not that*, quoting Iago. To my surprise, I realized I was only half joking.

But here was Richard to conduct me through the wings. At the unexpected touch of his warm hand through my wool coat, a shiver ran through me. He noticed and leaning close he said, 'Sorry about the cold.'

'Don't you freeze when you're performing?' I whispered.

'No, when the lights are turned up, it's far too hot.'

A shout from the stage distracted me and, looking past a piece of scenery, I saw a young man holding a sword to the throat of another young man who was lying on the floor. Adroitly the actor on the ground knocked the sword away with a dagger and sprang up to face his opponent. As they closed in, another actor rushed between them.

'That's me,' whispered Richard. 'Or rather, he's my stand-in for the rehearsal.'

Clutching his chest, the actor who must be Mercutio, I realized, died a horrible death. It was dramatic, but I thought he overdid it rather.

'That will do for today,' called a voice. 'James, perhaps tone down the death throes.'

I smiled to myself.

Laughing and joking, the three young men came off the stage, nodding at us cheerily as they passed.

'Come and meet Ma,' said Richard, beckoning to Sophie who was waiting in the shadows.

I hung back. 'Ma?'

'Mrs King. She's the guv'nor's wife – our leading lady and manager. Her name's Marjorie, but she likes everyone to call her Ma, and she *is* just like a mother to us. Come on.'

Reluctantly I allowed myself to be pulled on to the stage. At the very front, under a couple of flickering gas jets, a woman was gathering up her belongings, which lay scattered at her feet.

'Ma, may I introduce some friends? Miss Meriel Garland and Miss Sophie Casson.'

She came forward and seized our hands in turn in a firm handshake. 'How do you do, Miss Garland? Miss Casson?'

I couldn't help staring.

Wearing a smart tailored jacket and waistcoat over a silver-grey skirt, she looked businesslike, but there was also something attractive about her strong face and the direct way she spoke. 'You *are* the image of your sister, aren't you?' she said to me. Her voice was amazing, deep-toned, slightly husky yet rich.

I wanted to say something striking or clever to impress

her, but I couldn't think of anything so I just stood there smiling and nodding idiotically.

'Miss Garland is interested in a stage career,' said Richard.

'Are you?' She gave me a shrewd appraising glance. 'And are you, Miss Casson?'

'Oh no,' Sophie said hastily.

Mrs King turned back to me. 'Are you really hungry for it? So that nothing else matters?'

'Yes,' I said emphatically, looking her directly in the eye. 'It's what I want more than anything.'

'Hm, good voice,' she said, and I felt a thrill of pleasure.

'And have you any experience?'

My elation vanished. I didn't think she'd be impressed by my childhood efforts. 'Er, no . . . but I've practised and practised . . . I've learned a lot of Shakespeare by heart.'

'I was suggesting Miss Thorne's school,' said Richard.

She raised a finely arched eyebrow. 'Good idea.' She glanced at her watch, then looked at me. 'I haven't time now, but if you like come back after Christmas and I'll hear you. If I think you're any good, I'll recommend you to Sarah Thorne.'

I was almost struck dumb. I managed to gasp, 'Oh . . . thank you.'

She bestowed a smile on me that made me feel as if a goddess had favoured me with her attention. But then she said, 'I hope you don't mind if I give you a little piece of advice to think about before you come. I've seen countless young women who, because they can speak lines prettily and like performing, think they could be actresses. But acting is not about showing off – in a way it's the opposite: you have to forget yourself and become someone else so convincingly that the audience believes you *are* that person.

'To do that you have to have a sensitive awareness of other people, a deep sympathy with their feelings, even if they're very different from you. Have you that capacity for understanding others, Miss Garland?' She studied me for a moment, her gaze penetrating. Then she said briskly, 'I must be off. See you tonight, Richard,' and gliding with a queenly grace she disappeared into the wings.

I felt chastened, but only for a minute or two. After all, what had Richard said? That no girl in his company could deliver the Queen Margaret speech like me?

And now he was grinning at me. 'Well done.'

'What do you mean?'

'With Ma. You didn't gush. She hates gushers and, as she said, she's often plagued by them – empty-headed young ladies with a fancy for going on the stage when they don't know the first thing about it.'

'I'm not a gusher.'

'No, I guessed that.'

He gave me a penetrating glance and I suddenly felt embarrassed. To cover it up I said, 'To think that in a few hours' time you'll be here, and out there –' I indicated the auditorium with a sweep of my arm – 'hundreds of people will be watching. Do you get nervous?'

'Yes. But I'd be worried if I didn't. I think that's where the energy comes from – without it, I think I'd give a flat performance. Does that make sense?'

He looked from Sophie to me. She nodded and I said, 'Yes, I think so.'

'You said you like the play, Meriel. Which are your favourite parts?'

'Oh, I don't know . . . The ones with Romeo and Juliet in! I love the scene where they first meet.'

He took hold of my hand and I exchanged a glance with Sophie. He gazed soulfully at me, his eyes, sea-dark and mysterious in the half-light.

'*If I profane with my unworthiest hand*
This holy shrine, the gentle sin is this:
My lips, two blushing pilgrims, ready stand
To smooth that rough touch with a tender kiss.'

I recited back to him: '*Good pilgrim, you do wrong your hand too much*—'

But at that moment a door banged and voices sounded in the wings. A man in shirtsleeves appeared at the side of the stage.

'The stage-hands have come to set up. Excuse me, I need to speak to the limelight operator.' Richard went over to the man and, gesturing at various areas of the stage, he started talking animatedly.

Sophie came to my side and together we looked out past the footlights into the gloom of the auditorium, where now several women were moving along the rows, taking brown holland covers from the seats.

I was thinking about the scene Richard and I had just begun to act and wondering what would have happened if we hadn't been interrupted. Would he have done what the stage directions require and kissed me on the lips? My face went hot at the thought.

At my side Sophie stirred. 'Can you imagine it – performing Juliet here?'

I shut my eyes for a moment and conjured up a crowd of faces looking up at the stage, looking at me. I thought of the exciting future that seemed within my grasp, now that I knew about Miss Thorne's school and had met Ma King.

I opened my eyes and grinned at her. 'Oh yes,' I said. 'I certainly can.'

THIRTY-FOUR

The visit to the theatre left me in a state of euphoria . . .

I smiled at strangers in the train, at Sally when we met, even at Ponsonby when he opened the door to me . . .

I dreamed through the evening and on into sleep – cheers, wild applause as I took my leading man's hand and bowed a deep bow, perfectly in time with him . . .

I spent the morning before the looking glass, trying out gestures, speaking lines in different ways, practising that gliding, stately walk . . .

'You all right, miss?' asked Sally as, shivering, we tried unsuccessfully to shelter under the eaves of the closed-up boathouse from the hail stinging our faces and I smiled at the gunmetal sky, at the ice-bound lake, at the bedraggled ducks . . .

'Never better, thank you, Sally!'

I'd been thinking of Ma King. Here was a woman doing just what I wanted to do – acting, directing, managing a theatre company – and thus showing me that it wasn't just a silly dream . . .

The next morning when I reported to Grandfather after breakfast he waved a letter at me.

For a heart-jolting moment I thought it was from Papa about Kitty. But then I realized it was too soon; the letter from the Chirks couldn't have reached him yet. Maybe it was a Christmas letter, maybe he'd sent me some money . . .

Grandfather had said something.

'Pardon me?'

'Madame Marmot,' he said impatiently, 'the headmistress of the Château Bellevue. She's happy to take you.'

I stared at him, and my mouth went dry.

As time had passed, thoughts of school had drifted to the back of my mind. Visiting the Dionysus had banished it to oblivion.

'When?'

He glowered through his monocle. 'When what?'

'When do I have to go?'

'Term starts on January the eighteenth and it will take about three days to get there, so you'll be setting off on the fifteenth. Mrs Grimston will accompany you and . . .'

January the fifteenth. Unseen by Grandfather, I did rapid calculations on my fingers. Just under four weeks away.

'Pay attention, please, Meriel. There's a list here of things you'll need to take. I'll give it to Mrs Grimston to sort out and I'll get on with making the travel arrangements.'

'Yes, Grandfather.' I was still trying to take this in. Unless I could persuade him to change his mind, I was going to be exiled in Switzerland and my chance of going to Miss Thorne's School would vanish. And then I remembered what Mr Chirk had said. *I wouldn't like to make an enemy of Sir Osbert.* I swallowed. What if Grandfather was lying about the school? What if he was really plotting to send me to some dreadful place far away and I'd never be heard of again?

'Grandfather . . .'

'Yes?' He had his hand on a file of papers, his mind no longer on me.

'If I promise to work as hard as anything, can't I stay here?'

His expression softened. 'Well now, that's very touching, my dear . . .'

The old coot actually thought I didn't want to go because of *him*!

'. . . but I think this will be better for you. I thought you'd want to go.'

'I don't. I really, really don't want to go.'

He stared at me for a moment and then said, 'Well, I'm sorry. But it's all arranged, you see.' He tapped the letter.

'It could be un-arranged,' I pleaded.

His manner changed. 'Now then, Meriel, let's not have a fuss. Madame Marmot is expecting you and that's that.'

I stared at him, but I wasn't seeing his face – I was gazing into the darkness of my unknown future. 'Not have a fuss'? He had no idea of the trouble I could make, and would too, yes, I would . . . I opened my mouth to speak . . . Kitty's face appeared before me, Kitty's voice in my ear . . . *Please, Meriel.*

I shut it again.

'Though what she'll say when she sees the standard of your piano playing, I can't imagine.'

A vision flashed before me, Kitty playing beautifully, the centre of attention, loved by everyone. Why did I have to sacrifice myself for her? She had everything – *everything* – and I had nothing.

In that instant I made up my mind.

Setting my feet apart as though to root myself in the carpet, and drawing myself up to my full height, I said, 'Grandfather, I know.'

He frowned, puzzled.

'I know about Kitty.'

'Kitty?'

'My twin sister.'

There was a long silence.

My heart was beating wildly, but I stood my ground and held his gaze until he looked away. A thrill of victory went through me.

He straightened a pen so that it was parallel to the blotter. 'Her name is Katharine.' He spoke so quietly for a moment I wasn't sure I'd heard aright.

'Katharine Lydia Swann.'

I had no trouble hearing that. And even though it was the last thing in the world I would want, I felt a pang of jealousy that he'd bestowed his own name on Kitty, even if only in his own mind.

'They call her Kitty – the Chirks,' I insisted. 'Kitty Chirk.'

He waved his hand as if what the Chirks called anyone was irrelevant. 'How long have you known?'

'About three weeks.'

Did he relax a little?

He certainly wasn't blustering or looking alarmed, or denying he knew what I was talking about. He was lining up his silver pencil with the pen, as if tidying his desk was all that concerned him at that moment.

I licked my lips. 'And I know what you did. I know you took Kitty away from Mamma when she was just a few hours old and arranged for someone to nurse her till she was old enough to live with the Chirks.' I added, 'And you lied to them about who her parents were.'

His head went up then. 'Who is the source of your information?'

'It doesn't matter. It's true, isn't it?'

He didn't answer, but picked up a ruler.

'Did Mamma and Papa know? About Kitty.'

He froze, staring down at his desk. Eventually he said, in a neutral voice. 'No.'

Relief flooded me, a huge wave of it, washing away my deepest fear. But it was followed almost immediately by a bitterness on Mamma's behalf that stung my throat. 'How could you do such a cruel thing? How could you steal your own daughter's baby?'

I was glad to see he flinched, but he still wouldn't look

at me. The ruler was in place now, an exact distance from the other items, but he kept his fingers on it as if afraid it might jump out of line.

'Why did you do it? What was it *for*?'

No answer.

'I've met her,' I said. 'Kitty. And the Chirks.'

'Ah.' At last he looked at me. 'So they know about you.' He said it as much to himself as to me.

'Yes, they do.'

He moved swiftly, making me jump. I thought he was coming for me and I recoiled, but he only went to the bell pull, yanking it hard. Then he stood with his back to the fire surveying me speculatively. 'How is it that you've met them? When did you see them?'

I suddenly realized that if I wasn't careful I would implicate Sally. The last thing I wanted was for any blame to fall on her. I stared at him mutinously, my mouth shut tight.

With an impatient twitch of his head, he returned to his desk and opened a drawer.

'Does anyone else know?'

I thought of Sophie. 'No.'

He was taking things out and putting them in his pocket – some keys, his wallet, a small diary. It dawned on me that he was preparing to go out. Ponsonby came into the room and Grandfather said, 'Have the carriage brought round, please.'

Ponsonby coughed. 'Are you aware that it's been snowing for some time, sir?'

Grandfather swung round and drew aside the lace curtain. Fat flakes were drifting across the window, sticking to the glass.

'Nevertheless, I will go out.'

Ponsonby coughed again and withdrew.

I was filled with dismay. This wasn't how it was supposed to happen. It was supposed to be a big, dramatic scene, Grandfather cowering as I wielded the weapon of my knowledge. And here he was, calmly leaving the house.

A sudden thought almost floored me. 'Are you going to see the Chirks?'

He didn't answer. He was rummaging in the drawer again. He was *ignoring* me.

I sprang forward and shoved his careful arrangement so everything scattered across the desk. 'Didn't you hear me? Don't you understand? I *know* what you did, and because I know, you've got to let me do what I want.' I was shaking with fear and the desperate need to show him I meant what I said.

With a sigh he sat down and looked at me. 'What is it that you want?' His even tone betrayed no emotion at all.

I could scarcely believe it. He was actually *asking* me? I took a deep breath. 'I want to go to a theatre school. I want to be an actress.'

At last I'd shaken his composure – he screwed up his face as if he'd swallowed a draught of particularly loathsome medicine. He shook his head from side to side and uttered a single word. 'No.'

'Why not?'

'I'm not discussing it with you. It's completely out of the question.'

'But why?'

'Do you think that I would allow a granddaughter of mine to parade herself on a stage before a low and vulgar rabble, to put herself in a position where any scoundrel may go and look at her for a shilling? With one exception, there is nothing more degrading a woman can do.'

It took me a moment to understand what he meant, but when I did, I was shocked. He thought being an actress was hardly better than being a prostitute!

'How can you say that? Why, the Queen herself has attended a public performance and members of her family are often to be seen at the theatre.'

'Watching a play and taking part in it are very different things. Showing off in scanty costumes, impersonating immoral characters, not to mention spending time in the company of degenerate people from dubious backgrounds – an actress is a disgrace to her sex.' His tone was icy, chilling. 'I'm not prepared to discuss this any further.'

'Well, in that case I'm going to tell the world what you've done!' Triumphant, I watched to see the effect of my declaration.

It was disappointing.

He didn't shrivel into an abject heap, nor plead with me. Instead, raising an eyebrow, he smiled a horrible, ironic smile. 'Tell the world, Meriel? Just how do you propose to do that?'

I didn't falter. I'd rehearsed this so many times. 'I shall go to the newspapers.' I threw out my arm in a dramatic gesture.

He laughed. He actually laughed. Then he stood up, looked out of the window again – the snow was falling thickly now – straightened his chair and said, 'I want you to go to your room now. I suggest you make the best use of the short time remaining to remedy the deficiencies in your learning. Otherwise, I fear you will embarrass yourself before Madame Marmot and your fellow pupils.'

I persisted. 'Think of the scandal, of having your name in the headlines, of having it shouted by common newsvendors in the street.' I couldn't resist that last dig, knowing his abhorrence of anything 'low'.

His mouth twisted in another unnerving smile. 'My dear child, has it not occurred to you that as a person of some standing in the world I have more sway with newspaper proprietors than you do? And that if my status did not count, my money certainly would?'

My mouth fell open in dismay.

'And besides, do you know any newspaper proprietors or editors?'

The question hung in the air. I looked down at the carpet.

'I thought not.'

Crossing the room in a couple of strides, he went out.

I heard Ponsonby speaking to him in the hall, the front door opening and shutting. He'd gone.

The significance of being left alone in the library wasn't lost on me. I could rifle through his files as much as I liked – he had nothing to fear from me.

I lifted the lace curtain and saw the carriage driving away. Grandfather was on his way to the Chirks, I was sure of it. I stared out at the snowflakes falling from the steel-grey sky.

I had played what I thought was my trump card, and lost.

THIRTY-FIVE

There was a cough behind me as the library door opened. I spun round.

'Excuse me, Miss Meriel –' Ponsonby was all politeness, but there was an unpleasant glint in his hooded eyes. 'Sir Osbert has asked me to accompany you to your room.'

I stiffened. This was it. Once I was over the threshold, he would close the door, turn the key and I would be a prisoner.

'Thank you, Ponsonby,' I replied, equally polite.

He held the library door open for me and as I came out into the hall I glanced towards the front door. It was only five steps away, but Ponsonby slipped round me adroitly, putting himself between me and any chance of freedom.

Like a goatherd driving his flock, he shepherded me towards the stairs. I had no choice but to ascend them, acutely aware of him treading close behind me. Could I make a dash for the schoolroom and the fire escape? He would catch me before I could get the window open.

We'd reached the first floor, passed the drawing room and were continuing on and up. Ahead of me on the half-landing was the small room containing the water closet.

I said suddenly, 'Excuse me, I need to go in here,' and darted in and locked the door before he could stop me.

Closing the lid of the closet I sat down, praying that he'd go on and wait for me upstairs. But no, I could see his shadow on the etched glass pane in the door. Frantically I tugged at the window, but it was nailed shut. I sat there as long as I dared before pulling the chain. Then I washed and dried my hands slowly, all the time trying to think what I could do.

I could see one possible, risky chance.

Quietly sliding the bolt back, I paused a moment to gather my breath, then flung the door open as hard as I could. It smacked satisfyingly against something solid, and Ponsonby let out a pained cry. I didn't stop to see what damage I'd done – I was already halfway down the stairs. I raced along the passage, down the next flight and on to the front door. A brief struggle to get it open and then I was out. I nearly slid on the wet steps, but I managed to regain my balance and then I was off down the street, slithering in the snow.

There was no time to think where I was going – I just kept moving until I reached the main road, where the heavy traffic forced me to stop. The horses' hoofs were slipping, carriage wheels were churning up clouts of brown sludge and I was afraid that at any moment one might skid into me. With my heart in my throat I darted across as soon as a gap appeared, causing several drivers to shout and yank at their reins.

Regaining the footpath and stopping a minute to catch my breath I looked back. Because of the swirling snow I couldn't see if anyone was following me. If they were, here at least the slush bore the marks of many feet and my footprints would be lost among them. And ahead of me were the gates of Kensington Gardens – a good place to hide.

I set off into the park, but I soon came to halt. It was no good cutting across the open ground – on the pure whiteness my tracks would show up like anything. I thought I'd better stick to the path, but as I hesitated about which direction to take, a gust of wind sent a stinging shower of icy particles into my face. I became aware for the first time that it was bitterly cold, my dress was clinging damply to me, my thin, indoor shoes were soaked through and I couldn't stop shivering.

I wondered what on earth I was doing. If I stayed out here in the snow much longer, there was a strong likelihood I'd freeze to death, but without money I had no means of getting food, let alone shelter. For a moment I contemplated going back. But when I thought of what would happen, of being kept like a prisoner until I was bundled off to school or to somewhere worse . . . I couldn't bear it.

The answer came with a sudden flare of hope. Mrs Jolly. She'd take me in.

Setting my face against the wind, I began to trudge across the park.

My sudden arrival disrupted what had obviously been a peaceful morning.

Mrs Jolly put down her book and the girls jumped up

from the table, where they were occupied with cardboard and scissors. Minty reached me first. 'Meriel! Isn't the snow exciting? I've never seen it before. And Mamma says when it stops we can build a snowman! We're making a puppet theatre now. Come and see.' She seized my hand and exclaimed, 'You're freezing! She's freezing, Mamma,' she said over her shoulder, and then taking me in, 'and all wet. Why are you all wet?'

Mrs Jolly came forward and drew me to the fire. 'My dear girl, don't tell me you've come out dressed like that in this weather? Why didn't you put a coat on?'

My teeth were chattering unstoppably, but I managed to say, 'There wasn't time. I was going to be locked in.'

The consternation provoked by my words was very gratifying. The girls crowded round, eager to hear the story, but Mrs Jolly said, 'Amy, fetch a big towel and a blanket from the ottoman; Alice run and get my dressing gown and my red shawl; and, Minty, go and ask Varali to make Meriel a nice hot cup of cocoa.'

Minty sped off and Mrs Jolly said to me, 'Not another word till you're warm and dry. Take off those wet things before you catch your death of cold.'

In a remarkably short space of time my clothes were hanging on the clothes horse and I was ensconced in an armchair in front of the fire, toasting my toes on the fender and sipping cocoa. At which point Mrs Jolly said to her daughters, 'Now listen, girls. I want you to be very good and go to your room. Amy, will you read to the others until I call you?'

This set off wails of protest from Alice and Minty, but after a quick glance at me Amy spoke to them quietly and within seconds they were obediently following her out of the room.

'Now,' said Mrs Jolly when the door closed behind them, 'what's all this about?'

I took a deep breath and then paused. 'It's a long story.'

'We've plenty of time. Why don't you start at the beginning?'

Mrs Jolly listened without interrupting, for the most part, except for an occasional question. She was delightfully responsive, drawing in her breath when I related what Sophie had experienced with the locket, opening her eyes wide in shock when I told her about Kitty, tightening her mouth in disgust when I described what Grandfather had done.

When I stopped speaking she didn't say anything for a long time but sat staring into the fire. Finally she stirred and said quietly, 'Your poor mother – that's who I keep thinking about. How she would have loved to have you two girls, to see you growing up together.' Her eyes glistened and I could feel tears starting to prickle mine.

Blinking them back, I drained the last of my cocoa, though it was cold now. 'At first I couldn't believe Sophie was communicating with her spirit. It seems extraordinary, doesn't it?'

Mrs Jolly sighed. 'I don't know, Meriel, I really don't.

If you'd asked me before I'd probably have said I didn't imagine such things were possible, but . . .' She shook her head. 'I believe there are many mysteries in life that are beyond the scope of our knowledge.'

She got up and started rearranging my clothes, turning the damper parts towards the fire. 'I'm relieved, though, that you aren't going to attempt further communication with spirits. I think it could lead to a great deal of unhappiness.'

'That's what Sophie said.'

'She's a very wise young woman. I'm glad you have her as a friend, and I'm so glad you've found your sister. You must be overjoyed.'

'Mmm.' I turned to put my cup on a table so she couldn't see my face. I hadn't told her the full story. I'd left out the part about the Chirks asking me not to speak to Grandfather.

'And let me get this straight – your father knows about Kitty?'

'He will do, any day now. Mr Chirk has written to ask if they can keep her.'

'And how do you feel about that?'

I shrugged. 'It doesn't affect me, does it?'

She gave me a keen look before bending to move my shoes nearer the fire. Then she took her seat again. 'So why were you going to be locked in?'

'Grandfather's threatening to send me away. He says it's to Switzerland to a beastly boarding school for young ladies so I can be polished, but he might have a more sinister plan. Anyway, I told him I wanted to go to an acting school and he went berserk.'

Mrs Jolly frowned. 'I don't quite see . . .'

'I said if he didn't let me train to be an actress, I'd tell the newspapers what he'd done.'

Her eyebrows shot up. 'Tell the newspapers?'

'I thought the threat of scandal would frighten him.'

'I see. Blackmail, eh?' She didn't sound shocked. In fact, she was looking at me with mingled admiration and amusement. 'And did it work?'

'No.'

'It doesn't surprise me.' Her face became serious. 'What he did to Kitty suggests that he is someone who is prepared to take risks and might not care what people think. In other words someone not easily intimidated. So he threatened to lock you in to prevent you exposing him?'

'He didn't exactly threaten that,' I admitted. 'But I know he will so I ran away. And I'm never going back.'

'I see.'

Encouraged by her response, I added, 'You're right about Grandfather. He's a monster and I don't want to live with him any more. And I don't want to be sent away. I need somewhere to hide where he can't find me. I can stay here with you, can't I? Please say yes.'

'Whoa! Now, hold on, Meriel . . .' She made little suppressing gestures, like someone trying to stop a dog jumping up. 'I – well – no. I'm sorry, my dear, it's out of the question.'

I couldn't believe it. 'But why?' It came out as a horrible wail, but I couldn't help it.

Mrs Jolly put her hand to her forehead. She seemed lost for words.

'I thought you'd help me.'

She took a deep breath. 'Now listen to me, my dear. I do want to help you if I can, of course, but you can't stay here.'

I started to protest.

'No, listen, Meriel. You can't just run off and hide – your grandfather will be worried about you.'

'No, he won't. He doesn't care about me. He'd be glad if I just disappeared.'

'I don't think—'

'He will. Look what he did to Kitty. That's the kind of person he is.'

She looked at me gravely. 'Now, my dear, you must be sensible. Whatever your grandfather has done, I wouldn't invite you here without asking him—'

'But that's no good, he—'

She held up a hand to stop me. 'And much as I'd like to, I can't invite you, because there just isn't room. We're squashed as it is and – what are you doing?'

I was struggling to extricate myself from the layers of blanket and shawl. When I'd succeeded I took my chemise from the clotheshorse.

'You can't put that back on yet,' Mrs Jolly protested. 'It's still damp.'

'Please turn your back.'

'I can lend you some dry clothes.'

'Turn your back.'

With a sigh, she did as I said and, shuddering at the clammy feel of the wool, I dressed as quickly as I could.

Over her shoulder Mrs Jolly said, 'There's no need for this, you know. It's silly. By the time we've had lunch, everything will be dry.'

Lunch! If she didn't want me, and she plainly didn't, I wasn't staying a minute longer.

'Listen, my dear, perhaps going to boarding school might not be as terrible as you think. My girls like their school. You'd enjoy meeting other young women, wouldn't you? And perhaps there will be opportunities to act there.'

I squeezed my feet into my damp shoes and made for the door. 'Thank you for the cocoa.'

Mrs Jolly spun round. 'You're not going?'

'I do not care to outstay my welcome,' I said with as much dignity as I could muster.

'Oh, Meriel . . . At least let Varali get you a cab.'

'I'll get one myself, thank you.'

'Wait!' Picking up the shawl, she draped it over my shoulders. 'Take this – and this.' She pulled an umbrella from a tall ornamental container.

'Thank you,' I said grudgingly.

'You'll go straight home now, won't you?'

'Say goodbye to the girls for me.'

'I will. And, Meriel . . . I'm sure things won't be as bad as you fear.'

*

Outside it was snowing just as heavily. Although only just past noon, the sky was so dark it seemed more like late afternoon. Glancing up at the house, I saw Mrs Jolly looking out of the window. She waved, but I didn't wave back.

Putting up the umbrella and pulling the shawl tight around me, I set off towards the main road. Drifts blown by the wind had formed against the walls now and the sound of traffic was muffled. The snow was deep here and few people had passed this way – with every step I sank in up to my ankles. But I kept slogging on towards the only refuge left to me.

THIRTY-SIX

'. . . and I can't believe she could let me down like that, but I'm not going back to Grandfather's, not ever.'

'I see,' said Sophie gravely. From the moment I'd burst in on her and poured out my woes, she'd listened in her usual calm way. If I hadn't known her better, I would have thought my story was making no impact on her, but I knew she was taking it all in.

'Aren't you going to put some more coal on the fire?' While I'd been talking, it had gradually dawned on me that it was nearly as cold in the parlour as outside, and I noticed that Sophie was once again wearing her shawl and mitts. No wonder – in the grate the feeblest fire I'd ever seen scarcely flickered. The umbrella had protected me a little, but my skirt and shoes had got soaked again and my feet were frozen.

Sophie hesitated; then with the tongs she took one piece of coal from the scuttle and dropped it on the fire.

'It needs more than that! It'll go out in a minute.'

Sophie looked embarrassed. 'Mrs Quinn doesn't like me to use more coal than necessary.'

'She won't know.' Betsey had informed me somewhat grandly that Mrs Quinn was out, 'attending a luncheon'.

'She will.'

Something about the way Sophie spoke made me pause. Remembering Sophie's room, I again thought it strange that Mrs Quinn didn't treat her ward more generously. 'But aren't you cold?' I asked, shivering as I spoke.

Sophie rested her dark eyes on me a moment, then she suddenly stood up and shovelled a heap of coal into the grate.

I smiled at her gratefully. 'That's much better.'

On a small table beside her, there was a tray with the remnants of her lunch on it. 'Have you finished with that? Do you mind?' I nodded at the plate.

'Are you sure?' Sophie pulled a face as she passed it over. 'I'm sorry I can't offer you anything else.'

'That's all right.' I didn't care what I ate – I was ravenous. But when I saw what was on the plate – a fatty lump of cold mutton, and a dry-looking crust – I wasn't surprised Sophie had left it. As I chewed my way through it, I wondered about her relationship with Mrs Quinn. But I hesitated to bring it up – I didn't want to upset her.

I swallowed the last tough mouthful. 'So what do you think?'

Sophie gave me a guarded look. 'Do you really want to know?'

'Of course.'

She hesitated and then said, 'I can understand your distress about being sent away, and so I can see why you spoke out, but I think it's unfortunate that you revealed to Sir Osbert what you knew.'

'Yes, now I'm in this mess, I can see it was a mistake. Do you think I should have gone straight to the newspapers?'

Sophie's expression was enigmatic. 'No. I meant I was sorry you didn't wait for your father's response.'

'But it would have been too late! I'd have been in Switzerland or somewhere by then!'

'There are worse things than boarding school.'

'I know. That's what I'm afraid of!'

She looked at me levelly. 'You don't seriously think your grandfather could have you spirited away somehow, do you?'

'Why not?'

'Well, how would he explain to your father why he wasn't getting letters from you any more?'

'He could say I'd died.'

Sophie gave me one of her looks.

'Oh, all right. He probably is just sending me to school, but that's bad enough.'

'Yes, it is, but you can always come back.'

I stared at her. What was she getting at?

'If, as you suppose, Sir Osbert has gone to the Chirks, I'm concerned about Kitty and—'

'*Kitty?!*' I exploded. 'Not you too. You're like everyone else. "Poor Kitty." But she has everything – a home, a family who love her, whereas I—'

Sophie put up a hand to stop me. 'Whereas you,' she said quietly, 'are having a horrible time –'

'Exactly!'

'– but there's one important difference between you and Kitty.'

'Which is?'

'That you were brought up by your real parents, that you experienced your mother's love . . .' She broke off, and seemed to be struggling to keep some emotion under control. 'Forgive me, I'm speaking out of turn, but sometimes I think you don't appreciate how lucky you were.'

I stared at her. What right had she to speak to me like that? She had no idea what it was like, how I felt about Mamma, no one did. 'Lucky? How can you say that? Anyway, Mrs Chirk loves Kitty dearly – anyone can see that.'

'It's not the same.' Her dark eyes were insistent.

I wanted to shake her. 'Well, I haven't got the benefit of my mother's love any more, have I!'

'No, but you have a father.'

'Who doesn't care about me!'

'I know how painful that must be.'

The look of pity she gave me exasperated me even more. 'You say that, but how can you know? Your father's dead!'

She flinched, and at once I felt like a beast. And of course, I remembered too late, she'd lost her mother too. Perhaps she did know how I felt.

'I'm sorry,' I muttered. 'That was a mean thing to say.'

She looked down at her lap. An awkward silence fell. After a minute or two she raised her head, the expression in her eyes unfathomable. 'The point I'm trying to make is this: because your father is your legal guardian, you could appeal to him for protection if your grandfather seriously threatened you, whereas, until your father knows about her and acknowledges her, Kitty is vulnerable. Sir Osbert has already intervened once in her life. Who's to say he won't do it again?'

It was my turn to look down. She was right. I'd known it all along really, but in my concern about what was going to happen to me, I'd not let myself dwell on it. Now, hearing Sophie say it brought it home to me – I had no idea what I'd done, what danger I might have put Kitty in.

I squirmed in my seat, trying to squash my unease. 'I know I shouldn't have said anything, but it's done. There's no point in dwelling on it, is there?'

Some feeling flickered over her face, but all she said was, 'So what are you going to do now?'

I hesitated. Sophie thought badly of me because of Kitty, and I'd just been horrible to her, but even so . . . 'I don't suppose I can stay here with you, can I?' Her poky attic room wasn't inviting, but it was better than nothing.

One look at her pained expression and my heart sank. 'It's all right, you don't need to say anything. I know what I did was unforgivable.'

'No, it's not that—'

'If I could undo it, I would, you know.'

She shook her head. 'It's not because of you. Mrs Quinn –' She broke off.

'What's it got to do with Mrs Quinn?'

'She wouldn't like it.'

'Why should she have any say about who you invite to stay? It's not as if you're her servant.'

A red flush crept up Sophie's face.

'Well, you're not, are you?'

A long silence, during which she stared into the fire, threading and unthreading her fingers.

'Sophie, what is it?'

'I can't –' She paused, clenching her hands so tightly her knuckles were white.

I wondered what on earth was wrong. It wasn't like her to be so dramatic.

She turned suddenly, an anguished look on her face. 'I *shall* tell you. I believe Mrs Quinn has told you about my parents – my father the count, my mother's tragic death?'

I nodded.

'It's not true.'

'What?'

Her lip quivered. 'I know nothing about my father and very little about my mother.'

I stared at her, astonished. 'But Mrs Quinn said—'

'I was brought up in the Foundling Hospital.'

I must have looked blank because she said, 'You haven't heard of it?' She seemed to brace herself, but she kept her eyes fixed on mine as she said, 'It's a place for children whose mothers aren't married and can't look after them.'

It took me a minute to absorb what she was saying. *Sophie was illegitimate?*

There was a beat of silence as we looked at one another, Sophie's face taut.

'Oh.' It was all I could think of to say as I struggled to take it in. 'Why didn't you tell me before?'

She looked down. 'I wanted to, but I was afraid you might . . . think badly of me.'

At once Grandfather came into my mind. I imagined how he would react if he supposed Sophie to be the daughter of a count, how different his reaction would be if he knew the truth . . . and then I thought of Mamma and Papa and their revulsion at the way people treated the untouchables . . .

'No . . . *No!* It doesn't make any difference, honestly.'

She scanned my face and then her shoulders relaxed and she smiled, a small, tremulous smile.

My mind was whirring as I suddenly understood Sophie's reserve, the way she seemed to hold herself back all the time. Her childhood must have been so different from mine. 'Where is this place?'

'In Bloomsbury, very near to where Kitty lives.'

'No! So that's why you –'

She nodded. 'Yes, I know the area quite well.'

'And how old were you when you went there?'

'I don't know, but they don't accept babies over a year old.'

I gazed at her, a new understanding illuminating everything. 'So you never knew your mother at all?'

'No.' She twisted a corner of her shawl. 'One of the staff – a young woman more sympathetic than the others – once told me secretly that the token my mother had left with me was a silver thimble, worn with use, so perhaps she was a seamstress.'

'I don't understand. Why did she leave a token?'

'So that she could identify me, if she came back for me.' As she said this her voice trembled.

'But hadn't she given you a name?'

'I expect so, but when babies are admitted to the Hospital they're baptised with a new name.'

'Why?'

Sophie shrugged. 'I don't know. Perhaps to distance us from our mothers.'

I frowned, still not understanding.

'I suppose the idea was we were being given a fresh start in life.' She paused and her grip on the shawl tightened. 'But then they never let us forget that our mothers had done something wrong, and somehow we were at fault too.'

I'd never heard her speak with such bitterness.

'They used to make us sing this hymn written specially for the Hospital.'

She recited:

Left in the world's bleak waste forlorn,
in sin conceived, to sorrow born,
by guilt and shame foredoomed to share
no mother's love, no father's care.

'That's terrible! Making children sing that. Was it awful growing up there?'

Sophie shrugged again. 'I got used to it. Though at first it was a shock when I came back from the country. I found it hard to adjust to the rigid routine.'

Seeing my puzzled look, she explained. 'After the babies are admitted they're sent away to be nursed, and until I was four I lived in a village. I can't remember much about my life there, but my nurse was kind . . . I think she was fond of me. She made me a doll, but I had to leave it behind . . .' She broke off and it was a minute or two before she could resume. 'They cut off my hair, and we had to wear a brown uniform.' She pulled a face. 'They said it was to remind us of our poverty and of the need to be humble.'

'It sounds like a dreadful place.'

'It wasn't really. We were adequately fed and given a basic education. But if someone cried at night, no one came to see what was wrong. We were never kissed or hugged.'

Her tone was matter-of-fact, without the least hint of self-pity, but somehow that made it worse. I almost leaped up to hug her now, but I thought she wouldn't welcome it.

'There was one lovely thing . . .' She smiled. 'The Hospital choir. Sundays were special – the peace of the chapel, the organ playing and those beautiful voices . . .'

'So that's how you know so much about music!'

She nodded. 'It's the only thing I miss about being there . . .' She was quiet and thoughtful for a moment and then she seemed to shake herself out of her reverie and looked at me. 'I'm telling you all this so you'll understand my position here.'

'Your position? I thought you were Mrs Quinn's ward.'

Sophie shook her head. 'That's what she tells people. But the truth is I *am* her servant.'

I gaped at her. 'What?'

She sighed. 'I know it must sound bizarre, but I can explain. Most of the girls at the Hospital go into service. It's what we're trained for. When I was fifteen Mrs Quinn came looking for a maid. She chose me. I don't know whether it was chance or whether she sensed something about my gift.'

'You think she knew?'

'Well, if she didn't, it wasn't long before she found out. Soon after I arrived in the house, she was holding a private consultation and as I showed the visitor into the room I couldn't help noticing her brooch. The lady saw me looking and said, "My daughter gave that to me." At once she was there in the room, the daughter, and without thinking I said, "Carrie is here." '

I sucked in my breath sharply. 'What happened?'

Sophie pulled a face. 'I passed on Carrie's loving message to her mother, who was luckily more grateful than anything. Of course, Mrs Quinn realized at once how useful I could be to her. That's when she invented a new identity for me, one that would impress the rank of society in which she wants to make a name for herself.' Again there was that bitter note in her voice. 'And I ceased to be her servant and became her ward – in the eyes of the world, at least.' As she said this she looked at me, a steady clear-eyed look.

It all made sense now. Why she always wore the same dress, why she walked everywhere, why she seemed so secretive . . . 'You talk of my being an actress. You've played a part far more convincingly than I ever could.'

'Not from choice, I can assure you.' She sighed. 'I wish I'd never set eyes on that lady's brooch.'

I crinkled my forehead. 'But is it not better to go out in society and be taken for a lady, even if it's only for show?'

'No.' She spoke without hesitation looking directly at me. 'No, it isn't.'

I stared at her for a moment and then I remembered what she'd said before, about how much she disliked deceiving people. Perhaps pretending to be Mrs Quinn's ward was as distasteful to her as pretending to see spirits and passing on made-up messages. 'If you're not happy here, why don't you look for another position?'

Sophie sighed again. 'Because I'm not free. I'm bound as an apprentice here, and until I'm twenty-one I'm still a foundling. Once a year I have to report back to the Hospital, and if my conduct isn't satisfactory, Mrs Quinn can send me back. And if that happens –' She broke off and clasped her shawl tighter.

'What?'

'If that happens,' she said in a low voice, 'I could be sent to the workhouse.'

An image flashed into my mind – a bundle of rags propped up against a wall – and I shivered. 'Oh, Sophie, that's terrible.'

We gazed at one another for a moment and then she said, 'Perhaps you can see now how careful I have to be not to displease Mrs Quinn. That's why I haven't always been available when you needed me. I wanted to tell you, but I was too afraid. I'm sorry.'

I stared at her, absolutely stunned. Thinking of some of the things I'd said, the way I'd flounced off . . . I felt hot with shame.

'Sophie! You don't need to apologize. I've been beastly to you, absolutely beastly, and you've been a perfect brick.'

A pink flush crept into her face. 'You haven't been so bad,' she said with one of her little smiles.

'Oh yes, I have. And I'm really sorry.'

There was a pause – I think we both felt slightly awkward. Abruptly I said, 'Have you ever tried to find your mother?'

'No.'

'But, surely, if you ask at the Hospital, they might have some information about her. They'd have to tell you, wouldn't they?'

'They don't tell us anything – they won't. But even if they did, there'd be no point . . .' She turned her dark eyes on me. 'My mother's dead.'

'Dead?! But how do you know?' And then I realized. 'Oh.'

She gave a rueful smile. 'Yes. She appeared to me. That's when I was sure of my gift.' A beat of silence, then she looked at me intently. 'That's why I wanted to help you find Kitty, because . . . if you have family, well . . . it's important not to lose people, if you can.'

Her words pierced me, and I suddenly felt choked up. I didn't trust myself to speak.

Tactfully Sophie got up and busied herself for a minute or two, putting the plate back on the tray, sweeping up some coal dust from the hearth. She went to put some more coal on the fire. 'Don't,' I said. 'Don't get yourself into trouble.'

With a nod of acknowledgement she replaced the shovel. 'What will you do? You see now why I'm afraid I can't ask you to stay?'

'Yes, of course.' I cleared my throat, swallowed. 'I don't know what I'll do.' The idea of running away was appealing, but only if there was somewhere to run to. I thought about the world of the London streets out there, the beggars I'd seen even in Kensington, that girl in Whitechapel, the bundle of rags outside the work-house . . . What was it like for them today with the chill wind biting into their bones and nowhere to shelter? 'Go back to Grandfather's, I suppose . . . and see what happens.'

Sophie's face was full of sympathy. 'And will you try to see Kitty?'

I hung my head. 'I don't know. I don't imagine she'll want to see me.'

'I think she will.'

I looked up and our eyes met.

'And you'll want to see Richard again, won't you?'

Something in her tone made me pause before answering and I went pink. 'Sophie! I do like him . . . but not like that.'

It was true, I realized. I liked Richard's company and it was wonderful to have met someone as interested in the theatre as I was. I liked daydreaming about us acting together, but that was as far as my feelings went.

Sophie seemed relieved at my answer and my stomach contracted. '*You* like him, don't you?'

'Yes . . . He's very kind.'

'No, I mean, you like him *very much*.'

It was her turn to go pink. 'Oh no, of course not. It's nice of him to take an interest in me and I really like talking about music, but that's all.'

'You were jolly keen to come to the theatre with us.'

'Yes, but it wasn't because I wanted to see Richard.'

I scanned her face. Did she mean she wanted to see me? I felt a sudden rush of gladness. I understood now why I'd been so bothered about Sophie and Richard. I hadn't wanted her to be smitten by him, because it might have changed things between us, Sophie and me. I realized that I liked things the way they were, and from what she'd just said it seemed that Sophie felt the same.

Dear Sophie, however rotten I'd been to her, she'd always stayed loyal. She seemed to know what I was feeling better than anyone . . .

I opened my eyes wide.

All this time I'd been looking for someone who understood me, and she'd been there all along.

I grinned at her and she smiled shyly back.

It was gloomy in the parlour now – it must be getting late. 'I'd better go, you know.'

Sophie went over to the window and pulled the blind aside. 'It's stopped snowing, but it's treacherous out there. I'll get Betsey to fetch a cab.'

'Please don't.'

'You can't possibly walk back. It's nearly dark now.'

I held out my empty palms admitting, shamefaced, 'I haven't any money.'

At once she felt in her pocket. 'Here, I'll lend it you.'

'You mustn't, Sophie.'

She pushed a shilling into my hand. 'You can repay me when you receive your allowance.'

On an impulse I flung my arms round her and hugged her. For a second she held her body stiff, but then suddenly she relaxed and hugged me back.

'I don't know when I'll see you again. If I'm allowed out, I'll try to come . . .'

'You'll let me know what happens, won't you?' she said.

'Of course I will.'

THIRTY-SEVEN

It was a slow journey back to Queen's Gate Walk as the horses slipped and struggled in the dirty churned-up slush. I didn't mind. I was in no hurry to get there. I stared out into the dusk, seeing, but not taking in, the lamplighter struggling to steady his ladder, the men dealing with the telegraph wires brought down by the snow.

I couldn't stop thinking about the conversation that had just occurred.

I tried to imagine what it must have been like to be a child in the Foundling Hospital, but my imagination could not go beyond the idea that it must have been hideous. It explained so much about Sophie. That way she had, of seeming to say wordlessly, Don't come near me. It wasn't the aloofness of a sense of superiority, rather a shell she must have built in order to survive.

I suddenly remembered what she'd said once when I was suspicious about her wanting to help me: that she and I were alike. At the time I'd rejected the idea, but now I wondered if she'd sensed my loneliness. I had been lonely in England, but Sophie must have been lonely all her life, apart from those first few years with her nurse. And now, to be at Mrs Quinn's beck and call, having to do what she didn't want to do, living with the threat of the workhouse hanging over her head . . .

There are worse things than boarding school.

I felt stricken. The fuss I'd made – and yet what I had to put up with was nothing compared to Sophie. But it hadn't made *her* envious and resentful. Instead she'd done everything she could to help me. She was troubled by her gift, and yet she'd used it for me, letting Mamma's spirit speak through her. She'd wanted me to find my sister; she wanted us to be happy together.

Mamma would have wanted us to be happy too, I was sure of it . . .

Oh, God, what had I done to Kitty?

I was taken aback when the door was opened by Phoebe.

'Where's Sally?'

'Mrs Grimston says I'm to do her work from now on.' Phoebe gave a pert little bob, her expression smug.

I was aghast. Had Sally been dismissed?

'Sir Osbert wants to see you. As soon as you come in, he said.' From her tone I could tell she was ghoulishly pleased to be the bearer of bad news. She scanned my face.

I wouldn't give her the satisfaction of seeing my reaction. I looked at her levelly. 'Would you let my grandfather know I need to change out of these wet things and that I will come down as quickly as I can.'

'Yes, miss,' she said with a toss of her head.

I expected Grandfather to be at his iciest. Apart from trying to blackmail him and running off without telling anyone where I was going and staying out for hours, I'd also inflicted an injury on Ponsonby, at least as much to his pride as to his person. He wouldn't have wasted any time in complaining about me.

But when I appeared Grandfather leaped up and said, 'You're back!' He seized my shoulder and shook it. 'Don't ever do that again, do you hear? Where have you been?'

I wondered why he was in such a pother. He surely didn't think I'd run off to talk to some newspaper editor, did he? 'I've just been out.'

'But the weather's atrocious. You could have caught your death of cold.'

I shrugged.

He continued to stare at me, knitting his brows, until I felt embarrassed. 'What's happened to Sally, Grandfather?'

'Sally?'

'Parks, the upper housemaid.'

His face changed. 'She's been dismissed.' The familiar chilling tone was back.

'Why?'

'It's not my habit to discuss the management of the servants with you, Meriel, but I'll make an exception on this occasion, since it involves you. I would have thought you'd realize that there is no place in this household for someone guilty of such gross misconduct.'

'Do you mean she's being blamed for letting me go off on my own?'

'Indeed.'

'That's not fair! I wanted to go on my own and she was only doing what I told her – so it's my fault.'

'Your loyalty does you credit. It might interest you to know that Parks was equally loyal to you, refusing to divulge any information about your activities –'

Oh, Sally!

'– but such a gross breach of trust cannot be condoned. Anything might have happened to you. I'm not prepared to discuss it further.'

I wanted to discuss it further. I wanted to know whether Sally had already left the house and whether she'd been given a reference – she'd told me that without a 'character' a servant couldn't hope to get a decent position. I desperately wanted to know that she was all right.

'As to your own conduct –'

He seemed to have recovered his usual equanimity, jawing on about disobedience and foolhardiness. I expected him to stress the impropriety of going about unchaperoned, but to my surprise he seemed more concerned about my safety. More than once he repeated, 'Anything might have happened.' When at last he wound down he shook his head and said with a sigh, 'I suppose it's just as well you'll soon be at the Château Bellevue. You won't be able to get up to this sort of mischief there.'

I was puzzled by his tone. He seemed almost regretful, and I didn't understand why. At least I knew he still seemed set on going ahead with his original plan for me. But what about Kitty? What was going to happen to her?

'I know I shouldn't have behaved like that. I'm sorry, Grandfather.' And I was, though not for the reason he would think.

'Humph! Penitent, eh? Well, that's something, I suppose. Now, you'll apologize to Ponsonby, won't you?'

'Yes, Grandfather.' I swallowed. 'Have you been to see the Chirks today?'

He tensed immediately. 'If I have, what of it?'

That meant yes. 'What did they say – about me?'

'What took place between the Chirks and myself is private.'

'Can't you at least tell me what's going to happen to Kitty?'

He started shuffling papers. Always a bad sign. At any moment now he'd dismiss me. On the way home I'd racked my brains, trying to think of a way to make things all right. Now was the moment . . .

'Grandfather, please listen. This is all my fault. I found out about Kitty and went to see her. *I* did it, not her. She didn't know anything, so it's not fair to blame her. Do whatever you like to me, but please don't punish her! Don't take her away from the Chirks!'

He glanced up from the document he'd selected. 'Meriel –' he spoke remarkably gently – 'I have work to do.' And he turned his attention to the page.

At a loss, I stood there for a few moments longer and then walked out of the library, shutting the door quietly behind me.

*

Back in the schoolroom, I went to draw the curtains, but before I did so I looked out.

It had stopped snowing. Every branch, ledge and lamp post had been anointed with a mantle that shone blue-white in the cold light of the moon. Nothing moved in the eerily silent street.

I rested my forehead on the icy glass. I had failed. Whatever was going to happen to Kitty, I hadn't been able to prevent it.

THIRTY-EIGHT

The weeks that followed were horrible. I was forbidden to leave the house, and the weather – more snow followed by freezing fog – put a stop to any thoughts I had of trying to get out. In any case, it would have been hopeless – every time I left my room there was a servant sweeping the stairs or dusting pictures. Grandfather wasn't taking any chances.

For hours I stared out of the window. I'd never go to Mrs Jolly's again, but it would have been nice to see Sophie. Even writing to her would have been a comfort, but I'd lost my secret postal service.

Eventually, a gloating Phoebe told me that Sally had left the house the day I'd tried to run away. And I hadn't even had a chance to apologize, to say goodbye. When I asked Phoebe if she knew where Sally had gone all she said was, 'I couldn't say, miss,' with that little toss of her head that infuriated me.

I hadn't realized how much Sally meant to me until she wasn't there. I missed seeing her regularly throughout the day, hearing the latest gossip, 'having a lark', as she would put it. She'd been a patient audience for my acting, a sympathetic listener to my woes about Grandfather . . . Those days with her and dear old Tippy that had seemed so dull looked quite different now, and I wished like anything to have them back.

Grandfather was behaving very oddly. The morning inspection of my school books had ceased, but he dropped into the schoolroom nearly every day. He didn't seem to mind that I wasn't working, and he didn't seem to have any reason for coming either – he hung about, watching me as I pretended to read a book, sighing sometimes, and then he'd glide away like a ghost.

Christmas came and went and I wondered what it had been like at the Chirks's. Had they enjoyed their cheerful festivities or was the house quiet, with a horrible empty space where Kitty should have been?

January brought heavy rain and fierce gales that blew down more telegraph wires and lashed the trees. Night after night I lay awake, listening to the wind wailing down the chimney and the water running in the gutters, but it wasn't the weather that prevented me from sleeping. For hours I stared into the dark, wondering where Sally was and whether she was all right and wishing I knew that Kitty was safe. I was missing Sophie too, and I thought about Ma King and how my dream was slipping away . . .

As the day of my departure approached, I prayed for the snow to return – snow so deep it blocked the roads, prevented the trains from running – but every morning I woke to the sound of rain beating on the window and at last the morning came when I was to leave.

I couldn't eat the boiled egg Phoebe brought for my breakfast. I already had an egg-sized lump in my throat that prevented me from swallowing. The carriage which would take me to Victoria station to catch the Continental Express had been ordered for ten o'clock; my trunk was packed, locked and corded.

I was in my room stowing my treasures in the old carpet bag when I heard the clop of hoofs followed by the grating of wheels against the kerb. Surely it wasn't time to go yet? I went to the window and looked out. Drawn up outside the house was not Grandfather's carriage but a hansom cab. Probably someone visiting our neighbour. I was just about to turn away when something about the man paying the driver arrested me. My view of him was foreshortened . . . I couldn't be sure . . . but then he swung round and rapidly ascended the steps to our front door. There was no mistaking that gait.

My hand flew to my mouth and for a moment I was rooted to the spot. And then the doorbell pealed and I dashed out of my room, startling the new housemaid, who was dusting the banister, and ran down the three flights of stairs.

He was handing Phoebe his coat. He was thinner in the face and he seemed shorter than I remembered, but then of course I'd grown.

'Papa!'

He turned and his face lit up. 'Meriel, my darling girl! Thank God you're here.' He came towards me, his arms outstretched, and I was about to run to him when the library door opened and Grandfather came out.

Frowning, he peered at the figure before him. It was obvious he didn't know who it was. And then his eyebrows shot up and his monocle dropped. 'Francis Garland. Good Lord!'

Papa's face darkened. 'Yes, Osbert, it's me. I came to find my daughter.'

Did he mean me or Kitty?

'How dare you show your face here! Damn your brazen impudence.' Grandfather had lost his composure – he'd gone as red as a turkey.

'Where can we talk, Meriel?' Papa asked me, ignoring him.

I shot a glance at Grandfather. Why was he so angry with Papa? 'The dining room?'

Grandfather spluttered, his hands clenching into fists, but Papa said quietly, 'Calm yourself, Osbert, or you'll make yourself ill. I'll see you when I've spoken to Meriel.' He gestured to me to lead the way and we left Grandfather standing there.

Phoebe was still hovering, her mouth hanging open.

'Mind you don't catch a fly,' I hissed as we passed.

In the dining room Papa made a move to embrace me, but I shrank back and the smile died from his eyes.

I couldn't help it. That first impulse – to run and bury my head in his chest, to feel his arms round me – had been overwhelmed by the warring feelings churning inside me.

There was a moment's awkward silence and then Papa said, 'Well, shall we sit down?' and we perched on two of the stiff ornate chairs.

He glanced quickly around and then his eyes came back to me. 'Are you all right?'

'Quite well, Papa,' I said coolly. It was obvious why he'd come. He must have received Mr Chirk's letter and booked his passage immediately. He didn't have enough money to pay for my passage home or to come to see me, but when it came to Kitty, money had been found and he'd come at once. And if he could take only one of us home with him, of course he would choose her, especially when he found out that I'd betrayed her . . .

'Good, good, but I meant . . . Oh, my darling, I'm so glad to see you – I thought you might have gone.'

'I was just about to leave.'

'Oh, Meri, Meri. Have you been so very unhappy?'

I was taken aback – I was prepared for questions about Kitty, concern for her. But since he'd asked . . . I looked him in the eye. 'Yes.'

'I'm sorry, I'm so sorry, I –' He broke off and ruffled his hair distractedly in a gesture so familiar it brought a lump to my throat. I'd forgotten he did that.

Hardening my heart I said, 'But I told you – in my letter. I said it was horrible here and I wanted to come home.'

'You did . . . and I blame myself for not taking you seriously.'

'You didn't believe me!'

'I thought –' he ran his fingers through his hair again so it stuck up in tufts – 'because I couldn't do anything about it, it was easier to convince myself you were over-dramatizing. You've got to admit you tend to do that, don't you? You take after me in that respect.' He gave me a wry smile, but I wasn't smiling. 'I made myself believe you were better off here.'

'Because you didn't want me.'

'My darling, how can you say that? I'd have given anything to have kept you with me if I could.'

'Why didn't you then?'

He looked distraught. 'I can't – it's too . . .' He took a deep breath. 'When you're older perhaps you'll understand.'

'Papa, I'm sixteen. I'm not a child any more.'

He stared at me then as if he was looking at me properly for the first time, and something changed in his face. 'You're right.' He sounded sad.

If he was sorry he'd missed years of my life, whose fault was that? 'I want to know now.'

He looked at me helplessly. 'You will, but this is not the moment. I need to know what it's been like for you and then I must speak to Osbert.'

'*Tell* me.'

He almost smiled. 'I'd forgotten how fierce you can be. All right.' He cleared his throat. 'This is hard for me, you know.'

'Please, Papa.'

He paused a second and then, looking away as if he were ashamed of what he had to say, he began to speak in a low voice. 'After your mamma died, I had no money and little prospect of getting any. I could just about afford to rent a room in the bazaar – a squalid cockroach-infested hole. But it was no place for you, my darling –' he glanced at me – 'and I was at my wits' end worrying about what was going to happen. When Osbert offered to take you, it was like the answer to my prayers.'

'But we were all right, weren't we, before Mamma died? I mean, not well off but not poor. You could afford to rent the bungalow . . .'

He shook his head. 'We did our best to keep it from you, but by that time things were pretty bad. In that last year we only managed to survive by selling Eleanor's jewellery. Apart from her locket, of course, which she would never part with –'

Instinctively my hand went to it.

'Ah, I see you have it still – good, good. Well, by the time she died, the pearl-drop necklace – you remember it? – was all that was left.' A pause and then he said quietly, staring down at his lap, 'I sold it to pay for her funeral.'

In the silence that followed I studied him and it was as if, through my older eyes, I saw him clearly for the first time. I saw that the knees of his trousers were shiny with wear, his cuffs frayed. The lines on his forehead were deeper, and his face was etched with other lines that hadn't been there before. I thought about what it must have been like for him, and my heart twisted with sudden pity.

He looked at me. 'My darling, I hope you understand now why I had to send you away. It was the hardest thing I've ever done.' His voice broke. He put his hands to his face and I could barely hear what he said. 'I failed Mamma . . . and then I failed you . . . and I've gone on failing you.' His shoulders shook.

Slipping off my chair, I went to him and tentatively stroked his curly hair. It was going grey over his ears, I noticed. He seized my hand in both of his and gripped it as if he never wanted to let it go, and then somehow my other arm was round him, hugging him, and I was weeping, with a pain behind my breastbone as if something that had long been locked up had been wrenched open . . . but it felt good that whatever was shut up in there was let out at last.

After a while he gained control of himself and blew his nose loudly and I wiped my face.

'Tell me,' he said, searching my face, 'what were you going to do? Where were you going to go?'

I was surprised by his questions. 'Why, to boarding school. Didn't Grandfather tell you?'

He frowned. 'Boarding school? Oh, thank goodness.'

At once my stomach tightened. 'You're pleased about it?'

'What? No, I just meant . . . In her telegram Everina said you were talking about running away – I was afraid I might be too late.'

'Mrs Jolly sent you a telegram?'

'Yes, she said you'd come to her in a state of distress and she was very worried about you. It disturbed me no end, of course, all the more because I was stuck out there with no idea of what was going on. So it was like a miracle when Gussie offered me the commission the very next day . . .'

He must have seen the puzzled look on my face. He clapped his hand to his forehead, 'Oh, I was forgetting . . . of course, you don't know about that. Gussie, Mr Jolly, has asked me to paint his portrait, an official one for the School of Art entrance hall – apparently the trustees have come up with the money and Gussie gave me an advance. Now I've thought about it, of course, I suspect Everina put him up to it so I'd have enough money for the fare.'

All my resentment towards Mrs Jolly melted in an instant. She did care for me, after all. But something else was dawning on me, igniting a flicker of impossible hope in my chest.

'So you came because of Mrs Jolly's telegram, because you were anxious about me?'

Papa seemed surprised by the question. 'Yes, I told you – I was nearly out of my mind with worry.'

'But you'd received the letter?'

'What letter?'

The flicker burst into a blaze. He didn't know about Kitty. He hadn't come for her. *He'd come for me.*

A wild thought gripped me. I didn't have to tell him. I could go back to India with him – after all, he didn't live in a slum any more, he had rooms at the School of Art – and I could live there with him and it would be just the two of us, me and Papa. Of course he would find out about Kitty, because the letter would be waiting for him when we got back, but by then it would be too late . . .

'What letter, Meri?'

I looked at his face, his dear face, and a vision of Kitty rose in my mind. Kitty, my sister, who was stolen away and deprived of her parents' love; Kitty, the daughter he didn't know he had.

I swallowed, took a deep breath. 'There's something you need to know, Papa . . .'

Papa was so overcome by what I told him that he couldn't sit still but leaped up from his chair and prowled about. In the middle of the story I had to restrain him from going at once to confront Grandfather. By the time I'd finished, his hair stuck up in wild disarray.

'My God . . . I can't believe it . . . another daughter, kept from us all this time. Poor Eleanor, not to have known about her . . .' He almost broke down again, but then his face darkened and he looked towards the door.

'Take heed, Osbert Swann,' he murmured. 'You'll be sorry you did this!'

'Papa?' I touched him on the arm.

He looked startled and then his face cleared. 'Meri . . . my dear.'

He drifted over to the sideboard and absent-mindedly lifting the lid of a soup tureen he peered inside. 'What you must have felt when you discovered you had a sister! Unimaginable . . . It's astonishing, a miracle, that you found all this out. But I can't believe you were able to go about London on your own.'

'They thought Sally was with me.'

'But you must have been out for hours sometimes. And no one checked?'

I shook my head.

He blew out his breath. 'Such negligence.' With a sudden decisive movement he replaced the lid of the tureen. 'I'm going to speak to Osbert now.'

As he walked past me I seized his arm. 'Papa, you're not going to . . . to hurt Grandfather, are you?'

He laughed and patted my head. 'Don't worry, chick. I'm not going to risk my neck for him.'

Unconvinced, I reluctantly let him go. He went out, suggesting I returned to the schoolroom.

Of course I didn't. I waited a few minutes and then checking that no one was about, tiptoed to the library and put my ear against the door.

I heard an angry exclamation – that was Grandfather – and a sharp retort from Papa and then I heard him say, 'Wait a minute,' and the next moment the door opened.

I jumped back, trying to pretend I hadn't been eavesdropping. Looking amused, Papa said, 'Will you wait upstairs for me? Please?'

I nodded, but still I stood there.

'Meri?'

'You will come up, won't you? You won't leave without seeing me?'

'Good God, of course I won't. I'll be with you as soon as I can.'

He waited until I started up the stairs before going back into the library and shutting the door.

In the schoolroom I wandered about, picking things up and putting them down again. It seemed like forever as I waited, but finally I heard him calling me.

I went to the door. 'I'm here.'

He almost pushed me inside. 'Your grandfather – all these tests he's been doing – he hasn't hurt you?'

'No.'

'My God, when I think . . . I'm sorry – so, so sorry. If I'd known, I'd have never let you come; you do realize that, don't you?'

I was struggling to follow. 'If you'd known . . . ?'

'Why, that Osbert Swann is mad, completely cracked.'

I stared at him. I knew Grandfather was odd, but was he really mad?

Papa strode to the door. 'Come on, Meri. Is your coat downstairs?'

'Where are we going?'

'I think I should meet your sister, don't you?'

I stiffened. 'I can't come.'

'But don't you want to see Kitty?'

Wordlessly I shook my head.

'What's the matter?'

I swallowed and said slowly, 'Papa, Kitty might not be

there, you know. But if she is, I don't think she'll want to see me . . .'

'Why ever not? Come on, Meri, tell me what's bothering you.'

There was nothing for it. Taking a deep breath, I told him about breaking my promise to Kitty.

I thought he'd be shocked, outraged, disappointed in me. I thought he'd say, 'How on earth could you behave like that towards your sister?'

But he didn't. He put out his arms and drew me to him, rocking me as he used to do. 'Oh, Meri, Meri.'

'You're not angry with me?'

'Why should I be angry? You were all alone, desperate . . .'

His sympathy, the comfort of his arms . . . it was wonderful, but suddenly I pulled away. 'Did Grandfather say anything about Kitty?'

'What do you mean?'

'Mr Chirk was afraid he might take Kitty away.'

He stared at me. 'Take her away?'

'Yes, you know, hide her somewhere so he could go on being in charge of her without interference.'

His face changed. 'What?! The blackguard! Surely he wouldn't do that!' He made for the door. 'Meri, come on.'

THIRTY-NINE

Outside Papa looked up and down the street. 'Where's the nearest cab-stand?'

'This way.'

Turning up his coat collar, Papa grimaced at the rain. 'By jingo! I'd forgotten how cold it could be here. Let's walk fast, shall we?'

As we hurried towards the main road I heard hoofs behind me and looking round I saw Grandfather's carriage drawing up at the house. Papa glanced back too.

'It's come for me – to take me to the station.' I looked up at him anxiously. Would he say, Off you go then?

'Well, it isn't needed, is it? Your headmistress will be disappointed, mind. She'll have to find another pupil to fill the vacancy.' He winked and my heart expanded. So I wasn't going to school, at least not that one. But I didn't feel altogether like celebrating because I had no idea what was going to happen to me instead . . .

On the way to Eldon Square Papa told me more of what Grandfather had said. 'Can you believe it? The reason he gave for stealing our daughter from us, deliberately keeping the pair of you apart and subjecting you to experiments . . .'

I crinkled up my forehead. 'Experiments?'

'Yes, didn't you realize? A twin study. That's what he

said. The first perfect twin study there has ever been. The finest contribution to the understanding of heredity the world has ever known.'

'Keeping Kitty and me apart was going to achieve that?'

'He hoped so. And there was some rigmarole about wanting to prove that nature would always win out over nurture.'

'What does that mean?'

'I think it means that even though you and Kitty were brought up in different homes, he's hoping you're similar enough to show that the quality of your upbringing made no difference – it's what you've inherited that makes you who you are.'

'And that's important?'

'Your grandfather thinks so.' Papa shook his head and sighed. 'Of course, these ideas could be important, I suppose, but to try to investigate them by using his granddaughters like laboratory rabbits . . . He appears to have no shame about it, no grasp of the immorality of what he's done. That's what makes me question his sanity.'

Despite the unease I felt as the cab carried us nearer and nearer the Chirks's, part of me was enjoying this. I'd forgotten the pleasure it gave me when Papa shared his thoughts with me, something he'd done at times even when I was a little girl. It had always made me feel special and I realized how much I'd missed it.

'You know, Meri, what enrages me, apart from the fact

that he's done it at all, is that he claims his motive is, I quote, "the loftiest of all – the advancement of scientific knowledge". Bosh! I suspect he's just after personal glory, the kudos of being the first person to undertake such a study.'

He glanced sideways at me. 'Is she like you? Kitty.'

'Ye-es . . . in some ways. But not all. She's more placid than me . . . quieter.'

'Is she? Not like your mother or me then. Perhaps she takes after your grandmamma.'

'Her middle name's Lydia. Grandfather must have decided that.'

We were both quiet for a moment, thinking.

'She's nicer than me.' I pulled a face.

'Oh, Meri, don't be silly.' Papa squeezed my hand. 'I don't believe it for a minute. But, according to Osbert, if it's true, it's not your fault.'

I was puzzled by his ironic tone. 'What do you mean, Papa?'

'Why, he considers Kitty's upbringing to be the superior one and you, poor chick, were abandoned to a dreadful fate.'

I had no idea what he was talking about.

'You were brought up by me! And your mamma of course, but I was the bad egg – Irish and therefore innately inferior, an artist, the lowest of the low, and to compound it all I took you off to India where you were contaminated by contact with despicable natives. Didn't you realize you'd drawn the short straw?'

I couldn't help smiling. How absurd. Perhaps Grandfather really was mad.

We'd come to a standstill – the traffic locked both ways across Piccadilly Circus.

Papa had stopped laughing and his expression was serious now. 'The alarming thing is he really believes this twaddle – about the innate superiority of certain races and classes. I hadn't realized until today how strongly the idea has taken root in him. It explains why our marriage was anathema to him. But it's a dangerous creed. You know he wants to use the twin study to support his belief that the poor and feeble-minded should be prevented from marrying. It's a short step from that to justifying the elimination of anyone considered undesirable.'

'But that's awful.' I stared out at the stream of umbrellas passing up and down the footpath as I thought about what Papa had said. Grandfather would certainly consider Anila and our other Indian servants 'undesirable' . . . Sophie too, probably. 'Papa, even though I didn't know about it, I don't want to have contributed to something so cruel.'

'Don't worry. Osbert won't be publishing his study if I have anything to do with it.' Papa's mouth set in a grim line.

As the cab set off again I was still thinking. 'There's something I don't understand. Does he think Kitty and I are inferior because you're our father or superior because he's our grandfather?'

He shook his head. 'God knows. He did complain that your behaviour wasn't as good as Kitty's, so he probably puts that down to my influence on your upbringing. It's a good question. It shows what utter nonsense all this is. I think your grandmother's death must have driven him over the edge of reason.' He was silent for a moment and then he said, 'You know, he blames me for Mamma's death.'

'What? But that's ridiculous.'

He shrugged. 'He says if I hadn't taken her to India she wouldn't have died.'

'But Mamma wanted to go, didn't she?'

'She did. In fact it was she who persuaded me. She thought it would be an adventure.' He smiled wistfully. 'And so it was, for a long while.'

Neither of us spoke for a time until Papa suddenly sat up straight, as if shaking off sad thoughts. He gazed round him. 'Oh, look, we're passing the Drury Lane Theatre. Tell me – what plays have you seen?'

'None.'

'None at all? You've been in the theatrical capital of the world and you've not seen single play?'

'Grandfather doesn't approve of the theatre.'

Papa snorted and then when I told him about *Faust* his face darkened. 'Fancy denying you a harmless pleasure. And not approving of Everina Jolly, when she's the kindest, most generous of souls.'

'She wouldn't let me stay with her.' A twinge of bitterness returned as I said it.

'But, Meri, didn't you realize she's going back to India next week?'

'Oh? No, I didn't.' I felt aggrieved. 'She might have said.' But then I remembered how I'd flounced out, not giving her time to tell me anything. Sorry, Mrs Jolly, I said in my head.

I looked out of the window. We'd reached the British Museum. 'We're nearly there,' I said in a small voice.

'What's up, Meri? Are you worrying about Kitty?'

I nodded. Fluttering moths seemed to be trapped in my stomach.

'Chin up. It will be all right.'

Dear Papa, always the optimist. But I didn't share his certainty.

FORTY

The maid who opened the door told Papa that the master was at the university, but that Mrs Chirk was at home. No mention of Kitty. The moths in my stomach beat their wings.

Did I want to hear the worst? But it was no good – I couldn't bear to put it off any longer. 'Is Miss Kitty in?' I asked the maid.

'She's in the drawing room, I think, miss.'

'She's here? Oh, thank you.' I hardly knew what I was saying. I felt light-headed with relief. Kitty was safe. I didn't have to feel guilty any more. 'Kitty's here, Papa,' I said unnecessarily. Suddenly I wanted to be generous. 'Do you want to see her alone? I can wait here.'

'I do, but first I think I'll step along to the university and find out if Mr Chirk is free to see me, so why don't you go up?'

I ran up the stairs, but outside the drawing room I stopped.

How would she receive me? I wouldn't blame her if she never wanted to see me again. I wouldn't, if it had been the other way round. But then she wasn't like me . . .

I opened the door and went straight in without knocking.

Kitty was standing by the piano, turning over sheets

of music. She looked up, startled. My heart contracted. It was as if I was seeing her for the first time all over again.

In the whole world, she should be the person closest to me. Could we . . . ? Was it possible to start again?

'Kitty, I'm sorry.'

I hoped she'd hold out her hands to me, smile, show me she'd forgiven me, but she did none of these things. She stared at me, her face a mask. But I knew exactly what she was feeling. She was angry, no, probably furious, with me.

'I didn't mean to, but I was miserable and I kept thinking about you all here having a lovely time together, and then Grandfather said I was definitely going away to school and I couldn't bear it . . . don't you see? I couldn't . . .' I trailed off in the face of her stony silence.

She narrowed her eyes, a cat about to pounce on its prey. 'You told him.'

'Yes, well, I . . . I thought I could get him to change his mind about sending me away. I wasn't trying to make things difficult for you—'

'I asked you not to tell him, but you did.'

'Well,' I shot back, stung, 'I asked you not to tell anyone about meeting me and you told Richard and the Chirks.'

'That was different.'

'No, it wasn't. It was just the same.'

'It wasn't. I knew it would be all right if I told *them* . . . but you knew better than anyone that telling Sir Osbert was risky.'

She was right. I dropped my eyes, studied the red roses on the carpet.

'At any rate, you're still here,' I muttered.

'But I might not have been. You think it's all right just to turn up and say you're sorry, but you've no idea what it's been like.'

I made myself look at her. 'Has it been bad?'

'Bad?' She spat the word out. 'It's been awful. When Sir Osbert turned up like that, out of the blue, Mamma went quite white. I thought she was going to faint.'

'What did he say?'

'I don't know exactly. He saw Papa. Afterwards Papa tried to reassure us that everything would be all right as long as we didn't tell anyone what Sir Osbert had done. But I know he's beside himself with worry, though he does his best to hide it from us. Mamma's tried to pretend everything's normal too, but I know she hasn't been sleeping and her eyes are red from crying. We don't trust Sir Osbert. Every day we've been expecting him to come and take me away . . . can you imagine what that's been like?' Her eyes flashed.

I hung my head.

'I don't think you can. I don't suppose you know that the Chirks had a daughter, a little girl who died. That's why they were so glad to adopt me. I don't suppose you can imagine what they're going through. Especially my mother. She's already lost one child. And now, thanks to you, she's afraid she'll lose another.'

I felt flayed by her scorn; everything in me shrivelled. She hated me. My sister hated me.

Minutes ticked by as we stood there. I felt paralysed by the enormity of my guilt and I didn't know what to say. 'Sorry' was totally inadequate – it certainly wouldn't placate her. Such fierce passion. She was, I realized with a little shock of surprise, much more like me than I'd thought.

And then she took the wind out of my sails completely.

'I don't know why you hate me so much. I've done nothing to you.'

'I don't hate you, Kitty.'

'I don't think you like me very much.' She caught hold of her bottom lip with her teeth. I knew what that meant too. She was trying not to cry.

All the mean thoughts I'd had came back to me, and I felt even more ashamed. I'd had no idea that she knew what I was feeling, that she could understand me so well.

I looked into her eyes that were just like mine and I tried to find the words to say exactly, truthfully, what it had been like. 'It wasn't how I thought it was going to be – finding you. I thought it would be wonderful, but it was . . . strange.'

'I know.'

'You felt that too?'

She nodded. 'I thought it would be like . . . like playing a duet, where your music isn't the same but you blend together perfectly.'

'That's how *I* thought it would be. Like being incomplete apart but making something whole together?'

She nodded again.

'But I've been more of a discord.'

She smiled wryly, not disagreeing.

'I told you I was hopeless at music.'

At least she laughed.

It was a relief to be honest. It felt right. I didn't want to hide anything from her.

'Partly I was jealous.'

'Jealous?'

'Yes. You seem so happy here with the Chirks. Like a proper family. It made me feel more . . . alone.'

She smiled, an odd, bitter little smile. 'That's how I felt when they told me I was adopted . . . as if I didn't belong here really. I wondered what they'd been like . . . my real family. I really wanted to know, but I never thought I would.'

She gave me a reproachful look. 'That's why I was so glad when you came.'

I felt worse than ever. What could I say? All I could do was go on telling her the truth, as if the truth were an offering that might make her forgive me. 'I was jealous of you and Richard too.'

'Of me and Richard?'

'Yes, you seem to be such good friends.'

'We are, but then I've known him since I was a little girl. He's like a brother to me, you know.' Kitty was watching me closely, gauging the effect of her words. They stung as she surely meant them to. 'After Sir Osbert came, I talked to Richard about you. He was angry with you.'

I could see she took pleasure in stabbing me with that as well. I couldn't blame her – I'd have been the same.

'But,' she went on, 'he was more prepared to see your side of it than I was.'

Thank you, Richard, I thought.

'He wondered if you'd done it because you were desperate. Because of wanting to act.'

'He's right.' I seized on this eagerly. 'Kitty, I wasn't trying to hurt you . . . honestly. It was the thought of missing my chance . . . I realize now it was totally thoughtless and I know it doesn't alter what I've done, but I am truly, truly sorry.'

I waited, hoping against hope that she'd say she forgave me. Because I'd suddenly realized how much it mattered to me that she did.

But she didn't. Her mouth set in an obstinate line and she turned her back on me and started leafing through the music again.

'Kitty, listen, I have some good news. You don't need to worry any more.'

Though she didn't turn her head, I knew she was listening.

'About Grandfather, I mean. He can't do anything to you now.'

She turned to face me. 'What do you mean?'

I paused. 'Papa's here.'

'Papa?'

'Our father. Come from India today.'

All the colour drained from her face. 'Our father?' she whispered.

I felt for her, suddenly aware of the enormity of what she faced – seeing her own father for the first time. 'Yes. He's gone to the university to see Mr Chirk. They're probably arranging everything this minute.'

'Arranging what?' Her voice was sharp with alarm.

'I don't know . . .'

We gazed at one another. Her face mirrored all the trepidation I felt. What did the future hold for both of us?

'Don't worry,' I said, trying to sound confident. 'I'm sure it will be all right. Papa—'

The door opened.

Papa's jaw dropped as he stood looking from one to the other of us. 'My God!' he whispered. 'It's unbelievable.'

All three of us were frozen, for all the world as if we were taking part in a tableau. I kept my gaze on Papa, looking and looking to see what his feelings were as he laid eyes on his daughter for the first time. And even after all that had passed between Kitty and me, there was a little part of me that didn't want to see that he felt for her what he felt for me.

Papa recovered first. 'Kitty?' he said tentatively.

She seemed quite unable to speak. Her colour came and went as she stood immobilized, her eyes fixed on his face.

Papa smiled, a funny shy smile. 'I believe I'm your papa.' He went up to her and held out his hand. 'I'm very, very glad to meet you.'

Still gazing at him, still not speaking, she slowly raised her arm until her palm met his and suddenly their hands were clasped together.

I shuffled uncomfortably.

'Oh, Meri . . .' It seemed to me that Papa took his eyes from Kitty reluctantly. 'Mr and Mrs Chirk would like to see you.'

My heart sank. 'Oh, Papa, do I have to?'

Papa nodded. 'They're waiting for you in the morning room.' And as I hesitated, he added firmly, 'Off you go.'

All the way down the stairs my mind was on Papa and Kitty. What were they saying to one another? I'd have given anything to be an invisible observer and overhear their conversation.

FORTY-ONE

When I reached the morning room I stood for a moment outside the door preparing myself. Then I stepped over the threshold and, keeping my eyes on the floor, I started to mumble a broken apology. But I'd only managed a word or two before Mrs Chirk rushed forward, exclaiming, 'Oh, Meriel!' Laughing and crying at the same time, she gave me a big hug.

When she let go of me I dared to glance at Mr Chirk. He was polishing his spectacles and positively beaming at me. What was going on? Why weren't they furious?

'Your papa – such a lovely man, isn't he, my dear?' Mrs Chirk addressed her husband.

'He is indeed, my love.'

'And, Meriel, isn't it wonderful news?!'

'I'm sorry?'

'You don't know? He's happy –'

'– happy for Kitty to stay with us.'

'Isn't it marvellous!' Mrs Chirk literally bounced, twice.

I let my breath out in a great sigh as warmth flooded through me from the top of my head all the way down to my toes.

Papa wasn't taking Kitty back to India with him!

Mrs Chirk was still talking. '. . . make all the necessary

legal arrangements. From now on, Osbert Swann won't have any say about what we do, will he, my dear?'

'No indeed, my love.'

'And—'

'Careful, my love,' said Mr Chirk.

She clapped her hand to her mouth. 'Oh yes, I mustn't . . . no.' She took me by the hand and led me over to a chaise longue.

I looked at her wonderingly. What had she been going to say?

'Now, my dear, did you have a lovely Christmas?' And she rattled on as if nothing had happened, nothing had changed between us, while Mr Chirk listened and beamed and occasionally interjected a comment.

It seemed like a long time before Kitty appeared. She came through the door wreathed in smiles, and the three of them hugged and kissed while I sat there feeling awkward. It was only after much exclaiming that Kitty turned to me and said, 'Oh, I forgot. Your papa's waiting for you upstairs.'

Did she give that 'your' a little emphasis, or did I imagine it?

'So,' said Papa, 'I told you you didn't have anything to fear, didn't I?'

'You were right. They were amazing. They weren't even cross with me. But, Kitty . . .'

'Ah yes, well, that's another matter . . .'

'I don't think she'll ever forgive me.'

'Well, she is extraordinarily like you.' He smiled, teasing me.

I looked at him reproachfully. 'It's not funny.'

He drew me to him and gave me a hug. His jacket was rough on my cheek, but I stayed there, nestling against him. It was so lovely to feel the comfort of his arm around me. 'You know, I thought you'd want to take Kitty back to India with you and forget about me,' I confessed.

'I'd never do that. And in any case, I think Kitty will be happier here, don't you?'

I nodded.

'But you know, Meri –' Papa held me at arm's length so he could look me in the face – 'I *will* have to go back.'

This I'd known all along. I closed my eyes, waiting to hear what he would say next.

'And, my darling, I'm afraid I can't take you with me. I live in one room at the School of Art, and I can't give you the life you deserve. Do you understand?'

I bit my bottom lip to stop it quivering. I should have known, really. For one thing there was the evidence of Papa's worn clothes. But I'd made myself ignore it because I wanted so much to go home, and going home meant . . .

Shock made me open my eyes.

It wasn't India my heart was aching for, had been aching for all along. India didn't matter. Losing Papa did.

I clung to him. 'I'll miss you, Papa. I'll miss you so much.' Tears choked my voice.

He pressed me to him. I could hear he was fighting tears too. 'I'll miss you too, my darling.' Neither of us spoke for a long moment.

At last he stirred and, patting my head, he let go of me.

I gave him a watery smile. 'Papa, what *will* happen to me?'

'You'll have to be brave, Meri, and stay here in England.'

'You mean, with Grandfather?'

'Good God, no! Now, I want you to tell me the truth, all right? Promise?' His face was serious.

I nodded, wondering what was coming.

'How would you feel about living here with the Chirks? They've offered you a home, if you'd like it.'

'Oh.' I felt quite breathless. I hadn't expected that. The Chirks were lovely of course, but . . .

'Well, what do you say?'

'What about Kitty?'

'Of course the arrangement has to be agreeable to both of you. That's partly why I wanted to speak to Kitty on her own.'

'What did she say?'

'Well . . .'

'I knew it. She hates me. Oh, Papa, what am I going to do?'

He shook his head, laughing. 'That's my Meri, dramatic as ever. No, I told you she's like you . . . she has a loving heart.'

I stared at him, baffled, and then as he looked at me knowingly I understood. 'She said yes?'

And breaking into a smile, he nodded.

After that there was a great deal of confusion. We went down to the others and I was kissed and hugged by Mr and Mrs Chirk, and Papa was kissed and hugged and invited to lunch by Mrs Chirk, and everyone was talking at once. In the midst of it all, I pulled Kitty away and took her off into a corner.

'Are you sure about this? I don't want you to feel I'm intruding into your life. I'm not a very nice person, you know, and we'll probably have rows and fall out with each other all the time . . .'

'I expect we will,' said Kitty, shrugging. 'But I'm willing to try, if you are.'

I looked into her eyes and saw myself mirrored in them. Our faces were identical, but our expressions were not: mine was uncertain, Kitty's teasing.

Papa called across the room. 'Meri, I'm going back to Osbert's to tell him what we've arranged. You can stay here if you like. Your luggage is already packed, isn't it?'

I hesitated. There was no need to go back, not ever again, and yet . . .

'I'll come, Papa.'

Papa and I were quiet on the way back. He looked tired now, which wasn't surprising, given his long journey. And I felt shaken, wrung out. So much had happened in the short time since he'd arrived that morning, some of it positive, all of it unsettling.

I gazed at the rolling hindquarters of the horse toiling to pull us along.

'Papa, what was that saying you used to quote? Something about horses and courage.'

He thought a moment. '*The courage of the tiger is one, and of the horse another*.'

'Yes, that's it.'

'Emerson – Ralph Waldo Emerson. A great thinker. He spoke out against slavery, you know.'

'What does the saying mean?'

'Well, I might be wrong, but I take it to mean that though everyone's different, we all have courage in our own way, and that everyone should be accorded respect, whoever they might be.' He looked quizzical. 'Whatever put that into your head?'

I pointed at the horse and he smiled. 'Well, he certainly needs a lot of courage to cope in this traffic.'

I wondered if the horse in the saying represented people who weren't free to do as they wanted, who were forced to serve others. Like Sally . . . and Sophie. Maybe the saying meant that it took a kind of courage to plod on cheerfully, without complaining, as they did.

And maybe the tiger represented powerful people, like Grandfather, who were free to do as they wanted. Like a tiger, they could be dangerous – and trample all over everyone else . . .

I suddenly sat up straight.

'Are you all right, Meri?'

'Yes, Papa.' I answered him abstractedly. I felt as if someone had turned a white light on in my brain.

I used to try to be like a tiger, until I grew tired of being lonely and then I thought I'd stop. But now I could see that in some respects I hadn't stopped at all. I was no better than Grandfather.

All along I'd forged ahead, determined to get what I wanted without considering anyone else. Look at what I'd done to Sally. And Sophie had been a tower of strength, but I'd just taken it all for granted. Until she'd told me her story, I'd not given a thought to her situation or what she might be feeling. No wonder I hadn't guessed her secret.

As for Kitty . . . I winced, remembering the bitterness of her tone, how ashamed she'd made me feel. But I'd deserved it. I'd been hideously selfish; that was the truth of it.

Ma King's voice floated into my head. 'Have you that capacity for understanding others, Miss Garland?'

'Meri, are you sure you're all right? You're looking very doleful.'

'Papa, do you think people can change? Or are the horses bound to be horses and the tigers have to go on being tigers?'

He looked bemused. 'You're in a funny mood, chick. All these serious questions . . .'

'But what do you think? Can they change?'

He gazed at me thoughtfully. 'Well, you know, I think animals stay true to their nature – they have no choice.

But people – they're much more complicated. I think they can change if they really want to. Why do you ask?'

'Oh, nothing.' I sat back, thinking.

Living with Kitty, who, as it turned out, might not be my soulmate after all, I was probably going to have a lot of opportunity to practise understanding other people. I could try to be more sensitive and aware, like Sophie. In fact, I could start by being more sensitive *to* Sophie and try to be as loyal a friend to her as she'd been to me.

We'd reached the gates into Kensington Gardens; it wasn't far now to Queen's Gate Walk.

'Papa, you remember I told you about Sally, the housemaid? Can we try to find out what's happened to her and whether she's all right?'

'Yes, of course.'

'And after we've been to Grandfather's, can we call on my good friend Sophie? It's not far and I really want you to meet her.'

FORTY-TWO

'Will you tell Ponsonby my trunk needs fetching, please?' It gave me great pleasure to say that to Phoebe and see the pert look vanish from her face.

I turned to Papa. 'I'll get my bag from upstairs.'

'Right. I'll just have a word with your grandfather.'

Instead of going straight to my bedroom, I went up to the schoolroom. It was silly really. Mostly I'd been bored and exasperated here, but still I wanted to see it for one last time – the worn carpet, the globe, the ink-stained table I'd sat at for so many hours.

There were still some spellings on the blackboard written in Tippy's rather shaky hand and for a moment I felt sad. In my head I said, I'm sorry, Tippy, for all the trouble I caused you. Wherever you are and whatever you're doing, I hope you're all right.

And then I announced to the room, 'I won't be coming back,' and I felt a tingle of excitement.

It was harder to leave my bedroom, where I'd felt so close to Mamma. I went over to the dressing table and stared at my reflection. No need now to wait for that strange feeling of someone being close, but still I paused.

I knew it was pointless, but I couldn't help hoping. This might be her last chance. Would Mamma speak directly to me? Would she, just this once, whisper my name?

The room remained silent.

With a sigh I picked up her photograph, the last thing to be packed. I thought of her setting off from here for her new life in India, and as she smiled out at me I imagined her saying, 'Have courage, Meri.' And I remembered what Sophie had said and I felt comforted. I wasn't leaving Mamma behind. She was coming with me. She would always be with me.

Tucking the photograph into the old carpet bag, I carried it from the room without looking back.

I met Papa coming out of the library.

He said, 'I'm just going downstairs to see if anyone knows anything about Sally. You can wait in the cab, if you like.'

I could have walked out of the house just like that, without seeing Grandfather. But instead I knocked on the library door and went in.

Grandfather wasn't in his customary seat behind his desk; he was sitting in the armchair by the fire, staring into it. I was shocked at the change in him. Instead of holding himself upright, he was bowed over, like an old tree bent by the wind.

I stayed near the door. 'Grandfather, I've come to say goodbye.'

He turned his head then. 'Meriel, I meant it all for the best – you know that, don't you?' Even his voice was quieter, as if it had lost its power.

I stared at him, torn between outrage and scornful laughter. Even now, after all that had happened, he still thought he could justify himself. 'The best for you, you mean. You used Kitty and me because you wanted to be famous.'

He looked bewildered. 'Famous? No. Come . . . come.' He beckoned me towards him.

I went closer reluctantly. He seized my hand in his dry, scaly one and I couldn't help shivering at his touch. I had to bend my head to make out what he was saying.

'I did it for Eleanor, my darling Eleanor. It would have been too much . . . the burden of a disabled child . . . out in India . . . too much. I wanted to spare her.'

I gaped at him. Was this true? Or was he making it up? Pretending he wasn't a monster . . . 'You didn't say that to Papa.'

'No, I wouldn't tell *him.*' His eyes snapped in the old way. 'But you, you understand, don't you?' His grip on my hand tightened. 'It was only later that I saw the scientific possibilities, that the research could be important, its contribution incalculable. Your father has no idea of the cost of his intervention. If he permitted . . . if I could publish even the results I have so far, it would have far-reaching consequences . . .'

'What a shame you can't then.' I couldn't help gloating. After all the times I'd been in this room, furious with frustration and biting my tongue, at last the tables were turned and I felt a buzz of triumph.

I expected an icy retort, but all he did was look at me sadly and then he said, 'You don't have to go away, you know. You could stay here with me. I promise I won't do any more investigations.'

'But you don't want me. You were going to send me to school!' I tried to pull away, but he held me fast.

'Only because you were growing up and I realized I couldn't keep you safe. You were determined to go out into the world, and I knew that sooner or later someone would find out about you and Kitty. I had to make arrangements to send you away; you see that, Meriel, don't you? But I didn't want to. I knew the house would be empty without you.'

I stared at him. Did he mean it? I thought of all the times he'd visited the schoolroom and lingered there. I'd supposed he was spying on me, but maybe I was wrong.

'Grandfather, I've got to go.'

Just for a second, the look in his eyes tore at my heart. I knew what he was feeling because I'd felt it myself . . . that loneliness.

Gently disengaging my hand, I walked away from him.

At the door I turned and said, 'Goodbye, Grandfather.'

As I closed it behind me I heard his voice, suddenly distinct, cry out, 'Eleanor, don't go.'

EPILOGUE

I sat bolt upright on the edge of my seat, taking it all in.

Around me in the stalls people were laughing or chatting, shaking hands or waving to friends across the auditorium. I'd never seen so many wonderful dresses, so many bare shoulders, so many pearls and diamonds. I craned round to scan the crowded pit; I gazed at the dress circle and the boxes where the most jewellery was in evidence and then I peered up at the overflowing gallery, where the people must have been baking under the hot lights. I breathed in the scents of perfume and flowers and let out a sigh of satisfaction.

'All right, Meri?' Papa squeezed my hand.

I smiled up at him, a rather wobbly smile. This was the one shadow on my happiness – tomorrow he and Mrs Jolly were going back to India. I didn't know when I would see him again and the thought made my heart ache. But I pushed it aside. Tonight he was still here, still with me, and that's what mattered.

I looked past Papa at Kitty, who was talking to Richard. She and I had created quite a stir in the foyer as we came through. I was more than happy to be stared at, pleased to be wearing my new dress of blue silk that Kitty and Mrs Chirk had helped me choose.

Beside me Sophie was scanning the programme and

beyond her Mrs Jolly was saying something to Mr and Mrs Chirk that was making them laugh. Nearly everyone I cared about in the world was here, for now, and it gave me a warm feeling.

I was so glad Papa had insisted on talking to the kitchen maid at Grandfather's and discovered where Sally had gone. It was kind of Mrs Chirk to find her a new position with a friend of hers. I only wished we could do something for Sophie but Papa said we couldn't, not as long as she was bound to Mrs Quinn.

Just then Sophie looked up and, catching my eye, she smiled that little smile of hers. She looked different tonight – her face had some colour in it, her eyes were shining. This was her first-ever visit to a theatre, but I was determined it wouldn't be the last. And on Sunday we were going to the Foundling Hospital with Kitty to listen to the choir.

At least she'd have some nice things to look forward to from now on, and maybe at some time in the future she wouldn't have to be a servant any more.

I'd said, 'When I'm a famous actress you could be my dresser.' I'd been joking about the famous actress bit, but Sophie hadn't known there were such people as dressers in the theatre and she'd been interested in the idea.

It pleased me to imagine a future where we might be together, working in the same place, still friends . . .

I sighed to myself knowing there were a lot of obstacles to overcome before that dream could come true. Even though I'd finally confided my ambition to Papa and he and Mr Chirk had had a talk and said they thought it would be possible for me to go to Miss Thorne's School of Acting, I still had to be accepted.

Next week Richard was taking me to see Ma King, but what would she think of me? Sophie had said I didn't need to worry, but even so . . . my hand went instinctively to my locket.

Stop it, I told myself. Whatever the future has in store for you, you'll just have to face it when it comes. After all, you've survived so far. Unbidden, a vision of Grandfather came into my head; I imagined him all alone in that big empty house and I wondered whether he was all right.

But just then a bell rang, and after a second or two the orchestra, segregated behind their crimson cord, started playing. Soon, very soon, I would see her, Ellen Terry, there in front of me on the stage. A tremor of excitement went through me. Sophie must have felt it because she looked at me and smiled.

'Don't forget,' she whispered, 'Richard said we were to watch out for the special effects in the Brocken scene.'

I grinned back. I didn't need to be reminded – I didn't intend to miss a single detail. Settling back into my crimson plush seat, I turned my attention to the stage, as the curtain rose . . .

AUTHOR'S NOTE

In my depiction of Osbert Swann and his work, I have drawn on information about Sir Francis Galton, the Victorian scientist, but Osbert is in no way intended to be a portrait of Galton – I have taken considerable liberties with the truth here, as elsewhere, for the sake of the story.

ACKNOWLEDGEMENTS

Thank you to . . .

Penny Barber, for enlarging my understanding of spiritualism and, in particular, for an inspirational suggestion; Matt Eagland, for information about the theatre; and all the other people who helped by answering my questions, including several contributors to the invaluable Victoria list. Thanks also to the team at Macmillan, especially Emma Young, and to Lindsey Fraser, for her unfailing support.

ABOUT THE AUTHOR

I came late to writing or rather came back to it, because I loved making up stories as a child. I was born in a rather dull Essex town – long streets of houses that all looked the same – and reading and writing were ways of escaping to more exciting worlds. I taught for many years and I still do, part-time, though these days I help adults to develop their writing. I enjoy it hugely, but am also glad to have more time to myself, for there is nothing more absorbing than creating a story. I live in Lancashire now and can see hills from my window as I write.

It's ironic that I've written two historical novels, since I gave up History at school when I was thirteen. I've always regretted this, but happily it's something else I've been able to come back to. Like my first novel, *Wildthorn*, *Whisper My Name* was inspired by reading about the Victorian period; in particular I became fascinated by the extraordinary world of Victorian mediums and their preoccupation with what lies beyond . . .

Wildthorn Hall, where cruelty and madness meet . . .

Seventeen-year-old Louisa Cosgrove longs to break free from her respectable life as a Victorian doctor's daughter. But her dreams become a nightmare when she's sent to Wildthorn Hall. Labelled a lunatic, she is deprived of her liberty and even her real name. As she unravels the betrayal that led to her incarceration, Louisa realizes there are many kinds of prison. She must be honest with herself to have a chance of being set free. And love will be the key . . .

Exodus

Julie Bertagna

AS THE WATERS RISE, THE OLD WORLD IS LOST.

BUT A NEW WORLD WAITS TO BE FOUND . . .

Mara's island home is drowning beneath storm-tossed waves, as mighty icecaps melt and Earth loses its land to the ocean.

But Mara has seen something extraordinary – hints of a New World rising from the sea and reaching into the sky. Cities where frantic refugees might find safety.

In a desperate bid for survival, Mara and her friends set sail in the ultimate exodus. Their quest is a heart-wrenching story of love and loss, and a journey into humanity's capacity for good and evil . . .

EVA IBBOTSON

The Secret Countess

ST PETERSBURG, 1917

Anna's world is under threat. The eighteen-year-old countess has lived in luxury all her life, but revolution is tearing Russia apart – and her family must escape . . .

LONDON, 1919

Now penniless, Anna is working as a servant for the aristocratic Westerholmes. But as she falls in love with the young earl it becomes harder to keep her true identity a secret . . .

Previously published as *A Countess Below Stairs*

EVA IBBOTSON

The Morning Gift

They were not supposed to fall in love . . .

Ruth lives happily in the magnificent city of Vienna. Then the Nazis invade and her world is turned upside down. Her parents flee to London, but Ruth is accidentally left behind. A family friend offers her an escape route: a marriage of convenience to be dissolved as soon as they reach England. But Ruth's feelings for Quinn soon take her by surprise, and her efforts to set him free do not go quite as she had planned . . .